Sweet By and By is a wonderful novel about the Deep South that brings pleasure to the soul. The characters' lives were tested by adversity, strengthened by faith, and held fast by perseverance. I loved it!
—Jo Hubbard, Mt. Olive, MS

Very compelling and enjoyable. I stayed up and read it all in one night. I didn't want to put it down. Then I read it again and thought about what it said to me.
—Jackie Boss, Petal, MS

Sweet By and By was the best book we've read in a decade. After the first page we were mesmerized. It has a good balance of suspense and humor. As for the characters, we felt like we'd made new friends. We are anxiously awaiting the sequel.
—Michael and Deborah Sanford, Collins, MS

A story about a courageous woman weathering the worst storms of life, *Sweet By and By* was hard to put down.
—Dema Patterson, Sumrall, MS

Sweet By and By is a story about life-like characters told with Southern flair; highlighted with Scripture to remind us that God knows every human need, joy, and weakness, and just enough romance to spark the imagination.
—Kay McQueen, Collins, MS

Sweet By and By is a book you'll want to read over and over. Everything about the story is so vivid. As you read, you can smell and taste the food, feel the oppressive southern heat, feel the breeze in your hair. Best of all, you begin to believe you know the characters personally. In your mind, they become real people experiencing all of the tragedies, drudgery, suspense, and pure joy of living.

—Bettye Worrell, Magee MS

I am not an avid reader, but when I began reading *Sweet By and By* I found it impossible to put down. It was like watching a movie. I was sorry to see it end.

—Dorothy Jones. Seminary, MS

To: Ann —
... for the Father
waits over the way ...
    God Bless you,
    Ramona Bridges

SWEET BY AND BY

RAMONA BRIDGES

SWEET BY AND BY

A story about love

TATE PUBLISHING & *Enterprises*

Published by Tate Publishing & Enterprises, LLC
127 E. Trade Center Terrace | Mustang, Oklahoma 73064 USA
1.888.361.9473 | www.tatepublishing.com

Tate Publishing is committed to excellence in the publishing industry. The company reflects the philosophy established by the founders, based on Psalm 68:11,
"The Lord gave the word and great was the company of those who published it."

Book design copyright © 2009 by Tate Publishing, LLC. All rights reserved.
Cover design by Leah LeFlore
Interior design by Nathan Harmony

Published in the United States of America

ISBN: 978-1-61566-416-0
1. Fiction: Christianity: Romance
2. Fiction: Christian: Western
09.11.04

DEDICATION

This book is dedicated, with endearing memories,
to my grannies, Alvie Mae and Lutie.

ACKNOWLEDGEMENT

Mere words don't allow me to explain how important writing this book was for me. Throughout my life I have read about and heard countless sermons about the phenomenon of spiritual gifts, and the privilege and obligation we have as Christians to use the gifts God gives us to uplift the name of Jesus Christ, in hopes of inspiring others to follow Him. There have been times when I felt so inadequately equipped to be an effective witness for Him that I wondered whether or not I possessed such a gift. However, I've since realized that God doesn't call the qualified, He qualifies the called. Through prayer and spiritual growth, I discovered that I have indeed been blessed with an ability of sorts, one for storytelling and creative writing. I am humbled that God graciously inspired and tenderly encouraged me to write *Sweet By and By*. I give Him full credit for the story. Any errors or inadvertent misinterpretation of the Word, I take responsibility for.

Much love and many thanks to my husband, my family, and my friends for their earnest prayers and their fledging support. Theirs was a vision I did not anticipate.

May God bless and keep you all.

CHAPTER 1

"Come unto me, all ye that labor and are heavy laden, and I will give you rest." (Matthew 11:28).

The air was thick. The late-July night was alive with a loud, shrill chorus of chirping crickets and croaking tree frogs. Their voices lifted high and clear a song that begged for rain to quench the parched land and offer a blessed reprieve from the oppressive Mississippi summertime heat.

Addie Coulter lay in the dark on the side of the bed nearest to the window. Not even a hint of a breeze stirred. The day had been intolerably humid, making it seem overly long and laborious. She was bone-tired, but sleep would not come. She felt irritable and restless. Even the quest for comfort proved a wearisome task.

Within the house, it was stifling hot. Addie kicked at the covers until they were bunched up at the foot of the bed. The smell of dust filled her nostrils; the mere weight of her thin, cotton gown was suffocating. She tugged at it until the hem was gathered at her knees, baring her legs to welcome any relief, however slight, from the unbearable heat.

Her long hair was damp with perspiration. She pushed it away from her face and twisted it into a knot on top of her head. Some of the loose, silky strands stuck to the clammy skin on the back of her neck. She turned her pillow over, hoping the underside would be cooler.

Usually it is the dead stillness of night that has a way of carrying sound, making it travel across distance and fall upon the ears with a sharpness and clarity that is elusive by day. However, this particular night did not lie in quiet repose, and yet they were at least a half-mile away when she heard them coming from the direction of town.

The hour was late, probably midnight or better. She heard the distinct sound of Gent's hooves as he steadily clopped along on the packed clay road. It wasn't long until the horse and the rider rounded the bend, climbed the short hill, and came near. Then they veered toward the barn that was situated across the way in front of the house.

A few minutes later, Addie heard the loose gravel being ground beneath his boots as he walked across the road. He stopped in the yard at the big oak and relieved himself.

He entered the house through the back door into the keeping room. There he rummaged through the pie safe like a thieving rat searching for a scrap of food. She knew he found a few pieces of cold fried chicken and a couple of hard, crusty biscuits left over from supper. *If he'd come home earlier and eaten with us,* Addie mused inwardly, *he could have had crisp, juicy chicken and hot, fluffy biscuits.* Sadly, sitting down to supper with his family was of no importance to him.

Addie heard him bump into the edge of the table and curse. *There's no doubt,* she thought, *he's drunk as Cooter Brown.*

Only a few minutes later he stumbled into the room where she lay in the dark.

He made his way across the oak plank floor toward the bed as he'd done countless nights before. Addie kept still with her back turned to him. She quieted her breathing. He grunted as he removed his boots and then his dirty clothes. He dropped the boots and the garments onto the floor beside the bed.

The mattress sank with his weight. He moved fairly close to her on the bed, close enough that she felt his hot breath on the back of her neck. Close enough that she felt hemmed up, both body and mind. She didn't move or make any sound at all.

The man smelled of whiskey, stale tobacco, and sour sweat. And, like so many times before, she caught a faint odor of something else, too. The very thought made her ache. *No telling where he's been,* she thought, *or with whom . . .* She was grateful for the snores she heard a short time later. Her dread passed.

The man lying next to her in a drunken sleep was her husband, Alfred. Alfred Coulter. *Is it possible,* Addie marveled, *that we've been wed for sixteen years?* How many nights over the years had she lain awake wondering where he might be? *I'm thirty-three years old and have spent half my life like this, living with a man who cares naught for me.* Their entire marriage had been a charade, a mockery from what God intended. *We are but two fools living apart under the same roof.* Knowing there was nothing she could do to change this caused her spirit to wither.

She strained her ears and listened for any sound from the room across the hall where her ten-year-old daughter, Emily, and her invalid mother, Rachel, slept. All was quiet.

Two years before, Rachel had a light stroke that left her weak and unable to stay alone in her own house. She had been reluctant to leave her home, but Addie finally convinced Rachel to come to live with her so she could care for her. Five months ago she'd suffered a second stroke that left her bedbound. Now her body was gnarled and twisted, her stiff limbs useless.

Addie took a deep breath and stretched. Her back ached. It was necessary for her to reposition Rachel in the bed every hour or so throughout the day. It was toil to turn and lift her mama's rigid body. There was so much work in caring for her. She sighed inwardly and thought, *I'd never manage to get everything done if it wasn't for*

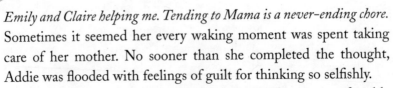

Emily and Claire helping me. Tending to Mama is a never-ending chore. Sometimes it seemed her every waking moment was spent taking care of her mother. No sooner than she completed the thought, Addie was flooded with feelings of guilt for thinking so selfishly.

She fought to clear her mind so she might get comfortable enough to fall asleep. She wondered if she might still be lying there awake when the rooster crowed to announce the break of day.

For a while, Addie lent her attention to the harp of the night— the chirping of crickets, the croaking of frogs, Alfred's snores, and the *thump* made when the old hound, Ben, dropped himself down heavily on one end of the porch. *It's a hot night indeed when even dogs won't prowl,* she thought as she drifted off into a dreamless sleep.

The Coulters lived roughly three miles northeast from the town of Collinsville on Monroe Road. The road was named in honor of James Monroe, who served as the fifth president of the United States between the years of 1817 to 1825. Collinsville was watered by Hutchins Creek, which powered both a sawmill and a gristmill built on the bank of the creek. A general store, a mercantile, a post office, a blacksmith shop, and several other structures, including a church and a schoolhouse, made up the town. On the outskirts of town was a cane mill, where folks brought their sugarcane in the fall to be ground and boiled into syrup.

About four miles out of town to the southeast, just off Monroe Road, was a Negro settlement known as Nigger Ridge. The area had been called that by whites and blacks alike for as long as anyone could remember. Ask any Negro around Collinsville where he lived and he was bound to say, "I stays up on Nigger Ridge." After Lincoln abolished slavery and the Civil War was fought many black families staked their claim on a homestead and mule allotted them by the government. In the years that followed, the population of the settlement had flourished.

Of course, anywhere human nature prevails, inevitable prejudices flourish as well. Among some people, blacks and whites alike, prejudice was held to as dearly and protected as furiously as a firstborn son.

However, it was rare, if ever, that trouble was heard of between the residents of the two communities living around and sharing the town of Collinsville. The reason being simple: it was a known fact that people, regardless of origin or color, were basically the same and generally strove for the common goals of eating, sleeping, reproducing, and dying.

Addie roused some time later when the weight of the baby made it necessary to get up. She slipped quietly from the bed and out the back door, barefoot. The warm, gentle embrace of the night enveloped her.

The fruity essence of the blooms of a nearby mimosa tree smelt intoxicating. The night air heightened their heady fragrance. During the day, when hummingbirds were on the wing, dozens of them swarmed the tree in a frenzy, hovering over its fuzzy, pink blossoms, gathering nectar.

As Addie passed under the big oak in the backyard, she heard a faint stirring from high in the tree. *Roosting guineas.* They waited out the night upon the lofty limbs, safely out of reach from foxes and bobcats.

Addie was fond of her guinea-fowl. Their gray and white feathers were layered so that the birds were made to look like they were sporting polka-dotted coats. Guineas made good guard dogs too, sounding an alarm of loud shrieks to announce any unexpected happening or visitor.

Somewhere in the distance a neighbor's dog barked, and closer, just beyond the woods' edge, an owl hooted. Leaves rustled as small critters scurried about. All these familiar sounds versed a song Addie knew by heart.

The grass beneath her feet was dry and wilted. *Lord, we so need rain. Please bless us and quench our need,* she prayed silently.

On her way back from the outhouse Addie stopped on the path and turned her face upward to gaze into the wondrous night sky. The vast blackness was illuminated by thousands of twinkling stars. She loved the sky at night; its serene beauty usually comforted her when nothing else could. She thought, *Pa said stars were the eyes of ten thousand angels keeping watch over us.*

Standing there, she took several long, deep breaths. She tried to will herself to be drawn into the tranquil depth of the midnight clear. *Dear God,* she asked, *why must life be so hard?*

Addie longed for His tender reassurance to fall upon her heart and soothe her worried soul. *In me ye might have peace...* But the thoughts that clouded her mind thundered so loudly that the peace He whispered to her was drowned out, leaving her feeling desperate and alone. The tender reassurance she sought was beyond her reach. *In the world ye shall have tribulation...*

Addie was caught in a haze of depression. She felt troubled on every side and wondered what was to become of them all. Alfred. Rachel. Her unborn baby. And, of course, Daniel. Oh, how she wished Daniel could come home! Her son belonged here, with her. The hardest thing she'd ever had to do was let go of her child. She'd been forced to let go of him *because of Alfred.* Feeling that she had in some ways failed Daniel, a familiar wave of hopelessness and utter despair washed through her whole being.

When she finally headed back toward the house, an overwhelming sense of sadness had settled in, and she was consumed by it. *But be of good cheer, I have overcome the world.*

Feeling tired and defeated, Addie ignored the voice from above that offered peace and hope to her spirit and gave in to her emotions. She leaned her back against the rough boards of the house and wept.

CHAPTER 2

"But he that is of a perverse heart shall be despised." (Proverbs 12:8)

Morning came.

In her bed, Rachel lay stiff as a corpse and stared at a red bird sitting on her windowsill. She'd awakened before dawn feeling tired and bored and desperately lonely. The chickens cackled, roosters crowed, a mule brayed, and the birds sang. She heard Addie milling about in the kitchen. Rachel made no sound except for breathing. Breathe in. Breathe out. Breathe in. Breathe out. She thought sadly, *I ain't no good to myself anymore, no good to anybody else either.* A tear slid from the corner of one eye.

The last stroke had left her right arm drawn up over her chest. Her hand was bent and looked like a bird's claw. The muscles of her face were drawn and locked, leaving her to appear to be wearing an expressionless mask. Her flesh had shrunk tightly and molded to her bone structure, giving her an almost skeletal appearance. She'd lost her ability to speak. The only sounds she made now were either incoherent grunts and throaty groans or embarrassing, involuntary noises that escaped from somewhere within her. Rachel felt like a snared rabbit, trapped in a useless cage of a body.

When Addie went outside to throw feed to the chickens, Alfred instantly appeared in her doorway. Rachel cringed as he sidled over to her bed, chomping on a biscuit, split and filled with butter and ham. In a mocking lilt, he sang, "Good mornin' to you, good mornin' to you…" When he bored of singing, he moved on to other theatrics. He jeered, "Granny, you smell like what the cat covered up." Her infirmity had robbed her of all dignity.

Rachel's hatred for Alfred was pure and simple. Her mind screamed, *Get thee hence, Satan!* She shifted her eyes toward the wall, flatly refusing to look at the man, despising the very sight of him. She'd known the first time she'd laid eyes on him that he was sorry as carrion, and it hadn't taken fifteen years, or fifteen minutes, for that matter, for him to prove her right. He was a mean, crazy drunk.

She thought nervously, *The mangy cur used to make hisself scarce as hens' teeth 'round me. Wonder why all of a sudden he's took to sneakin' in here?* Alfred's presence put her on edge. *I'd rejoice if he went back to leavin' me be.*

She flinched when Alfred moved closer to her bed. He dangled the last bite of ham just under Rachel's nose.

"Granny, you want a taste of this here? *M'mmm!*" He smacked. An oily sheen of pork grease coated his lips.

He was deliberately antagonizing her, knowing full well that since the stroke she could no longer chew or swallow solid food. Everything she ate had to be mashed up. The smell of the biscuit and ham made her mouth water. In her mind, she hollered at him, *Git from me, you ignorant cuss! You ain't got the sense God give a mule— though it sure befell you to be a jackass!* What she wouldn't give to be able to get up and kill the sorry wood's colt.

"Eh? I didn't hear you. No, you say?" Alfred continued to taunt and mock her. "Well, all righty, then. Jus' you be that a-way. Yer

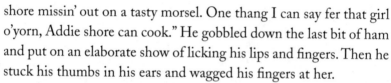

shore missin' out on a tasty morsel. One thang I can say fer that girl o'yorn, Addie shore can cook." He gobbled down the last bit of ham and put on an elaborate show of licking his lips and fingers. Then he stuck his thumbs in his ears and wagged his fingers at her.

For a minute, Alfred loomed over Rachel's slight body with his arms folded, gawking at her, sucking his teeth. He amused himself by intimidating her. *The wickedness of man was great… every imagination of the thoughts of his heart was evil.*

Knowing he risked being seen if he tarried much longer, Alfred leaned over and put his mouth near to Rachel's ear, making her skin crawl. She shuddered as he made her a sinister promise.

"Granny, on account o' you bein' s' nice to me, one day real soon I'm a-gonna brang you a present."

For another long moment, he stood there and silently stared at her. All of a sudden, his expression turned to stone, and in one swift movement he clutched the bedcovers with both hands and gave them a mighty jerk. Rachel fell off the bed and landed headfirst onto the hard floor.

A few seconds later, Alfred fled the house, unseen.

Addie came from the henhouse with her apron bunched up to carry the still-warm eggs. Emily would gather up the rest of them directly since she knew all the hiding places of the hens that refused to lay their eggs in the nests inside the coop.

She had risen long before the sun, and today being washday, she'd woken Emily up a little earlier than usual, too. She wanted them to get an early start. The day was heating up fast, and working around a blazing fire this time of year was tortuous.

Even though he hadn't said a word to her before he left, she figured Alfred had headed out to the woods where his crew was logging. Though it wasn't unusual, he'd grumbled all through breakfast this morning, aggravated at her about having to milk the cow before he went to work. Emily usually did the milking, but lately Daisy's temperament had grown unpredictable, and if she was feeling particularly skittish, she got the notion to kick.

He'd set the bucket of milk on the back step, and Emily had already poured it into a crock and left it in the clabber cupboard to sour. Hot as it was, they could churn tomorrow and have fresh butter.

Earlier, Addie had started a fire around the big, cast iron pot in the backyard, and Emily filled it with water. Now she was drawing more buckets from the well for the rinsing. She had her sleeves pushed up, and the front of her dress was wet from where the water sloshed over the rim as she clumsily carried the heavy, water-laden buckets. Her cheeks were flushed pink from exertion, but she was humming a tune as she worked. Always wearing a smile, Emily was of fair countenance and disposition, an independent and obedient child. She had a natural curiosity to explore the world around her, and if one had passions at this so tender a bloom, hers were books and cats.

When Addie walked past Emily on the way to take the eggs into the house, she cautioned her, "Hon, you be careful around that fire."

"Yes, ma'am, I will," was the cheerful reply.

Just as Addie was about to enter the back door, Claire Ellis rounded the corner of the house.

"My, you're stirring early," Addie greeted her old friend with a smile.

"When you get my age, you stir when the body's willin'." Claire noticed the shadow of fatigue on Addie's face and the lingering puffiness from what she suspected was wasted tears. She thought, *As surely as Noah shoveled manure, I'd cry too if I was married to Alfred Coulter.* Even if she lived to be a hundred, she would never understand why Addie chose to marry that confounded devil in the first place.

Back when she'd spout off disapprovingly about Alfred to her husband, even though he didn't care for him either, Luke would always warn her not to interfere in other folks' business by quoting one of his favorite sayings: every folk hoes their row a little different. Whereas she liked to speak her mind, Luke had been more disciplined and hoarded his judgment of others for his own entertainment.

So she'd held her tongue and lived to regret it. Thinking Rachel might have said more to dissuade her daughter from courting Alfred, Claire just about had a fit when the two ran off and got married. As far as she was concerned, the man was unsuitable to be called a human being, so she most certainly considered him unbefitting as a husband for her sweet Addie.

Grateful for opportune timing, as she walked up, she'd glimpsed Gent's tail end trotting off toward town and thought, *Now there goes a horse with an ass sittin' high in its saddle.*

She said, "I figured y'all might could use a spare pair of hands, it being washday." Inwardly she speculated, *It'll be a sight to see how Addie's gonna be able to keep everything stirrin' once this lit'lun gets added to the stew! She's gonna need all the help she can get an' then some!* Claire could skin Alfred alive for not helping her more and carousing less.

"God bless you, Claire! You're sure to have many stars in your crown up in Heaven!" Addie exclaimed. "Truth be told, I was as restless as an ant on a hot pile of ashes last night; wore myself out trying to get to sleep. For the good it did me to lie down, I should have just stayed up and did the wash, and that way we wouldn't be worried with it this morning."

Claire remarked, "I thought you looked a little peak-ed." She figured she had a better chance of capturing the wind in her fists but suggested it anyway. "Why don't you go in and rest a spell. Let me help Emily with the wash."

Addie protested. "Fiddle! I feel fine. We'll do the wash while you go in and sit with Mama. The company will do her good."

Claire put forth a sincere effort to be a friend to Rachel, a feat which had not always proved simple. Prone to bouts of extreme emotional highs and lows that alternately and unpredictably rose and fell, Rachel was one inclined, at times, to impolitely bend the expected boundaries of human kinships. Because of this unconven-

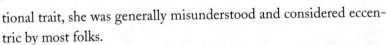

tional trait, she was generally misunderstood and considered eccentric by most folks.

Yet Claire still made an effort because, after all, it was her beloved Luke that had brought them all together. On a day that seemed so long ago, Claire had tearfully watched as Luke marched off to the war. Two and a half years later, he'd soldiered back home accompanied by a man he'd befriended along the way named Samuel Warren. Before a week was out, Samuel and Rachel were completely infatuated with each other; a week later they were married.

Luke had been gone for twelve years now. Habited to going out and sitting on the porch every evening after supper to puff on his pipe and watch the sun set, one such evening, while Claire was cleaning up the dishes, she heard his chair fall over. When she rushed out to the porch to investigate, she found him lying dead with his pipe still in his mouth, his face contorted and as red as a sugar beet. Doc Hughes said he'd most likely died of a heart attack. After all those years of living, he was gone—just like that.

Luke Ellis had been a kind and generous man, very well-thought of in the community, and his funeral was largely attended. In the solitude of the evening after his burial, Claire did something she'd never thought of doing before. In honor of his memory and in preservation of her husband's daily ritual, she sat quietly on the porch and watched the sun set. When night fell, she rose from the chair feeling relaxed and gratified—and enlightened—having discovered the pleasure of smoking his pipe.

Following Luke's death, a few old widowers presented themselves in vain, mistakenly assuming Claire might be flattered by their efforts to court her. One or two even overstepped their bounds with the presumption she might have an interest in remarrying. She promptly let it be known she wasn't in the market for another husband. From time to time, Addie would tease her about getting remarried, sending Claire off and snorting, "Never in my life have I heard the likes of such a silly notion! There's not a man alive that could take Luke's place! Some things are meant to be endured once in a lifetime, an' I plan on enjoyin' what's left of mine without some broke down ol' Hank slowin' me down!"

A few months before Luke passed away, Claire quit teaching school. She saw her fiftieth birthday that year. She'd taught Addie and her brother, Wesley, at the one-room schoolhouse in Collinsville. When she was a girl, Addie loved to read and went to the Ellis home regularly to search the shelves in Claire's back room for books to borrow. Along one wall was row upon row of books of poetry and history, old school books, and novels.

Wesley was in and out of the Ellis house, too. He liked to sit around and listen while Luke and Samuel told stories of places they'd been, and he shared the fish he caught in the creek with Luke and Claire. Sometimes, when no one else was around, Luke let Wesley smoke his pipe. And, of course, they all loved Claire's famous teacakes.

A few years after Samuel and Rachel were married, a tragic event occurred that tested the strengths and weaknesses of the two families. From that day forth, Rachel's heart was as one crying in the wilderness. Luke and Claire had not been blessed with children of their own, but on days when Rachel was down in the valley with realities too hard for her to endure, Claire's house became the natural place for Wesley and Addie to migrate to.

As it turned out, Claire and Addie discovered they were alike in many ways. "Birds of a feather," Claire would say. Both were strong-willed and decisive, they shared the same humor and spirit for life. From their similarities grew a special bond; and despite the difference in their ages, over the years, Claire and Addie became best friends and loved each other dearly. "How is my old gal Rachel this morning?" Claire asked.

"Mama's the same, I reckon. She still won't eat hardly a thing. When I fed her earlier, she only took a few bites of grits and molasses. She's fell off even more since the last time you were here. She's nothing but skin and bones."

Claire could tell Addie was discouraged. She followed her into the house where she took a thick-rimmed bowl down from a shelf for her to put the eggs in. Then she went across the hall toward Rachel's room.

A moment later, she hollered, "Addie, come in here quick! Rachel's fallen off the bed!" When Claire first saw Rachel lying on the floor, she thought she might be dead, until she made an attempt to raise her head. The first thing she did was turn Rachel over onto her back, and then she made sure she didn't have anything in her mouth to choke on.

Addie went hastily to where Rachel lay and gasped. Her nose had bled, there was dried blood smeared on her face. An odor hung over the room; Rachel had soiled herself.

"She was facedown when I found her." Claire was bent over Rachel.

Addie knelt beside her mama, her hands were trembling. She crooned, "Oh, Mama, are you all right? It's going to be all right."

There was a raised bump on Rachel's forehead and an angry-looking bruise had begun to form.

Addie couldn't bear to seeing her mama this way, so pitiful and wasted. She cried, "I'm so sorry, Mama. I didn't mean to let you fall." *In a fleeting moment, she was reminded that Rebekah, too, had fallen…* "I'm so, so sorry." She smoothed Rachel's thin hair away from her weathered face.

Rachel grunted. She wished she could speak. It riled her to see Addie's tears and have her thinking it was her fault that she'd ended up on the floor, when Alfred was really the one to blame. She thought, *Oh, Addie, I didn't fall off the bed. It was that godless villain, Alfred. He comes in here on the sly just to work my nerves. He yanked me off the bed an' knocked the wind out of me… left me here on the floor just to be mean an' to trick you.*

His plan had succeeded.

With this, paired with the lack of sleep, Addie went to pieces.

She struggled with guilt and wiped her tears on her apron. Emily heard the commotion and ran inside to see what had happened.

"Claire, Emily, help me with Mama's mattress. Let's put it down here on the floor and lay her on it so she'll be more comfortable." Working together, the two women and Emily dragged the mattress to the floor and lifted Rachel's stiff body onto it. Rachel wasn't that heavy, but she was dead weight. She groaned when they moved her. Addie was worried that she might have some broken bones.

"I'll take the bed frame apart later and move it into Daniel's room, out of the way. At least being on the floor will save Mama from another fall." Addie's mind was racing. "All this time, it never occurred to me that she might roll off the bed. I should've thought of that."

Claire consoled her, gently patting her arm. "She's fine, dear. She's just gonna be bruised and stove up for a few days. Stop blaming yourself. It's not your fault. I never gave a thought to her falling either." Claire coaxed mildly, "You go on now and help Emily with the wash. Let me tend to Rachel."

Addie wouldn't hear of it. "No, I'll tend to Mama."

Claire knew there was no point in arguing with her. "I'll be right back with you a pan of warm water." She and Emily left Addie alone with Rachel.

Rays of morning sun came through the window and bathed the room in light as Addie lovingly bathed her mama. *Truly the light is sweet, and a pleasant thing it is for the eyes to behold the sun.*

She removed the soiled nightgown and diaper and washed Rachel just as she would an infant. She turned her onto her side to put a clean dressing on the bedsore on her left hip. The odor was foul, especially in this heat, and the stench of it promptly attracted a multitude of annoying, buzzing flies that danced about and lit on the filthy rags.

With that completed, Addie gently turned Rachel onto her back. She propped her head upon a pillow and spread a thin sheet over her. Being careful with the bruised area, she kissed her forehead.

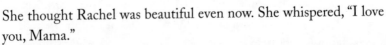

She thought Rachel was beautiful even now. She whispered, "I love you, Mama."

Rachel wished for a voice to say to Addie, *You don't know how good it feels to be clean. You are a good daughter, and I love you so very much.*

"Mama, I'll be right back." Addie pushed her pregnant body up awkwardly from the floor and went outside to throw out the dirty bath water and put the smelly rags in the fire. The rags disintegrated and burned up quickly, sending the disappointed flies on their way.

Claire and Emily were wrestling with a water-weighted bedsheet. Emily held one end, while Claire held the other. Emily giggled as they stretched and twisted it between them, wringing out as much water as they could, careful not to let it touch the ground and get dirty again. Then they hung the sheet on the line to dry.

Addie drank from a pitcher of freshly-drawn, sparkling-clear water. Sweet and refreshing, it was so cold it hurt her teeth. She went back inside the house with the water pitcher and knelt again on the floor beside Rachel.

"Mama." Rachel opened her eyes when Addie touched her shoulder. She held the tin cup to her lips and let her drink of the cool water. Rachel took two sips before closing her eyes again. The ordeal with Alfred and the bath had tired her out.

While Addie was knelt on the floor ministering to Rachel's needs, she realized that there was irony in circumstance. She thought, *Mama and I haven't been this close since I was eight years old. Grief may have taken her far from us, but it was she who kept us far from her.* An onslaught of memories darted through her mind. *The accident changed everything.* A burst of yellow flitted across her thoughts like autumnal butterflies.

Addie chased the memory off and said aloud, "Sufficient unto this day is its own troubles." Seeing that Rachel was resting comfortably, she pushed herself up from the floor and made ready to go about the rest of the day. She felt like she'd already done a full day's work and there was a mountain of things still to be done. First on the agenda, go out to the shed and get the tools to take the bed apart.

CHAPTER 3

"They that sow in tears shall reap in joy." (Psalms 126:5).

About the same time Addie was tending to Rachel in Collinsville, her fifteen-year-old son, Daniel, was busy at work in a woodshop miles away in the community known as Golden Meadow. The shop belonged to a man named Hiram Graham. Mr. Hiram, as Daniel referred to him, had offered him a job during the first week of May as a cabinet-making apprentice; he himself was a talented craftsman who made furniture of any style to order.

Daniel, a tall young man, serious in his ways, was living with his Uncle Wesley and Aunt Laura and his three cousins at their place just down the road a mile or so from the woodshop. Mr. Hiram and his uncle were good friends.

Daniel loved working for Hiram. A door had opened to a world he'd previously been a stranger to. In two and a half months, he'd already learned a fair share about the certain characteristics of the woods they worked with—pine, cedar, oak, pecan, and cherry. He was learning to identify wood by its smell and color. He was intrigued by the variable strengths and textures of the different kinds of wood and had gained an appreciation for the beauty of its grain. But, more importantly to Daniel, he considered himself fortunate to have been hired by such a man as Hiram Graham, figuring it unlikely he'd ever run up on a more just person anywhere. They worked long and tediously, but his boss was even tempered and went about things slow and easy. The hours passed quickly, even though neither of them were big talkers. However, Hiram listened to what little bit Daniel did say, and he seemed interested in knowing him as a person. Compared to how his pa had treated him, this was a far cry from what he was used to. Alfred had thrived on blaming him for everything that was wrong with the world.

Eager to make a good impression, Daniel had arrived several minutes early the first day on the job. He'd stood nervously outside the shop waiting on Hiram. Hiram finally ambled up a few minutes after six o'clock and drawled, "Daniel, just so you know, I'm ahabited to readin' my Bible ever mornin' between five-thirty an' six. If you happen to get here before me, you're welcome to go on in an' get started if you feel inclined to such."

Hiram had headed out early this particular morning to Oakdale to tend to some business and was yet to return. Daniel was glad for the solitude. He was carefully sanding the top of an oak drop-leaf table. As he rhythmically rubbed the wood, fine particles of sawdust accumulated on the table's surface. Daniel either wiped or blew the dust away and lightly ran his hand across the wood to determine its smoothness. His hands steadily worked on the table, but his mind was miles away.

He tried to pour his soul into the task at hand to keep from thinking about Amelia, but it was useless. Amelia was all he could think about. Amelia Rose Riley—just thinking her name made his heart ache. Today was July 27, Amelia's fifteenth birthday.

Daniel couldn't remember anything about himself up until the day he met Amelia, and it was the same for her. It was as if they'd

been wandering around aimlessly, awaiting the moment their paths would cross so they could begin their lives. That being the case, they began their lives the summer of their eighth year.

They had a special place down by the creek. If they'd planned to meet, and Amelia was late because of chores, Daniel patiently waited for her. Sometimes she'd run to join him and arrive slightly out of breath, with her face all flushed. They spent hours fishing, sitting quietly side by side on the shady bank of Hutchins Creek. Usually they sat so close that their legs touched. Daniel always insisted on baiting her hook, even though Amelia had no objection to handling worms.

They could talk about most anything or about nothing at all. Their friendship sustained them, urged them toward a private, still place neither knew of elsewhere. They shared their hopes and disappointments, some unspoken yet not secret from the other. His pa and hers, both drunks, roundered and stilled liquor together. Daniel felt bad for Amelia. She had it worse than him; at least he had a good mama. Amelia had often said how she wished Bonnie was nice and pretty like Addie. Bonnie treated Amelia mostly with indifference, usually referring to her as "that crumb-snatching brat." When they were drinking, Pete and Bonnie had other names they called her that sounded much worse, names that Daniel had only heard otherwise when they spewed forth from his own pa's mouth.

At a very young age, Amelia realized if she were to survive, she'd have to fend for herself.

If there was any food in the house to cook, Amelia cooked it. Amelia toted water and washed clothes. In winter, she gathered the kindling to build the fires to chase away the chill from their drafty house. One night, she awoke to rain dripping on her face; the roof was leaking. She found a pot to try and catch the water, but by morning her cot was soaked through. When she told her ma, Bonnie growled, "Do I look like a roofer? Go an' tell yer pa!" Amelia looked around the place. There was no use in expecting Pete to fix the roof or anything else. Their house was in shambles; it looked more like a lean-to than a house. Amelia just rearranged her small room so that her bed was no longer under the leak.

She never complained about things being hard, nor did she tell him they rarely had food in the house, but Daniel figured that out early on. On days when they were able to meet, Daniel always brought along something for Amelia to eat. Whatever he presented to her—whether it be a piece of chicken, an apple, a piece of pie, or whatever it was—Amelia would always unwrap the offering, break it in two, and give half to Daniel. If there were two cookies, she handed one to him. They would sit side by side and eat together, sometimes talking, sometimes in silence, but always content. Theirs was a friendship that shone brightly through years of small, sweet, unselfish gestures, as they shared of themselves one to the other.

Remembering Amelia's birthday reminded Daniel of the birthday she had five years ago when she was ten. He'd pleaded with his mama to help him get her a present. Something special. Addie gave him enough money to buy her a gift, and he bought her a porcelain doll from the mercantile in town. She gasped when she saw it. She'd never had a doll before. She exclaimed it was the most beautiful thing she'd ever held in her hands, much less owned.

The years went by. Adolescent changes and awakenings were inevitable, but even as his boyhood waned and Daniel became acutely aware that Amelia was no longer a little girl, their friendship remained innocent and pure, clean as spring rain. On their last night together before Daniel had argued with Alfred and left home, he and Amelia had lain on the grass under a canopy of stars and spoke in whispers. Daniel rolled over onto his side facing her and gently said, "Amelia Rose Riley, you promise me that you'll marry me one day, when the time gets right."

Amelia smiled and murmured, "I promise you, Daniel."

When he walked her home that night, they kissed for the first and only time. Daniel swore to himself if he died that night it'd be fine, because he was for certain and without a doubt, even if he lived to be a thousand, that there could be nothing more sweet to come than that kiss.

Three days later Daniel had a huge argument with his pa. Alfred had jumped on Daniel and bore him into the ground. The two rolled and struggled and grunted, evenly matched at first, until Alfred broke free and grabbed the horsewhip. He dealt several lashes to Daniel's back and made him a serious threat. He told Daniel to leave and never come back. Alfred didn't have to tell him that, for he never intended to go back. Now he only wished for a day when he didn't *look* back.

Daniel's hate for Alfred had given him the will and the strength to walk all through the night and most of the next day until he arrived at Wesley's. He was a haggard, hungry, dirty, bloody sight. Laura insisted a doctor be sent for, but Daniel refused. The worst of his wounds were on the inside, in his heart and in his mind. He hated Alfred passionately, and he was depending on that hate to sustain him as he strove toward a goal, toward fulfillment of a promise.

Frantic to get word to Amelia, three weeks later the opportunity finally came when he went into town with Hiram. He mailed a letter to her from the post office in Oakdale. The letter was not very detailed. He just told her where he was, that he was all right, and that he'd found a job. He assured her that as soon as he'd saved a little money, he would go back for her and they'd have the life they'd been counting on since they were eight. He asked her to write back to him as soon as possible.

He waited two weeks without hearing from Amelia. When no word came, he was worried and wrote to her again. He pleaded with her to respond. Three long weeks later, the letter arrived.

Daniel could hardly wait to open it. He tore into the envelope and saw Amelia's familiar handwriting and scanned the note. When he finished reading it, the paper he held in his hand was shaking. He stared at it like it was a poison that had drained half the life from his body. He sat there for a long time, not knowing what to do next. The very reason and purpose for his existence had suddenly become extinct. He was numb, his heart wrenched. His pain poured from his eyes and streaked his young face; the teardrops stained the front of his shirt.

He'd folded the note, put it back in the envelope, and hid it away in his pocket. He would keep it forever, but he'd never have to read it again, for the words were branded across his mind.

> Daniel,
>   By the time you read this, I will have moved away. I have found Mama and am moving from here today to go and live with her. I want you to know, even though I probably won't ever see you again, I'll never forget what a good friend you were to me. I hope for you a happy life.
>
> Amelia

Daniel blamed himself for not going by the Rileys' the day he left and explaining things to her then. He was sure that Amelia would have left with him. Now it was too late.

He continued to sand the table. He could feel the weight of Amelia's note in his pocket, heavy as a millstone; however, it was nowhere near as heavy as the sorrow he felt in his heart. The folded piece of paper he'd received in the mail two weeks ago was the only thing he had that he could hold in his hands that she'd held in hers. He missed her so, felt so empty and lonely without her. Alone in the woodshop, with no one around to see, he surrendered to his despair and wept with abandon.

Over supper that night, Alfred was hunkered over his plate, half listening as Addie replayed the ordeal of Rachel falling off the bed. He pretended to be surprised, but what he really felt was equal between amusement and irritation. Amused, since he had a clearer account than she did, since it was his doings; and irritated, because he didn't care to hear about every single detail right down to the bump on the old hag's head and how she and old lady Ellis took the bed frame down and left poor Granny's mattress on the floor to keep her from taking another tumble. It irked him to no end to have such endless babble heaped on his ears after a long, hot day of cutting logs and fighting horseflies. All he wanted was to enjoy his vittles in peace. He gobbled down his food like a starved dog, gulped down his buttermilk, and drained the last of his coffee. When he finished, he wiped his mouth across his shirtsleeve and belched.

Addie had fretted over Rachel's fall most of the day. When Claire went into town, she'd asked her to stop by the doctor's office and tell him what had happened. She told Alfred, "Travis came by and examined Mama this afternoon. Luckily, he said there are no broken bones, but it might take two weeks or better for the bruises to fade away."

The mere mention of Travis made Alfred's ears turn red. He grunted. Perturbed, he said, "Travis, is it? Don't you mean Doc Hughes?"

At first glance, Dr. Travis Hughes didn't strike most folks as being the doctor type. His usual attire was jeans, a vest, cowboy boots, and a hat. Nor did he fit the suit of decorum sometimes expected of one of his chosen profession. Travis had a natural bluntness about him that sometimes made him come across as rough as a dry cob. Barring the fact that he was ever so lively in the presentation of his person, his bedside manner might have been construed a bit salty for the taste of some. Still, he was reputed to be a fine doctor and was well-liked and in good standing with the community. Some of his patients referred to him as Doc, but those who knew him best just called him Travis.

By age thirty, Travis's hair had turned snowy white. Now in his midfifties, he was still a vital man with youthful posture and carriage, a tad cocky in his self-deceit, and never without a good cigar. Outwardly, Travis seemed dry and bland in his humor, but his blue eyes held a diverted glint that gave him away as never being inwardly dull or idle of mind. Life itself held plenty to keep him sharp and entertained.

Depending upon how far he was going to see patients and what mode of transportation suited him at the time, sometimes Travis made calls in his buggy; otherwise, he cantered about the country-side on horseback.

Travis had known Addie and Wesley practically all their lives. He'd delivered Daniel, but Emily had been in such a hurry to enter the world that by the time he arrived at the Coulter house on that October night, he had to give her birthing rights to Claire.

Presently, Addie ignored Alfred's sarcasm. It was no secret that he disliked Travis, but she'd known the man all her life, a whole lot longer than she'd known Alfred, and if she chose to call him by his given name, she would.

Alfred stared at Addie impassively for a minute while in his mind he measured his contempt for Doctor Travis Hughes. Then he steered his thoughts back to Rachel and chuckled. "If that don't beat all I've heard…Granny fell off the bed. Well, I reckon she's learnt her a lesson. If she'd a-laid still like she ort to- of, she'd still be a-layin' on a nice, soft bed instead of havin' to sleep on the hard ground like ol' Ben. She jus' messed in 'er nest." When he realized the ungraceful reality of that last part, he guffawed, taking nourishment from his own crude wit.

Addie found nothing funny about it and felt her temper rise. For a minute, she glared at Alfred. She felt like slapping him. Galled by his crassness, she vowed inwardly, *One of these days…*

Her tone held a sharp edge. "Alfred, what makes you so mean? It's hard for me to believe you can be so unfeeling toward another human being, especially somebody as helpless as Mama."

Nag, nag, nag. Alfred ignored her and pushed away from the table thinking, *You ain't seen mean yet! Tomorrow you'll be swangin' from the rafters tryin' to save yerself!* His eyes glittered in anticipation.

As he walked from the kitchen whistling, Addie said, "Tonight, when I say my prayers, I'm going to pray that the Lord changes your hateful ways. He might yet make a saint out of you." *In whom we have redemption through his blood, the forgiveness of sins, according to the riches of his grace.*

Alfred replied gruffly over his shoulder, "If I's you, I wouldn't waste my breath. Truth be told, the Lord knows I'm aways beyond redemption."

The next morning was Friday. Addie went about clearing the table and was wiping the skillet when Emily burst through the back door with a basketful of eggs. She set them down on the table without ever breaking her stride and continued through the house toward the front door. She sang out, "I'm headed to the barn to see Callie's kittens!"

Addie called a reminder to the back of Emily's head, "Don't forget the churning."

"Yes, ma'am!"

Addie glanced at the hands of the mantel clock. It was almost seven. *Time to feed Mama.*

She fixed Rachel a bowl of grits and went to her room. Rachel was wide awake, and as soon as Addie knelt on the floor beside her mattress, she started making loud, unintelligible sounds. She was trying hard to tell her something.

Addie bent over Rachel and kissed her, wincing at the sight of her bruised forehead.

"Here, Mama, let's put another pillow under your head so you can eat." She couldn't help but notice how different Rachel was acting this morning—she was so alert, her eyes were wide and roving. *Maybe she feels a little stronger today,* Addie thought hopefully. As she recalled, Rachel hadn't been this animated since one morning this past spring. That particular day she'd raised a ruckus similar to how she was behaving now.

Addie remembered how she had scanned her surroundings for a clue to Rachel's agitation, and it took only a few seconds before her eyes lit upon the culprit sitting on the windowsill. Before Emily had left for school, she'd put a water jar filled with pretty wildflowers nearby for her granny to enjoy. *Yellow wildflowers.* Emily was innocent in her thoughtfulness. Emily didn't know, and Addie would never confuse her by trying to explain to a child what she herself hadn't been able to understand when she'd been a child. She simply took the bouquet from the windowsill and relocated it to the kitchen table. Once the yellow flowers were out of sight, Rachel settled down.

But there were no yellow flowers in here this morning.

Addie guided the spoon toward Rachel's mouth, but she clamped her lips shut and turned her head. She rocked her shoulders and let out a high-pitched wailing sound.

It was all very frustrating for Addie not to be able to understand what Rachel was trying to tell her.

"Mama, I don't understand." Suddenly Rachel became quiet, and Addie noticed that she was staring, unblinking, at something across the room. Addie turned her gaze in the same direction, toward Emily's bed, to see what had captured her attention.

At first Addie thought there was a shadow of some sort in the dark corner, but then she decided it was a pile of something. Something black. *Odd.* A slight movement caused her to look more closely when the pile started changing shape. Realization dawned in an instant!

Addie froze and then fell backward, horrified. Cold fear ran up her spine! She dropped the bowl of grits and scrambled clumsily on her hands and heels in a frenzied attempt to push her cumbersome form backward toward the door to get out of the room as quickly as possible. When she was able to find her voice, she started screaming for Emily.

All the noise and vibrations caused by her scampering across the floor and hollering alarmed the huge snake. It uncoiled and raised its ugly head a few inches off the floor and flicked its forked tongue at them. It was as big around as Addie's arm! Having a terrible, mortal fear of snakes, she continued to scream.

The snake began crawling about in frantic search for an escape from the hysterical humans.

The screams were bloodcurdling. "*Emily! Emily Victoria!*"

Emily sprinted into the house quick as a deer, not knowing what to expect. One glance at the scene told her all she needed to know. She hurried to get a broom.

The more commotion there was in the enclosed space, the more entrapped the frightened serpent felt. It slithered and slid all around the room. Its sleek, muscular body slinked across Rachel twice. Addie was so filled with terror, she was completely irrational. She wanted to help Rachel, but her mind was paralyzed with fear. All she could do was scream and roll about on the floor, trying to dodge the snake's path.

Emily closed all the doors leading from the hallway and propped the front door open wide. Using the broom, she chased the snake from the house onto the porch. The snake didn't stop on the porch, but Emily caught up with it in its mad dash to get away and chopped its head off with a hoe.

Panting, Addie collapsed beside Rachel on her mattress. Rachel thought, *If I could move my arms and get my hands around your neck, I'd choke you for lettin' that snake crawl all over me!* Addie would not have blamed her one bit.

Her chest heaved with every breath. She was shaking, sweating, dizzy, and felt like she needed to vomit. She believed there was a distinct possibility she might die. She laid her head down on Rachel's chest and broke down and sobbed with relief. The encounter with the snake had gotten the best of her nerves. She hated snakes. As silly as it was to be that afraid of a thing, she just was, and that was that.

Rachel was upset, too, but not near as much as Addie.

"Now I know what you were trying to tell me," Addie said.

Rachel wished she could tell her that Alfred had played this heartless joke on them. *While you was puttin' breakfast on the table for your sorry husband, your sorry husband was in here drapin' that snake around my neck!* She thought, *She probably wouldn't believe me. I talked 'til I was blue in the face … tried to warn her about his kind, but she wouldn't listen to her crazy ol' mama.*

Alfred knew Rachel and Addie both despised snakes more than anything.

If the door had been latched, Claire would have knocked it off the hinges. She bounded up into the house completely out of breath. She'd heard Addie's screams all the way from her house, and when she saw Addie lying on the floor cradling Rachel, naturally she thought the obvious. *I never imagined she would take it this hard and carry on so, though.* She reasoned, *I suppose she overreacted on account of she's expectin.'*

"Oh, Addie, we're gonna miss her something awful, but she's finally at peace with the Lord," Claire consoled.

When Addie heard Claire's *condolences* and realized what she was thinking, hysteria set in. She clutched her chest as peals of uncontrollable laughter burst forth. She couldn't stop laughing long enough to explain herself. Claire thought Addie had surely lost her mind.

Wiping her eyes, Addie was finally able to say, "Mama's not dead!" Then she added, "But don't be surprised if I have this baby today!" Even Rachel's sounds were distinguishable as laughter.

Claire was confused. "There better be a good reason for all this since I ran all this way without any drawers!"

Emily came running in, pigtails flying. She couldn't wait to tell the tale. Addie was more than happy to let her. She was too worn out to do it justice.

Emily was on the lookout and could hardly contain her excitement as she rushed to greet her pa when he returned home from work. In explicit detail, she told Alfred the story of the snake being in Granny's room and led him to where she'd hung it on the fence so he could see for himself how big it was.

Still rattled from the morning's big event, Addie was finishing up supper. She'd made every effort to put the ordeal behind her, but so far the memory hadn't faded. She'd teetered around on wobbly knees, while she and Emily spent half the day going through the house, searching every nook and cranny for any more snakes that might have been hiding. They also looked for any ports of entry that a snake might be able to fit through.

She heard Alfred bellowing with laughter, carrying on like an idiot. She also noticed he'd tied Gent to a bush in the yard, which meant he was planning on riding off somewhere directly. He got paid today, so she figured he had it in mind to play cards tonight.

"That's for shore the funniest dang thang I've heard tell of in all my born days. Dog, I can just see it now—I bet y'all scattered like a covey of quail." He slapped his hat on his thigh and bent over laughing, thinking, *What I would've give to been a fly on the wall!*

Convinced he'd been hatched out by the sun and raised by boar hogs, Addie turned back to the stove. His callousness incensed her. In defense of Rachel's feelings, as well as her own, she said, "There's nothing funny about it, Alfred. Has it occurred to you that Mama and me were scared to death? Thank goodness Emily was here."

"Now, Addie, you gone tell me two grown women are *that* scared of a little ol' rat snake? Why, they ain't even poison," he pointed out. "You're just upset 'cause the Lord gave you a test today, an' you failed it."

Addie wouldn't speak to him anymore. She left the room carrying a plate of creamed potatoes and gravy and mashed-up peas and a cup of sweet tea. She wondered what he would do if she dumped it over his stupid head, but she had to feed Rachel. It was doubtful that she'd eat more than a bite or two, but she had to try.

The sun finally set upon the clamorous day, and night enfolded in quiet respite. Addie settled into a comfortable chair to pray and read her Bible. *Feed on the Word of God…*

Claire offered to sit with Rachel come this Sunday so she could go to church, and she gratefully accepted. Since the last stroke, most of the time Addie was confined to the house, devoted to taking care of her mama, so she missed going to worship services. She felt a need to go to church and feed her soul, spend some time in the fellowship of other believers; she needed a spiritual uplifting.

As written in the Scriptures, Addie knew it was important for them to worship together as a family, and Emily was excited, looking forward to them sitting together on a pew like in times past and singing hymns. One of her favorite Bible verses was *Make a joyful noise unto the Lord... Come before His presence with singing...*

As Addie let her mind wander, she suddenly found herself pondering the whereabouts of Amelia Riley, Pete and Bonnie's fifteen-year-old daughter. Amelia used to come by and sit with Rachel from time to time, but she realized the girl hadn't visited in weeks now, leastwise not since Daniel went to stay with Wesley and Laura in Golden Meadow.

Daniel and Amelia had been best friends since they were little children. Addie hoped there was nothing wrong. A dozing current carried with it her thoughts, *Amelia's young. I'm sure she's got better things to do with her time than sit around and keep company with us old folks.*

As Rachel lay on her mattress waiting for Emily to get ready for bed, she found herself again pining away for her beloved grandson. She missed Daniel terribly and hadn't been able to get him off her mind for days. Weeks had gone by since Alfred sashayed into her room one morning, boasting of how he'd stripped the shirt off Daniel's back with a horsewhip and run him off for good. She lamented, *Where in the world is he? I do wish somebody would tell me. And what has come of my sweet, precious Amelia? I miss her so.* She was worried sick about them both.

Rachel remembered how the girl was just about starved to death when she'd first come around. *There was not one ounce of meat on her bones!* Her thin shoulders could barely keep her raggedy, little dresses hanging on that wisp of a body. Rachel thought, *But I saw to it she ate.*

Most every day, under the guise of an afternoon tea party, Amelia got fed. And, Rachel sewed the waif-like girl a new dress just about every week for as long as she was able to see well enough to thread a needle. *Pete an' Bonnie deserved to be strung up for the way they mistreated that baby!*

Amelia didn't get loved at home, but Rachel certainly loved her. And, through her wise grandmotherly eyes, she'd seen the undisputable love between Daniel and Amelia when they were but young'uns. She believed in her heart that God intended for Daniel and Amelia to grow up to someday marry. *But Alfred's ruint all that. Daniel's gone. And poor Amelia.*

The day Alfred told her what he'd done, Rachel was distraught. She moaned and cried and carried on like she was in dire agony, for indeed she was. Thinking the worst, Addie sent for Doc Hughes. It was easy to determine that Rachel was in some sort of pain, but after he examined her, he was stumped, unable to diagnose the cause of her apparent suffering. Etiology unknown, he'd said.

Travis told Addie it was his opinion that Rachel wasn't experiencing actual physical pain. He believed it to be in her head. To him, it seemed she was grieving over something. But of course, since Rachel couldn't communicate what she was feeling to them, he couldn't say for sure.

The piercing blade Alfred had plunged and twisted into the depths of Rachel's heart was not palpable by anyone but her. The wailing continued for hours until she tired herself out and surrendered to exhaustion.

When Emily had washed up and donned a fresh cotton nightgown, she went to the front room and sat on a stool while Addie plaited her hair. With that done, they kissed goodnight and exchanged "sweet dreams" wishes. Emily retired to the room she shared with her granny and, kneeling at Rachel's head, she plumped the pillow under her neck

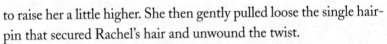

to raise her a little higher. She then gently pulled loose the single hairpin that secured Rachel's hair and unwound the twist.

With long, slow strokes, Emily started brushing the fine, sparse threads of her granny's hair. She complimented her.

"Granny, you've sure got pretty hair."

The whole time she was grooming her grandmother, the vivacious ten-year-old prattled nonstop about the various happenings of the day. Earlier this evening, she'd brought a tiny striped kitten inside and placed it in Rachel's hand, letting her touch its soft fur. As she'd rubbed the docile kitten, its gentle purring made the tired, old woman feel happy.

Emily frequently laid such gifts in Rachel's hand—a smooth, cool rock; a colorful feather; a bird's nest. One day she gathered a bouquet of trailing wild roses, and before she set them in the window, she held the velvety, pink blooms near to Rachel's nose so she could sniff their sweet perfume.

Just as Jesus multiplied five loaves and two fishes from a boy's dinner-basket to feed a multitude, the child offered what little she had, and God blessed it, and through her, He created small miracles and used them for good.

It wasn't long until the methodical stroking of her granddaughter's hands soothed Rachel into relaxed sleep. Emily whispered "night-night" and kissed the top of her head. She left her head propped up, just like Mama taught her, so her granny wouldn't choke on her own spit during the night.

After she tucked a light, soft quilt around Rachel, Emily said her prayers. After she said her prayers, she blew out the lamp and crawled into bed and closed her eyes.

CHAPTER 4

"Be still and know that I am God:" (Psalms 46:10).

Monday morning, Addie went in to Rachel and tended to her like every other morning. She was mindful of Rachel's inevitable feelings of loneliness and isolation and always tried to approach her cheerfully. Like Emily, she talked to her mama constantly while she carried out the familiar ritual of bathing and diapering her frail, deteriorating body and while dressing her wound. Sometimes she would sing to her or read to her from the Scriptures; sometimes she just sat and held her hands comfortingly in her own.

"Here, Mama, drink some water," Addie encouraged her.

Rachel took a few small sips from the cool metal dipper before closing her eyes again.

"Mama, I'm fixin' to go to the field to pick us a mess of peas for dinner. I'll be back shortly." Rachel's eyes remained closed, and her breathing was soft and regular. Addie kissed her on the forehead. "I love you, Mama."

I love you, Addie.

Addie left Rachel resting quietly on her mattress. From a peg at the back door, she took a bonnet and covered her head, leaving the strings untied. Emily was in the backyard under the oak tree playing with two of the barn cats. Callie, a calico mama cat, had mewled her litter out of hiding and was giving them a hunting lesson. The playful kittens toyed with a fat field rat Callie had maimed into a crippled condition, such that prevented its escape. She tossed the rodent about, encouraging the kittens to paw at it. She'd pretend to let the rat go free, only to recapture it and give it another swift swat. Now and again the rat would squeal, begging for mercy, but escape proved impossible.

A lazy, black-and-white tom Emily called Coppy was crouched a few feet away curiously watching the game of cat-and-mouse. His tail twitched with aggravation as he wished to have the smell of feathers on his breath. From a nearby bush, a pestering mockingbird cawed noisily at the cats, bravely swooping down every so often to taunt them.

"Emily, I'll be back directly," Addie told the girl as she walked barefooted in the direction of the pea patch, carrying a dented dishpan.

Crossing the distance between the back of the house and the path to the field, Addie was greeted by the loud crowing of roosters and cackling of hens. A couple of the guineas shrieked at her and bluffed her in mock attack with their wings hiked back when she disturbed their dust baths. After they'd made a show, and fools of themselves, they rejoined the flock of pot-rackers that were fighting over beetles and crickets.

Two fig trees grew just beyond the shed. Addie noticed they were abuzz with wasps and bees—the fruit was ripening. *There's another hot job for me,* she thought. In the next couple of days, she'd need to make fig preserves.

Even this early in the day it was plenty hot and humid enough to make her skin clammy and cause the fabric of her dress to cling to her back and chest. The path was so dry the dirt felt like talc beneath her feet. The warm, powdery feel of it lent an odd cushiony sensation to her feet and toes. The grass on either side of the lane was wilted and drab and crackled when the skirt of her dress brushed against it. Grasshoppers hopped from one stalk to another, staying just ahead of her in a race they intended to win. A few white clouds hung in a sky seemingly still and endlessly blue, the clouds held in place by the weight of the heat. The plaintive coo of a lone mourning dove echoed across the field.

There was no dew on the peas Addie picked. It'd been a hot, dry season, and the summer crop was almost gone, the hulls were drying up and the plants were strangling from the tight grasp of morning glory vines.

As her hands moved over the plants and picked with a natural and easy will of their own, she used this quiet time alone to talk to and listen to the Lord.

Lying on her mattress, Rachel thought of Addie out in the hot field picking peas. *Peas she'll no doubt force down my throat later,* she thought. Not that she wasn't grateful to Addie for all her effort; there just simply wasn't any joy for her in living like this. Most of her solace now came from an asylum of sleep and dreams. *Bless her heart, she means well, but food holds no appeal for me anymore. I'm too wore out from livin' to care about eatin'.*

She wondered how Addie was going to be able to manage with yet another baby to take care of. *She's seven months along with Satan's seed, child of Lucifer.*

It had been less than a week ago, one morning while Addie was at the well drawing water, that Alfred had come into her room and dropped his pants and exposed himself in a shameful way. Watching him wiggle and swing his hips from side to side, dancing around the room like an evil madman, she'd thought, *Oh for a kettle of boiling water an' a strong arm!*

Inwardly she sighed. *But I have no choice but to lie here an' wait for him.*

For she knew he was coming.

CHAPTER 5

"A man's heart deviseth his way:" (Proverbs 16:9).

I got a notion in my head. The voice inside Alfred wouldn't let up.

Trying to size up the man's strange behavior, a fluffy buff hen cocked her head to one side and gawked at him suspiciously with beady, glasslike eyes. She wondered why he tarried this morning. Usually he was long gone by this hour.

He kept out of sight behind the barn, like a boy who'd been sent out by his mama to cut a peach-limb switch for a butt-whooping.

Alfred peeked around the corner, cautiously watching the house. His forehead glistened with sweat. A drop rolled into his eye. He removed his hat and wiped his brow and ran his hand through his thick, black hair. His collar was wet, as was the waist band of his britches. He thought, *The sun ain't even up good, an' dang if it ain't hotter'n the devil's poker!* He cursed and muttered to himself. He'd been chewing on a hay straw and suddenly grew aggravated with it and pitched it to the ground. He was growing impatient and fidgety.

The hen rushed over greedily to investigate the straw, tapping it a time or two with her beak; it then retreated, disappointed when it yielded nothing of interest.

The man licked his salty lips and smacked. His mouth felt like it was full of sand. *My mouth's so dry I ain't got enough spit to swaller,* he told himself. He craved a smoke. *I didn't figure on havin' to wait 'til Gabriel blowed his horn!*

Finally!

He saw Addie start toward the field toting a pan. *She's headed to the pea patch,* he told himself as anticipation swept through him, *an' Emily's out behind the house playin' with them triflin' fur balls.*

A few minutes later, stepping out of the shadow of the barn, he left his hiding place and made his way cunningly across the road to the house. His heart was beating so wildly he thought his chest might bust wide open. He took the front steps two at a time and tiptoed across the porch. Once inside the dog-trot that ran through the middle of the house, he crept down the hall, past Daniel's empty room, and edged his way along the wall toward hers. It was the next one on the right.

Quietly, quietly, quietly, he took the last few steps. With every step he took, he felt more powerful. The door was ajar. Alfred looked around and listened. Sure that he hadn't been seen, he stepped across the threshold and went over to where Rachel lay.

She was wide awake; she'd sensed his coming long before she heard his footsteps crossing the porch. Her eyes warily followed his every move.

The way she looked at him gave Alfred an uncanny feeling.

"Was you waitin' on me, Granny?" he asked.

It seemed so.

Rachel's mind had reached a place of tired resolve. She was helpless; she couldn't move, couldn't say a word. There was nothing she could do but lie there and wait for whatever he was about to do. She'd give anything to be able to claw him, kick him, curse him, or spit on him, but she couldn't do anything but lie there. And wait.

She knew. Intuition told her his intent.

She knew she was about to leave here, but she was ready. Of course, if the choice was hers, she wouldn't have it happen this way for the world, but the choice wasn't hers. She was completely at his mercy; her helplessness gave him complete power over her.

Then suddenly she felt their presence; turning her eyes toward the ceiling, she saw them, hovering. She smiled. *Praise the Lord!* There would be no more pain; she would have a new body and a new life, an eternal life with them in Paradise. This was not the end, it was just the beginning. She prayed, *Lord, I'm much obliged to you for the life you gave me on this earth an' all the blessings you bestowed on me o're the years. You can see I'm just a wore out, useless bag o' bones now. Nothin' but a burden and a hindrance to Addie. Samuel and my baby, Rebekah, are waitin' for me on the other side, an' I long to be with them and with you. Watch o're Addie an' Wesley an' all their young'uns … but especially Addie 'cause you know this here man is the devil hisself. But I know you are just, and I beseech you, oh my God, let Alfred die a horrible death quick as you see fit.*

With an air of blessed assurance, she looked at Alfred for the last time with the culmination of hatred she'd held dear for him all through the years. Without fear or regret, her eyes invited him to get on with it. *I dare you, you cowardly cuss. I've got nothin' to fear 'cause I've been washed in the blood of the Lamb. Another thing is sure; after this day, I won't ever again have to lay eyes on your sorry hide.*

Alfred stared at her, disappointed to see no fear in her eyes. He had thought she would be afraid and at least cower from him. Without a solitary word, he took the pillow from underneath her head and covered her face with it. Breathing fast and hard, he pressed down and held it there firmly until she crossed over into Glory. *O death, where is thy sting … O grave, where is thy victory?*

In a hurry to put some distance between himself and the house, Alfred ran through the woods to where he'd left Gent. Minutes later, the horse was galloping down the hard clay road toward town.

Feeling an explosion of energy and pride, Alfred laughed and sucked a deep breath of air into his lungs, never having been more pleased with himself than he was at this moment.

Elated by the brute exhilaration of the killing, he thought, *Shoot! Best day's work I ever done an' caint brag about it to a single soul!*

CHAPTER 6

"Whereas ye know not what shall be on the morrow. For what is your life? It is even a vapor that appeareth for a little time, and then vanisheth away." (James 4:14)

When Addie returned from the garden toting the pan overflowing with peas, she was winded. She sat down at the table under the oak in the backyard to catch her breath and cool off. The sun had only begun to climb, and the day was already blistering hot. With Emily's help, it didn't take long for them to shell the mess of peas.

While Emily carried the hulls across the road to the barnyard and dumped them in the trough for Daisy, Addie put the peas on to boil. Five years ago, when Rachel came to live with them, they moved her old cookstove from her kitchen and set it in the backyard near the smokehouse to use during the hot summer months for cooking and canning. The house was aptly unbearable this time of year as it was, without the additional heat of a cooking fire making it even more so. However, in winter, the warmth from the woodstove was a blessing.

It was not until the peas started to cook that she went inside the house and discovered that Rachel had passed away. If not for the waxen discoloration of her skin, and, of course, the absence of breath, she may have simply been sleeping or perhaps praying. She looked so at peace the way she was lying there with her head resting on her pillow, her eyes closed, and her hands folded across her chest. Addie felt a deep sense of loss, but was not hysterical. Kneeling on the floor at Rachel's side, she stroked her mama's cold face and cried, "Oh, Mama, if only I had known … I would have stayed with you." When she left to go to the peapatch, Rachel's breathing seemed normal; in fact, nothing had seemed awry on this morn. It grieved her that Rachel had died alone.

Addie sent Emily to tell Claire, who then sent Emily for Travis. He, upon hearing Addie's sorrowful regret about not being with the old woman when she expired, reassured her by saying, "Sometimes death comes softly, Addie. Rachel suffered a long time, but now her suffering's met an end. Lay hold to the comfort of knowin' she slipped away peacefully in her sleep."

Addie nodded. Travis was right, for this she could be thankful.

Customarily, word of important happenings, such as that of a death, was spread throughout the county and over distance by word of mouth from one house to another. Neighbors would ungrudgingly stop whatever they were doing long enough to carry a message to his nearest neighbor. The grapevine of information was kept alive this way until the news fell upon the intended ears.

It was by this means of communication that Wesley received the news of his mother's death around evenings' twilight the last Monday of July.

Wesley Charles Warren and his wife, Laura, and their three children lived in the community of Golden Meadow, which lay midway between the town of Oakdale and the smaller township of Pine Bluff.

Asher Bradley was Laura's brother. Asher—his wife, Anna—and

their eight-year-old daughter, Libby, lived about a mile, give or take a few paces, west of Wesley's place. Asher had fixed fence most of the day and was gathering up his tools to head home for supper when his neighbor, Algie Thomason, rode up and relayed what sketchy details he'd received about Rachel's death.

Asher inwardly wished the task of delivering the solemn news of Rachel's passing hadn't fallen on him, but after a brief exchange of idle talk that consisted primarily of speculation over whether or not there was possibility of rain in the forecast, Algie steered his horse around and galloped off back in the direction from whence he'd come. Asher propped his tools up against a fencepost and set out walking toward his brother-in-law's house.

Asher and Wesley had been friends longer than they'd been kin. In fact, during the two years Wesley had to wait for Laura to turn seventeen so their father, Amos, would allow them to marry, he'd helped him build their house.

Wesley was unharnessing the team of mules when Laura entered the barn with her brother, and at a glance, he clearly read the seriousness on both their faces and knew there was a purpose for the untimely visit.

"Evenin', Wes."

"Asher."

Asher fumbled with his hat and turned it in his hands.

He said gravely, "Like I told Laura, I sure hate to be the bearer of bad news, but Algie ain't long left my place tellin' how your ma passed away this mornin' over at your sister's house in Collinsville."

Asher shifted his weight from one leg to the other, the circumstance making him feel awkward and ill at ease. True to his gender, he was more comfortable and practiced at presiding over practical matters than those of a personal nature.

"I shore am sorry for your loss."

Laura reached out and put her hand on her husband's arm while

he took a minute and weighed out the news in his mind before saying aloud what he was thinking.

"Well, I cain't say I didn't know this day was comin.' That last stroke all but put her down. She's in a better place now…better off than the rest of us, I reckon."

Though he may have sounded all too practical about it, there was ample sadness in his voice as he spoke the words. No matter how difficult—or rather how insane—Rachel had been, she was still his mother.

As he stood there reflecting, he thought of the time when he and Laura had journeyed to Collinsville a few weeks after Meggie was born so that Rachel might see her new granddaughter. Since she'd always doted on Sarah Beth and Jesse in a manner that would make one think they made the sun rise and set for her, it was naturally assumed she'd act accordingly toward Meggie. In fact, in a letter to them, she thusly expressed her excitement over seeing the baby and declared she was counting the very hours in anticipation of their arrival.

When they got there, Rachel was standing on the porch step to greet them, Addie next to her, also eager to finally lay eyes and hands on her new niece. Laura proudly presented the baby to Rachel, placing their new bundle of joy into her arms. Rachel took one look at Meggie's beautiful little face and gasped. The smile fled from her face, and in her haste to pass the baby over to Addie, she almost dropped her. She broke away from her and, for the duration of their stay, made no move to approach the sweet child again, withholding any show of affection or endearment for her whatsoever, even to the extreme of avoiding being in the same room with her whenever possible.

After traveling all that way only to be received so, Laura's feelings were, of course, crushed. She was both miffed and perplexed. What would make a woman reject her own flesh and blood and not want to cuddle and rock her own grandchild? For the next couple of days, it proved difficult for her not to nurse some degree of resentment along with the baby.

Wesley was mad but not surprised. He remembered all too well what it'd been like living with Rachel's irrational behavior and drastic mood swings. She'd forever ran hot and cold. *Even before the accident.* Not one to nurture dissension or old hurts, he just reminded himself, *Mama's crazy ways are the very reason I live in Golden Meadow instead of someplace around here.*

It was Claire who later inadvertently shed light on the reason for Rachel's alienation of Meggie; nevertheless, as far as Wesley was concerned, it was still a poor excuse for the ridiculous way she'd acted toward an innocent baby. He figured, if anything, Rachel should be glad of the likeness Meggie bore.

In the long run, there were no residual hard feelings, instead more of an unsympathetic acceptance of the situation, and when Rachel suffered her first stroke, Wesley and Laura willingly extended her an invitation to move to Golden Meadow and live with them. Rachel snubbed their offer, citing that she'd be better suited at Addie's since Doc Hughes was just a holler away should she need a doctor. Anyway, Laura already had her hands full with three children, and her mother lived with them as well. Rachel had met Stell Roberts on occasion and ironically considered her to be an old, contrary grump who disregarded conventional manners when it suited her, which was always. Of course, Rachel couldn't stand Alfred either. She wouldn't cross the road to spit in his eye, but on the other hand, Collinsville was home to her.

Truth be told, she could have made excuses all day long, but at the end of the day, they would all boil down to the only one she really couldn't contend with.

Meggie.

Even after all this time, it pained Rachel to look at her, for the beautiful, little, dark-haired Meggie was the spitting image of her beloved Rebekah.

As his thoughts returned to the present, Wesley said, "Mosey on up to the house an' set with us a spell, Asher...I 'spect Laura's got some coffee made."

Asher was tired and hungry and had a considerable distance to walk home. He politely declined by saying, "Much obliged, but I guess I need to be gettin' on home. Anna will have supper waitin.' She's probably wonderin' right now what's keepin' me." He made ready to leave and added, "If there's anything we can do for y'all, just say. We'll help out any way we can."

"Much obliged to you, but right now I don't know of a thing."

The men shook hands. Laura smiled at her brother and thanked him for coming. Before departing, Asher asked, "By the way, Wesley, how old was your ma?"

Wesley frowned in thought while he figured his answer. "If she'd lived 'til the tenth of September, she would'da seen fifty-six."

Wesley finished putting the tack away while he and Laura discussed their traveling plans. It was decided they would set out at daybreak for Collinsville. Sarah Beth and Jesse would go with them to their granny's funeral, but since Meggie was so young and didn't know her anyway, Stell could just look after her there for a couple of days.

They thought it was best if Daniel didn't go. It was probably a good idea for him to stay as far away as possible from Alfred.

With these things settled, they left the barn and walked hand in hand toward the house to tell the children and prepare for their long journey.

Regardless of the occasion, it became a glad reunion when Wesley and Laura and the children arrived on Tuesday afternoon. When they climbed down off the wagon, Addie managed to grab Jesse and Sarah Beth and plant a kiss on each of them before they went flying into the house on the wings of curiosity to stare at their dead grandmother just long enough to satisfy their fascination before they ran off to play. Emily was overheard promising her cousins that she'd also show them a dead snake.

Then came the enthusiastic greetings and embraces, the tears and the laughter, the questions and the answers. Laura whispered her sympathy softly, "I'm so sorry you've lost your mama."

"Thank you, Laura. It's kind of you to say." Addie had always been fond of her sister-in-law. Laura was a lively, genuinely sweet and good-hearted person.

Laura drew back to look at her and said, "You look wonderful." She placed her hand on Addie's round belly. Her pretty brown eyes danced when she asked, "Oh, won't it be exciting for you to have a new baby in the house? What are you hoping for—a boy or a girl?"

Addie accepted the compliment while considering the question. If she'd answered honestly, Laura would no doubt be taken aback, for she might very well have said she'd been so busy taking care of Rachel she'd not given much thought at all to the baby. A second truth would sound far worse. She was ashamed to admit she had yet to decide whether to be happy or sad about this baby, considering the sorry way things stood between her and Alfred. But there was no need to concern Laura with such an admission, thus Addie answered, "Don't ask me why, but I just have a feeling it's a boy, which will be fine with me."

Addie turned to her brother. Wesley drew her close, and she clung to him and cried, "I've missed y'all so."

As Addie brushed her tears away, he replied, "I'm glad to see you too, sister."

Their eyes met in understanding when Addie said to Wesley, "I know y'all are tired and hungry. We'll talk later."

She was impatient for them to get off to themselves, out of earshot of everyone, so he could give her news of Daniel.

Wesley nodded. "First, I want to go in an' see Mama. Then I'll come back out an' move the wagon an' see to the horses."

Addie escorted them inside the house. Claire had requested to be allowed the honor of preparing Rachel's body to be laid out. Bathing and dressing her for burial was the last act of kindness she would be able to do for her old friend. Rachel's coffin was set up on sawhorses in the front room for her corpse to be viewed by the thoughtful and the morbidly curious—both of who would most certainly be coming to call within the next two days.

Wesley had last seen Rachel some four months ago in the spring. When he went over to the coffin and looked down on the mortal remains before him, a lump crept up unexpectedly in his throat. He could hardly make the frail, wasted body he beheld be his mama. It was unbelievable how she had deteriorated in such a short length of time. Gazing at her in quiet reflection caused him to feel the full impact of her death, giving him a prickling sense of his own mortality. *As it is appointed unto men once to die.* After a few minutes, he squeezed Laura's hand, and seeing the emotion on his face, her compassionate gaze followed him as he slipped quietly from the room.

Shifting their attention to happier talk, Addie steered Laura toward the kitchen. "There's already enough food here to feed an army." She handed her a plate and a fork, and while Laura helped herself to a slice of ham, a heaping spoonful of string beans, and a piece of cornbread, she poured them some tea and cleared a space at the table for them to sit down.

Laura was very perceptive. Regarding Addie for a minute or two, she sensed her weary spirit, a loss of heart that didn't ordinarily belong to her sister-in-law. While her head was bowed in a silent prayer of thanks for her food, she earnestly asked God to restore and strengthen Addie.

When she raised her head, she looked across the table at her and suggested gently, "I can't imagine how hard the last few months have been, Addie. I can tell you need a rest. I wish I could have been more help to you."

Addie shook her head and, thinking mainly of Daniel, struggled to keep her voice steady. "You are good. You've been more than a help to me, Laura. I can't put words on what it means to me that you've opened your home and your hearts to Daniel. For this, I am truly grateful."

"You are welcome." Laura smiled as she reached across the table and patted Addie's hand. "We don't visit together nearly enough."

For a while, the two women found much to talk about. They cast all things, from the simplest and mundane to some they wouldn't dare mention to any other, into the course of conversation. As they caught up with each other's news, the barriers of separation, the passing of time and distance of miles, seemed to dissolve in the current and were taken far from them.

It was under the last rays and long shadows of the evening sun that Addie and Wesley finally had the opportunity to talk.

"Tell me all about Daniel. How is he? I miss him so. And what's this I hear about him having a job in a cabinet shop?"

"Daniel's fine, sister," Wesley assured her. "A fifteen-year-old boy's shy about such, but he said, 'Be sure to tell Mama I love her an' I miss her.'" Daniel made Wesley promise not to tell Addie how badly Alfred had hurt him. He didn't want her to worry any more than she already did.

"I've already said this to Laura, but thank you, Wesley. Y'all are so good to take Daniel in like you have."

"He's more than welcome to stay as long as he needs to." Wesley added, "He misses his sister, too." He was leading up to saying something.

Addie replied, "I know. Even though they fussed like cats and dogs, Emily misses having her big brother around."

Wesley hesitated, waiting to see if Addie planned to say more on the subject. When she didn't, he proceeded with caution.

"Families need to be together, Addie."

Daniel wouldn't tell Wesley what set Alfred off the day they argued. He just said that his pa was drunk, and he didn't want to talk about it ever again. He didn't want Alfred to know where he was either. Wesley had sent word to Addie in a letter mailed to Claire to let her know her son was with them. After seeing first hand what

Alfred had done to the boy, Wesley was concerned for Addie's safety as well. He deliberately turned the topic another way. "We'd be glad to have you an' Emily go home with us tomorrow. You know we've got plenty of room."

There was no mistaking his meaning. It rang out loud and clear. Addie sighed. "Let's just give it time for the water to clear."

He came back with, "You can't get the water cleared up 'til you get the hog out of the creek!"

Addie couldn't suppress her laughter at the old expression. "God bless us Southerners and our silly sayings!" She felt happy and content to have Wesley there. She looped her arm through her brother's, and they walked slowly toward the house to join the others.

"You worry too much."

You didn't see Daniel's back, Wesley silently told her.

He repeated in a gentler tone, "I mean what I said, Addie. There'll always be room for you and Emily at our house if you change your mind."

She was touched by his concern but evaded his persistence on the matter and coaxed him in a different direction, saying, "Let's go have some sweet tea and a peach tart. Or better still, a while ago Claire brought over some freshly-baked teacakes!"

Wesley suddenly remembered that he hadn't answered her question. "Oh yeah, you asked about Daniel's job. He works for our neighbor, Hiram Graham, just down the road at his woodshop. Hiram's a good man. You'll meet him tomorrow. Now tell me, how are my old friends … Claire … Travis … ?"

In part due to the relentless heat and given the fact that Wesley and Laura needed several hours of daylight to return home, it was decided that Rachel be laid to final rest at nine o'clock Wednesday morning.

Getting dressed, Addie contemplated wearing a cool summer frock for the funeral, knowing that Mama wouldn't care what she wore—that is, so long as it wasn't yellow. But instead she let propriety and decorum and, what is perceived by some as respect for the dead, win out. She thought, *Some folks carry more judgments under their wings than a Baptist preacher, judging others much more harshly than God judges them.* But she wouldn't give way to tongue-wagging. She abandoned comfort and sensibility and donned a drab, dark-gray dress with a crisp, white, starched collar, while Emily wore a simple church dress and tied her hair back with a black ribbon.

During the graveside service, Addie looked out at the faces of the congregation until she spotted him. *Alfred.* He was standing off to himself, wearing a look that would scare birds off their roost, almost hidden behind the very last row of those in attendance. Nowhere near her or any of the family. Appearing distracted, he didn't even look her way.

Addie thought to herself, *If anybody wanted to spread gossip, there's a crude figure of just cause, given the fact he stayed out all night!* Alfred had made himself all but absent ever since Rachel died. Addie sighed. She'd given up trying to understand him.

At thirteen Alfred had walked away from his father's poor farm in Missouri and never looked back. Most of his youth, he drifted from one place to another; where he called home was wherever he happened to be at the time. Smart and not afraid of hard work, he went from job to job earning enough to feed and clothe himself, picking up a variety of useful skills along the way. Eventually he found himself in Mississippi, a logger in the timber business, harvesting mighty pine trees for lumber.

Addie had never been anywhere exciting her whole life. During their courtship, such that it was, the handsome, wild-eyed dreamer swept her off her feet as he told with pride in his voice of the wonderous adventures he'd had in places like Savannah and Jacksonville. He'd even talked of them maybe going to New Orleans together.

Addie was young, bored, and lonely; Alfred, carefree and careless. He made her laugh and sparked her imagination. Despite his past ramblings, like many a misguided bride, she had believed Alfred would make a suitable husband, fully believing once they were married he would settle down and they would live happily ever after, in love.

She had been wrong.

Thinking back now, Addie remembered that the first few weeks of their marriage had been the happiest of her life. Her happiness, however, was too soon lost. They had barely been married a month until one night he didn't come home for supper then later staggered in drunk. Hurt and bewildered, the next morning she'd made sure to tell him that she would be cooking his favorite meal that evening. That night, not only did he not come home for supper, he didn't come home at all. Fighting back her panic, she'd waited up for him until after midnight before she finally went to bed, alone.

As time passed and she was stripped of her dreams, she found it was simpler just to shield herself from his drinking and cheating by wearing blinders, simpler to handle the hurt and disappointments with quiet dignity—and denial.

Then Daniel came along, and she didn't need anything more…

As the preacher spoke of the hope that is laid up in Heaven, Addie gazed past the wrought-iron fence bordering the cemetery. Just beyond was where County Line Road ran into Monroe Road. She loved the story of how Samuel and Rachel met up where the roads forked and then walked together the rest of the way to the church where they became husband and wife. She thought sadly, *Their life together on this earth has now come full circle and ended at the same place it started from.* Tears of the remembrance blurred her vision.

Rev. William Harris officiated the simple but touching service. He was generous with kind words of comfort, saying all the things one expected and needed to hear at a loved one's funeral. He was also smart and merciful to keep the sermon short.

It was especially stirring at the conclusion when the group of mourners who'd congregated in Eminence Cemetery sang a hymn in closing. Addie held Emily close and consoled the tender-hearted girl as she sobbed openly and unashamed as her granny's coffin was lowered into the grave.

As it were, the meal following Rachel's funeral turned into a social event. Having never expected so many folks, to Addie it seemed like half the town attended Rachel's service, and most of those headed back to her house afterward to further extend their condolences and partake of the bountiful bereavement feast.

Adhering to the tradition that good food can heal most any hurt and bring comfort to the soul, there was plenty of good food to go around. There was fried chicken, chicken and dumplings, ham, butterbeans, snapped beans, peas, rice and gravy, potato salad, deviled eggs, cornbread, and biscuits. There was a table just for sweets laden with pecan pie, sweet potato pie, apple and peach pies, jam cake, and sliced watermelon. Seeing that some poor soul had brought a hickory nut pie, Addie made a mental note to seek out whoever made it, since hickory nuts were little more than a nuisance even to squirrels. Considering how hard a hickory nut was to crack, much less the puny reward inside for all the trouble; to have shelled out enough to make a whole pie surely had been a labor of love.

Addie didn't have to put on manners to be a gracious hostess. She meandered around the yard greeting everyone she saw, appreciative to everyone for coming and for their kind words of encouragement.

A group of children were gathered in a fit of laughter, having a time over a watermelon seed-spitting contest. Most of the participants were boys, but Emily was being cheered on by the girls. Addie was glad to see she was over her crying spell and was enjoying being with the other children.

The funeral provided Hiram Graham a dual opportunity. He could pay his respects to Wesley's family and also make a trip into

Collinsville to acquaint himself with the town's sawmill. He needed to buy some cherry wood for a piece of furniture he was working on and had heard they had a ready supply.

When Wesley insisted that he go by his sister's house after the funeral to be introduced to her formally and have a meal before he traveled home, Hiram agreed.

In late spring, he'd hired Wesley's nephew to work for him in his woodshop, and he was really impressed with the boy. He was well-mannered and a hard worker, and though Hiram didn't know all the particulars, he knew Daniel left home over some trouble with his pa. He was intrigued to have a chance to meet his mother.

Addie saw Wesley standing with a tall stranger and knew this must be the man he'd mentioned yesterday. She cut across the yard and walked toward them. As she approached, they turned to greet her, and she smiled as Wesley introduced her to Hiram Graham.

Their eyes met. Eventually the day would come when she would remember his tanned, handsome face and find herself unexpectedly thinking about the depth of his startlingly blue eyes, and how they crinkled at the corners when he smiled at her. But for now she was just appreciative of the chance to have any contact with the man who worked with her son. "I'm very pleased to meet you, Mr. Graham. Wesley and I are touched that you came all this way to pay your respects."

When he spoke, his voice possessed a deep, warm quality. "It's been my pleasure. I enjoyed traveling over this way and getting to know another part of this country."

"Where are you from?"

"Virginia, ma'am." Hiram was thinking about how Wesley never mentioned how pretty and gracious his sister was. His eyes swept the entire length of her, not disrespectfully, but appreciatively. Noting her condition, his eyes trailed off, and for a moment, he fixed his gaze on something nondescript on the horizon. Whenever Addie crossed his mind in the future, he would be careful to remind himself she was a married woman. A *pregnant* married woman at that.

He looked back at her when she said to him, "It's kind of you to give Daniel a job. Thank you."

Hiram nodded. Their eyes held for another long moment. "Daniel's a mighty fine young man." He made ready to depart. "Wesley, ma'am, again, I'm sorry for your loss, but it's high time I head back toward Golden Meadow." To Addie he said, "Much obliged for the meal." She placed her soft hand in the strong one he extended for a brief and gentle handshake. "Again, it's a pleasure to have met you."

Addie stood watching as Hiram and Wesley made their way across the road to where he'd left his rig. There was an easy unhurriedness about the man that she really liked. When he and Wesley shook hands in parting, she glimpsed beyond the gesture and witnessed a certain exchange of like respect between them, a sentiment of brotherly love.

She wasn't sure why exactly, but suddenly Addie felt reassured knowing Daniel was working for this friend of her brother, this genteel man from Virginia.

Inside the house, Claire and Laura were helping keep a clean supply of plates and forks ready. Laura looked out the window and noticed a couple of stern-looking elderly ladies standing in the yard. She nudged Claire and indicated toward the two. "Miss Claire, they're the ones I told you about earlier. I overheard them ask Addie if they might have something of Rachel's. 'Some little trinket to remember her by' were their exact words, if I remember correctly." Laura had been appalled at their nerve to be so blatantly insensitive to Addie's feelings so soon after burying her mother.

Claire looked in the direction where Laura pointed and frowned. She knew the two all too well. "I swanee! Kill the fatted calf! That's

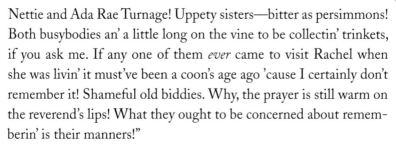

Nettie and Ada Rae Turnage! Uppety sisters—bitter as persimmons! Both busybodies an' a little long on the vine to be collectin' trinkets, if you ask me. If any one of them *ever* came to visit Rachel when she was livin' it must've been a coon's age ago 'cause I certainly don't remember it! Shameful old biddies. Why, the prayer is still warm on the reverend's lips! What they ought to be concerned about remem-berin' is their manners!"

Laura laughed when Claire chirped, "Confounded buzzards! I tell you, it's a proven fact. There ain't nothin' like a corpse and a free meal to get company to call—most of whom, on any other day of the week, would most likely pass by with their noses up in the air!"

Laura thought, *I do declare! Mama and Claire Ellis must be kin!*

Travis and Wesley paused under a chinaberry tree at the edge of the yard. The tree resembled a huge open parasol and was useless, save for providing a nice shade in summer and a slew of hard, amber-colored berries that boys used for slingshot ammunition in the fall.

Travis held out a cigar. "Have one," he offered, "it'll cure what ails you."

"If that's the case, give me a handful of 'em," Wesley replied. They lit up to enjoy a smoke.

A comfortable silence followed. Finally Travis said, "I was right proud of old Preacher Harris today. He said a fair piece over Rachel." Wesley nodded. Travis asked, "How's the boy?" Of course he was referring to Daniel.

The answer was, "Better off now that he's away from his so-called pa. He was a sight, though, when he first got to us."

En route to Golden Meadow, fleeing from Alfred, Daniel had soaked in the creek to ease the burning cuts on his back and smeared himself down with mud to keep the thirsty mosquitoes at bay. Wesley was quiet-natured to the eye, but under his skin, he was strong and fiercely protective of his family. Thinking about the ugly, red welts on Daniel's back from the lashing Alfred had given him made his blood rise all over again.

Wesley remarked, "Travis, I've had to raise my hand a time or two to discipline our young'uns, but what Alfred did to Daniel was pure savage."

Travis drew deeply on his cigar and lost himself in thoughtful silence. He didn't like what he was hearing. He already knew enough about Alfred's carryings-on to hold him in high contempt. Along with doctoring came territorial knowledge of most anything and everything there was to know about folks. *Good God-a-mighty, that Alfred is a bad seed,* he thought.

Wesley said, "I swear if I live to be as old as Moses, I won't ever understand what come over Addie to take up with the likes of him."

Travis determined dryly, in what meager defense he had to offer, "I'm speakin' strictly for myself, but I've been known to come to under a strange sheet...maybe two, in my life. Of course, I was deeper in the cups back then..."

Wesley couldn't help but laugh. Travis was insane! "Dang, Travis! You don't have to tell all you know." Travis just shrugged.

When Wesley and Travis spotted Alfred on the opposite side of the yard in the midst of a group of men, it was obvious he was in the middle of telling a tall tale, taking advantage of the occasion to dominant the stage.

It was oppressively hot. Wesley squatted down and wiped away the sweat that collected on his brow. A trail of smoke curled from his mouth. "Yessir, that's one sorry feller yonder," he commented. "I wouldn't give him the sweat that's in the crack of my butt right now if he was dyin' of thirst." Wesley wondered where Alfred had slept last night, since he knew he hadn't come home.

The statement brought a smile to Travis's eyes. He nodded his agreement and approval. "It appears we host a mutual disdain for ol' Alfred. As I recall, your mama didn't have much use for him either. Rachel tickled me with some of the things she'd come out with about him. I remember years back, one mornin' at church, old lady Weems asked Addie, 'Where's Alfred at this mornin'?' Before she could answer, Rachel chimed in an' said, 'The heathen's at the house sittin' by the fire practicin' up for Eternity!'"

Wesley chuckled at the account.

Alfred was loud and boisterous as he continued to tell his tale. The two men heard him say, "I told him no, no, no, you ignorant fool! Don't let on to God we bin a-drankin'! He hears that, he won't help us out of this here ditch!" The men laughed at his ignorance.

Enticed by his knowledge of Alfred's violent nature, Wesley seethed. "I've a mind to use the same whip on that good-for-nothin' cuss that he used on Daniel. I be-dogged, if I don't!"

Wesley was a man of calm countenance, but in the way of a green-broke horse. Under his hide, he had plenty of roughness reserved to kick out of the traces if crossed just right.

Travis tossed down a verbal restraint. "You can deputize me, brother, but this ain't the time or place for us to leave him for dead."

In an attempt to lighten the mood, Travis brought up another ancient memory. "Yep, I can just hear old Samuel sayin', 'You boys know when Alfred was born they was twins—a boy and a turd.' Then he'd pause just long enough to spit and say, 'And the boy died!'"

As riled up as Wesley was over Alfred, he couldn't help but grin. "I hear what you're steppin' in, dude." He just shook his head and let the moment pass, for now.

The sun was dazzlingly bright. Wesley squinted up at Travis and took off in an opposite direction. "I'm a little surprised you ain't found yourself a wife after all this time."

Travis lost his wife, Carolyn, to pneumonia nine winters ago. His only son was thirty years old and lived in Memphis near his wife's family. Travis drawled slowly, "Ain't been lookin' for a wife. Trouble enough finds me as it is. Anyway, we ain't all lucky enough to be thrown in the ring with the woman of our dreams like you are."

In truth, Travis did have a deep, unrequited love for the woman of his dreams. However, this was a lonely secret that he protected and kept locked away in his heart.

Wesley snorted. "Yep, I'm one lucky man. I'm lucky enough to be blessed with the wife of my dreams an' cursed with the mother-in-law of my nightmares." Laura's mother, Stell Roberts, had been living with them now for almost two years. "Miss Stell may look as solemn as a settin' hen, but she can flat pitch a fit when she takes a notion. You can take to heart Proverbs 21:19, my friend: It is better to dwell in the wilderness than with a contentious and angry woman!"

Travis howled.

CHAPTER 7

"I will never leave thee, nor forsake thee." (Hebrews 13:5).

The house was quieter than it had ever been. Addie was alone. Everyone had gone home, returned to their own. It seemed the whole world had retreated to some far off place, taking with them everything and leaving only grief behind for her alone to tend.

Emily and Sarah Beth had schemed, then begged and pleaded, for her to permit Emily to go home and stay with them for a couple of weeks. Addie pretended to have to think about it, making them wait an unbearable minute with their faces frozen in a half-anxious expression as they held their breath in anticipation of her answer. Wesley and Laura had already said yes so naturally she agreed. The girls jumped up and down and kissed her on the cheek before their squeals of excitement echoed down the hall as they took off running to Emily's room to pack her things. Emily was practically beside herself at the prospect of seeing her brother again and spending two whole weeks away from home at her cousins' house. It was a child's dream come true.

Addie knew the children needed this time together. Brothers and sisters and cousins should run and play and laugh together, celebrate being young.

The hardest thing she'd ever done in her life was packing Daniel's clothes so Wesley and Laura could take them to him. The task made her face a finality she'd denied until now. Daniel wasn't coming back home. She'd lost him, just as she had lost Rachel. She loved her son to the depth of her soul, yet she couldn't help but feel she'd failed him. She wasn't ready to let him go, but in reality, he was already gone, had been gone for weeks.

She also sent his arrowhead collection, a spinning top, a bag of glass marbles, an old slingshot, and all his favorite books—familiar things. She was glad Daniel couldn't see the tears that poured down her face as she handled these childhood treasures of his. She realized he'd long since outgrown the toys, but she imagined he'd be happy to pass them on to his younger cousin Jesse. Jesse was almost nine years old, just the right age to glean joy from such things.

Addie was reluctant, for she knew she would miss his presence around the place, but she sent Ben, too. The dog, in fact, belonged to Daniel. He'd raised him from a puppy. She'd give anything to have seen the look on his face when his little sister *and* Ben jumped off the wagon this evening.

Alfred had ridden off on Gent hours ago.

It must be around nine o'clock, Addie thought. In the dark room, the ticking of the clock on the mantel sounded unusually loud.

Darkness had fallen around her while she sat in Rachel's old rocker. In her hand she held an old, still photograph, a likeness of her with Pa and Mama, Wesley, and Rebekah. They'd sat for the photograph about three months before Rebekah died. As she'd looked at it, she thought, *A photograph of a happy family.*

Addie kept it pressed safely within the worn pages of Rachel's old family Bible. The Bible chronicled the names and dates of births, baptisms, marriages, and deaths of members of both Samuel's family and Rachel's, dating back over a century. *Now she could write in another death.*

As she sat alone in the dark hours of the day she'd buried her mama, Addie realized she already missed Rachel terribly. About this same time night before last, she'd bathed her and dressed her for bed, and Emily had brushed her hair. Now, just two nights later, her mama was gone. The nightly ritual was gone. Everything had changed, nevermore to be the same.

The overwhelmingly empty feeling made her thoughts turn to another dear one she missed terribly, his twinkling eyes etched upon her memory forever. She missed how he'd made her and Wesley laugh by pretending to make his tongue wiggle from side to side by tugging on his ears.

Pa taught me so much about life, she thought. Samuel Warren had loved people. *He taught me and Wesley to 'love thy neighbor.'* Thinking back, she realized hardly a day passed that she didn't tag along with her pa to visit someone. He was one to just stop by a neighbor's house to say "howdy" and see how they were getting by, and he was forever sharing produce with them—apples, pears, squash, peaches.

"You never see Samuel Warren without a bucket in his hands," folks would say. He had a heart big as a washtub and full of understanding. Samuel was the one who made certain that she and Wesley felt loved—without feeling guilty—after Rebekah died. There was never any doubt in their minds that he loved them both dearly.

Samuel loved to play his fiddle. It was a beautiful, old instrument that had belonged to his father before him. The body of it was made from fine wood that was smooth to the touch, its patina glowed rich with age. With the bow guided by his hand, the fiddle begat the ability to breathe and sing a delicate overture and crescendo into a symphony of a heartsong unable to beguile the ears, for the tone and tempo of the music expressed accordingly the sentiment of the musician. The mood of his spirit was revealed through his playing.

Samuel had meant everything to her; it had been so hard for her to let him go. Addie hugged herself as she remembered the night her beloved father died. She was only fourteen years old. She recalled how she'd sat so close to him on the bed and held on so tightly to his big, strong hands—hands that could set most anything right. How she'd prayed, held fast to hope, desperate to keep him here with her on this earth. *Please, God, don't take him; I need him here with me.*

But she'd held on in vain, for while she was trying to hold him here, God was pulling him ever so gently toward a more glorious destination, beckoning him toward Heaven. She stayed right there with him until the end, and when he slipped from her grasp, she lingered for a time, holding onto his lifeless hands long after he'd gone home. It was so hard to let him go. Her pa had been the one she could always count on.

It wasn't until later that Addie realized what Samuel had done all along. Throughout the years, and in each minute they'd spent together, he'd showed her with subtle acts of love and kindness to those around him how to imitate the ways of one she could always count on. *And be ye kind one to another…*

He'd taught her to look to the one whose gentle heart was full of infinite understanding.

He'd taught her to love the one who loves unconditionally— *beareth all things*—and had hands able to set anything right—*I will make crooked things straight…*

Because of him, Addie learned to lay hold to the hope set before her, build her hopes on things eternal. Her pa taught her to hold on to her Father's unchanging hand. With tears pouring down her cheeks, she got up to put the photograph away.

Had one ever required Addie to name a possession that she could hold in her hands upon which she placed particular sentimental value, or any physical object that bore significant importance to her, three things would come to mind. One was Pa's fiddle, another was Rachel's Bible, and the third and last was the photograph of her family.

Those three irreplaceable treasures all represented to her a time in her life as it once had been, and reminded her of people she loved as they once were; both accounts irretrievable and no longer existent—except where she had harbored them in the recesses of her heart. There were times she found it comforting just to look at or touch those three treasures, all which were displayed on the mantelpiece over the fireplace in the front room.

Addie's tears wouldn't stop. She felt so lonesome; she missed them all—Pa, Mama, Daniel, Emily, even Ben. She whispered, "Lord, sometimes *home* is the loneliest place there is." Finally the silence was too loud for her to bear. She found solace in and began softly singing the song that had been sung that morning at Rachel's funeral:

"There's a land that is fairer than day, and by faith we can see it afar, for the Father waits over the way, to prepare us a dwelling place there. In the sweet by and by, we shall meet on that beautiful shore … in the sweet by and by we shall meet on that beautiful shore."

CHAPTER 8

Fear and shame had kept fifteen-year-old Amelia Riley away from Rachel's funeral. She didn't want to believe Rachel was gone; she felt like screaming at the unfairness of her death, the unfairness of having lost her endeared friend.

It was true that Rachel was Daniel's grandmother, not her own, but she'd always treated Amelia like she was her very own, too. She'd been so good to her over the years, so generous and compassionate.

Amelia wondered how many times she'd walked the well-worn path through the woods in the middle of the night when Pete and Bonnie were drunk and fighting. When things got too rough, she would crawl through her window to escape the chaos and go in search of a quiet refuge from the war that raged out of control at their house.

She'd been just eight years old the first time an unseen force guided her tiny feet toward the security of Rachel's peaceful home. She remembered how she would tiptoe quietly into her room and slip beneath the warm, protective covers of her bed. It became her sanctuary, her haven from the drunkards and the disorderly world they created.

Even though she and Daniel had loved each other, such was never spoken between them; it simply *was*. In Amelia's whole life, Rachel was the only one who had ever said the words "I love you" to her.

In a gentle, broken voice, Amelia whispered, "Miss Rachel, I'm so sad you had to die. I'll be lost without you." First she'd lost Daniel, and now Miss Rachel. Now, she had nobody. She felt so isolated and alone in her pain.

Amelia had waited for the moon to ascend before coming here. A whippoorwill called out, and a prompt imitation answered from somewhere across the hollow. Night's mysterious current caused the rusty gate of the cemetery to creak mournfully. Nevertheless, she was not spooked by such trite sounds and movement. Life had already taught her there were dreads far less ordinary to be afraid of.

Kneeling, she ran her fingers through the soft, loose dirt of the new grave. She buried her face in the bend of her arm, and her tears flowed freely as her broken heart grieved for Rachel.

Amelia needed a friend now more than ever before. She needed someone to talk to, but she was all alone and had nowhere to turn.

CHAPTER 9

"A soft answer turneth away wrath; but grievous words stir up anger." (Proverbs 15:1).

The corn in the lower field had long since yielded its harvest, and whatever ears were still on the stalks would be shelled off the cob and used for feed for the stock and chickens in the coming winter. It was time to pull the corn stalks for fodder, haul them up to the barn, and pile them up so the soil could be plowed under to prepare for fall planting.

Pete Riley was at the house early the Saturday morning after Rachel's funeral. He and Alfred stood around in back of the house drinking coffee and swapping lies. They were waiting on the two Negroes Alfred had hired to help him and Pete pull the fodder.

Some men didn't care to have dealings with Alfred because his roughness had the tendency to put folks off. However, those willing to put up with his brusqueness knew he'd pay a fair wage for a fair day's work.

When the Negroes arrived shortly, they too had a cup of coffee

before the work got underway. One of the men was Cleve Walls. He was tall, muscular, and dark-skinned, black as coal. Even though Cleve kept quiet manners, there was an air about him which Addie disliked. He was deliberate in the way of making his mocking, hooded stare follow her in bold appraisal, seeming satisfied if ever he sensed his carefully veiled suggestiveness made her uncomfortable.

Ap Carver, on the other hand, was a joy to be around. He was always laughing and carrying on about something, or about nothing. Ap's skin was light and reddish and gleamed like burnished copper. He'd been born with a disfigurement that marked the skin on one of his arms and on the left side of his face and neck with patches of white, giving him an odd, dappled appearance. If he was self-conscious about the strange discoloration, he certainly didn't let on. Ap claimed to be part Indian, and while he was free to claim whatever he chose all day long, everyone knew, in those parts, even one drop of black blood coursing through his veins made him a Negro.

Claire paid Ap a little all along to do heavy work for her. He'd plow and haul up firewood and split and stack it for her. Claire told Addie on more than one occasion, "That Ap talks 'til my ears turn blue. I have to tell him sometimes, 'I don't pay you to talk, Ap.' I do know he'd worry the horns off my billygoat if I had one, but thank God I don't!" She claimed him aggravating as a fly, but also as harmless; so on account of his good nature, she could tolerate his jabbering.

When the workers went to the field, Addie wrung a hen's neck. She plucked and dressed it and put it into a pot to stew on the stove outside. After that, she picked a pan full of figs, poured some sugar over them, and put them on to cook. It seemed to take forever for a fig to cook down, but at the end of the day, she'd have a few jars of preserves.

When the chicken was so tender it fell apart, she separated the meat from the skin and bones. With Ben gone, the cats had a feast with the scraps all to themselves.

She ladled enough of the chicken broth into a bowl of flour to mix into a soft ball of dough. Then she rolled the dough out and cut it into strips and dropped them into the boiling chicken broth to make dumplings. She poured in a cupful of milk, dropped in a hunk of butter, and threw in some salt and pepper to season it up. She covered the pot with a lid and set it off the burner to simmer until the men came up for dinner.

For a month and a half Addie and Emily had spent the better part of their time canning vegetables. Last week they'd pickled cucumbers and okra. They had several dozens of jars lined up on the shelves of the root cellar to show for their hard work. Addie reminded herself to put out a jar of the sweet, vinegary pickles for them to have with their dinner.

A little while later, she shielded her eyes from the glaring sun and looked in the direction of the field. A great flock of crows were cawing and dancing around on the limbs of the trees in line with the fence rails. She supposed they were quarreling in protest to Alfred and the men who were pulling corn, but the sound filled her with a forlorn feeling. Her eyes misted over. It was all still so fresh. She felt lost as she stared out across the field. She hardly knew what to do with herself now that Rachel was gone. For so long most of her time and energy had been spent taking care of her, and now she had all this empty time on her hands and an empty feeling in her heart. She had become so habited to their daily ritual, she'd caught herself a couple of times going to look in on Rachel before she realized she was no longer there. Oh, how she missed her!

Tuesday morning, she and Claire had walked into town where she'd bought several yards of cloth; since then, she'd sown several articles of clothing for the baby. And, it'd been months since she'd been able to go to church, but tomorrow would be Sunday, and she was looking forward to attending. *For where two or three are gathered together in my name, there am I in the midst.*

Addie picked up a knife and looped the handle of a bucket over her arm and went to the garden. The prickly okra stalks towered well above her head. After about a half hour, she'd cut a good mess of the green pods. She returned to the well, drew a bucket of water, and washed the okra.

After putting more wood in the stove, she sat down and brushed a strand of hair out of her eyes and wiped the sweat from her face on the hem of her apron. The baby inside her kicked furiously. She chipped the okra into bite-sized pieces and sprinkled it with salt. Then, she moistened it with a little buttermilk and dumped in a cup each of flour and cornmeal, and stirred it to coat each piece. When the grease in the heavy skillet was hot, she fried the okra until it was tender, the crust brown and crisp.

The oppressive heat drained her energy; the chore of standing over the hot stove made it even worse. It seemed to take more effort to do the simplest of things these days. Addie told herself, "At least when I'm done here, I'll be done with cooking for the rest of this day." She hoped to spend a couple more hours that afternoon sewing for the baby.

Three counties away, on this bright Saturday morning, Hiram was busying himself with piddling repairs he'd been saving up for such a day as this. He was fixing a window casing on the front of his house and saw them coming, but he didn't let on. Sarah Beth and her cousin Emily were trying to sneak up behind him. Of course, the way they were giggling, they couldn't sneak up on a dead mule. He nonchalantly finished driving a nail and then turned around and acted surprised to see them.

"Mister Hiram, we brought you something," Sarah Beth said in a sing-song voice. She held out a small basket.

Hiram reached into his pocket and took out a handkerchief and dried his wet neck.

"Well, now, what have we here?" he asked as he peered with interest at the basket and took it from her. "I wager there's a nickel in here to pay me to hide you from those buzzards circling overhead."

In unison, the girls turned their faces upward, expecting to see nothing, simply playing along with his jest. But, sure enough, they saw several buzzards with wings outspread gliding along on the wind's current. First, they shrieked. Then they giggled again at his teasing.

"Emily an' me baked a big batch of oatmeal cookies. There's a jar of tea in there, too," Sarah Beth told him prissily.

He invited them to sit on the steps and share the cookies. "*Mmm, Mmm!* Best cookies to ever set sail across my lips." He exaggerated over their efforts while he thought to himself how both the girls were cute as buttons. That Emily was just a miniature of her mama—shiny, brown hair; her sweet face framed with wheat-colored highlights bleached by the sun; dark blue eyes. In contrast, Daniel's hair was dark and wavy. He looked more like his pa, Hiram contemplated.

"Whatcha been hammerin' on, Mister Hiram?" Sarah Beth inquired.

He pointed, chewing. "Just fixin' that window over there. I've got plenty to do today. If y'all plan on bein' here long, I'll put a hammer in your hands an' put you to work. Let you hit your thumbs a time or two like I did. It feels good." He held up a bruised thumbnail for them to see. The girls leaned in close to study it.

Emily piped up and said, "My mama says the surest way to see clean through to a man's heart is by way of a hammered thumb."

Hiram guffawed. "Your mama says that, does she?"

Emily nodded and said, "Yes, sir."

"It sounds to me like she knows what she's talkin' about," he complied. He'd have a hard time arguing that fact.

Emily reasoned, "Mama's smart about a lot of things, since she's so old. She's thirty-three." She emphasized the numbers in such a way one would have believed the words actually weighed thirty-three pounds. "How old are you, Mr. Hiram?"

"Oh, I'm a lot older than your ma. I'll soon be thirty-seven. I been studyin' on whittlin' myself a walkin' cane since I'm lookin' any day now to be needin' one."

Emily asked with wide eyes, "Ain't you scared—bein' so old an'

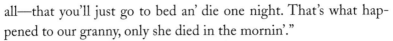

all—that you'll just go to bed an' die one night. That's what happened to our granny, only she died in the mornin'."

What a precocious child! Her unvarnished philosophy humored him. Hiram rubbed his beard a minute like he had to give a fair share of consideration to her question.

"Well, Miss Emily, to tell you the truth, I'd never thought about it quite like that before. But I 'spect now that you've laid it before me just so, I'll most likely ponder that possibility every night now when I lie down to try an' go to sleep ... for this, I thank you."

His playful sarcasm was wasted on Emily. She plowed ahead and said, "I'll be eleven come my next birthday, October 20."

Sarah Beth sighed. Her vanity had heard quite enough of this useless prattle. Not being the center of attention made her feel ignored and bored. Standing up, she commanded, "Let's go, Emily."

As the girls started down the steps, Hiram told Emily in a serious tone, "Miss Emily, if what your mama says is fact," and he knew it was, "I reckon I'd best remember to lay my hammer aside if she ever comes 'round me when I'm workin' ... else she's libel to see a side of my heart that'll make her ears burn."

"Mister Hiram, you sure are funny," Emily called back to him.

There wasn't a crumb left in the basket when the girls went skipping home. Hiram raised his eyes to the sky. A line of thick, low-hanging clouds was moving in, and the wind was starting to kick up a bit. With the heavy air, conditions were favoring a much-needed rain.

He took up his hammer and went back to work.

Back at the Coulter place, Ap was grinning like a possum when he headed to the table with his plate full of chicken and dumplings.

"Miz Addie, I smell dis all da way to da field! My guts bin growlin' all mawnin'! Lawd knows I'z fixin' to have me a time over dis!"

Addie smiled. She couldn't say that she'd ever received a more spirited compliment for her cooking. Ap's exuberance was unequivocal.

A pan of hot biscuits, a bowl of fried okra, a jar of pickles, and a bowl of figs were on the table. The men sat under the shade of the oak and enjoyed a scrumptious meal.

It was past dusk when Addie looked out the window and saw Alfred trudging toward the house. He stomped up the back steps and came through the door, letting it close with a slam. He was filthy, tired, and seemed as irritated as a hive of angry bees.

She went to the stove and fixed him a plate and asked, "Y'all get done?"

"Y'all git done, you say?" Alfred mocked her. He collapsed into a chair at the end of the table. "We got a right smart done, but we ain't nowhere near finished. Daylight give out on us…They's still a ton o' work out yonder yet to be done."

Addie set him a cup of coffee down on the table.

"'Tween hearin' them dang squawkin' crows an' Ap's flappin' gums all day, my head feels ready to bust wide open," he complained. "Crows! I reckon we're in for us either a death or a rain tonight."

An involuntary chill ran down Addie's back. "We sure need rain."

A slow smile crept up Alfred face. *We done had us a death, I reckon.*

Addie sat down with her plate and bowed her head to give thanks to the Lord for her supper.

Again, Alfred's tone was surly and mocking. "I swear, the way you pray over food don't make a lick o' sense to me!" He shook his head, vexed. "This here ain't fixin' to kill me is it?"

"Probably not, but if it did, I would indeed have reason to lift up a prayer of thanksgiving, wouldn't I?" Her attempt at a joke was wasted. Alfred didn't find humor in anyone's foolery but his own.

He stared at her for a moment and then sneered and went on, "You women folk got it made in the shade, sittin' 'round sewin' all dang day." He gulped his coffee.

Addie straightened her back. The belittling remark barbed her.

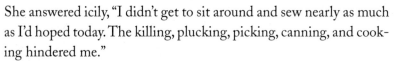

She answered icily, "I didn't get to sit around and sew nearly as much as I'd hoped today. The killing, plucking, picking, canning, and cooking hindered me."

He ignored her and griped, "It galls me like hell to have to hire niggers to work my own place."

She didn't comment. She didn't feel like quarreling, and his language was offensive to her, especially at the supper table.

"We fixin' to start cuttin' on yer mama's ol' place next week. Bet that brother of yorn fetched a purty penny for that piece-a-land. They's some mighty fine timber in them woods." She knew Alfred was testing her mettle, baiting her. He waited to see what she would say. She ate quietly without replying.

He finally came right out and asked, "When he wuz here this week, he ain't said nothin' 'bout givin' you yer part from the sale?"

Addie was careful with her words. She felt it would be a betrayal speaking to Alfred of Wesley's financial matters.

"You know, Alfred, when we got married, Mama gave us this place. This was my grandpa's old home place. Wesley told me if we ever need anything, all we have to do is ask." Nothing she said was a lie. And she knew Alfred wouldn't ask Wesley for the time of day.

He grunted. "I bet Mr. High-and-Mighty did say that." Then, "Winter'll be here directly. Looks like I'll be havin' to hire me a nigger or two to cut an' haul us up some wood so we won't freeze an' catch our death." He wanted to argue so bad he could taste it.

Addie didn't say anything else to him. *Talking to him serves no more purpose than arguing with a fencepost.*

He bit into a biscuit sullenly. Still, he wouldn't relent. He snorted. "Like I got money to give niggers."

They ate in silence for a few minutes, but he knew how to rile her.

"My point bein', Addie, if that worthless, lily-livered boy of yorn hadn't up an' run off…faced me like a man…" He spit the word *boy* out like it was bitter on his tongue. "I'd have me some help right now…an' I've a idie where he's hidin' out."

83

There was the proverbial straw that laid the camel flat. Addie lost her temper and rose to defend Daniel like a tiger she-cat defending her cub. She hadn't been there with them in the field that day to know exactly what happened, but she certainly knew Alfred, and for some unknown reason, he had always been especially hard on Daniel.

"That *boy* as you call him—that *boy* is *our* son. And yes, he was a big help around here until *you* ran him off with your hatefulness. He'd be here today where he belongs, in *this* house eating supper at *this* table, if you hadn't treated him so mean. I reckon just because he didn't bow down and kiss your feet you decided to get rid of him!" Hot, angry tears rolled down her cheeks.

Alfred stood up with such force the chair turned over and hit the floor with a loud slap. His voiced boomed, "Don't holler at me, woman!" His fist came down hard upon the table.

Addie didn't even flinch. All the words she'd kept pent up for three months flew out of her mouth.

"If you'd treated him the way a father is supposed to treat his son, he wouldn't have left! But that's not in you, is it? All you ever did was find fault with anything Daniel did. You always had to criticize every little thing he did, hurt him and keep his spirit beat down, with words and fists! You should hope to someday be the man that *boy* already is!"

Alfred lost control. He was like a madman. He raked the plates off the table, and they shattered on the floor. In his rage, he lunged at Addie and shoved her with all his strength.

She was cast off balance and began to fall; the floor seemingly rose to meet her. It was too late, but Alfred reached out and tried to grab her flailing arm, only to have his fingers barely brush the sleeve of her dress. She fell solidly against the unyielding cast iron stove; the full length of her right side struck it hard. Afterward, she lay in a crumpled heap on the floor.

For a few minutes, Addie lay there dazed and trembling. Her breath was ragged. She tried to sit up, but a sharp pain shot through her side and lower back. She wondered if her ribs might be broken.

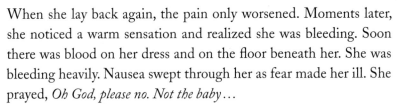

When she lay back again, the pain only worsened. Moments later, she noticed a warm sensation and realized she was bleeding. Soon there was blood on her dress and on the floor beneath her. She was bleeding heavily. Nausea swept through her as fear made her ill. She prayed, *Oh God, please no. Not the baby…*

Within moments, she became so cold that she was shaking. Then, the most incredible thing happened. There were people on the ceiling, waving to her. *Pa! Mama! Rebekah!* Addie felt drugged; she was floating. She heard, *I'z fixin' to have me a time, Miz Addie.* She was so tired and so cold. Her teeth were chattering. *Got to hire me some niggers before I catch my death.*

Her mind coaxed her to give in, kept beckoning her into a warm, seductive sleep. *Just close your eyes…*

Rebekah called to her, *Come on, Addie, come and play with me!*

But Addie was too tired to play. She wanted to sleep, not play… *But first I have to wring the chicken's neck…*

Just before she lost consciousness completely, she whispered, "Go fetch Travis and Claire."

But Alfred was already on his way.

She sank lower and lower, until she felt nothing.

Just before midnight, thunder clapped and rumbled across the hollows. Lightning flashed and fierce gusts of wind pushed upon the house, causing its boards to creak and pop and moan against the force of it. The house seemed to wail its own fury and resentment against the intrusion of the tumultuous storm that waged within its walls.

Finally, the bottom fell out of the clouds, and a torrential, drenching rain fell upon the earth and answered the hopes and prayers of many a folk. Drops of sorrow in the form of rain were mercifully flung from above for the tears Addie couldn't spill, as in the dark hours of early morning she gave birth to a tiny, dead baby boy.

CHAPTER 10

"The heart knoweth his own bitterness." (Proverbs 14:10).

It was the sixth day of August. Claire sat in a chair by the window near the bed embroidering while Addie napped. For five days she'd fussed over her friend, nursed her body, and ministered to her soul. She'd helped Addie bathe and dress, cooked her every meal, and made her eat, even when she protested she wasn't hungry. In an earnest attempt to draw her thoughts, she'd told endless stories and read to her from the Bible; however, Claire knew there were some hurts that only time could heal.

She and Travis were haunted by Alfred's account of the accident. When questioned, he'd been too evasive about the details to suit them, and of course neither of them believed half of what he said anyway. Addie had yet to speak of what happened, and they dared not press her in such a fragile state. However, as suspicious as they were, and as badly as they wanted answers to what caused her to fall, and as hard as it was for them to *let all bitterness be put away*, the only thing that really mattered to them right now was for Addie to get well.

A slight stirring from the bed made Claire look up from her stitches and glance at Addie as she slept. With the morning light on her face, her skin was so pale it looked translucent. Claire shuddered as she reflected upon the past days and was again reminded of how close they'd come to losing her. That first night, they couldn't tell if she would live, but each passing day brought with it the reassurance and hope that she would. *But… we lost the baby.*

Addie's eyes fluttered as she awoke. She opened her eyes but lay still. Even though she'd slept for hours, she felt tired. Her insides felt like a basket of busted eggs. For a moment, her thoughts tossed about in a whirlwind of feelings. She wondered if maybe it all could've just been a bad dream. *No… it's no dream.* Her arms longed for the comfort of something they couldn't have. *My baby is dead.* A tear slid from the corner of an eye.

From somewhere beyond the window, a dove called out. The room was so quiet that she thought for a minute she was alone, but when she struggled to sit up, Claire laid her hoop aside and was there in a flash to put a pillow behind her back. Addie gave her a weak smile and said, "Thank you."

"Feelin' better?" Claire asked, her voice soft but chipper.

Addie lied with a nod of her head.

Claire left and came back with two cups of tea. Resettling in the chair near the window, she said, "I just happened to think, today is Rachel and Samuel's anniversary. Why is it I can remember something that happened forty years ago like it was yesterday but couldn't remember what I ate for breakfast this morning if it weren't for what's stuck between my teeth?

"Lebanon Baptist Church was havin' their big meetin', and a gang of us took off walkin' to church that evening. If it weren't hot an' dusty, I'm not settin' here on the grave side of old an' ugly! I swanee, I can still taste the grit in my mouth!"

She continued the story. "Samuel set out walkin' with us. Me and

Luke were already married. Rachel met up with us where the roads meet at the Eminence graveyard."

She sighed dreamily. "Your mama was pretty as a picture, wearing a voile dress she'd sown herself. They hadn't breathed it to a soul that they were gettin' married that night. Old Preacher Harper did the ceremony, such that it was, right after he closed the revival service. Later on, Rachel swore that was the long-winded-est sermon she'd ever suffered through."

Addie had heard the story a dozen times, but it never got old.

Claire picked her embroidery hoop back up. "They went back to Samuel's little shotgun-shanty of a house. We all went over there in the middle of the night to serenade them. We banged on pots and pans, rang cow bells, hollered, an' carried on like a bunch of hoodlums. We all had such fun back then . . ." Claire's voice trailed off reminiscently.

For a few minutes, the only sounds heard were the persistent ticking of the clock and the mournful call of the dove. It brought to Addie's mind the crows and what Alfred had said about them having either rain or a death. She shuddered. *How many days ago was that?*

Claire noticed she was drifting and drew her attention back. "You were probably too little to remember, but did Rachel ever tell you about the trip she took to New Orleans? She was expecting Rebekah at the time."

Addie gave Claire a vague look and shook her head. She had no knowledge of this. "No, she never told me. I had no idea Mama ever went to New Orleans."

This made Claire happy. She had a fresh story to tell.

"Well, Rachel was about four months pregnant. Your great-uncle, Estus, a crook he was, invited her to go with him to visit his sister, Ida. Rachel wanted to go, but they didn't have the money for such frivolity. A jaunt like that was considered sure 'nough high-falutin' back in them days.

"But Samuel couldn't deny his beloved Rachel a blessed thing. He worshipped the ground she walked on. If that man didn't beat all . . ." This was true; Samuel was twenty years Rachel's senior and had saved his love all his life, waiting to find his true mate. "Your pa sold a yearlin' to Milton Collins for six dollars and gave that money to your mama so she could go to New Orleans with Estus."

Addie nodded. "That sounds just like Pa, always giving to someone else."

Claire went on. "The stage fare was some'ers around two dollars. Rachel went on an' on about how big the city was; so many people you couldn't stir 'em with a stick! Es hired a carriage and rode her and Ida around, takin' in the sights. They had coffee at a popular café down in the French Quarters and went to see a beautiful cathedral down by the Mississippi River. That girl had the time of her life and still had two dollars in her purse when she came home!"

What a romantic story! It made Addie sad to think about how once upon a time her parents had been so full of life and so in love. Now they were lying side-by-side in Eminence Cemetery. Bitterly considering her plight, she thought, *Soon as I'm able, either my dead marriage or my dead husband will be lying in that very graveyard.*

Addie knew she'd cheated herself out of such a romance by foolishly marrying a man she barely knew. In hindsight, it was all perfectly clear; at the tender age of sixteen she'd been in love with the fanciful idea of being in love, but she'd not been in love with Alfred. Alfred had been worldly and convincing; she, naïve and inexperienced. He made her feel loved, and in exchange she let him corrupt her innocence, let him persuade her to take the sensual passage from girlhood to womanhood in his arms. *What a horrible mistake!*

Looking back, she could see how rebellious and angry she'd been. Samuel had died; Rachel's moods were up and down, up and down; she was stark raving mad. *I thought if I didn't get out of that house I'd end up crazier than Mama!*

More significantly, though, at the time she and Alfred got married, Addie was spiritually lost. It wasn't until two years later that she accepted Jesus Christ as her Lord and Savior—*for He so loved the world*... After she was saved, there was no question; she and Alfred

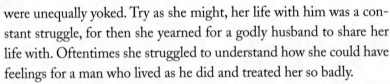

were unequally yoked. Try as she might, her life with him was a constant struggle, for then she yearned for a godly husband to share her life with. Oftentimes she struggled to understand how she could have feelings for a man who lived as he did and treated her so badly.

For years she'd tried to win him over to Christ. If only he would believe in Him and ask Him into his heart, he could be saved, and he'd change; for in the Bible it says, "Therefore if any man be in Christ, he is a new creature; old things are passed away; behold, all things are become new."

But she had not gotten what she prayed for. She'd finally come to accept that God's answer to her fervent prayer for a godly husband was no. She supposed it was just punishment for dishonoring God and dishonoring herself. A good girl didn't lie with a man unless she was married to him. *Why didn't I listen to my mother?* Regrettably, she had come to her senses too late.

She told Claire, "Thank you for telling me that story. I never dreamed Mama had such an adventurous side."

When she was young, Addie had read about the exciting city of New Orleans in the books she borrowed from Claire. Once upon a time, she'd even fancied she might someday be able to go there. Before they were married, one time she and Alfred had even talked about going there together. She sighed wistfully as she realized the likelihood of her ever making such a trip was now nothing more than a fantasy.

She was crying again, unable to help herself. She turned on her side with her back to Claire. A few seconds later, in a small voice that gave away her anguish, she whispered, "Claire, you're a dear friend, and I love you."

Claire didn't have to see Addie's face to know that she was crying, and knowing this hurt her heart. The way she felt about Addie— well, she should have been her own daughter. She wished she could take her sorrow from her, but she also knew that sometimes crying was good for the soul.

Claire didn't pause from her sewing; she simply said, "I love you too, child."

The following day, Addie penned a letter and gave it to Claire to take to the post office. It read:

Dearest Wesley and Laura,

First, let me bid you well and tell you how wonderful it was to see you last week, even though the occasion was sad. Thanks again to both of you for welcoming both Daniel and Emily into your home. I am looking forward to Emily's homecoming, so she can share with me each and every detail about her visit there.

I will not further delay in telling you that we've had to face the difficulty of yet another tragedy here. A few days ago, I lost the baby. He came too early and arrived stillborn.

Don't fret—I'm in the best of hands. Travis and Claire are taking very good care of me, and I am regaining strength with each passing day.

It is for this reason I write, asking you to allow Emily to extend her stay with you by two or three weeks. School will not begin until the middle of September, and it will be good for her to have the additional time with Daniel and her cousins.

Please do not feel you need to journey here. I assure you, I am on the mend, and of course, I am not alone. Our precious Lord has not forsaken me. He is nigh.

Truth be told, I need some time to myself for my broken heart to heal. It is said that time alters circumstance, and I need time to grieve, not only for the child I've lost but also for Mama. The next time my children see me, I don't want to greet them with a look reflecting only sadness and sorrow. Wesley, I know you especially understand what I am saying.

I ask you to withhold this letter from Daniel and Emily, but tell them the news of the baby. It will be better, at least for me, if they hear it from you, spoken in kind and soft words;

there, in a home where joy and love abide.

Press upon Daniel and Emily that I am doing well so they will not worry needlessly about me. Give them both a kiss from me.

Please remember me in your prayers, as I do you in mine.

With love, your sister, Addie Virginia

CHAPTER 11

"O my God, I trust in thee; ... let not mine enemies triumph over me." (Psalms 25:2).

A few mornings later, not long after she heard Alfred leave the house, Addie got up and put on a dress. She felt weak but knew she wouldn't get her strength back by lying in bed the rest of her life.

She took the back steps slowly. Every muscle in her body was still sore, but she didn't feel near as battered as she had in days past. She had a huge, black bruise spreading from her right side across her back, but her physical pain was beginning to gradually fade away.

She walked the short distance across the yard to the chicken run. It took all her energy, but she managed to corner one of the birds up and grab it. With one twist, she wrung its neck. While it flopped around on the ground dying, she sat down to rest. A little while later, she willed herself to pluck and dress the chicken. Then she had to rest some more, thinking, *I'm weak as a kitten.*

When she got her wind, she drew a bucket of water and washed the chicken before she cut it up. She emptied the pan of bloody water in the grass and then drew a fresh bucket to keep the chicken from spoiling until she was ready to cook it. Near exhausted, she filled a pan and lathered up her hands and splashed her face and neck. It was oppressively hot. After drinking a dipper full of the cold, sweet water and feeling somewhat revived, she went inside the house.

Claire was encouraged when she dropped in just after noon to find Addie sitting on the porch with her feet propped up and some degree of noticeable color back to her cheeks. She'd baked fresh bread and brought Addie a loaf along with a jar of canned peaches.

"You spoil me!" Addie exclaimed. She offered to brew a pot of coffee, but Claire shook her head stubbornly.

"Don't have time to set long. The devil did his work when he made sawbriars. I've got Ap comin' to help me clear a fence row, an' if I'm not there to keep an eye on him, he's libel to hack down my rosebushes. I just had to skip over here and assure myself you're not overdoin.'" She would have been outraged if she'd known what Addie had been up to all morning.

As soon as Claire left, Addie made a fire in the stove out by the smokehouse, determined to finish what she set out to do.

A half hour later, she put a peach pie in the oven. Then she seasoned the chicken with salt and pepper, dredged it in flour, and browned it in a little bacon grease. Next, she mixed a cup of apple cider with some molasses and a little vinegar and poured it over the chicken in a cast iron skillet. She covered it with a heavy lid and slid it in the oven to bake for about an hour and a half.

She cut a few potatoes into thin slices and pan-fried them with a large onion in the skillet where she'd cooked a couple strips of bacon. When the potatoes were tender and crisp, she crumbled the bacon on top of them.

Preparing the meal claimed the better part of Addie's day, and just to her expectations, it did sorely taunt her physical endurance. But she'd made up her mind before she got out of bed that morning that she was ready to take on whatever bullying the day might bring, and she'd let no doubt give her pause.

Anger and bitterness toward Alfred consumed her. Of all the things he'd ever done to hurt her, this time he'd gone too far. *He'd senselessly taken the life of an innocent baby—murderer!*

She'd suffered loss before, but just the thought of her dead baby was almost more than she could bear. She almost wished Alfred was dead. And, if God was expecting her to forgive him for this, He was expecting too much. She'd never forgive him of this, not this. This was unforgivable. *Surely God understands how I feel.*

With supper accomplished and laid ready, Addie was filled with a renewed sense of confidence in herself and convinced of at least one truth—that she held within herself her greatest source of strength. *It is God that girdeth me with strength.* In spite of Alfred, and for the sake of Daniel and Emily, she was determined to persevere.

Alfred came in around dark from cutting timber on Rachel's old place. He hung his hat on a nail just inside the back door and sniffed the air in the kitchen. Mumbling a greeting to her, he sat down at the table. He had yet to make mention of the loss of the baby.

Addie served his plate in silence. The chicken was tender and covered with a thick, sweet glaze; the potatoes were perfectly browned. The peach pie was cooled and sat atop the stove.

She poured them both a cup of steaming, strong, black coffee. The loaf of bread Claire had brought was near the center of the table, loosely wrapped in a cloth. Beside the bread lay the largest knife Addie could find. Earlier in the day, she'd spent almost an hour sharpening it until it was razor-edged.

She stood deliberately close to Alfred and picked up the knife. One of her hands held firm the loaf, while the other cut through the bread with slow, sawing strokes. The aroma of the freshly baked yeast rose to meet her nose in promise. *A promise of a reckoning,* she thought.

She laid two slices of bread near the edge of Alfred's plate and set the butter dish within his reach. She fixed herself a plate and sat down in a ladder-back chair at the opposite end of the pine-planked table.

She bowed her head and said a quiet blessing before she started eating. Alfred's attention fell immediately to his food. For a while, the only sounds in the house were his fork scraping against his plate, his chewing and smacking, and the methodical ticking of the mantel clock.

The supper was savory, well-seasoned, and satisfying. *Comfort food.*

For some reason, Addie felt clearer of mind and more focused than she'd ever recalled. In fact, to have been so tired earlier, she felt surprisingly well now. *God is great, God is good.*

When she felt prompted, she laid down her fork and stared for a moment at her half-eaten food while deciding what to say.

"Alfred." She paused and waited for him to look at her. She wanted to be sure she had his full attention. He raised his eyes and glanced over at her. In a soft but controlled and steady voice, she stated simply, "It's not my intent to waste words on you, so you listen and hear me well. If you ever again lay hands on me, *for any reason,* as God as my witness, I aim to kill you."

Any other time a smirk would have come to play on his face, and he most likely would have come back on her with some hateful or sarcastic remark. But not this time. Alfred caught a glimpse of something in Addie's eyes he'd not seen there before. As her gaze bore into his, he felt the scorch of her implication burn across his very soul. She stared him down, locking him into a sure understanding. Plain and simple, her intent was his demise if he ever so crossed her again.

The slightest movement upon the table drew his eyes. Addie's hand had moved to rest near the large butcher knife. She fingered its handle ever so lightly.

In thoughtful recompense of the situation, Alfred was inwardly respectful of, even if not fully convinced of, the seriousness of Addie's threat. In the back of his mind, he granted himself credit for knowing one thing for absolute certain—a mad woman branishing a knife could be a formidable force to reason with. At least for now, he chose the safer position and did the smart thing. He kept his mouth shut and let the meal end without further exchange.

Considering all, it seemed a small victory, but a victory nonetheless. That night, Alfred began sleeping in Daniel's old room across the hall.

CHAPTER 12

"Now faith is the substance of things hoped for, the evidence of things not seen." (Hebrews 11:1).

A light, balmy breeze made the heat pleasantly tolerable Friday morning. Addie was sitting in a rocker in the yard with her face upturned to catch the soothing warmth of the sun's rays. The recent rains left behind a clean, sweet smell, and it felt good to be breathing the fresh air. Rachel's Bible was lying open on her lap.

Lantana was blooming. A drove of butterflies flitted around the bush, and watching them was almost hypnotic. Callie brushed against Addie's leg, purring. She reached down and stroked the cat's soft fur.

When Daniel was a small boy, he'd carved his initials into the arm of the chair she was sitting in. Addie idly traced the letters *DC* with her finger.

She was glad for the solitude. Claire, dear soul that she was, had blessedly cut back on the frequency and length of her visits since she'd seen the dark circles were gone from underneath her eyes

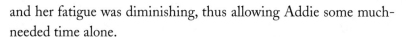

and her fatigue was diminishing, thus allowing Addie some much-needed time alone.

She put her hand up to shield her eyes from the sun when Travis pulled his buggy off the road and stopped in front of the house. He was extremely pleased to see her up and around.

He crossed the yard toward her and said, "The sun is powerful medicine."

Addie smiled at him and thought inwardly, *Yes, the Son is the Great Healer.*

Aloud, she greeted him cheerfully, "Mornin', Travis."

He couldn't get over how well she looked. He was amazed, actually, since he knew it was a wonder she'd survived at all. *So much blood lost.* The night of the storm, he'd feared he was going to lose her. He stayed right by her side through the whole ordeal, dozing off and on in a chair until he was sure she was out of the woods. He'd even bargained with God for her life a couple of times, made a few promises no mortal man could possibly live up to. Of course, in the end, he knew she hadn't pulled through because of anything he'd done as her doctor, and certainly not beholden any promises he made to God. However, he believed Addie was alive for a purpose known only to God; he spared her for a reason. *A real pity about the baby, though.*

"How're you feelin', Addie?"

"Stronger every day," she replied. "I finally convinced Claire to go home, though I hate to admit I already miss her teacakes." Claire was near famous in these parts for her delicious teacakes.

Travis drawled, "Well, knowin' Claire, you won't be missin' 'em long. I'd bet she's probably bakin' a batch right now. They'll show up here directly."

Addie smiled sadly and said, "While I'm thinking about it, Claire told me you saw to it that the baby was buried next to Mama. I appreciate you doing that for me, Travis." Her voice cracked a little, her feelings visible in her eyes.

Travis didn't make a comment; he just nodded. He felt sorry for

Addie; she'd lost Rachel and the baby both in the same week. Of course, he wouldn't tell her that he felt sorry for her. He knew the last thing Addie Coulter wanted was his pity, nor was she one to sit around and feel sorry for herself.

They engaged in a few minutes of community small talk.

Travis pushed his hat back and looked out across the way. His brows drew together in a frown. Inwardly, he swore, *I'll eat my confounded hat if Alfred ain't to blame for her fallin'.* Even though she hadn't said as much, he could feel it in his bones. Alfred had proved what he was capable of when he attacked Daniel with a horsewhip. *Alfred's a dangerous lunatic who needs the hell beat out of him, an' I'm thinkin' I just might be the man for the job.*

Besides for being worried about her, Travis was also mad. He'd always been of the notion that if he had something to say, it was usually better just to go on and say it and get if off his chest rather than letting it fester 'til it came to a head. He and Addie were a lot alike in this respect.

"Addie, I say it's past time you pissed on the fire an' called the dog on Alfred." *He doesn't deserve her; she deserves better.*

Addie's reply came quick. "Yes, I suppose it is. But haven't I also heard you say, 'Everybody knows how to handle a kickin' mule 'til they get one of their own?'"

Travis gave an affirmative nod. "Yep, I reckon you have at that." He looked at her with obvious concern and released a weary sigh. "Don't begrudge me for bein' concerned about you, Addie. I want you to live to be as old as I am, and I'm not exaggeratin' when I say you was rattlin' hard on Heaven's gate the other night. You about died, an' your baby did." Though he meant well, the words sounded harsh, even to his own ears.

Addie didn't need him reminding her of things she'd sooner forget. Today just wasn't the day for it. She retorted sharply, "You know, Travis, it wouldn't hurt for you to buff up your bedside manner to at least a dull shine. I'll have you know, I made a vow before God, and that's not the sort of thing I take lightly!" Did he not realize how badly she wished she could turn back the clock?

Travis was apologetic and thought about what she said for a minute and replied tenderly, "Addie, God wants you to be happy. You remember that."

He couldn't imagine how she was struggling. *Lord, you know I am struggling!* If her heart's voice of reason hadn't wrestled the butcher knife from the mind of her hands, Alfred would be stabbed full of holes right now. She had no intention of things continuing on as before with Alfred, but she needed time to sort it all out in her mind, come to some semblance of peace with it all.

She had been diligently trying to lift herself out of her depression, was trying to trust God to guide her way in this—*walk by faith*—but right now everything else seemed to wan in comparison to the overwhelming pain she was feeling over losing her mama and her baby. In her heart, she knew *without faith it was impossible to have peace,* and oh how she longed for peace, yet she was angry, her faith was wavering. *God, where were you through all this? Why didn't you stop Alfred from pushing me? Why did my poor baby have to die?*

At times when she prayed, she found herself wondering if God was even listening to her or cared that she was hurting.

When she spoke again, her voice had lost its annoyance. Now she just sounded tired. "Travis, God has never let me down. With a little faith, I can be as happy as I allow myself to be. It's really all up to me now."

Travis had misgivings. He hadn't meant to cast a cloud over her day. He reached over and placed his hand lightly on her shoulder.

"I'm sorry, Addie, forgive me. I got no right to meddle an' less right to preach. I just care about you; that's all."

Addie knew Travis cared about her deeply, and she was fortunate to have a friend like him watching out for her. In gesture of this sentiment, she reached up and took his hand and pressed it tenderly to her cheek. She held it there but a moment, but it might have been an eternity. In the midst of the silence that fell about them, the butterflies seemed to grow nervous as they flitted about the lantana.

Finally she gave his hand a reassuring squeeze before withdrawing hers and placing it on the Bible in her lap.

She was smiling at him. "Travis, please don't worry. I'm going to be fine; everything is going to be fine." She added, "Thank you for caring about me. I'm lucky to have you for a friend."

Travis let out a deep breath and changed the subject. "I tell you, it's such a hot day. I believe when I get back to the creek, I'm gonna shuck down to the cob, jump in, an' cool off. You ought to come with me," he invited jokingly.

Addie knew he was kidding. "Shoot! Hutchins Creek is way too cold for me! Daniel and Emily are always trying to get me to swim with them, but I can't stand that icy water!"

"Aw, it might be cold when you first jump in, but after you've been in it a while, you get used to it," Travis coaxed playfully.

She realized what he said and busted out laughing. "Why, Travis Hughes! You just described my marriage!"

He gave her a puzzled look.

She explained, "My marriage. It might be cold, but now that I've been in it for a while, I've gotten used to it!"

Travis chuckled and shook his head. At least she was able to joke about it. "Well, on that note, I'd better be going. I've got a few more patients to see before I head back into town. See you in a few days. Stay off your feet." He was walking toward his rig.

Addie stopped him. "Wait. I have something to give you." She got up and went inside the house. When she returned, she was carrying a stack of baby clothes. Holding them out to him, she said, "Here, I want to donate these to a worthy cause. I figure you might know someone that needs them."

Travis took the baby things and started back toward his buggy. "I just might at that."

Addie called out, "I'm planning to be in church next Sunday, and I'm expecting to see you there!"

Travis waved good-bye and headed down the road. He glanced down at the baby clothes on the seat beside him and thought about who he was going to give them to. *There's another situation that warrants me cause for worry.* He'd hoped the baby belonged to Daniel—both Amelia and the baby would've been better off. But Amelia adamantly denied it was his. That being the case, Travis figured it would kill Daniel to know she was pregnant. They'd been close as two peas in a pod all their lives. Amelia made him swear on a Bible he wouldn't tell Addie or Daniel she was expecting. Of course, he'd never break the confidence of a patient. He shook his head sadly. *Amelia's barely fifteen! How Bonnie could run off and leave that girl to survive on her own with that piece of white trash Pete Riley is beyond me.*

Travis slapped the reins on his horse's rump and urged him into a livelier trot.

Addie went back to her rocker and again sat to be soothed by the sun. She whispered to God, "Lord, in the book of Matthew, you said, 'All things, whatsoever ye shall ask in prayer, believing, ye shall receive.' You know my desires and the needs of my heart. You have promised to comfort and heal. Help me, for I am downcast. My faith is tried and tempted. Draw me near and restore me. Oh God, help me hold fast to hope."

She opened Rachel's Bible to the eleventh chapter of Hebrews and began to read:

> "By faith, Abel offered unto God a sacrifice …
> "By faith, Enoch pleased God …
> "By faith, Noah became heir of righteousness …
> "By faith, Abraham obeyed …
> "By faith, Sara herself received strength …

"By faith, Isaac blessed Jacob and Esau...
"By faith, Jacob...
"By faith, Joseph...
"By faith, Moses passed through the
Red Sea by way of dry land...
"By faith, the walls of Jericho fell...
"By faith, the harlot Rahab...
" ...faith is the substance of things hoped for, the evidence
of things not seen... if ye have faith... nothing shall be
impossible unto you."

CHAPTER 13

"A whip for the horse, a bridle for the ass, and a rod for the fool's back." (Proverbs 26:3).

Later by evening's fading shadows, as fate would have it, Travis and Alfred met up on the road. Travis's virile ego defied the voice in his mind that charged him to *keep on riding*. When Alfred saw Travis tighten the reins and bring his buggy to a halt, even though he despised the sight of him, he urged Gent close enough so that the two could exchange greetings.

Alfred pushed his hat back. A grin spread across his stubbly face. "Howdy, Doc. You bin out at my place… seein' my wife when I weren't home?" He said it rudely but without challenge.

Travis felt the hair on the back of his neck bristle. In his eyes, the bawdy insinuation was far more disrespectful to Addie than himself, which made it even more insulting. He had a wild instinct to guard her honor from being attacked.

He refused Alfred the satisfaction of seeing his contempt. Letting his face show nothing, he replied lazily, "It'd appear so." He deliberately didn't offer more of an explanation, which drew the desired reaction from Alfred. Travis saw a flicker of agitation run across his features, and his jaw set hard. His knuckles were white as he held tight to Gent's reins.

A long moment later, Alfred sneered, "Well, strictly speakin', as my wife's *doctor,* would you advise me to turn Gent 'round an' head back to town for a new suit, or you reckon she's gonna live?" Not that he cared one way or the other.

Right now, Travis could think of no reason not to kill the bastard. Pairing up his wife's recent brush with death and the devastating loss of the baby, he couldn't believe the man's irreverent posture. He took his time about answering. Squinting at him, he said, "Strictly speakin', as her doctor, you can bet your bottom dollar that Addie will long outlive the both of us. But it might be a good idie for you to buy one to bury yourself in."

Alfred shifted in the saddle as Addie's words suddenly echoed in the back of his mind, *As God as my witness, I aim to kill you.*

Travis was glad he'd chanced up on this cussed thug out here by himself. Figuring he was as good a man today as he ever was, here was his opportunity to boldly, perhaps foolishly, bend some fury. Inwardly, he resigned, *I reckon I'll be affirmed here shortly.*

"Here's some doctorly advice for you, Alfred." He paused for effect. "Next time that pesterin' mad itch of yours flares up, an' you get the notion to horsewhip somebody, or beat somebody up, I'll thank you for lettin' me give you the cure. But be warned, you'll get a dose of medicine from the ol' doc here you're not used to gettin' from a boy…or a woman."

Alfred's eyes narrowed and grew cold as the implication registered and swirled around in his mind unsettled for several seconds. Neither spoke, but their faces wore warning enough, as the two men squared off with stares as hard as forged steel. The brief minute that passed seemed like an hour. Gent snorted and stomped the ground impatiently. Travis could feel his chest pounding as he assessed Alfred's

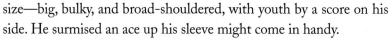

size—big, bulky, and broad-shouldered, with youth by a score on his side. He surmised an ace up his sleeve might come in handy.

But just when Travis thought Alfred might call his hand; for some reason, he decided to fold. He readjusted the wad of tobacco in his mouth from one cheek to the other and spit on the wheel of Travis's buggy.

He managed an unconvincing grin, but it didn't hide his murderous expression. "I'll keep yer idie in mind, Doc."

"Much obliged if you do," Travis reiterated to make the point understood.

There'd clearly been a meeting of the minds in the eyes held steady between Travis Hughes and Alfred Coulter.

Alfred jerked Gent's reins and gave his sides a swift kick. The horses' hooves kicked up a cloud of dust and slung gravel as he quickly put a respectable distance between his master and the man in the buggy back there on the road.

Relieved, Travis relaxed back on his seat and laughed, amused with himself. He reached into his vest pocket and drew out a cigar and lit it. Shaking his head, he said right out loud, "Travis, you crazy son-of-a-gun! You 'bout overplayed your hand this time." He scratched his crotch and told himself, *You gone yet fool around an' let these thangs get you killed!*

Chuckling, he exhaled a big billow of smoke, slapped the reins, and hollered, "Giddy-up!"

CHAPTER 14

Summer's last days breezed by. In the middle of September, proud spikes of goldenrod bloomed plentifully in fields and alongside roads. Seemingly overnight, red spider lilies appeared on gangly stems, a true sign the nights had turned chilly despite the lingering warm days.

"Mama!" Emily's face was bright as a sunbeam.

When Wesley pulled the wagon to a stop, Addie stretched her arms wide and caught Emily in a welcoming embrace, the force of which almost knocked her off her feet. She hugged her daughter tightly and then pulled away so she could take a good look at her. She hugged her again and tearfully exclaimed, "Oh, I've missed you!"

Just as he might have expected, Wesley found his sister looking remarkably well, seemingly recovered of body and in command of her emotions. He thought wonderingly, *Such a one is Addie, tough as nails.*

Sarah Beth and Jesse accompanied him on the trip, and despite her insistence, Addie couldn't convince him to stay the night. So, while she and Claire cooked a hearty dinner for them all, Wesley took a sentimental walk down by the creek with the children to stretch his legs before heading back toward Golden Meadow. By the time they ate, the horse was rested and they set out for home.

It took hours for Emily to tell Addie all about what she and her cousins had done during her stay. She didn't leave out a single detail, right down to what Laura cooked for supper every night and how Granny Stell was forever griping about every little thing. She described watching Daniel make a table and talked incessantly about Mr. Hiram, and how he teased her constantly. After she'd listened to Emily go on and on about the man for almost an hour, there was no disputing that he'd captivated her daughter's favor.

That night over supper, Emily asked quietly, "Mama, are you sad about the baby?"

Addie had expected she would bring it up eventually. After all, there was no way for them not to talk about it. She answered, "Sometimes." Inwardly, she thought, *There's nothing sadder than the loss of a child.* She almost couldn't bear what had happened, but she had to live with it and go on.

Emily never raised her eyes up from her food when she asked, "Is Pa sad too?"

Maybe she imagined it, but to Addie, Emily sounded skeptical. She hesitated only a moment, and for Emily's sake, she lied. "I'm sure he is, honey."

There were tears in Emily's eyes as she explained it all to her as simply as possible. For a few minutes, the girl focused on her food, seemingly lost in her own thoughts.

In an attempt to move on from an awkward subject to a happy one, Addie reminded her, "You, young lady, will be starting back to school in a few days. Won't you be glad?"

Emily smiled and nodded. Addie saw that she looked pleased. Emily liked school and was looking forward to going back.

Where Daniel was concerned, she mildly suggested that unless Alfred specifically inquired of her brother, it was probably best for a while not to mention him or his whereabouts to her pa. Emily needed little instruction in regards to this situation. Her perception was extremely agile for a child her age. She didn't understand the basis for their arguing, but she had long since figured out there was serious trouble between her pa and brother.

On the first night of her homecoming, Emily fell asleep laughing and talking in her mama's bed. The following night, she went down the hall to her own room, but the room was too empty, too quiet. It spoke to her only of loss and sadness. For two years, she and Rachel had shared this space, had shared a nightly ritual. *Now Granny is gone.* Her chin trembled, and her eyes filled with tears. She ran back and threw her arms around Addie and let her console her. A while later, Addie lay still, listening as the sounds of the night penetrated the room and Emily snored lightly. Comforted by her presence, she yawned, and soon she slept.

Thereafter, they settled comfortably into a new ritual, replacing the one which was lost. It felt only natural that Emily sleep in her bed, and on the nights he ventured home, Alfred continued to occupy Daniel's room.

Every fall Addie took on a sewing project for the mercantile in Collinsville. The store's owner, Yancy Neelson, had discovered there was a demand for quality, ready-made merchandise, especially around Christmastime, and he gladly paid a fair sum for various household items such as doilies and embroidered tablecloths to stock his shelves.

Not much seemed to be going on in town as Emily sat on the wooden steps of the store, gazing out across the road, with her elbows propped on her knees. While Addie was inside choosing materials, she sucked on a peppermint stick, delighting in its cool sweetness.

She soon noticed a woman and a girl coming her way. They were not familiar to her. The girl, who looked about her age, lagged a step behind the woman. The woman was black as soot, her face round as a melon. She had a broad, flat nose. A scarf that matched her calico dress covered most of her nappy hair. She was carrying a bundle of what appeared to be men's shirts.

The girl, Emily decided, looked a little peculiar, but in a pretty way. Her skin was light, hardly darker than hers. *Like coffee with a lot of cream stirred in,* she thought. She had clear, green eyes, and her hair wasn't the least bit kinky. Instead it hung loose and curly. Still, Emily guessed the Negro woman must be the girl's mama.

When they reached the mercantile, the woman's command was firm but soft, "You wait fo' me out here. I won't be long."

"Yessum," the girl answered obediently. The woman went inside the store.

The girl immediately started twirling around and around one of the posts supporting the storefront. Every time she came around to face Emily, she eyed her inquisitively, letting her gaze rest on the candy as though wishing she had a piece of it, too.

Emily was just as curious about her, but tried not to be obvious about it. A few minutes later, her generous nature revealed itself. She unfolded the brown-paper wrapping on her lap and held out a sweet offering to the post-twirler.

"Want one?" she asked.

The girl struck out a hand and snatched the candy quick as lightning, distrustful that Emily just might change her mind. The gesture of sharing the candy served as the tender; it had the effect of bringing them together, prompting the girl to also accept the implied invitation that came along with the peppermint stick. She plopped down next to Emily on the center step.

"Who you iz?" the girl asked between licks.

"I'm Emily Coulter. What's your name?"

"I'z Sassie Boone," she replied.

Emily blurted out matter-of-factly, "I never heard of anybody named Sassie before."

"It short fo' Sassafras," she clarified.

Emily said, "Sometimes we make sassafras tea."

Sassie considered this and shrugged. "Mama say the name suit me 'cauze I bin sassy since a'fo' I'z born."

Emily giggled. So did Sassie. Youth did this.

"How old are you?" Emily asked. "I'm ten."

"I'z 'leven." Sassie smacked her lips. "Dis candy sho' iz good. If I knew how dey cook't it, I'd cook me up some mo' when we git home."

Emily was in agreement with her. Peppermint was her favorite. "I help Mama cook sometimes," she said.

Sassie boasted, "I loves to cook, an' I'z a good cook! My Autie Dorrie show me how." After a brief reflection, she said, "She dead now, dough."

With a wistful expression, Emily said, "My granny died not too long ago too." She didn't mention anything about the baby.

Suddenly Sassie remembered something. "Auntie Dorrie say white folk don't eat no pig ears, no pig feets, no pig snouts. She say y'all waste da best thangs on a hog."

Emily made a face that proved Auntie Dorrie was right.

They laughed some more at their own silliness and happily crunched their candy.

Inside the store Addie and Creenie Boone smiled in silent greeting. They didn't really know each other except for meeting a time or two in the mercantile last fall.

From a few feet away, Addie discreetly watched Creenie out the corner of her eye as she searched through the neatly folded stacks of fabric piled high on a table. As she watched her, she was suddenly overcome with the oddest feeling. For some unexplained reason, a small voice inside prompted her to invite the woman to join in with her and Claire on an idea they'd come up with a few days before.

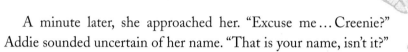

A minute later, she approached her. "Excuse me...Creenie?" Addie sounded uncertain of her name. "That is your name, isn't it?"

"Yessum. I'z Creenie Boone," she answered softly, wondering what Addie wanted with her.

Addie went on to introduce herself, but Creenie already knew who she was.

Addie started, "The other day Claire Ellis and I were talking, and we came up with what we think is a good idea. So I have a business proposition I'd like to share with you." She had admired some of Creenie's intricate needlework in the store, and admittedly, she was indeed an accomplished dressmaker.

Creenie kept her eyes averted from Addie's face, but she was listening intently. Addie didn't regard the mannerism as impolite, she just assumed Creenie either to be shy or perhaps reluctant to look her in the face simply because she was white, knowing that some Negroes still did that out of habit passed down from the old ways.

She went on and explained further. "Mostly all the women sew only small items to sell to Mr. Neelson. Claire and I couldn't think of anyone else who might be willing to invest a lot of time and work into a quilt they're not going to use themselves. We thought if we work together, we can make a couple of quilts in half the time and earn a good bit more money doing so. If we devote a few hours to quilting each Saturday, we could probably have them finished in a matter of weeks."

Creenie quietly turned the plan over in her mind. It was certainly an enterprising idea, and she certainly could use the money, but she felt reluctant to enlist her participation with two practically total strangers. Also, they were white, and ordinarily she didn't socialize with whites. She was usually *hired* by them, to work *for* them, not *with* them. Anyway, she wouldn't feel comfortable in Addie's house; it wouldn't be right.

She gave her answer. "I don't know, Miz Addie. I'll thank on it."

Addie detected her hesitation and continued her pitch. "We'd work on the quilts at Claire's house. She has a rack suspended from her ceiling, so we can raise them up out of the way when we're not working on them. Ap Carver—I believe you and he are cousins—does odd jobs for Claire from time to time. Maybe he could bring you to her house in his wagon, if it's too far for you to walk." Addie had no idea why it seemed so important to her that Creenie agree to come, or why she felt so drawn to her.

She was persuasive, but Creenie still wasn't entirely ready to commit. She made another excuse. "I'z got Sassie—"

Addie interrupted her. "She and my daughter, Emily, can play while we quilt. They'll have a good time together."

It was tempting, the money would sure come in handy, and Ap did speak highly of Mrs. Ellis. Somewhat reserved, she told Addie, "All right. I'll come."

An almost-smile passed across her features when Addie clapped her hands enthusiastically. "I can't wait to tell Claire! She'll be so happy you're going to join us." This would give her something to look forward to. "Why don't we start the first Saturday in October? That's two weeks away. That'll give us plenty of time between now and then to piece together our quilt tops."

It being settled, Creenie collected payment for the shirts she'd sown and left the store. Both girls were sorry when she told Sassie it was time to leave.

As they walked away and were halfway across the road, Emily called out, "See ya later, Sassie Boone!"

Sassie turned, walking backward in a quick, dancing way, and hollered back, "See ya later, Emily Coulter!"

Since there was no one else on the road to take notice, Creenie angled her head around and stole a quick, curious glance at Emily.

It was shortly after four thirty when Addie and Emily walked to Claire's. They found her zealously chopping down a hedge bush near the road. Her yard was swept clean, a pile of leaves burning. It

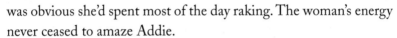

was obvious she'd spent most of the day raking. The woman's energy never ceased to amaze Addie.

Claire would never admit to it, but she was just about used up for one day. Slightly out of breath, she fussed, "Besides for a black gnat, I do know this old hedge is the hateful-est thing God put on the face of this earth!" Then in afterthought, she recanted, saying, "Same as a sawbriar, I 'spect they could be the devil's doin', though!"

Addie agreed with her about the hedge. "It certainly is worrisome." In the spring, the blooms made the air pungent and sickly sweet; each flower then became a bluish-gray berry that resembled a tick buried in a dog's ruff.

Addie tried to take the hoe from Claire. "Here, let me help you. If you don't dig up the root, you're just wasting your time and effort."

Claire wrestled the hoe back from her grasp and ranted on, "Well, I've wasted it anyway, for as sure as a coon sucks eggs, you can bet ever' last one of these confounded berries will take root and sprout. This time next year I'll be fightin' a whole new crop of the mess. It takes a place over quicker than you can cuss a cat!"

Determined not to let it get the best of her, Claire bent over and twisted the hedge root until she finally wrenched it from the ground. She held it up with a look of triumph. Slinging it into the fire, she straightened her back and smoothed her hair in place and said, "I must look a sight! My old hair looks like last year's bird nest."

Giggling at the funny comparison, Emily held out a bucket of pecans to her. "We brought these to you, Miss Claire."

"Oh, much obliged. I'm proud to have them. I'll have to shell us out a pie. My, just look at my filthy hands! My fingernails look like I've been to a tater diggin'!"

Her flight of ideas continued. "It's gettin' cool out here, now that the sun's goin' down. Let's all go in the house, and I'll put us on a pot of coffee. Emily, honey, we'll find you something, too."

Claire clucked her tongue and told Addie, "I had to give three

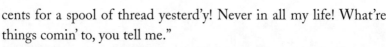

cents for a spool of thread yesterd'y! Never in all my life! What're things comin' to, you tell me."

They went into the house, and when Addie could finally get a word in edgewise, she told Claire, "Don't worry with making coffee; we don't intend to stay long." She proceeded to tell her about seeing Creenie in town and that she'd agreed to quilt with them.

"Oh, I'm so glad to hear that," Claire exclaimed. "And I'll stay glad if she doesn't turn out to have beans for brains like that crazy cousin of hers!"

Addie smiled. Despite all her complaining of him, she knew Claire really was fond of Ap. She said, "Emily's glad, too. She made a new friend today ... Sassie."

Putting on a kettle of water for the coffee, Claire commented, "From what I've seen, that Sassie's a ball of fire, but my heart goes out to her. A mixed young'un sticks out like a sore thumb; has a time of it bein' accepted in this world, by both whites and coloreds."

Much later, as they walked home holding hands, the road lit only by the moon, Addie told Emily assuredly, "You can't give dear Miss Claire a blessed thing. You can be sure that tomorrow we'll be eating pecan pie."

The following day was Saturday. In the evening, not long before it got dark, Alfred was standing with a gourd dipper held midway to his mouth, gazing out the window. He seemed lost in thought when Addie walked up and startled him. He hurriedly gulped down a big swallow of water, mumbling something about going out to the barn to brush Gent. As he left hastily, Addie thought, *He spends more time with that blame horse than he ever did with me.*

A little while later, she happened by the same window that Alfred had been staring through and tossed a glance through the filmy curtain. In the next instant, her heart ceased. Along with the alarming realization came a queasiness in the pit of her stomach. In that instant, she realized that she must take Emily away from there. She didn't know how yet, but she would find a way.

Like Addie, Emily loved to indulge herself in nice, long baths. On this warm morning, the girl had drawn enough water to fill a washtub within a few inches from its brim. Heated by the sun all day, by this time of evening, it set waiting, warm and inviting.

From this viewpoint, through the window where Alfred had stood staring out, Addie glimpsed her ten-year-old daughter innocently enjoying a soak in the tub.

CHAPTER 15

"O taste and see that the Lord is good..." (Psalms 34:8).

The first Saturday of October dawned fair and autumnal. Claire's cozy kitchen was filled with the rich, aromatic smell of freshly-brewed coffee as she sat down to her usual breakfast of grits and a fried egg. After she poured herself a steaming cup, she set the coffee pot a little to the side on top of the stove to keep what remained hot. She ate and rinsed and dried her plate and fork and put them away, but she kept her cup handy.

She felt especially chipper this morning. She had company coming later on. From a shelf over the table, she took down a large crockery bowl and a wooden spoon, and then she set about gathering up the ingredients needed to stir up a batch of teacakes. There was no need to look at a recipe; the process was so familiar to her she could have gone through it with her eyes closed.

She dipped a cup into the flour can and measured out about four cups. To the flour, she added a teaspoon of soda, two of baking powder, and a couple of cups of sugar. Then, she beat in two eggs. She poured in just over half a cup of buttermilk and added two logs of butter and a splash of vanilla. All these mixed together made a soft dough.

After sprinkling the table with flour, she turned the dough out onto it, and using a large floured pin, she rolled it to about the thickness of the wooden spoon's handle. She cut some of the dough into good-sized squares, some she cut round, using the mouth of a jar. There was just enough raw dough left to nibble on while the teacakes baked for about ten or twelve minutes. Straight from the oven, while they were hot and chewy, Claire took one to the porch swing so she could sit and enjoy it at leisure with that last steamy cup of coffee.

In a similar, homey kitchen, a few miles out from the other side of town, another cook was preparing to bake. Even if she'd been able to read, she, like Claire, didn't need to look at a written recipe. She relied upon a heritage of recipes kneaded to memory, a legacy passed down from the preceding generations.

With the sleeves of her calico dress pushed above her elbows, she separated the yolks from the whites of six eggs. She measured precise handfuls and pinches of selected dry ingredients and combined them with the beaten egg yolks, butter, and soured milk. Then she gently folded the whipped egg whites into the creamy batter. Hands coated with a dusting of fine white flour greased the baking pan. A while later, the heavenly aroma of the baking cake wafted through the air up on Nigger Ridge.

It was just after noon when Ap pulled up slowly and delivered Creenie and Sassie to Claire's door. As they stepped onto the porch, Claire poked her head out and welcomed them warmly to her home. She'd been eager for them to arrive all morning. Entering the house, Creenie handed Claire a basket covered with a flour sack cloth.

"What's this?" Claire asked as she eyed the basket.

"I'z thankin' we might have some cake later on," Creenie replied shyly.

A smile crossed Claire's face. "Why, bless your heart! We sure will!" She took the basket and set it on the table in the kitchen.

Addie and Emily waved to Ap as he circled back around and pulled out onto the road and headed back toward town. Knowing Creenie and Sassie were already there, they quickened their steps toward Claire's house.

It had taken them hours to piece together their quilt tops. Addie's was a log cabin design in warm, earthy colors. Creenie used bright fabric scraps to piece together a star pattern. They could scarcely wait to get busy and decided to start on Creenie's first.

Emily and Sassie were put to carding a sack of cotton. They worked the hard balls of cotton between the wiry bristles of two wooden paddles until it was separated and fluffy. The women used the cotton to fill the quilts to add weight to them and to define their stitches. As soon as the girls finished their task, they left the room giggling and wandered down the hall into Claire's back room library to plunder through the bookshelves.

Emily confided to Sassie that her favorite place to read was in a nest of sweet-smelling hay in the barn loft.

"My cats love for me to read to them."

Even though she felt a little reluctant, for fear of shame, Sassie admitted, "I'z caint read or write."

As the fact registered, Emily's interest was sparked, and soon an idea was born.

As the women started working on the quilts, at first Creenie's demeanor was polite but reserved. She devoted quiet attention to her stitches, only speaking in response to the specific questions Addie and Claire aimed at her in an attempt to draw her into the conversation. But before long, her shyness had abandoned her and flown out the window, leaving her surprised at how much they all had in common, despite their many differences. Regardless of their color, indeed God had created them equally, basically the same—*in His own image and likeness.*

Over the next few pleasant hours, the three of them sowed all manner of thoughts and ideas as they quilted. A latent bud sprouted and a new friendship flowered as they tended the gardens of their hearts in fellowship and laughter—and tears.

When Addie asked Creenie about her family, without pause from her sewing, she replied, "My Mama bin gone fo' a long time. My Auntie Dorrie die jus' las' February."

Claire broke in and professed, "I knew Dorrie Boone, but I knew her as Dorthea. She used to cook for Milton and Tressie Collins. You know, Milton was Stanton Collins's boy. Old Stanton was the founding father of Collinsville. Milton and Tressie didn't have a son, so the Collins name died off with them. Course, I didn't think Milton would ever die. That man seemed determined to live forever. Just goes to show how things can turn. On this day, there's not a single soul by the name of Collins living in a town named after them!" This was a fact she found amusing.

Addie asked her, "Do you have any brothers or sisters?"

Creenie didn't look up as she answered. In a hushed voice, she said, "I had a brother name Isaiah . . . but I caint remember him. I'z jus' a baby when he died. He fell in da river . . . drown when he wuz three."

Addie could certainly sympathize. "How troubling that was for your family. I should know. My little sister, Rebekah, died when she was three. It was a terrible time for us. Mama never did . . ." Her voice trailed off. *Life is so precious and fragile . . .* "Well, thank the Lord Pa was there. What about your father; is he still living?"

Creenie hesitated a minute. The answer was almost too incredibly sad for her to say, too sad to hear herself say. Her voice wavered slightly as she said, "I never knew my daddy. They say when Isaiah went in da river, he jump in to save him. He couldn't swim. He drown wif Isaiah." A single, plump tear rolled down her cheek and left a wet line on the side of her face.

For a minute, silence hung over the room. Addie swallowed hard. The story was so tragic she couldn't think of what to say. She felt bad that she'd trespassed upon such a very private place. A verse from John came to mind. *In the world ye shall have tribulation...*

Creenie forced a smile and said shakily, "Sassie all I got in dis world. She mostly all spice, but sometime she be sweet as huckleberry pie." Her love for the girl glistened on her face, along with the wet line from the tear.

Claire stood up and stretched. On a more positive note, she said, "I think it's high time we sample that pound cake. I'll put on a fresh pot of coffee." She headed off toward the kitchen.

Addie went to the hallway and called out to the girls, interrupting the bursts of laughter coming from the back room, asking if they wanted some refreshment.

"No, ma'am! Not right now!" they called back in unison.

Following Creenie to the kitchen, she said, "The way those two get along, you'd almost think they were sisters. We've hardly heard a peep out of them for hours. They're bound to be conspiring over some secret plot."

As they gathered around the table, Claire served the cake and coffee.

Creenie knew of incidences where white folks allowed Negroes to eat from their dishes, but only from ones with flaws. However, she noticed the china plate and cup and saucer Claire handed her were without crack or chip.

The buttery pound cake was so delicious it melted in their mouths. Claire took one bite of it and proclaimed, "Creenie, you sure put your foot in that one! I insist you give me the recipe."

What she said astonished them. "Y'all haf to talk to Sassie 'bout dat. She da one make it. Auntie Dorrie taught Sassie all she knew 'bout cookin' afo' she passed on."

The day flew by; the women were pleased with the progress they made on the quilt. As they admired what they had done, they talked about where they would begin next time they met. Ap came back for Creenie and Sassie in time to get them home before dark.

After everyone said their good-byes, as they strolled home in the coolness of the evening, Emily told Addie confidently, "I've decided, when I grow up, I'm gonna be a schoolteacher—just like Miss Claire."

Addie praised her ambition. "That sounds like a wonderful idea."

"Yep, an' I've already got my first pupil," Emily told her earnestly. "Sassie can't read or write, so every Saturday, while y'all work on the quilts, I'm gonna teach her. She's real smart. Today we had our first lesson, an' she's already learned to spell and write her name. *S-A-S-S-I-E B-O-O-N-E.*" She was proud of what they'd accomplished, and they'd had fun doing it.

So that's what they were doing. Addie pulled her fringed shawl closer and smiled. God had truly poured out his blessings on this day, the first Saturday in October.

Already, they were all looking forward to the next time.

CHAPTER 16

"I returned and saw under the sun that the race is not to the swift, nor the battle to the strong, neither yet bread to the wise, nor yet riches to men of understanding, nor yet favour to men of skill; but time and chance happeneth to them all." (Ecclesiastes 9:11).

The weather turned off cold. In past weeks there had been a few heavy frosts, but by the beginning of November, as it always did each year, a freeze came and the weather held cold for several straight days. At the break of dawn on Saturday morning, Addie and Emily set out on foot into the woods to squirrel hunt.

Though Daniel would fervently deny it, his little sister could outshoot him with a .22 caliber rifle. Emily was a little too delicate to be considered a tomboy, yet rough enough around the edges to be set a distance apart from most of her gender. Addie encouraged her to learn how to do everything, from shooting to sewing. She wanted her daughter to be independent and able to take care of herself, fearing any possibility—though she prayed ardently against it—that she may make the same mistake she did and marry a man like Alfred.

Addie shortened an empty feed sack and sewed a strap to it, fashioning a bag for their harvest. Emily wore the sack across her chest like a sling and carried the rifle. Addie packed a pocketful of extra shot.

The clear, fall morning held a certain crispness; the air was clean and cold and fragrant with the scent of pine. Every breath was satisfying and invigorating. They could see their warm breaths before them. It was the kind of day that made one glad to be alive.

October's rich palette of red, gold, orange, and yellow was quickly fading to brown, but all the trees seemed to shout for joy of the season as they strolled under a canopy of sprawling branches. Rays of sunlight filtered through. A thick carpet of fallen leaves and pine needles covered the woods' floor, and the damp ground underneath smelled of earthy richness and sweet decay.

For a distance, they walked along the creek bank. Leaves swirled in the tea-colored water as they drifted downstream in the idle current. Around a bend, a fallen log created a small cascade that gurgled and spilled into a larger pool. This pool was the fishing hole where Daniel and Amelia had caught many a string of shell crackers on a cane pole, using night crawlers and crickets for bait.

Rolled in cornmeal and fried crisp in a kettle of hot grease, the fish made for some mighty fine eating.

There was no hint of wind. The stillness of the morning was disturbed only by the slight rustling of the hunters' steps as they quietly trod through the woods, and the sharp, intermittent tapping of a woodpecker as he persistently knocked on the dull wood of a hollow tree somewhere across the way.

From the time they left the house, they'd spoken only once, in a low whisper, when Emily pointed out a spot and declared it to be the finest place she knew to lie down and daydream. Addie nodded in agreement.

It didn't take long for them to reach the shallow vale where a big

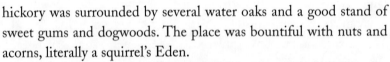

hickory was surrounded by several water oaks and a good stand of sweet gums and dogwoods. The place was bountiful with nuts and acorns, literally a squirrel's Eden.

Amid the music of their noisy chattering, the bushy-tailed rodents scurried around tree trunks and sailed from limb to limb with the skill of a blue jay. Dozens of their leafy homes were nestled in the forks of towering branches. Emily drew a bead on her first target and pulled back on the trigger. The gun's report broke the peacefulness and tranquility of the wooded sanctuary, and for the next half hour, high-pitched thunder echoed across the hollow again and again until the feedsack bag was weighted down with their supper.

In unspoken agreement, when they started home, they went the back way that led to Samuel and Rachel's old place, the place where Addie and Wesley grew up. After years of neglect, the house and grounds lay in ruin. Uninhabited since Rachel's first stroke, the old dwelling was rundown and falling in, its face partially hidden behind an overgrown camellia shrub. Addie suspected the house might cave in on any given day, if not for the fact that it was held up by the cordage of wisteria vine that climbed the crumbling brick chimney and trailed across the sagging roof. The old smokehouse and barn had long since collapsed and lay camouflaged under a heavy growth of weeds and briars.

When Emily ran into the house to explore, Addie strolled around to the back and stopped under an ancient oak, the branches overhead created a rambling trellis for a tangle of wisteria and ivy. When she was a little girl, she had made mud pies in this very spot. She smiled at the memory.

Gazing out toward the old well, she thought of the daffodils that so faithfully came back there every spring and spread a buttery trail of bouquets across the yard. This, of course, brought to mind another more unpleasant memory of how Rachel used to attack the tender plants with a hoe, chopping them to bits before they had a chance to bloom. *Mama used to scare me half to death*, she thought.

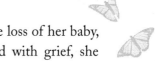

On the day Rebekah died, driven mad over the loss of her baby, Rachel went into a raging fit of despair. Crazed with grief, she grabbed up a shovel, dug a deep hole, and ceremoniously buried Rebekah's bloody, yellow dress. From that day on, yellow dresses were strictly forbidden, forever banished, never to be worn again by either she or Addie.

Even nature was denied immunity from Rachel's scorn for the color yellow. Longsuffering in its attempt to make amends, and relentless in its humble offerings of peace, the very ground fell under attack from her bitterness. Year after year, season after season, beautiful yellow flowers were sent forth in gentle remembrance of Rebekah, all for naught, for Rachel illogically regarded the seasonal gesture as merely trite and mocking.

Quite understandably, when a child dies, some*one* or some*thing* must take blame. Unfortunately, the effects of Rachel's bitterness rippled far beyond the inanimate.

Suddenly Addie's mind was flooded with the memory of that day—and the terrible accident. Even after all these years, her heart pounded so loudly she could hear it as she recalled:

It was summer—June. Wesley was ten; I was eight. Rebekah was almost three. Us young'uns were in the backyard with Mama 'round the table in the shade of the big oak. The table spilt over with bushels of the sweet, juicy peaches we'd picked in the cool of morning. Wesley had drawn several buckets of water and filled the big, black pot about halfway. Mama had a fire going around the pot. Jars for canning were kept on the shelves in the store shed, and she went in the shed and took some down to boil for the canning.

The day heated up fast. I'd dreaded this day just like I dreaded all the ones like it to come. Canning was tiresome and seemed to last all summer long. Peeling peaches was especially messy. The juice ran down my arms. In no time, my dress was wet and sticky. Flies were immediately drawn to the ripe-peach smell; several chickens too. They flocked under the table around our feet to peck at the sweet, succulent peels we dropped in the dirt. When their greedy beaks got too close to each other, the squawking birds turned on each other and feathers flew. When Mama wasn't tending the jars, she helped me and Wesley with the peeling; she knew it'd take us all day to peel that mountain of peaches on our own.

Rebekah was humming and skipping around, here and yonder, chasing after the chickens with a stick. They scattered over the yard, running from her. Rebekah was spoiled, Mama saw to it, and I was jealous of her. Since she was still just a baby, that excused her from the tedious, messy chores I got stuck doing.

She had dark, curly hair and real fair skin. She looked like a porcelain doll, running around in that pretty yellow dress trimmed with lace. The dress was handed down to her from when I was little, but I only got to wear the dress to church. Rebekah was outside playing in it, getting it dirty.

When she failed to catch the hen she fancied, her attention turned to the cats. She managed to capture one of the better-natured ones and menaced it for a while, dragging it around by its neck.

The cat quickly grew tired of being choked and squeezed and having its fur pulled. It twisted in her grasp and threatened to claw if not set free. Rebekah flung the cat to the ground. Quick as its paws hit the dirt, the cat escaped into the shed. Rebekah headed off toward a patch of dandelions and daisies at the edge of the yard.

I sighed heavily and propped my elbows on the table, wishing I could run and play. It wasn't fair! Wesley grumbled under his breath, too. He said fish would bite a bare hook on a day such as this. The creek would've sure felt good. While sweat ran down my neck, I daydreamed about how nice it would be to jump into the icy water. It was torturous to have to sit there and peel peaches and swat at a swarm of annoying gnats and flies all day.

Wesley shooed and kicked at a couple of roosters that had paired off to fight under the table. Just to be mean, he stomped on my toes and mashed them. I huffed and stuck my tongue out at him. We were miserable. Mama glanced over at us. She didn't scold us, but we got the message loud and clear. She went back to watching the jars and the fire. No one paid attention when Rebekah went poking around in the shed.

A short time later, the sound of breaking glass stole me away from my daydreaming and the mundane chore of peeling peaches.

All around the base of the big oak, gnarly roots protruded from the ground. There, on the hard gnarly roots, was where Rebekah tripped and fell.

Not one of us—not me or Mama or Wesley—had noticed when Rebekah came from the shed toting a gallon jug she'd taken down from the shelf. To carry it, she'd had to wrap both her chubby little arms around it and hug it close to her body. Her gait would have been awkward and clumsy from the size and weight of the big jug.

She stubbed her toe on the roots, her tiny feet tripped. She stumbled and fell on the jug as it broke against the base of the tree.

A moment later, Rebekah pushed herself up from the ground with her gritty, little hands. She seemed fine, at first. In one hand she was clutching a withering bouquet of weeds and flowers. With the other, she reached up and swept the wispy curls back off her face. Her hand went to smooth down the hem of her dress where it was turned up. She wiped the dirt off her hand on the front of her dress. Where her fingers pressed against her dress, an ugly stain suddenly soaked through. Bright red spread across the pretty yellow.

Rebekah turned and looked at us, wide-eyed. First, she looked surprised, and then, confused. She stretched her hand out toward us so we could see it was covered with something strange and red and sticky. A thin line of blood trickled down her short, fat legs. Mama screamed and ran toward her.

Rebekah was scared. She thought Mama was mad at her for taking the jug down to put her pretty flowers in. And, she also thought she was mad because she broke it, and ruined her pretty dress. Rebekah started whimpering and dropped the weeds.

Then she was crying hard. The searing pain from where the big, jagged shard of glass sliced into her made her feel dizzy and sick. There was a gaping wound in her stomach; a piece of glass was lodged there, stabbing her.

Mama held Rebekah in her arms and tried to comfort her. She held pressure to the deep cut place and hollered at Wesley to run to town and fetch the doctor. She hollered at me to run to the field and get Pa, but I couldn't ... I couldn't move. It was like my feet were tied to the ground.

Rebekah was fading away fast. Mama was panicked and screaming. In just minutes, they were both covered with blood. All the time, Mama was wailing, "Oh God, why Rebekah ... why Rebekah ... why Rebekah?"

God was merciful to Rebekah. She didn't have to suffer long. She bled to death within a few minutes and was dead way before Wesley came back with the doctor.

When I finally got my legs to move, I took off running to the barn and climbed the ladder to the loft. That's where I stayed hid until Pa found me.

Pa had to've been pulled in a hundred directions all at once, his mind and presence required by more than just me. There were others to see to, others to comfort, dreadful, horrendous things that needed tending.

But, he laid all those other things aside long enough to see to me, because he knew I needed seeing to. He sat up in the hay with me and did his best to soothe me and calm my fears, to help a scared, confused eight-year-old girl try to grasp on to what had happened.

And, he also came because he knew that when we climbed down from the loft and stepped off the bottom rung of the ladder, we'd be stepping down onto unfamiliar soil and into deep manure.

I never expected the sun would come up again, but it did, the very next morning. How could the sun rise when the world had

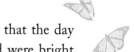

ended? It just didn't make sense. It didn't seem right that the day Rebekah died and the next day when she was buried were bright and sunny. It was all too unbelievable and unfair. Rebekah was dead, and time dared to continue. The rest of the world, except for us, just went on as before.

A mule-drawn wagon carried the coffin—a small and simple wooden box—to the graveyard. I remember being chilled to the bone. Even though it was June, when we got back to the house, Pa lit a fire in the fireplace to warm us.

For days, an unbearable quietness hung over the place, except for Mama's crying; I don't think the hens even cackled.

I think Mama wished she'd died with Rebekah, and honest to God, in some ways she did. As for me, I struggled to climb the same steep hill every day, never quite able to reach the top. Some days I wondered if Mama wished I had died instead of Rebekah. She had loved Rebekah so much and acted so different after she was gone.

Pa carried us on. We just had to be patient and wait on Mama to catch up. By and by, she made it to a tolerable place but never came back to the place where we'd all been before. That place was no more. The light in her eyes seemed forever dim, her laugh was never as melodious.

It seems like when a family loses a child, the earth gets atilt of its axis and the universe never again seems to regain perfect alignment. Folks don't know what to say to those who grieve for a child. Only God knows and understands their pain. *For God so loved the world that He gave His only begotten son …*

Satisfied that she had twirled a stick through every cobweb in the house, Emily bounded through the rickety back door and brought Addie's mind back to the present. Addie took a deep breath and put on a bright face, hoping Emily wouldn't see anything different.

She didn't. Emily had something else on her mind. She asked

hopefully, "I was thinkin' maybe me an' Sassie could fix this old house up an' pretend it's a schoolhouse."

Considering the dilapidated structure and its secluded location, Addie replied, "I don't think that's a very good idea. It's not safe here. You and Sassie will have to find somewhere else to play." Before Emily could protest, she added, "Let's go home, honey-child. We've got squirrels to clean."

While they were skinning and gutting the squirrels, the cats and chickens fought over the furry hides and bloody innards. Addie put the dressed squirrels in a pan of saltwater brine. After they'd soaked a while, she floured and fried the youngest and tenderest of the legs. The rest she made into a savory stew, seasoned with onions and simmered in thick, brown gravy. Emily made a pan of biscuits for sopping.

Not that he had one coming, but as a favor to Alfred, since he considered the brains a treat, Addie boiled the squirrel heads in salted water for him. Throughout the meal, he made sport of slamming the small, walnut-sized skulls down hard on the table, cracking them open for the sweet meat inside.

Grinning, he said, "Y'all gals musta read my mind. I've had me a hankerin' for a fine mess o' squirrels here lately." He cracked another head open and held it out toward Emily. She wrinkled her nose and shook her head in disgust.

"No, thank you!" she squealed. He was making her sick, she was making him laugh, and they were both eating it up.

More aware than ever that she must keep a cautious and watchful eye on Emily around him, Addie paid particular attention to the interaction between her and Alfred. Still very disturbed over it, she was yet to decide what to say to him about his invasion of the girl's privacy the other evening as she was bathing. *I must take Emily away from here...* However, despite his perversion, she wouldn't rob Emily of this rare, happy moment with her pa for anything. After all, her feelings were typical of any child's toward her parents. All she knew was that Alfred was her pa, and that in itself was reason enough for her to love and trust him.

It had been weeks since Addie carted Ben off to live with Daniel, but as luck would have it, Alfred hadn't noticed the hound missing until today. In between chewing, he made the comment, "Ol' Ben must've gone off in the woods with y'all this mornin' a-huntin'. I ain't seen him on the place all day."

Emily glanced over at Addie expectantly, waiting to let her give him the answer. What Addie said was not a lie. "No, Ben didn't go hunting with us this morning."

Suddenly it dawned on him. Alfred nodded, having solved the mystery on his own. "That ol' scamp's most likely caught wind of a split-tail an's run off a-courtin'. He'll drag hisself back up in a few days."

CHAPTER 17

The following Monday evening, the sky was a vision of exceptional beauty. Addie stood on the end of the porch facing westward, admiring the incredible sight, thinking, *Pa always said sunset must be Heaven's door left ajar.*

In the distance, stately hardwoods, now barren of their leaves, stood as black filigree silhouettes against a brilliant rosy-orange canvas streaked with diagonal slashes of maize. As night approached softly, a sea of muted purplish-gray settled itself above the vivid display. To the onlooker, night descended as a gentle but persuasive lover, its soft weight languidly stretched out and lay upon the brilliant hues. Alas, the remnant of the day long spent surrendered and slowly faded as it sank lower and lower, slipping completely from sight, absorbed into the earth.

Addie drew a deep, cleansing breath and pulled her woolen shawl tightly around her shoulders against the chill from the cold air. Nightfall came quickly this time of year. It was the third day of

November. She turned to go inside the house but stopped just short of the door, when a peculiar noise drew her attention. She turned and went to stand at the top step and watched the road in the direction of town and waited.

Odd, she thought as the sound of a wagon being driven fast and hard came closer and closer. A few minutes later, the clamoring rig rounded the bend and came into view. When she recognized the horse and buggy as that belonging to Travis, and saw the driver to be Ap, she immediately sensed alarm. Before Ap even saw her standing on the porch, he started hollering, "Miz Addie! Miz Addie!"

Addie didn't wait for Ap to reach the house. She knew for certain whatever message he was bringing her on the wings of such urgency in Travis's rig had to be of a gravely serious nature. Apprehension compelled her to act immediately. Heart pounding, she ran into the house and grabbed her cloak, making ready to leave. Before heading back out to the porch, she shouted, "Emily, put your coat on now! Hurry!"

The child obeyed. She dropped her lesson book and tablet and sprang from the floor. She grabbed her coat and put it on, fumbling with her buttons. The tone of Addie's voice told her that something was awfully wrong.

Ap drove up into the yard so fast he was barely able to bring the horse to a stop before hitting the front of the house. He was a fool out of control—of the buggy and himself. He was out of breath, gulping for air, waving his arms wildly, yelling to the top of his lungs, "Miz Addie! Miz Addie! Doc say I'z ta git you! Lawd, it Missa Alfred! A tree fall on him, an' he hurt bad! Yessum, *bad!* Doc say I'z ta come fo' you quick! *Come on now!* Doc say fo' us ta *hurry!* Oh, Lawd Jezus, help me *pleaze!*"

Against her better judgment, but because she had no choice, Addie climbed onto the seat beside a crazed Ap. He was still standing as he slapped the reins against the horse's flanks, urging it forward. The wagon jerked, and he took a free fall backward, landing on the seat, his legs flying over his head. He was still struggling for balance as the wheels rolled back onto the road.

Addie hollered over her shoulder to Emily, "Go directly to Claire's and stay there 'til I come for you! Go, now!"

Emily went running as fast as a lizard toward Claire's house, worried and scared to death over what she'd heard Ap say about a tree falling on her pa.

On the rough, reckless ride back to town, Addie tried to get an account of what had happened from Ap, since she knew he'd been in the woods working with Alfred at the time of the accident. However, that proved hopeless. It was beyond impossible to glean any useful information from Ap's idiotic babbling. All he could say was, "Lawd, this" and "Lawd, that." He was overcome with the excitement of it all, not only the incidence of the tree falling on Alfred but also the esteemed responsibility of fetching Addie for Doc. Together, it had got the best of him. He kept saying over and over aloud, as a reminder to himself, "I'z ta brang Miz Addie to da doc's office ... I'z ta brang Miz Addie to da doc's office ..."

Ap's rambling gibberish was frustrating, not to mention aggravating. As the buggy swerved all over the road, Addie grasped the seat and held on for dear life. She thought, *If I had a free hand, I'd use it to smack him. A well-placed blow to the head might knock a little sense into him and calm him down some before he runs off the road and kills us both.* But it was all she could do, holding on tight with both hands, to keep herself from being thrown from the bouncing rig.

Thankfully, the ride to town took only a few minutes, but it was almost completely dark when Ap braked to a screeching halt in front of Doc's office. Addie jumped down and rushed into the house, letting the door shut loudly behind her. Travis heard her and called out from the back room, where he saw patients.

She ran down the hall to the room, which was dimly aglow, lit by two kerosene lamps. Alfred was lying flat of his back on the table. The smell of blood was frank. Addie walked toward him slowly and pensively, unprepared for the gruesome sight that lay before her.

Alfred was stripped naked from his waist down, a sheet covering part of him. His eyes were closed, and he was moaning. He was pale as rice. His body shook violently, in spite of a heavy quilt draped over his torso. Addie saw that his left lower leg was covered with blood; a leather tourniquet was bound tightly around his thigh, just above his knee. There was blood on the table and some on the floor, where his blood-soaked trousers lay in a shredded heap.

Addie glanced over at Travis and saw there was blood all over his shirt, too. His sleeves were rolled up, and he was readying a tray with antiseptic and an array of tools and instruments. Nearby was a stack of clean rags. A big pot of water was coming to a boil on the stove.

"What in the world happened?" she asked in a small, feeble voice.

Travis answered matter-of-factly, "Tree fell on him." Right now, he was Doc, not Travis, as he went about in preparation of his work.

"Will he be all right?" she asked. Her eyes searched his face for some sign of encouragement.

He answered flatly, "To be honest with you, Addie, it's hard to say. He's pretty bad off."

On the table, Alfred mumbled deliriously, like he was having a terrible nightmare. Addie was close enough that she smelled whiskey on his breath.

"Is he drunk?" She said it more as a statement than a question, relieved for a moment, thinking this explained at least part of the cause for the pathetic state he was in. *Not to worry*, she thought, for she'd dealt with his drunkenness on plenty of previous occasions.

Travis looked down at Alfred and nodded.

"Drunk as a skunk. The men liquored him up good an' proper out at the site. Good for numbin' the pain, but bad 'cause the whiskey makes it hard to control the bleedin'." He looked at her squarely and said, "I can't do this by myself, Addie. I'm gonna need your help."

Glancing toward the door at a moving shadow he caught sight of Ap peeking in nervously. He addressed him so sternly he made him jump.

"Ap, come on in here. We can sure use an extra set of hands. You stay an' help, an' I'll dance at your weddin'." It was more of a command than a request.

The whites of Ap's eyes were as big and shiny as doorknobs. "Naw, suh, Doc, I ain't got no extra hands, an' I'z ain't gittin' married! I'z got ta git goin'!" He wanted no further part in what was happening here. He'd already seen more than a plenty to whet his curiosity. Quick as he was to answer, he was quicker in taking leave. Ap darted from the place like a scalded dog.

Travis knew he couldn't expect too much help from one of Ap's intellectual faculties. He mumbled something under his breath before turning to Addie and echoed her own thoughts, "He wouldn't've been any help to us anyway. He'd a-fainted an' hit the floor like a wet sack. Then I'd have two patients on my hands. Wild as Ap is right now, he'll hop around like a jack rabbit till the sun comes up." Shaking his head, Travis added, "That Ap's crazier than an outhouse mouse."

Addie took a deep breath. "Tell me, what can I do?" She waited for instructions.

Travis went over to a cabinet with glass doors and came back carrying a small bottle of medicine. Again, he looked at her squarely and said, "It's gonna take more than whiskey to keep Alfred down during the surgery." He held up the bottle. "This is ether. Addie, you listen to me an' listen good. You *must* do exactly what I say." He reached over and picked up a cloth. "I'm goin' to put some ether on this cloth an' put it over Alfred's mouth and nose. This'll put him in a deep sleep. We have to keep him asleep so he won't move. I need him to lie completely still. You understand me?"

Addie nodded silently, but her expression was so blank, he couldn't help but wonder if she was staring at his mouth just to watch his lips move. He needn't worry, though. She was hanging on to his every word.

"Now, you must—I repeat *must*—hold this lantern as *high* as you can over Alfred so I can see what I'm doing. I'll work as fast as I can, but you'll have to hold it high for a good, long while. Your arm will no doubt get tired. At the same time, you have to keep an eye on Alfred. An' if he starts comin' 'round, you'll need to give him some more ether. I'll tell you about how much when the time comes."

Travis stressed the next point carefully. "Addie, you *must* keep the lantern held high. You *cannot* let the flame near the fumes of the ether. If you do, we'll be blown to kingdom come. There won't be enough of us left for the choir to sing over; somebody's libel to run across our teeth over in the next county. You understand what I'm sayin'?" He spelled everything out to her just like she was a child, because once they got started, then wouldn't be the time for any distracting questions.

Addie nodded again, her eyes big as saucers. Her heart was pounding so loudly she was sure Travis must hear it too.

He was dreading the job ahead. It was getting late, and he was already tired from seeing patients all day long. He couldn't tell it to another living soul, and he'd certainly never done such a thing, but he'd toyed briefly with the idea of letting Alfred bleed on out, just letting him die. He tried to justify his thinking by convincing himself that Addie would be better off. Already convinced of that fact, he ultimately shoved the notion aside, sober in knowing the call wasn't his to make. Anyway, he didn't really have a stomach for killing. He'd taken a Hippocratic oath to preserve life, not take it. Inwardly, he thought, *If ever the night comes when my conscious keeps me up hootin' with the owls over somebody wrapped up in a sheet, I'll be-dogged if she ain't a sight more fetchin' than Alfred Coulter.*

Travis looked at Addie hopefully. "Are you all right with this? You think you can handle it?" He could hear her heart pounding.

Addie nodded. "I think so."

Her voice lacked conviction, but Travis had confidence in her. At least he did until she asked, "Once you give him the ether, and I lift the lantern, how long do you guess it'll take for you to sew his leg up?"

Travis looked at her over his glasses. It became clear that he hadn't done a very good job of explaining the nature of Alfred's condition to her after all. He'd assumed she understood the extent of his injury, but obviously she had no real comprehension of the unpleasant predicament lying ahead. Judging by her tone of voice and the question she just asked, he realized she hadn't fully grasped what he was fixing to do.

In a sharper voice, somewhat impatient and without his usual humor or manners, he explained, "Addie, I'm not plannin' on sewin' Alfred's leg back *on*. I'm figurin' on sawin' what's left of it *off*." He pointed. "Right about here at his knee. *Then* I plan on sewin' the stump up.

"With that done, I'll be much obliged to you if you'll hold that rag over my face an' give me a snort or two of that ether so I can get some shut-eye. If not, least I'll be willin' to settle for is a few hearty drops of fine bourbon for my trouble. By then, you might consider some for yourself, while we wait around to see if Alfred lives or not. I won't lie to you, we're in for a long night."

Addie swayed. The room suddenly felt smaller, and her mind went as blank as a spent shell. It took her a moment to regain some sense.

"Are you sure you have to cut it off? Are you sure there's no other way?"

Travis held the lantern over Alfred's leg. "Take a good look, Addie, an' you'll see there's nothin' else I can do."

Inwardly he thought, *Ain't like I'm amputatin' his leg 'cause I need the practice. The war saw to that.* He knew he was being harsh, but he didn't know any other way to make her understand.

He told her, "Ever' bone down there is ground up like meal. The tree that fell on him was big as a barn. It took right near an hour for two teams of horses to pull it off him."

Addie swallowed hard and stared at Alfred's leg. The lower part of it was mashed flat as a fritter. Shards of shattered bone protruded from the pulpy flesh. The limb was partially severed and barely attached just below his knee, held on only by cracked bone and threads of stringy muscle and pieces of torn skin. A large bone stuck out in an awkward position near what had been his ankle. The whole

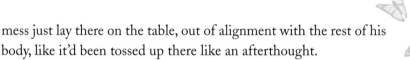

mess just lay there on the table, out of alignment with the rest of his body, like it'd been tossed up there like an afterthought.

She felt like vomiting.

Travis softened his overall tone a bit but kept his blunt edge.

"Not tryin' to steal any hope you might be hangin' on to, but Alfred's lost a bucket of blood, and he's in shock. I'd say it ain't nothin' short of a miracle the man's made it this long. I admit, it's a risky thing we're about to do, an' I can't guarantee you he'll make it through the surgery. In fact, there's a mighty good chance he won't. And even if he does, I still can't guarantee he'll live to see the sun rise. In fact, I can't really assure you of but one thing—if I don't take the leg off, he ain't got a snowball's chance of survivin'.'"

Her teary eyes were fixed on Alfred, and she was trembling. Travis wondered what she was thinking. *Not the same as me, I'd wager. I'm thinkin' the reapin's hell.*

"The night's not gettin' any younger, Addie. We need to get busy, and only steady hands can save any of us now. You in?" he asked.

She blinked rapidly and wiped her sweaty palms on her skirt, thinking, *In sickness and in health...* Her mind was spinning as she considered the potential consequence of what lay ahead. She seriously doubted her nerves or her marriage could withstand the storm they were in for, dependent on her decision. *If he lives.* But what choice was there? *Trust in the Lord.* Addie sighed and replied resolutely, "I'm in." *I'm trapped.*

At the last minute, she whispered a prayer for Alfred, and one for Travis and herself. Before she said amen, she afforded herself a small, selfish request. *Lord, when this is all over and done with, please help me to be able to remember that sunset you painted for me today.*

Later, Travis was dreaming. He was surrounded by a sea of bodies lying in various stages of existence. Wounded, dying, dead. Going, going, gone. An overpowering stink shrouded not only the inside of

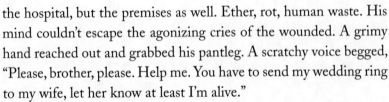

the hospital, but the premises as well. Ether, rot, human waste. His mind couldn't escape the agonizing cries of the wounded. A grimy hand reached out and grabbed his pantleg. A scratchy voice begged, "Please, brother, please. Help me. You have to send my wedding ring to my wife, let her know at least I'm alive."

He guessed they were about the same age. Twenty? Twenty-two? Too young to be suspended in the atrocities of this place and time. He couldn't deny the desperation in the soldier's pleading eyes. It was an understandable request, the least he could do for one in such dire predicament. He nodded and promised to return. He went out to the patch of ground—once a tended rose garden, now a refuse pile for decaying corpses, waiting to be hauled off to the field for unceremonious burial.

In one corner of the yard, discarded limbs were stacked up like cordwood. It took but a few minutes for him to find what he was looking for. Not but one there wearing a wedding ring. He went back inside and located a tablet of paper to write the letter for the soldier. If nothing else, through this simple act of human kindness, he might at least feel he'd actually helped a suffering soul today in the midst of this grotesque catastrophe.

He returned and sat down next to the soldier then realized the young reb had surrendered to the battle. He searched his pockets for identification papers. There were none. He didn't even know what state he was from. Travis sighed wearily. He'd done all he could do, all for nothing.

He awoke, chased from his dreams by a barrage of haunting images from a past he unwillingly lived and remembered from time to time. He took a moment to get his bearings and then arose from the cot where he'd dozed off and went into the next room to check on his patient. Alfred was in a fitful sleep but alive. Travis thought, *Seein' he's made it this far, he'll more than likely pull on through, live to make us regret it.*

He went over to his desk and glanced at his pocket watch. *Two in the morning.* He pulled open the top drawer of his desk and emptied the contents of his pockets. It was there, right where it always was, squirreled away in a dusty corner of the drawer: a small symbol of patriotism, improbable and unassuming in form, yet uncommon and remarkable in cost. *The unknown soldier's gold wedding band.* Travis had kept it all these years in the unlikely event he should ever need a reminder of the sacrifices made in the name of liberty and justice for all.

Exhausted, he turned the wick down and extinguished the lamp and undressed in the dark.

CHAPTER 18

"Render therefore their due ... honor to whom honor is due."
(Romans 13:7).

On the return trip from the mill in Oakdale, Hiram decided to take the shortcut and turned off the main course onto the less-traveled Rocky Creek Road. He was ready to get home. He couldn't recall a day that'd dragged by any slower than this one. The sky was unclouded, and there was no wind to speak of, but it was downright biting cold for November. He was looking forward to shucking his boots and kicking back in front of a roaring fire for a while.

Pulling the collar of his coat higher around his neck, he glanced over at Daniel riding shotgun. He could tell just by looking at him that he was in a strangle-hold. There was a stony cast to his features as he stared out across the passing wintry landscape. His hands and cheeks were red from the chilly air, yet he seemed oblivious to the cold.

Words had been sparse between them all day. In fact, Daniel had been in a black mood for several days now. He had been preoccupied in thought and quieter than usual, ever since last Thursday

when the doctor from Collinsville came to Wesley's with the news that Daniel's pa was in a terrible accident. Seems he'd lost a leg after being wedged underneath a tree.

Hiram knew the reason Daniel left home last spring and came to live with Wesley was due, at least in part, to bad blood between him and his pa. This he was able to gather only from what little Wesley told him, since Daniel hadn't ever confided to anyone exactly what had happened. For certain, though, he knew the two of them had fought.

Hiram noticed Wesley had always seemed to come up a few words short in having anything favorable to say about his brother-in-law. It'd always been obvious the two didn't much care for each other. However, Wesley and his sister were close.

As she came to mind, though the encounter had been brief, Hiram's memory of meeting Addie a few months ago, back in July, was pleasing. Now, deemed the fact that her husband had become a cripple, he thought, *There's a woman with just cause for grievance.* It hadn't been long ago her mother passed away, and only a week or so later, she'd lost her baby; and now this. *It'd take a certain measure of faith and determination to see clear of all that's been set on her lately.* Even though Addie was a stranger to him, Hiram felt a sudden stirring of prayerful concern for her. *It's a sad thing when a family hurts.*

Considering Daniel, he thought, *Daniel's faced with some tough choices at a tough time in his life.* Hiram went back in his mind to when he was about Daniel's age—no longer a boy, not yet a man. If he remembered correctly, coming of age was a complex malady of sorts. A strange and mystical adventure guided by all manner of feelings: restlessness, uncertainty, desire, exhilaration. Some days could be more riddling than others when being expected to take on the ways of a man, when the thing you'd practiced most at was being a boy. With that time at hand, there was nothing else to do except let that tarrying boy and the man forthcoming journey together and blindly stumble toward an unseen destination, steadfast and hopeful in the search, ever longing to come up on that place of recompense and proof known as manhood.

They approached an abandoned farmstead, the old Lewis place, located just over a half a mile from Hiram's. Daniel stared out sullenly across the open field. The sting of recent frosts left the field stark and barren, except for a random dotting of rust-colored clumps of feathery broom sage. Hiram gestured to the field, and in an attempt to make conversation, said, "Seems like just last week that field was knee-deep in clover. Nothin' there now but brown grass."

The brooding silence was broken long enough for Daniel to reply, "I like the look of a died-off field ... got a particular feel to it. You see the land for what it is—nothin' covered up or hidden."

Of course, Hiram knew a deeper meaning lay beneath Daniel's analogy of the field. He was no doubt hinting toward something altogether different. It sounded to Hiram like he was making a correlation of sorts between the field and maybe a secret, or perhaps a lie. Even though he couldn't help but wonder about it, he wasn't one to pry into another feller's business and was respectful of Daniel's space when he chose not to elaborate on the subject.

When they pulled up to the woodshop, Daniel jumped down from the seat and hurried to swing the door open to let Hiram drive the wagon in. Once inside, Hiram started unhitching the horses. He told Daniel, "We'll unload the wagon come mornin', but I'd be obliged if you'd help me with the team before you go."

They led the horses across to the barn in silence. Hiram went to the feed bin for a bucket of grain, and when he returned, Daniel was in a stall rubbing down one of the geldings. Hiram thought, *I'm sure gonna hate to see him go.* A moment later, he felt his chest tighten up when the truth of the matter washed over him and he had to admit to himself, *I'm gonna hate to see him go 'cause he's come to be like a son to me.* He stood watching him for a minute, reluctant to leave. He could almost feel the heaviness of Daniel's expression. It was obvious he needed to talk to someone. No way was he just going to walk out of there without at least trying to say something that might lift his spirits and let him know he cared about him and the problems he faced.

He ventured in. "Daniel, not to be meddlesome, but I can see you're worried sick about your pa. You must be feelin' like you're totin' the weight of the world on your shoulders."

Daniel kept on brushing Kit with long, rough strokes. When he didn't reply, Hiram continued. "I reckon you'll be leavin' here soon—goin' back home to help out on the place." He hoped Daniel would still find time to use the talent God gave to him to work with wood. "For what it's worth to you, I want you to know, you've done a fine job for me over the past few months, and as bad as I hate to see you go, I understand and respect that you have to do what's best for your family."

As Daniel quietly listened, he was quick to detect the tinge of regret in Hiram's voice. *Mr. Hiram's been good to me.* However, he'd unknowingly jumped to the wrong conclusion. Daniel found it hard to breathe as he blurted, "Mister Hiram, there ain't never been a meaner, sorrier man than my pa. There ain't a drop of good in him. You needn't think I'm goin' back there. An' if I's you, I wouldn't waste a minute pityin' him. He just got some of what he had comin.' God's punishin' him in favor of my prayers, an' I'm trustin' the Good Lord ain't done with him yet."

Hiram was taken back, disturbed by what he was hearing. This was not the Daniel he knew. Surely he didn't really feel this bitter toward his own father. A verse quickly ran through his mind. *Honor thy father and thy mother . . .* Hiram had to think carefully about how to respond. He moved to stand in front of Kit where he could see Daniel's face. The boy's eyes were blazing.

"Daniel, I don't know your pa. He's no doubt made some mistakes—we all do—but even if I had differin' ideas with a man, I'd still be sorry if he lost his leg. I guess what I'm tryin' to say is that sometimes folks change, especially when they hit on hard times, an' it takes a man to go back and help someone who's wronged him; it takes a man to forgive."

Daniel hung his head as he thought about Alfred. He couldn't recall a time when there'd been anything but conflict between the two of them. From his earliest recollections, his pa had never shown any measure of kindness toward him, and as far as he knew, Daniel had never done a blessed thing to please him. Even if he was a mind to pretty up his opinion of his pa for Mr. Hiram's sake, at best he'd still be nothing more than a godless drunkard. *Mr. Hiram mistook me 'cause he don't know about what happened. If he knew what happened, he'd understand.*

The words spilt from Daniel's lips in a faltering voice. "Sometimes I feel like I want to see him again—maybe tell him somethin'—but I don't know what. What's there to say to somebody that did what he did? Mostly, though, I just think about killin' him."

Hiram saw the raw emotion on Daniel's face. He hoped he trusted him enough to say whatever it was he'd kept pent up inside all this time; for whatever it was, he could tell he needed to let it out.

Daniel was breathing so hard his shoulders were heaving, "Mister Hiram, I saw them…"

Hiram waited quietly for him to go on.

Daniel took a deep breath, and his voice came out in ragged gasps. "I'd been fishin' on the creek behind Miss Claire's. I stayed as long as I could, but Amelia never came, so I headed home. I cut through the woods like ever' other time."

Daniel let out another trembling breath. "I came out at the bottom field." Apprehensively, he started retracing his steps in his mind. Even the pollen that fell from the pines that day seemed to fall upon him now. As he walked along the path, the atmosphere crackled with a sense of disquiet, an expectation of doom. His mind was racing ahead toward the clearing, but the fearsome dread of what lay waiting there made him reluctant to move forward. Daniel was panting. It was taking him forever to get to the clearing. When he finally got there, what he came upon made him feel faint, ill.

"Mister Hiram, that's when I saw them, there—at the edge of the clearin'." Daniel's eyes blurred from the vision in his head. The

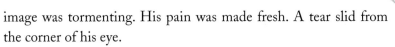

image was tormenting. His pain was made fresh. A tear slid from the corner of his eye.

The pounding of Hiram's heart was deafening to his own ears. He felt a little queasy. Instinctively, he imagined he might know where Daniel's story was leading them. He started praying he was wrong. Subconsciously, he planted his feet firmly, preparing himself to hear the rest.

Tears streamed down Daniel's face. He was pale as a sheet. He wished he could hush himself up, but he couldn't. *I've come too far to turn back. I'm already at the clearin'. It'll be all right, 'cause Mister Hiram's here with me.* Daniel so looked up to him and was ashamed for him to know his horrible secret. He was afraid Hiram would think badly of him just from coming from the seed of a man such as Alfred, and he certainly wouldn't blame him if he did. Still, he had to tell him.

"From the woods, I saw them. Pa, Cleve, an' Pete. They were all drunk. She was fightin', kickin' at 'em ... they were laughin'. I could see she was just a- cryin', beggin' them to quit. They just kept on. I hollered out across the field as loud as I could for them to stop an' let her go, but they didn't hear me. No sound came out. I took off runnin' toward her, but my feet didn't move." Daniel wiped his eyes, but the tears continued to fall like rain. "Amelia, *my Amelia,* kept on fightin' ... Pa tore her dress an' pushed her to the ground. He got on her. Pete, *her own pa Pete,* Cleve, they all held her down ... I knew what was comin.' I couldn't watch." He choked on the words. "I'd been lookin' after Amelia, had *loved* Amelia since she was eight years old; but the day she needed me the most, I let her down. Why, oh why, didn't I save her?" He looked so defeated.

Hiram's heart went out to him. He wanted to reach out and hug Daniel, but he hadn't finished his story.

Now that he'd gotten past the worst part, it was easier for him to tell Hiram the rest. "It was gettin' on dark when Pa came out to the field where I was. He was drunk, yellin', just a cussin' 'cause the plowin' wasn't nowhere near done. I told him what I'd seen an' how I'd just

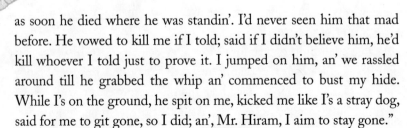

as soon he died where he was standin'. I'd never seen him that mad before. He vowed to kill me if I told; said if I didn't believe him, he'd kill whoever I told just to prove it. I jumped on him, an' we rassled around till he grabbed the whip an' commenced to bust my hide. While I's on the ground, he spit on me, kicked me like I's a stray dog, said for me to git gone, so I did; an', Mr. Hiram, I aim to stay gone."

When Daniel finally stopped talking, Hiram took a deep breath and let it out slowly. For a moment, he came up lacking for a reply. While trying to let it all soak in, he wondered, *What manner of men commit such an act?* Of course the answer was *men separated from God.* He burned with anger at the kind of men these were and for the vile thing they had done, *one of them the girl's own father!* It was beyond his comprehension. Also, he couldn't help wondering what had become of the poor girl—Amelia. *Daniel's sweetheart.* But now he understood why Daniel never paid special attention to the flirtatious advances of girls his own age at church. *Amelia owns his heart.*

His own thoughts were interrupted when Daniel asked, "Now you see why I don't give a hoot about Pa? You see why I can't go back there? Amelia's the only one that matters to me. She's the one I care about; she's the one I worry about." *And she's the one I love with all my heart,* he added silently. "It's my fault she got hurt. I should have stopped them before..." His voice trailed off. He couldn't bear to say it. Guilt was tearing him apart.

Hiram looked into Daniel's wounded eyes. He understood well the pain of losing one you love. After all, hadn't he lost Madeline, his wife, *twice.*

"Son, you've got to stop blamin' yourself for what happened. These kinds of things happen because folks give themselves over to Satan and let sin control their lives. And in that case, there is no control. You hear me when I say that what they did to that girl is *not* your fault." *Drunkenness leads to other vices, their heart shall utter perverse things.*

"I sent Amelia a letter," Daniel said. "I didn't tell her what I'd seen.

Only that I'd found work, an' as soon as I saved up some money, we'd get married. I'd even found us a place to live—the old Lewis place. I know nothin' can change what happened, but what happened didn't change the way I feel about her one bit. I figured we could still be happy so long as we were together. So long as we were together, I believe Amelia an' me would've been just fine."

He told Hiram wistfully, "Now I don't even know where she is. She wrote me back to tell me she'd moved away from Collinsville. I've probably lost her forever, but maybe she's better off without me. I sure did let her down."

Hiram reached out and put his hand on Daniel's shoulder. "I'm sorry for what happened, and you won't want to hear this, but under the circumstances, her leavin' there was probably the best thing for Amelia." He added, "I know this is hard for you, Daniel, but I'm glad you told me." He felt compelled to offer Daniel some advice. "Son, I can tell you from experience, if you let a thing like this dwell in your mind, it'll eat you alive. You need to turn it all over to the Lord."

Daniel shook his head. "The day might come when I can do that, but for certain, this ain't that day." But he did feel better now that he got it off his chest.

Hiram didn't press him. This would no doubt take some time. Right now, even he couldn't imagine what good, if any, could come from such a terrible mess.

"Mister Hiram, you have to promise me you won't ever tell this to another livin' soul. No one else knows, not even Uncle Wesley—just you an' me. Mama can't ever know. It'd worry her to death, and she's already got enough worries, just livin' with Pa." Daniel said firmly, "*Promise me*." His eyes were pleading.

Hiram understood. He understood that Daniel felt responsible for what had happened to Amelia. It was only natural that he felt he'd failed to protect her from being hurt by those men, particularly his father. Now he felt like the only way he could protect his mother from being hurt was by sparing her the truth. Hiram slowly nodded his head in agreement. He didn't know what else to do, at least not right now, and Daniel desperately needed to trust someone.

Daniel knew without a shadow of a doubt that Hiram was a man of his word, but in this incidence, a nod wasn't good enough. "I need you to say it, please."

Hiram could see how important it was to him. "I promise, son. I won't tell a soul." When he heard Daniel's stomach rumble, he saw it as an opportunity. "I don't know about you, but I'm about ready to rustle up some grub. What'd you say we call it a day an' get a fresh start in the mornin'?"

A few minutes later, Daniel had left the barn and was headed home for supper. He was worn out yet felt better than he had in a long time. As he walked down the road in the crisp night air, he suddenly remembered something. His face broke into a grin from ear to ear. A mere word, small and simple, yet it'd never been spoken to him in that particular tongue before. The way the word sounded when *he* said it made it take on a whole new meaning. *Son. Mr. Hiram called me son!*

Back inside the barn, Hiram stretched out an arm and steadied himself against a post. In spite of the down-right biting cold of this November evening, there was sweat on his forehead and the back of his neck. In his thirty-seven years, he'd bore witness to many a tale, but none matched the one he'd just heard. He swore aloud, "Sweet Lord, have mercy. Now I've heard it all!"

Hours later, when the night was far spent, Hiram did as he always did before he turned in. He got down on his knees to still his mind. Kneeling in the soft glow of a dying fire, he gave thanks for a blessed life and praise to a living Savior. He asked God to bestow divine comfort and healing upon the girl, Amelia, and upon Daniel.

So long as he was praying, he figured a prayer couldn't be put to better use than one aimed at Alfred and all the wicked men like him. Yet, given what the scripture says about praying for one's enemies, he found himself at odds about approaching the Throne to ask for the particular lot he felt should befall them. He wasn't altogether sure if he could square up such a notion in the eyes of the Lord. So rather than chance committing treason against him, he settled on simply asking for strength and understanding for himself, and for peace upon the home of Daniel's mother, Addie Coulter.

CHAPTER 19

"For our God is a consuming fire." (Hebrews 12:29).

It was late in the evening. Alfred flopped around on the bed like a bucketful of shiners. He was miserable. His mood was rotten, putrid as Satan's breath. His leg throbbed. He actually looked down for proof it was gone, even though he knew dang well it was. He swore he could feel it. But no, his leg wasn't there. It was sure enough gone. *My wife saw to that,* he thought bitterly. He cringed at the sight of it; despised the way it looked, despised the way *he* looked.

Alfred was at odds with himself. He spent every waking minute trying to decide who he hated the most—Addie or Doc. Just thinking about them made him seethe. *Them two done this to me.* After hours of deliberation, he finally reached his verdict. He laid more blame on Addie. Since he hadn't been able to speak up for himself at the time, she, being his wife, should have intervened on his behalf—on behalf of his leg. She should have forbade the ignorant doctor to remove it, insisted he leave him whole. *Yessir, I will see to it they suffer greatly. Them two will pay dearly for what they done.* His head thudded.

After three weeks, the ugly nub of a stump still pained him to no end, but overall, Alfred was mending remarkably well. At first, he'd panicked, felt powerless, went rabidly mad. He'd always been a strong man, done as he pleased. He couldn't stand feeling weak as rainwater and hated being confined. He couldn't stand having someone tell him what to do and when to do it. He despised his dependence on the very one who'd destroyed his life, stole his dignity.

Alfred had to be in control. He had no intention of lying around like a freak the rest of his life. He'd rather be lying dead. He could not, would not, live like this. Once that was decided, he set about devising a plan. Stoked by his lust for vengeance, he became determined to get well, obsessed to regain his strength.

Emily ran in excitedly to check the mantel clock to see what time it was. At school, they had been studying genealogy, and her teacher had given them an assignment to trace their ancestors and family history as far back as possible. Each pupil would present a short story about their family during the harvest meal that night after prayer meeting. (The ladies' assignment was to bring a pie or a cake.)

Emily was chomping at the bit to get there. "Mine will be the best; I just know it," she sang. She'd been preparing her story all week. Addie was letting her take Rachel's Bible and the photograph of her taken with Samuel, Rachel, Wesley, and Rebekah to show everyone.

They were going to meet up with Claire at the end of her road, and since Emily was so impatient to leave, Addie gave her permission to go on ahead and wait for her there. Emily put her coat on, waved good-bye to her pa, and skipped out the front door, hugging the cherished Bible in both hands.

Addie came into the room and set a covered basket containing a sweet potato pie on the small fireside table while she donned her coat.

"Alfred, won't you change your mind and come with us? I'll be glad to hitch up the wagon," she offered in a fake, cheery voice as she fastened her buttons.

All Alfred wanted was for them to leave. *I'm in hell*, he thought.

Between Addie's incessant puttering in and out of the house all day and the girl's unceasing prattle, he was ready to jump out of his skin. He growled at her impatiently, "I done told you *no*, Addie. They's meager charm in the idie of settin' 'round bein' gawked at by a bunch of do-gooders. I'd sooner git greased up with molasses an' perch on a hill of fire ants than have to suffer through such." He could just imagine a roomful of jeering, pathetic eyes turning to stare at him as he hopped through the door like a one-legged crane on his crutches. Just the thought of it made him burn with humiliation. *I don't want me nothin' to do with them pityin' fools!*

Addie knew she was wasting her breath trying to convince him to go. He'd been surly and hateful toward her all day. As for her, she was glad to be getting out of the house for a while. Her nerves were unraveling. Alfred's constant complaining and demands were tiresome and left her frayed around the edges. Her tongue was sore from her biting it in an effort to keep some degree of peace in the house. She hadn't been able to say or do anything right in his eyes since he'd come to and discovered his leg was gone. "Well, then, we'll be back directly. I've banked up the fire so you won't have to get up to put on more wood." *Taking care of Mama was never this trying,* she affirmed inwardly.

She glanced at him. He was stretched out on the bed. "Maybe you'll be able to get some rest while we're gone."

He shot back, "*Hmph!* If I git any rest it'll be while you're gone. I'm a-feared to shut my eyes anymore, thankin' you an' yer ol' buddy, *Travis,* is jus' waitin' to catch me unawares so y'all can finish butcherin' me. Maybe cut off my other leg!"

Exasperated, Addie picked up the basket and turned to go. She knew Alfred blamed her for the loss of his leg, but she could think of nothing more to say that might lessen his contempt for her in any way. She couldn't give him what he wanted. She couldn't give him back his leg.

Midway from the room, she stopped abruptly.

Without turning to face him, she asked, "Alfred, where's Pa's fiddle?" It wasn't on the mantel in its usual place.

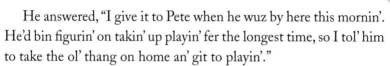

He answered, "I give it to Pete when he wuz by here this mornin'. He'd bin figurin' on takin' up playin' fer the longest time, so I tol' him to take the ol' thang on home an' git to playin'.'"

Addie felt like crying. *How did I ever end up with such a heartless man?* "You had no right to give that fiddle away—that belonged to my father."

Alfred replied sarcastically, "Well, now, Addie, your pa's been dead a spell now, ain't he? I reckon he ain't got no more use for a fiddle any more'n I got use fer my missin' leg."

The back of her head smarted from being struck by the smirk on his face. She didn't have to turn around to see how pleased he was with himself, or how pleased he was for hurting her. He'd do anything to get even with her for the loss of his leg.

She told herself, *No use in worrying over it, there's not a thing I can do about it tonight.* She just sighed heavily and, without another word, left the house to catch up with Emily and Claire and head to the church.

As soon as they were gone, Alfred pulled himself over to the side of the bed and sat up. He grabbed one of the crutches that was propped against the wall at the head of the bed. It took all his effort, but he managed to stand. He winced and groaned from the pain in his leg and became lightheaded. *Dang, I'm weak!* He began an unsteady hop toward the tall, blue-green wardrobe in the corner of the room.

He made it halfway there before he lost his balance and fell. He threw a flailing arm out frantically in search of something to grab hold of. The small, round table near the fireplace broke the weight of his fall, but it overturned. Everything on the table, and Alfred, crashed to the floor. He cried out; the pain in his leg was searing. He cursed long and loud. He rested a moment and then dragged himself over to the wall. Using the crutch, he managed to pull himself up again. His heart pounded. He gasped for breath. The pain was excruciating. He made it to the wardrobe and swung its door open.

He reached inside and pulled out a bottle of whiskey and muttered triumphantly, "Now here's what I'd say's a fair trade—two fifths of whiskey for a useless ol' fiddle!"

Holding tight to the bottle of whiskey, Alfred hopped back to the bed and plopped down, heaving. He had broken a sweat; a thin line trickled down the side of his face. He threw the crutch on the floor beside the bed and twisted the cap off the bottle. He brought it to his lips and took several long swigs, and then he wiped his sleeve across his mouth. For a few seconds he reveled in the warmth that spread down his throat and into his belly. He took several more long pulls from the bottle, for medicinal purposes, of course, and dropped his head wearily upon his pillow. A short time later, he dozed off with the half-empty bottle resting in the crook of his arm. His loud, drunken snores resounded in the room.

Alfred had given no heed to the overturned table. Overcome by his single-minded goal for the taste of whiskey, he'd foolishly disregarded the shattered oil lamp lying on the floor in a puddle of kerosene. Even while he sat on the bed, drinking to his destiny, the oil was seeping into the floor and inching slowly toward the hearth along the cracks between the planks.

The fire caught and spread quickly. It swept through the entire house and burned with a raging fury. The old house crackled and hissed as hot resin oozed from the fat timbers of the foundation and fueled the flames, intensifying the blaze, making it burn even hotter and more ferociously.

Before it burned itself out, every board was greedily devoured by the voracious fire, not one splinter spared. Had Alfred awoke and cried out for mercy, it was unlikely he was heard. The roar of the hellish inferno would surely have consumed his screams.

Local folklore claimed it to be a horrible death. Thus, the death became prophetic in nature, an answer to Rachel's prayer, the prayer she'd uttered in her mind only a few months before as she lay helplessly waiting for Alfred to smother her with her own pillow.

CHAPTER 20

"A new commandment I give unto you, that ye love one another, as I have loved you, that ye also love one another." (John 13:34).

It was after the childrens' presentations, when some of the menfolk wandered outside into the churchyard to smoke and measure lies, that they noticed the orange glow of light in the distance.

Something was burning on Monroe Road!

By the time everyone reached the Coulter place, the entire house was ablaze. To have tried to fight such a great fire would have proved to be a futile waste of time and energy. The house and everything within it were well beyond saving. The intense heat radiated by the enormous fire commanded both caution and respect from the crowd that gathered. Hugging themselves against the cold, the awe-struck audience could do nothing but stand back and shake their heads in disbelief. As they watched the awful event take place from a safe distance, pieces of ash settled on their faces and clothing; their eyes burned from the dense, acrid smoke that permeated the air.

As soon as Addie saw the house burning with such furor, she knew all was lost, even before it was confirmed Alfred was unaccounted for. In his disabled state, she knew he'd had little hope of escaping. As she thought about his being trapped in the hellish blaze, the horror of him being burned alive coursed through her veins, and she felt hysteria take rise within her very soul. *Burned alive.* She stood mummified, stunned. For a moment she wondered what slight comfort insanity might provide, but she quickly dismissed the thought. She refused to give to it; she had to be strong. She repeated the mantra over and over in her mind: *I must be strong. I must be strong. I must be strong…*

It was the sound of Emily's heartrending cries that brought her back to herself. The terrified girl soon realized what had happened to her pa. As Addie ran to her, Emily went rigid and fell to the ground as the shock of it sliced through her core. For a long while, Addie sat on the ground cradling her, consoling her with a sweet whispered lullaby, stroking her hair, remembering all too well how sad and abandoned and alone she felt the night her own father died. Knowing her child's heart was breaking, Addie prayed, *Be merciful to my child. Hide her under the shadow of thy wings… Breathe joy into her heart…*

When Emily's emotions were spent, and she was exhausted of tears, she drifted to sleep. A man rolled up his coat and put it under her head for a pillow. Another covered her with his, until Claire returned from her house with a heavy quilt. It was suggested that she take Emily to Claire's house to a comfortable bed, but Addie thought it best if she kept watch over her there. She wanted to be near her.

All those present testified solemnly among themselves. The consensus was unanimous. A more terrific occurrence had never taken place in the history of Collinsville. This would be something they all remembered for the rest of their lives. The fire was the worst any of them had ever witnessed, but that a man was gruesomely burned alive in it made the story even more sensational. Even those who hadn't cared a copper cent for Alfred wouldn't dare speak an unkind word against him now, after he'd perished in such a grisly manner.

With Emily asleep, Addie arose from the ground and looked

around, now aware of those who'd gathered about to offer their support to her. Like Samuel, Addie loved all people. Black, white—it was of no matter to her. She'd always made an earnest attempt to see folks as God saw them and treat them accordingly. And as a result, this was not forgotten by the people on this night, *in such a time as this.*

Addie was sustained and encouraged by the heavy outpouring of compassion and concern that flowed freely from her neighbors and the surrounding communities. The seeds of kindness she'd sowed over the years returned to her *like bread cast upon the waters.*

A messenger set out swiftly on horseback to fetch Wesley, and within a half hour of receiving the news, he, Daniel, and Hiram had dressed and were hastily saddling their horses. By the light of the moon, they could see the road fairly well and trusted the horses' instincts and sure-footedness to sense the terrain. They urged them toward Collinsville in a thundering gallop.

The men arrived by the faint, misty gray of daybreak. Daniel dismounted and went hurriedly to Addie. Upon seeing him, she grabbed and held her son fiercely and wept. Seven months had slipped past since she'd last seen him. She marveled at how he'd changed. Where a boy once stood now presented a half-grown man. He looked a foot taller, and his features were cut with a new maturity.

Upon first glimpsing the desolation, Daniel was shocked. Speaking to no one in particular, he exclaimed somberly, "God have mercy!"

By then the fire had died down considerably, reduced to a huge mound of smoking embers. Little was distinguishable except for the foundation joists that lay upon the massive bed of glowing coals. Besides the smoldering beams, the only other thing left standing was the chimney. The mighty oaks closest to the house stood blackened and charred.

Lost in his own thoughts, Daniel continued to stare at the coals for a minute or two with an arm around Addie's shoulders. He pulled Addie to him and kissed her forehead. "Mama, are you all right? Where's Emily?"

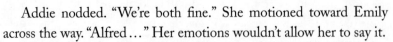

Addie nodded. "We're both fine." She motioned toward Emily across the way. "Alfred..." Her emotions wouldn't allow her to say it.

Daniel didn't look at her. There was no need for her to say more. He gazed at the remains of the house thoughtfully. "How'd this happen?"

She shook her head and answered, "I don't know. We were at church. I tried to get him to go with us. When we left the house, he was in bed. A piece of wood must have rolled out of the fireplace onto the floor."

Hiram kept a polite distance while Wesley, Daniel, and Addie discussed their plans. As he surveyed the fire, he couldn't keep from thinking, *Lord, I'll let this serve as a lesson. From now on, I'll be more specific. When I asked you to grant peace upon this house, this wasn't the particular brand I had in mind.* He was a firm believer in the infinite power of prayer.

With one look at Addie's disheveled appearance—her hair in disarray and her face, hands, and clothes smudged with smut and soot—Wesley urged her gently, "Go to Claire's and lie down. Let us tend to things here." He was worried about his sister. How much more could she take?

"Nonsense! I'm fine," she replied adamantly. The tone of her voice convinced him it was pointless to pursue the suggestion any further. He knew better than anyone how willful she could be.

Daniel and Hiram walked away to go see Emily. Wesley paused for a moment and looked around, remembering days gone by. He'd known this place all his life. The old house that he'd taken to be ageless and indestructible now existed only as an image in his mind. He blew out a long breath and said slowly, "I swear, it all looks different now."

Addie nodded. She understood her brother's sentiment. So she in turn shared one with him. "I wish things hadn't been left as they were between Alfred and me." She told him with an air of regret about the quarrel they had over Samuel's fiddle. It sounded so trifling now.

Wesley hated seeing her in such distress. The fire was indeed a terrible tragedy. He realized she'd lost her home and all her posses-

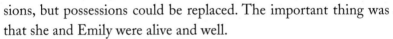

sions, but possessions could be replaced. The important thing was that she and Emily were alive and well.

He quietly reassured her. "We have to accept this as one of those things that seem to happen sometimes without reason. I know at first it won't be like home, but you can live with us for as long as you can stand sharing a room with Stell. At least you, Daniel, and Emily will be together."

She tried to smile at his attempt to humor her, but Addie almost couldn't bear the realization that she'd lost her home. As with the loss of the baby, she thought ruefully, *I'll just have to live with it and go on*. Alas, what choice did she have?

As for Alfred, Wesley's opinion of him remained calloused. If put forth for him to speculate, he would've guessed Alfred's last minutes on earth proved a blistering foretaste of what lay in wait for him in eternity, *the place God went and prepared for him*.

Addie's mind raced. There was so much that needed doing, and in light of circumstance, she amazed everyone with her presence of mind and fevered energy. During the night, in her restlessness, she went about here and yon, her way lit by a lantern, as she made fair assessment of what was in the outbuildings. When morning came, she was in charge.

"Daniel, you and Mr. Graham can gather up all the tools, feed, and tack from the barn and load onto our wagon. We can borrow another one from Travis.

"Wesley, you help me catch up as many of the chickens as we can. It shouldn't be that hard. We'll throw some corn out in the hen yard. I know there's no hope of capturing any of the guineas—they'll just have to roam.

"Of the stock, Daniel, of course, Gent belongs to you now. He's a fine horse. We'll take the mules with us. Daisy's too old and slow. She'd give out long before we got to Golden Meadow. We'll give her to someone who needs a good milk cow. Claire's getting pots and jars from the shed.

"Emily, it's your job to run down any cats you want to take. Put them in a crate. They'll be wild. You best nail the top down, or they'll escape on the way..."

And so on, and so on.

Every now and then, her voice would falter and it seemed she might break down, but then she'd manage to collect herself and go on. Wesley tried to convince her that not everything had to be done in one day, but she worked tirelessly and didn't stop to rest all morning.

During the course of the morning, as callers came and went paying their respects and offering their sympathy, Addie was reassured time and again. *People are so good,* she thought. She was touched by the outpouring of encouragement and generosity from the people of her community. They brought her gifts and offerings of every sort. Folks readily did whatever they could to be of help.

She overheard an elderly Negro woman tell Claire, "Po' thang! Ain't got a pot to pee in or a winder to tho' it out of! I'z didn't know what to brang, but I sho hopes she can use dees thangs!"

She didn't recognize the lady or pay particular attention to what she brought. What did it matter? The true gift was that she had given so unselfishly of herself and come there. Before the woman got away, Addie strode toward her with outstretched hands. They embraced and clung to each other tightly for several moments. Addie held the old woman in arms of heart-felt gratitude, while the old woman armed her up in compassion. No word was spoken. There was no need for words, for the Lord directed their hearts, and the love made possible through the blood of Jesus Christ flowed between them, one to the other.

About this same time, not too far away, a girl crouched in some bushes just beyond the woods' edge and watched the activity. She took care to keep herself hidden from view. She'd walked quite a distance to get there. Several times along the way, she'd had to stop and sit down on a stump or fallen log to catch her breath and rest.

News of the fire spread throughout the town. It was all anyone could talk about. As soon as she'd heard, she had no choice but to come. She was drawn to this place, and to *him*.

She knew he was down there even before she caught sight of him. She'd felt his presence. From her viewpoint, she could barely see his face, but just knowing he was near was a comfort to her. *Daniel.* Her heart was made happy upon seeing him. Then it ached. Oh, she missed him so! Her eyes filled with tears.

Amelia watched as Daniel carried things from the barn and loaded them onto a wagon. How she wished she could go right up to him, wrap her arms around his neck, and proclaim her love for him! But that was impossible now. Her body was changing so. She felt so ashamed. She could never bear letting him see her like this. How disappointed and disgusted he would be if he found this out. *I am surely a disgrace to us both,* she thought as tears slid down her cheeks.

There was one thing Amelia could be thankful for, and all things considered, she actually looked upon it as somewhat of a small miracle. *No lips besides Daniel's had ever touched hers. No, none.* Even on that cruel, cruel day, only rough hands had covered her mouth to stifle her protests. Her first and only kiss belonged to Daniel, as it should be, as it was predestined. In her mind, she could taste the gentle sweetness of his mouth on hers still to this day. The memory of the kiss they'd shared had become like a magical thread of hope she held fast to whenever she felt she might otherwise go insane.

Remembering how far she must walk to return to her Aunt Jennie's house, with a sad and heavy heart, Amelia left her hiding spot and went deeper into the woods to head back the way she'd come. *I must leave him again.* Tears poured down her face.

Understandably, no feeling of care ever crossed her mind for the man who had died in the fire.

Conditions attending, it deemed only logical that Alfred's funeral be held at the site now referred to as his final resting place. Around noon, work stopped when Rev. Harris called everyone to gather around. All those present joined with him near the smoldering pile of ashes for a short, impromptu burial ceremony.

Addie reached over for Emily's hand while the old preacher read the Twenty-third Psalm:

"The Lord is my shepherd; I shall not want. He maketh me to lie down in green pastures, He leadeth me beside the still waters. He restoreth my soul, He leadeth me in the paths of righteousness for His name's sake. Yea, though I walk through the valley of the shadow of death, I will fear no evil, for Thou art with me. Thy rod and Thy staff they comfort me. Thou preparest a table before me in the presence of mine enemies, Thou anointest my head with oil, my cup runneth over. Surely goodness and mercy shall follow me all the days of my life and I will dwell in the house of the Lord forever."

During the scripture reading, Addie and Daniel's eyes met. She wondered what he was thinking. *There will be plenty of time for us to talk soon,* she promised herself.

Her mind wandered. Maybe it was the air of devastation surrounding her, or perhaps the magnitude of the tragedy was such that she hadn't fully comprehended it yet. Or maybe she was becoming desensitized to disaster. *I don't feel anything.* Maybe there was a limit to the sum of grief allowed a person during a lifetime, and maybe she had spent her allowance. Could it be that she'd reached the point of insensibility because she was just plain worn out? *That must be it.* Whatever the reason, the words coming from the preacher's mouth seemed to fall upon wooden ears. To her, the sermon sounded both inappropriate and void of any special meaning. Based on her opinion, the tragedy of Alfred's death lay more in regret than in sorrow; regret over what should have and could have been, but never was.

Just in time to rescue her from her memories, Emily yanked on her hand and whispered, "Pa's in Heaven now." *Behold, the dreamer.* Addie nodded reassuringly to Emily. *She can only hope.*

With the final prayer said, Ap, of all people, humbly offered to sing a benediction hymn. In a strong, baritone voice, he paid homage to the Lord with a soulful rendition of "What a Friend We Have in Jesus." His performance was unexpectedly moving, and God did truly approve. While Ap sang, the gentlest of breezes picked up and caused the smoke to drift downwind away from their faces. No other animal on the face of the earth made a sound for the duration of the song. Even the fowl wandering about were daunted by his singing and stopped to listen. No guinea trilled, no chicken cackled, and no birds warbled.

Then it was over.

Tables of food sat ready. There was nowhere to sit but on the ground, but everyone ate a gracious plenty.

A little while later, Addie watched as Claire scampered about, acting spry as a cat but appearing to be worn to a nub.

She coaxed, "For goodness sake, Claire, won't you sit down and rest?" kindly pointing out, "You'll be so give out, you'll need help getting out of bed in the morning." *And I'll be miles away.*

Claire retorted, "Poppycock! I can rest when I'm dead."

An idea suddenly flickered across Addie's mind. There *was* something Claire could tend to for her.

Alfred had never demonstrated a rightful sense of responsibility or obligation when it came to most things, finances not withstanding. Addie knew full well that anytime he got his hands on money, it burnt a hole in his pocket until he managed to squander it on card games and whiskey. Finding a shovel someone had propped up against the chinaberry tree, she took it and went behind the smokehouse. On the ground underneath one of the fig trees was a heavy sandstone rock. She rolled the rock aside and dug in the loose soil, unearthing what she'd buried there a few months back. She bent down and brushed the dirt from the blue quart fruit jar sealed with paraffin. In her hands, she held more money than she'd seen in her entire lifetime—her half of the money from the sale of Rachel's land.

Thank heavens I hid it away!

She went immediately to find Claire. "Claire, please go with Emily to the mercantile and let her choose enough material for three or four dresses." Emily heard and came running to her side excitedly. "Emily, pay attention to the time of year you're buying for. Claire, help her pick right. And while you're there, y'all might go on and get some material for me, too, and put me a sewing basket together—scissors, thread, needles, thimbles—you know what all I'll need." She gave Claire enough money for the purchase. "Let Ap drive y'all in his wagon."

"Brother Harris!" Addie proceeded toward the portly gentleman as he walked toward his buggy, coat slung over his arm. "Before you go, might I have a word with you … privately."

The preacher followed her until they were out of earshot from everyone. He presumed she sought religious instruction or spiritual reassurance. *Her faith is faltering, and understandably so,* he thought. *Judging by all the persecution she's suffered lately, Job was undoubtedly on more favorable terms with the Lord than she.*

Once they were alone, Addie looked at him and said, "You're aware that for months now I've been unable to attend church services as I would have liked, taking care of Mama and—"

The reverend smiled and butted in, "The Lord understands and pardons such things."

She ignored his interruption. "*However,* I've been waiting for the opportunity to give this to you." Addie withdrew her hand from her dress pocket and placed a thick wad of folded money in his hand.

He looked at her quizzically and asked, "What's this?"

"It's my tithe—at least a tenth of the money I got when Wesley sold Mama's place. It's an offering to the church... to be used to glorify God."

For the tenth shall be holy unto the Lord...

Brother Harris's eyes shifted around. Folks were here at the site of a burned-out home bearing offerings to *her*. After all, she'd lost everything in the fire.

She read his thoughts, "No need to worry. God is making provisions for me even as we speak." She gestured to all those milling about. "He'll continue to take care of me as He always has. The money belongs to God anyway."

He stammered, completely taken by surprise. "Why, I don't know what to say, Addie. Is there anything in particular you wish for me to do with the money?"

"No. In Malachi it says, 'Bring ye all tithes into the storehouse.' I've given it to you in obedience to God. I trust you, as shepherd of the storehouse, to use it accordingly, to minister to the needs of your flock."

Her spirit of generosity was like a breath of fresh air to him. So many people hid the Lord's money for themselves. He'd never been the administrator of such a gift before. Ideas were swimming in his mind. "For your faithfulness to him, the Lord will surely open the windows of Heaven and pour you out a blessing."

Addie did ask him to grant her one favor. "Whatever you feel led to do with the money, I'd be much obliged if you do it in the name of Jesus. Let this be just between us." *Take heed that ye do not your alms before men, to be seen of them.*

He nodded. He understood and whole-heartedly agreed.

It was some time later when Travis approached her. Looking into Addie's tired eyes, he didn't beat around the bush. With tender sincerity, he said, "This may not be the best time, but you know you don't have to go. You could stay on here and make me a happy man. There's a place for you ... and, of course, for Emily ... with me."

Addie was stunned. For a second, her mind stopped, her insides twisted. There was no questioning what he proposed. Although it was no secret to her that Travis held her up on a pedestal of sorts, it had not occurred to her that his feelings for her might be deeper, that maybe he loved her *in that way*. She blinked back the tears. She wished she could feel the same way about him—for Travis was a fine, admirable man. He'd no doubt be good to her, yet she knew he'd be better off with someone else. He deserved a woman who could return the same kind of love to him. Addie did indeed love Travis, but she only loved him as a dear friend. And she didn't want to jeopardize their friendship for anything.

She managed a half-hearted smile and replied softly, "I don't know what to say." The last thing she wanted was to hurt him. "Let there be no misunderstanding, I love you. Your friendship means the world to me, but we both know I could never marry you, Travis. It wouldn't be fair ... to you."

Even though this was exactly what he'd expected her to say, he had needed to hear her say it. He reiterated firmly, "Just so you know." He reached out and touched her cheek and brushed away a single tear.

Addie nodded and smiled in answer. Their eyes held in a warm exchange of friendship.

True to his form, Travis was undaunted. He smiled, his blue eyes twinkling, and said, "You know, I travel to Oakdale at least once a month. With your permission, I'll look in on you from time to time."

"I'll be looking forward to it."

Usually, when Claire entered her front door, her house greeted her with a familiar feeling of warmth and hospitality, welcomed her like an old friend. Now, its walls offered meager solace.

After she and Emily returned from town, she had deliberately

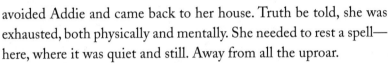

avoided Addie and came back to her house. Truth be told, she was exhausted, both physically and mentally. She needed to rest a spell—here, where it was quiet and still. Away from all the uproar.

Now that she was alone, Claire went to the kitchen and started a fire in the stove to heat up a kettle of water. *I believe I'll make me some coffee.* A few minutes later, she decided coffee held no appeal to her at the present. She set the kettle aside. Aimlessly, she went to the back door and looked out. A blue jay was perched on the limb of a plum tree. After staring at the bird for a minute, she turned and went to the sitting room and looked at the mantel clock. *Not even two o'clock.*

Dread imprisoned her. She went to the front door and looked out. Her yard needed sweeping. She decided what she needed was several hours of hard work. Another minute dragged by. As she stood looking, she thought what a long, bitter day it had already been. She sighed. *And it's just now only two o'clock.*

Suddenly Claire found herself feeling every which way but right. Her sense of purpose waned. The emptiness she felt inside was overwhelming. Without warning, a little sob caught in her throat. Her hand flew to her mouth to suppress it.

Ever since Addie had been a little girl, younger than Emily, she'd added light to Claire's days, had brought a rare and radiant energy into her life. Up until now, Claire had simply taken for granted that it would always be thus. Now, the reality of it all had sunk in. Addie was leaving, moving away... *Oh, God, I'll be lost without my Addie! How will I endure it?*

Not knowing what to do with all these unfamiliar feelings of helplessness, dismay, and self-pity, Claire did something she'd done precious few times in her entire life. She sat down in a rocking chair, and for a long time, in her solitary confinement, she wept.

Daniel owned no comfort or closure from being back here. With part misery and part relief, he finished securing the load on the wagon. More than once today he had a strong sense that Amelia was nearby, watching him. More than once he'd glanced over his shoulder with the expectation of seeing her standing there with a fishing pole. Just like old times.

He'd resisted the urge to revisit the spot where they had lain in the grass under the stars their last night together. *The spot where she'd promised to someday marry me*, he thought wistfully. He was afraid just walking down the trail and being there again would make him feel even lonelier than he felt before. *Why torment myself?* He was going to have to wake up to the fact that the tracks of their love had gone cold. Amelia was gone.

In the last few hours, he'd said her name in his mind at least a hundred times. Now, looking out toward the edge of the woods, he whispered it aloud. "I sure do miss you, Amelia." He stood there another minute, hoping to hear the echo of her thoughts come back to him. He yearned to know, *Do you miss me too?*

Fighting back the memories, he saw Mr. Hiram climb up on the seat of the wagon. It was time to leave.

By early afternoon, everything salvageable had been loaded onto two wagons. Addie waved to Daniel as he and Hiram pulled the first wagon slowly onto Monroe Road.

She took a deep breath, suddenly filled with the emptiness of having to leave. Apprehension and dread rose within her. She'd put off the worst and hardest thing for last, but the time had come. *This would be the crowning blow.* Her heart was pounding in her ears, her eyes searched the yard, but she didn't see a trace of her anywhere.

Wesley came up beside her and told her gently, "Addie, Claire went home a while ago. She said to tell you her heart ain't strong enough to watch you leave. She said she'll write to you soon."

Addie's emotions caught in her throat. She knew what Claire had done. She'd gone home to spare *Addie* the unbearable pain of bidding her farewell. Claire knew how difficult it would be for her

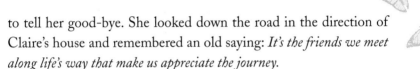

to tell her good-bye. She looked down the road in the direction of Claire's house and remembered an old saying: *It's the friends we meet along life's way that make us appreciate the journey.*

In her mind, she whispered, *Good-bye, my beloved friend.* Her throat ached.

Wesley could almost hear her heart breaking. He held something out toward her, wrapped up in a piece of cloth.

"Here," he said, "take this.... consider it an early Christmas present." He watched her face. "I made a trade ... swapped your old cow for this old thing."

Addie's eyes met his as she reached out and took it. Up until now, she'd been able to deny her tears, but as she clutched Samuel's fiddle close, they came. For a moment, overwrought with emotion, she stood there and sobbed like a small child.

Wesley told her, "Mama's Bible is settin' on the seat right by Emily. Come on, let's go home, little sister." They had a ways to go before reaching Golden Meadow.

Before she climbed onto the wagon, Addie took a moment and looked around one last time. She did her best to see beyond the aftermath of calamity before her. She closed her eyes and in her mind envisioned everything as it once had been. She'd grown up loving this place. She bore her children in this house. She thought about how four generations of her family had lived there. And, taking into account her grandparents, Rachel, Alfred, and her baby, four generations of her family had also died there. A part of her had died there, too.

At last, numb from exhaustion and laden with uncertainty, Addie climbed onto the wagon. *Forgetting those things which are behind, and reaching forth unto those things which are before. As thou goest, thy way shall be opened up step by step before thee.*

She had not closed her eyes all night nor stopped all day. Her mind was as tired as her body. Before they'd gone a half mile, she was sound asleep.

No one had dared to mention it, but today was Thanksgiving Day.

CHAPTER 21

"For no man understandeth Him; howbeit in the spirit He speakest mysteries." (1 Corinthians 14:2).

Wesley and Laura lived on Longview Road, the main thoroughfare between the town of Oakdale and the smaller town of Pine Bluff. Whereas the roads around Collinsville climbed over small hills and through wooded hollows, the character of the land in these parts was vastly different, offering a vista of sprawling cultivated fields and acres upon acres of rich pastureland alternated with tracts of woods. In a particularly flat, straight stretch, for a distance of a few miles, Longview Road and the Leaf River ran almost parallel. About a mile from Wesley's house, a bridge crossed over a branch of Cedar Creek.

Laura's parents, Amos and Dinah Bradley, had owned and farmed seventy acres and lived in a five-room house that was plain as rice. Dinah suited Amos in every way. She was soft and pretty, always cheerful. Sometimes he felt guilty for being so blessed. They'd been married nigh to a year when Dinah told him she was pregnant. His heart leapt; he felt a child would make their happiness complete, perfect.

When her time grew near, her older sister, Stell Roberts, came for a visit to be there for the baby's arrival. This was indeed unexpected, for Dinah knew Stell had always gone out of her way to avoid being around babies, or most people in general for that matter. In fact, Dinah and her sister were opposite in every way. Whereas she was good-tempered and friendly, Stell, an old woman since birth, was of a courser constitution, cantankerous by nature and casually rough of tongue. She usually said whatever came to mind without the slightest qualm as to how her outspoken opinions and snappish remarks might settle upon others. Imparted thusly, not surprising, Stell had not married.

However, Dinah turned a blind eye and a deaf ear to her sister's shortfalls and was thrilled to have her come be with her during such a celebratory time. After all, to those who knew and loved her, Stell was just Stell.

As it were, the event turned into an unforeseen nightmare. Dinah had a difficult childbirth. Her labor seemed never-ending, the pangs overly excruciating. Amos left the house like a madman to fetch the doctor, and while he was gone, Stell did every thing she could to help, but something was terribly wrong. She finally realized the baby was positioned wrong, breach. Dinah was in dire trouble!

By the time Amos returned with the doctor, his wife was near gone. His sweet, happy flower was fading quickly from him, and he was powerless in deterring her ascension. The doctor set about with grim hope, doing his best to save Dinah and the baby, but Dinah hemorrhaged greatly. She could barely speak, but even as she was being courted by the next world, she fought to hold on. If she couldn't live, she at least wanted her baby to live, for Amos. *Stell, please help Amos take care of my baby…*

Dinah managed to cling to life until she heard her son's first cries. He was tiny, yet perfect and strong. Moments later, she ceased to breathe and passed peacefully from this world into life everlasting, meeting with a glorious welcome. *Well done, thou good and faithful servant…*

A stunned, tumultuous silence fell about the room. The very walls threatened to give way under the weight of the medley of emotions constrained within. At first, the doctor thought the second baby that emerged from her mother's womb was stillborn. She was listless, not breathing and blue. He turned her over and rubbed her vigorously. A second later, she made a slight whimpering sound, like a puppy. She was alive! The tiny girl awoke and kicked her spindly limbs and squalled angrily. *Praise be!* Like her brother, she was perfectly formed and fine.

Both devastated and puzzled by Dinah's death, Amos felt trapped in a heavy fog. The next day he rode back on his horse from the burial service that accomplished little in the way of relief from his heart's suffering. He went directly to the room where the infants lay cuddled together in the same crib. Careful not to wake them, he gently gathered them up in his arms and went to sit in a nearby chair.

Remembering the names he and Dinah had talked about, their son was called Asher. He named their precious daughter Laura. He was overcome as he stared at the twins in awe. Dinah had bequeathed him two babies to love. In them, he still had her. As he gazed at them lovingly, the sweet peace of sleep on their tiny faces reached out and pierced his heart. Amos wept for joy; tears streamed down his cheeks and painted the front of his shirt.

It was a desperate situation, and Stell seemed to be the only plausible solution. As a matter of utter necessity, she humbly succumbed to the call and set about the tremendous undertaking, devoting herself to help Amos take care of the newborns and manage his house. *Stell, please help Amos take care of my baby...*

Following the doctor's instructions, she fed the babies with bottles of sugar water and goat's milk, and against all odds, they miraculously survived and flourished. Stingily endowed with maternal instincts, and with an awkward approach to any true expression of warmth, she loved her sister's children and raised them as her own to the best of her ability.

When the festering conflict between the states finally came to

a head, Amos dutifully rendered himself and went off to serve in a war he had only a vague understanding of and, for the most part, was opposed to. Asher and Laura were about ten years old when he wearily reappeared from a ravaged world of killing to the quiet serenity of the farm. Not ever did Amos speak of the war or the fighting, he just praised God for being merciful in seeing fit that he return safely home to his family, to his beautiful children and his wonderfully obstinate sister-in-law.

It was around that same time that he summoned it appropriate that Asher and Laura should know the truth about their biological mother. It was understandable that Stell was nervous and considered the notion venturous. She inwardly worried, *How will they react?* Asher and Laura had become her life. *Will this compromise their affection for me?*

However, all fear and uncertainty was laid aside; all hope was made manifest. For upon hearing the account of the births, both children kissed and hugged Stell and pledged their loyalty to her, singing, "I love you, Mama! I love you, Mama!" The disclosure proved irrelevant. Were they not still flesh and blood? So what if they both (fortunately) inherited Dinah's disposition and energy for life? The only fact that really mattered held unchanged. *Stell* was the only mother they'd ever known. It was *she* they loved and looked to.

Of course there had been talk, none of which was ever brought directly to their attention, about Amos and Stell living together, them unmarried. Through the years, their feelings toward each other grew in complexity yet remained platonic. Theirs was a relationship literally born and raised from terrible tragedy and a deep sense of obligation for the welfare of two children. Amos never pined after Stell, nor did she encourage him. However, when Amos died a few years later during an epidemic of yellow fever, Stell grieved for him savagely in secret as would a wife upon learning her beloved husband had been killed in battle.

Wesley was eighteen when he and a few of the rowdy boys he ran around with invited themselves to a barn dance one Saturday

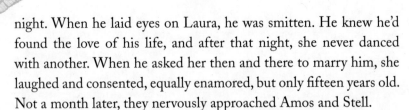

night. When he laid eyes on Laura, he was smitten. He knew he'd found the love of his life, and after that night, she never danced with another. When he asked her then and there to marry him, she laughed and consented, equally enamored, but only fifteen years old. Not a month later, they nervously approached Amos and Stell.

Not to say Amos had anything against Wesley, he in fact liked him, but he felt his daughter hadn't yet spent enough time being a girl. He wasn't ready for her to become a wife, a woman. He was agreeable to their courtship and even to Wesley's request for his daughter's hand in marriage, but not without condition. He put their doe-eyed infatuation to a test of time. This rearing buck of a boy who was posturing and pawing the ground at his daughter's feet must first prove himself. Laura and Wesley would not have his blessing to marry until she turned seventeen.

Inwardly disappointed and a bit touchy over the man's strict provision, with clear sight and a willful determination, Wesley set out to prove himself worthy of the prize. First, he took a job at the mill in Oakdale, his labor in exchange for cypress lumber and bead board. On the corner of the land Amos gave him, he started building a house. For two long years, when he wasn't working at the mill or courting Laura, every waking moment was spent on the house he was building for him and his bride. Some days it would peeve Stell to no end to look out her window and see Amos and Asher, hammers in hand, helping her future son-in-law with the construction. Near to two years later, upon completion of the house, Amos was pleased and satisfied that Wesley would make a fine husband for his little girl.

The whitewashed house set aways off the road. A long avenue of crepe myrtles lined one side of the property. The front steps led onto a deep, covered porch. To the left was a large, semi-octagon shaped room with tall windows. This room served as the sitting room. The porch that fronted the house extended to and wrapped around the right corner and ran the entire length of the dwelling. Six large cypress posts supported the porch. The side porch opened directly into a wide center hall which, off either side, led to the kitchen, dining room, and bedrooms. Most of the activity of the household gravitated to the side porch; its door handled most of the comings and goings.

A well was located a few yards from the house. Several outbuildings led in succession from the main house to the huge barn. Inside the barn were tack and tool rooms and multiple stalls for housing farm implements and stock. Above each stall was a slatted hay shoot which the children loved to climb to access the loft; the ordinary, sensible stairs were much too under deserving of their imaginative adventures.

Married now for fifteen years, Wesley and Laura had three children: thirteen-year-old Sarah Beth, nine-year-old Jesse, and three-year-old Meggie. Their place was home to a menagerie of animals—cows, pigs, several horses, mules, three dogs, at least a dozen barn cats, chickens, and a flock of guineas. The newest additions, Gent, Ben, Coppy, and Callie, all fit right into the scheme of things at their new home in Golden Meadow.

The first few days after the fire were the hardest. Every morning, Addie awoke tired, filled with a sense of foreboding, with a premonition that something bad was about to happen. *What else could happen?* She ate little, if nothing, and kept to herself as much as possible. When she looked into the mirror, she didn't recognize the eyes that stared back at her. They were the eyes of a stranger. She felt hollow and strange. Loss overcame her. It seemed there was only loss and sorrow in her life. Her house had burned. She'd left her home. She left Claire. Alfred was dead. Rachel was dead. Her baby was dead. She tried to pray but received no reassurance that God even heard her. *God, are you ignoring me? Have you forsaken me? Why won't you comfort me?* She was filled with a sick, empty feeling. Her whole life had changed. Except for Emily, there was nothing. Daniel was practically grown and didn't really need her anymore. He had long since established himself here; he had his own life now and loved working for Mr. Graham.

She fell into a black abyss.

Lying in bed in Wesley's arms late one night, Laura whispered, "It is indeed a mournful sound when a heart cries." She was so worried about Addie.

Two weeks passed.

Addie slowly began accepting and adjusting to, or at least working around, things as they were now; if nothing else but in an automatic way. Little by little, she once again recognized there were reasons to be grateful. One being, for instance, that children are, in some ways, so resilient. Emily seemed happy. After all, she had a newly acquired *sister* about her own age. She and Sarah Beth were delighted to be sharing a room and their girlhood secrets. Also, she loved her new school and her new teacher, Miss Bernice, and couldn't wait to get home every afternoon to tell Addie about a new friend she'd met or what she'd learned that day.

One morning, Addie ventured out of the house for a walk. As she strolled slowly along the road in the fresh air and sunshine, she found herself drawn to the woodshop where Daniel worked. As soon as she entered, there was something about the atmosphere there that welcomed her. It seemed comforting, somehow.

She lingered awhile and sat on a stool and watched with keen interest as Hiram and Daniel put the finishing touches on a beautiful oak chiffonier. It didn't take long for her to realize the skill required of them by their trade merited genuine respect. They talked very little as they worked, but when she decided it was time to depart and stepped back out into the sunshine, for the first time in a long time, she noticed how blue the sky was. She was slowly beginning to come back to life.

It was a few mornings later, after she'd bathed and dressed and ate breakfast, that she went outside to further explore her new surroundings and spied Stell's old house a couple hundred yards away set amidst a stand of oak trees. Suddenly a revelation flickered across her mind. *Of course!* She immediately took matters in hand.

She found Wesley in the barn repairing a wheel. She motioned to him and said, "Come, walk with me. I want you to go with me to look at something."

"Right now?" But she had already gone out ahead of him and started with determination toward the narrow lane that ran alongside the fence leading to the house. He quickly laid aside what he was doing, willing to humor her, reminding himself, *She's goin' through a rough time.* He followed, ran, and caught up with his sister.

When they reached Stell's old house, Addie noticed the outbuildings were in bad shape, but no matter there. She observed out loud, "The yard needs to be raked and swept." There were fallen limbs lying about, leaves scattered.

Wesley followed her into the house, where she proceeded to walk through each and every room, assessing and calculating. "Five rooms in all. Just right." She said it more to herself than to him. "I'll need some shelves built over there on that wall." *For her books.* "Daniel can handle that. I think I counted two broken windows." She was pleased and excited with what she saw. "For the most part, I'd say it just needs a good cleaning."

She turned to Wesley. "I'm going to talk to Stell today. If she has no objection, Emily and Sarah Beth can help me. We'll get busy up here in the next couple of days. With a little work, it'll take shape in no time."

Wesley had heard enough now to put it all together. There was no doubt in his mind what she was up to, what she was planning. He fixed his mouth to dissuade her.

"Addie, I can assure you that Stell couldn't care less what you do up here, but what's the all-fired hurry? We've got plenty of room for now. When spring gets here—" He stopped in midsentence.

Addie was shaking her head. She would not be denied this. Her mind was made up. Wesley and Laura were kind and gracious hosts, but she wasn't used to living like this, dependent on somebody else for every little thing. Nor did she have any intention or desire of getting used to it. She needed her own place, needed to make decisions again. She felt displaced and smothered, and she felt like an intruder in someone else's house, in someone else's life.

A few nights before, when Stell's grizzly snores drove her from their room, she'd padded down the hallway toward the kitchen for a dipper of water. A lamp was lit, and Wesley was sitting in a chair. Laura moved about him slowly, her body occasionally brushing against her husband's as she gave him a shave. The act was so sensual, so intimate, that she may as well have discovered them making love. Thankfully, they were too enthralled with each other to even notice her, and she'd quietly turned away and gone back to bed.

Recalling this, she said, "You and Laura deserve to have some privacy."

He laughed incredulously. "Privacy! My lord, Addie! Me an' Laura ain't had no privacy since Stell moved in!"

"Precisely my point, and now you have even less," she pointed out.

He let out a heavy sigh. *Dang, if she ain't headstrong.*

She decided to just say what was on her mind. "I want Claire and Travis to come and spend Christmas with us here."

He relaxed a little, admittedly surprised. He thought vaguely, *Is that all this is?* "Addie, that sounds like a dandy idea. Laura will be tickled pink for them to spend Christmas here, but I still don't see—"

"I want this place presentable enough by then. When Claire is here at Christmastime, I'm going to invite her to come here ... *move* here and live with me, with us. This is the practical place for Claire, Emily, and me to live, and of course, Daniel too, if he's not opposed to living with a houseful of women."

Caught off guard for a minute, Wesley didn't know what to say. He sure hadn't seen this coming. He'd figured Addie wanted the house just for herself and Emily. He let out his breath with exasperation and asked, "Addie, don't you think that's puttin' the cart a ways before the horse? What in tarnation makes you think Claire Ellis will leave the only home she's ever known to move way over here to live with us?"

Addie had every confidence. "Why, that's simple, Wesley. *Home* is where your family is, and *we* are Claire's family. Trust me, she'll come."

She took a deep, satisfying breath as her spirit took flight and soared just a little. All of a sudden, she felt like something she'd forgotten, like a pleasant dream lost to waking, had somehow come back to memory.

Wesley couldn't help but notice that she *was* actually smiling.

CHAPTER 22

"And the voice spake unto him again the second time, What God hath cleansed, that call not thou common." (Acts 10:15).

The following week, they had what folks called a bark-buster. Winter arrived and stayed with temperatures well below freezing every night. Wesley came into the house for supper and brought with him some of the cold air and a hearty declaration, "It's hog-killin' time!"

Tuesday morning, at the crack of dawn, he went outside and started a fire around a big washpot in the backyard and drew several buckets of water and filled it. Shortly thereafter, he, Daniel, and Hiram walked to the hogpen across a frost that made the grass crunch beneath their boots and stunned a hog they'd hemmed up the night before with an ax blow before slitting its throat. After it bled out, they half-toted, half-dragged the hog's enormous carcass to where they'd laid out a pallet of scalding boards. It took the muscles of all three men to heave the heavy swine onto the boards. Directly, Laura and Addie would pour scalding water over it to soften its bristles to be scraped away.

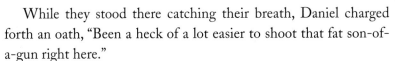

While they stood there catching their breath, Daniel charged forth an oath, "Been a heck of a lot easier to shoot that fat son-of-a-gun right here."

Wesley scratched his head thoughtfully. A thing he knew from misfortunate experience—herding pigs could prove a precarious endeavor. He didn't put much stock in Daniel's brainstorm and remarked dryly, "Yep, but it'd shore been the devil convincin' him to trot over to this spot an' stand still for his execution."

Their breath made smoke. Wesley reminded them, "Y'all caint run off just yet. After he gets scraped on this side, we'll have to roll this heathen over. An' soon as he's all shaved down, I'll dang sure need some help hangin' him up on that limb over yonder." He nodded toward a gambrel stick and a pole leaned against a big tree. Not one of the men cared for butchering hogs, but not one of them could deny the reward at the end of the day would amply justify their laborious efforts.

The children begged to stay home from school for the hog-killing, but Laura said an emphatic "no," knowing they'd be more of a hindrance than a help.

Even with everyone doing their part, it was a long day of heavy work, but Addie was grateful for it. Staying busy helped keep her mind off her troubles. Yesterday, when Daniel and Hiram rode into Oakdale, they mailed the letters she'd written to Claire and Travis inviting them for Christmas, assuring them that there was plenty of room to accommodate them overnight. She could hardly wait for their reply and to see what would come of her idea.

While the backbreaking work went on all day, Meggie had the best time kicking around a ball made from the inflated bladder of the deceased.

Stell was put in charge of fixing supper, and she outdid herself! Hiram joined them, of course, and when they sat down to eat, Wesley asked him to say the blessing. Just before he bowed his head, his and Addie's eyes met for just a second. During her first days here, she'd quickly noticed he was such a familiar sight around the

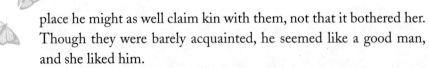
place he might as well claim kin with them, not that it bothered her. Though they were barely acquainted, he seemed like a good man, and she liked him.

Everyone ate their fill of fried tenderloin, cracklin' bread, rice and gravy, and biscuits. As Addie ate quietly, her thoughts strayed back to Collinsville as she remembered how much Claire loved fresh pork loin. She missed her friend so and couldn't help but wonder how she was doing way over there, all by herself. She wondered if Creenie and she had managed to finish the quilts. And how Travis was? And since she'd been forced to abandon them, what had become of her flock of guineas? A growing sense of melancholy set up in her heart, and she again found herself homesick.

During the meal, Wesley looked around the long table and said in jest, "If my family keeps growin' like it has here lately, next time we have a hog-killin', we'll have to slaughter two of 'em." He just didn't know it yet, but Biblical prophets had not uttered a proclamation any closer to the truth.

Stell finished eating and quipped, "I made the coffee extra strong so you young folks can set up renderin' lard. As for me, neither strong coffee nor a guilty conscious will keep me up tonight. I'm plumb used up." She pushed her chair back and stood up and said, "I believe I'll stagger on back here to my grave an' get some shuteye."

Leaving the kitchen, she slowed her exit long enough to snort, "An' if I *was* to finish dyin' before I wake up, I'll come back an' skin alive the one that lets Lizzie Ainsworth sang over my corpse." It had been over thirty years since old Lizzie Ainsworth had made the mistake of setting her cap for Amos after Dinah's death, a breach for which Stell still held a grudge against the poor woman for to that day.

Not until way after nightfall was the smokehouse host to fresh ham, sausage, and salted fatback. Hog-killing was indeed a job!

CHAPTER 23

The first time Addie wandered into the woodshop, it was mainly out of curiosity to see where Daniel worked, but today she found herself entering it for no particular reason other than the fact she just liked being there. She found the woodsy scents of pine and cedar mingled with the fragrant aroma of citrus oil and beeswax pleasing to be around. That being true, there was, however, another underlying but *unrealized* reason for her going there.

A tender force within her was drawn to and searched out Hiram's quiet ways. She liked his easy, unhurried manner and his unassuming wit. Wesley and Laura had been agreeing with each other in private that they sensed a subtle note of partiality between the two. In truth, Hiram and Addie were unaware of the fact that they were both desperately lonely and starved for friendship.

Hiram looked up when she whisked in. His voice was deep as he said, "Mornin'."

She noticed flecks of sawdust on his pant legs and boots and in his beard. "Mornin' to you. I realize Daniel's helping Wesley pull fence today, but I thought I'd stop in and see what it is he's been working on that keeps him here to all hours of the night."

He smiled at her and teased, "And here I was thinkin' you were just cravin' my company."

Addie played along with his good-natured banter. "Hardly." She added, "But if you must know, I've been in worse company."

He immediately thought of her late husband and nodded. "I figured as much."

Hiram pointed to a five-drawer chest. "Daniel made that. Toward the end of the week, I'll be delivering *most* of these pieces to a store in Oakdale."

He watched Addie walk over to examine the chest. His eyes rested on her, and for a moment, he framed up his thoughts of her. Everything about her seemed decent and ladylike, but it was her essential nature, her subtle display of inner strength, that he found most distinctive. *In quietness and confidence shall be our strength…*

She ran her hand across the smooth surface of the chest and admired the intricate cutwork. "It's lovely. I had no idea Daniel was so talented." After a pause, she added, "I suppose the Lord had a hand in him coming here after all."

Remembering Daniel's account of what Alfred had done to the girl Amelia, Hiram considered her statement at least in part subject to speculation. Before he could stop himself, he said, "Not meaning to rob God of any credit or speak ill of the dead, but I'd venture off and say it's closer to the truth that the hand of Daniel's pa brought him here."

He hadn't planned on saying such a thing out loud. *What's wrong with me, and what made me say such?* A pang of regret stabbed him instantly. He didn't want to upset her. "I'm sorry. I had no right to say such a rude thing. Ordinarily I don't talk this much, but the good news is it'll be especially hard now with my boot in my mouth."

His candor was surprising to her, yet what he said in apology

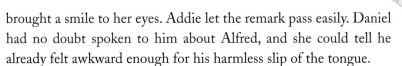

brought a smile to her eyes. Addie let the remark pass easily. Daniel had no doubt spoken to him about Alfred, and she could tell he already felt awkward enough for his harmless slip of the tongue.

"You needn't apologize. It's a well-known fact Alfred could be a mean man."

It was an understatement at best, but he again reminded himself there were things she didn't know. He shook his head and replied, "Still, that's poor excuse for what I said. It's best I left judgments about things that are none of my business off to the side."

He looked at her quietly for a moment and considered everything she'd been through lately. Suddenly he felt compelled to let her know he understood how strange life could be. Sounding contemplative, he said, "Some folks think pain and disappointment are just things you feel, but I can say from knowin'—sometimes a face can be put to them. There for a time, I saw their reflection every time I looked into my own eyes."

Given what Wesley had told her, Addie glanced at him and said softly, "I heard about what happened to your wife and child. I'm sorry for your loss. I know it must be hard for you." If there was anything she understood, it was loss.

"It was a long time ago."

What he said next, he'd never put into another's keeping, nor had he ever expected to, but for some reason, he felt he had to confide it to Addie. He trusted her without really even knowing her and wanted her to know how he'd come to this place.

"The baby my wife carried wasn't mine."

Addie felt the slackness of her jaw. For a moment, the comment hung suspended in dead air. With eyes full of surprise, she stammered, "Wesley ... d-didn't say anyth—"

"He doesn't know. When I first met Wesley, I told him Madeline died in childbirth and that the baby perished as well. He made the obvious assumption, and I've never felt obliged to tell him different.

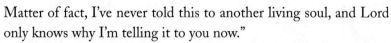
Matter of fact, I've never told this to another living soul, and Lord only knows why I'm telling it to you now."

Addie searched his face.

He sighed and said, "It's a long story." One he felt obligated to share with her now. "Madeline was a good woman, but she could be a mite impatient at times. She wanted things—things that cost money. So to give her the things I thought she wanted, I spent a lot more time making and selling furniture than I spent with my wife. I don't care to recall how many times she accused me of neglecting her. I see now where she had a right to feel that way, but at the time, I felt like I was doing my best to make her happy.

"A man came along. He made her feel special in a way I failed to. Madeline fell into temptation … lost her way." He paused thoughtfully. "When I learned there was to be a baby, I knew it couldn't be mine, and Madeline knew I knew it couldn't be mine, for she'd ceased to yearn for me in the ways of a wife."

Addie felt her cheeks flush. The particulars of what he was telling her seemed almost too personal, too revealing. It bore a tone of intimacy that verged on inappropriateness between a man and woman of mere acquaintance. She felt as though Hiram had stripped down and was standing before her naked. Instinctively, she averted her eyes. Without looking at him, she asked, "What did your wife say?"

"As unbelievable as this sounds, we didn't speak of it. We took the cowardly route, avoided confrontation, lived in denial. Proves what kind of marriage we had, huh?"

Addie looked at Hiram. His eyes were filled with the story he was telling her. She saw he had been badly hurt.

He being a well-read man, when he sat back and stretched his long legs out before him, he couldn't help but recognize the irony in the simile, the long story he was stretching out before Addie. He continued. "What can I say? I got the pride knocked out of me, fell down, and landed hard on my knees. I asked God to show me the way, make me a better a husband, and help me forgive Madeline. And I prayed that I'd be able to love the child, see it not with my eyes but with my heart. I'd always wanted a child, and the child was innocent."

Addie let out a long breath she'd been holding. "You must have loved her very much."

He considered that for a moment. Hers was a natural conclusion not entirely false. "I did love Madeline, but I despised her a little bit, too. Together we lived through some of our highest and lowest times. You know, sometimes in a marriage you have to fall in love more than once with the same person."

In retrospect, he said, "I used to wonder what would have happened if she and the baby had survived. It would have been complicated, to say the least. It took me more than a minute, but I eventually forgave the man, too. I figured it would serve no useful purpose to hold dear to a rope of thorns. Course, that was between me an' the Lord. I never let on to the man I knew about him and Madeline. Funny thing, we can forgive a stranger most any slight, but a grudge against family we guard to the grave. It took some soul searchin', but I have been able to forgive my brother for seducin' my wife."

Too astonished to speak, Addie thought, *The spirit of man is the candle of the Lord.*

When he'd finished laying everything out in the open, Hiram waited for her response. After mulling it over for a minute, she simply told him, "Madeline was fortunate to have had a husband like you." Here was no ordinary man.

"While she lived, I never stopped praying for *us* to heal. I hoped tenderness would be restored between her and me and there would be a peaceful place for our hearts to come together, a place where I could hold my wife in my arms again and tell her how much she meant to me and mean it, but that wasn't to be. Madeline raised a hedge of guilt and regret around her, denied herself forgiveness. In the end, I was sorry for her."

His compassion for Madeline was so overwhelming, it made her want to cry. Addie could barely whisper the words, "How sad that after all you went through, you still lost them both."

"Addie, as I just explained to you, I lost Madeline a good long while before she died. I wished a thousand times I'd done things different, but I realized my mistakes too late." He sounded wise and old when he said, "Like I said before, it's a long time gone."

The story stirred her; tears welled up. Addie's eyes consoled him.

"I didn't mean to make you sad. I guess I just felt like you'd understand."

"You never thought on remarrying?"

He raised his eyebrows at her and broke into an amused grin. "Now, Addie, given the facts you've just heard, can't you see how I might consider such a notion a bit contrary to sensible thinking?"

She couldn't help but smile at him and affirm, "Believe me when I say, I understand completely!" Had she not spent fifteen insensible years in a travesty of a marriage?

Remembering something he'd said earlier, she changed the subject. Diving in head first before she lost her nerve, she asked, "I wonder…Might I accompany you to Oakdale at the end of the week when you make your delivery? There're some purchases I need to make for Christmas."

This question came pleasant and unexpected. He assured her, "I'll be glad for the company."

"You're certain I won't be putting you out?"

"Not unless you change your mind and decide not to go."

A few minutes later, Addie walked home in the brisk December air carrying a cheerful song on her lips and a deepening regard for Hiram in her heart, glad that their paths had crossed and glad that they were friends.

Later, with supper cleared, Addie sat at the table over coffee with Wesley and Laura as the house settled about them for the night.

Abruptly, she said, "I may have stretched the boundaries of propriety today." In answer to their quizzical looks, she asked, "Tell me, would either of you think it improper if I travel to Oakdale on Thursday with Hiram?" She hurried to explain, lest her reasons be misinterpreted. "I have some purchases to tend to, and he was going anyway, to make a delivery…"

Laura was shaking her head while Wesley spoke for both of them, "Ain't a thing improper about it far's I can see."

"Good, then it's settled. Come Thursday, that's what we've got planned."

Laura stole a glance toward Wesley, and their eyes met briefly over the rims of their cups. A satisfied smile played ever so slightly upon Wesley's lips.

CHAPTER 24

"And the angel said unto them, fear not; for behold, I bring you good tidings of great joy, which shall be to all people. For unto you is born this day in the city of David a Savior, which is Christ the Lord." (Luke 2:10–11).

The Christmas season was Laura's favorite time of year, and despite the deaths of Rachel and Alfred having had occurred so recently, she felt it imperative they celebrate the birth of Jesus Christ. Still, in consideration of Addie's feelings, before proceeding with plans to observe the holiday in the traditional manner, she first approached her sister-in-law for her nod of approval. However, Addie needed no persuasion. She herself was counting the days, ever impatient for the blessed day to arrive ever since receiving a letter from Claire confirming that both she and Travis were looking forward to spending Christmas with them. They, too, could hardly wait to see everyone again.

With that settled, Laura set about with childlike enthusiasm in preparation.

Daniel and Jesse went to the woods and cut a cedar as tall as the ceil-

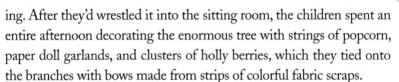

ing. After they'd wrestled it into the sitting room, the children spent an entire afternoon decorating the enormous tree with strings of popcorn, paper doll garlands, and clusters of holly berries, which they tied onto the branches with bows made from strips of colorful fabric scraps.

Laura decorated the mantle with evergreen boughs, pine cones, and sweet gum balls all swathed with red ribbon. Tall, taper candles stood on either end, waiting to be lit. Five socks were hung in a row over the fireplace—one for each child. Addie wreathed muscadine vines and magnolia leaves to adorn the doorways and made evergreen swags to drape the windows.

Throughout the week before Christmas, each afternoon the kitchen bustled with activity, as Laura and Addie supervised the girls in the making of all sorts of holiday sweets. They baked gingerbread, fruitcake, and molasses cookies. They sugared pecans and parched peanuts and made popcorn clusters. Meggie's favorite day was when they made a big batch of thumbprint cookies and filled them with fruit preserves. After several days of baking, they had an abundant variety of goodies stored in wooden cheese boxes. Of course, the sweetest part of all was the fun they shared in the process.

The entire house was festive and inviting with its heavenly, tantalizingly aromatic of cinnamon, spice, and pine. Everything looked, smelled, and felt just like Christmas should. The excitement was contagious, and soon everyone was pulled into the spirit of the season.

Early on Christmas morning, when Daniel and Jesse went hunting near the old Lewis place, it was Jesse who came home grinning ear to ear with the trophy—a huge gobbler! At eight years old, the boy dearly loved to hunt, and each time he retold the tale of shooting his first turkey, it became more outrageous. He kept the spent shell as a keepsake to commemorate the special event and stashed it in his box of treasures. Even though Laura was baking a ham, the roasted turkey would be the centerpiece of their Christmas feast.

And, oh! what a joyous reunion it was when their guests arrived! When Travis's buggy clattered to a halt in front of the house that afternoon, the entire household fell into grand commotion. It was an emotional time as old friends exchanged greetings, and new acquaintances were introduced in a rapid production of handshakes and smiles and tears.

While she and Claire embraced, Travis smiled at Addie warmly, and their eyes held. He reached and took her outstretched hand in his, and they held onto each other possessively for several moments, neither of them wanting to let go. At least for a time, all sorrow was vanquished, transformed into a vapor that drifted away in a cloud forgotten. At least for a time, Addie was happy.

They lingered over the meal for nearly two hours, enjoying the nearness and fellowship with one another until they could no longer stall the rambunctious children who were jumping up and down, begging to be allowed to open their presents.

Before they opened gifts, everyone gathered, while all the children, except Meggie, who was too young to read, took turns reading the Christmas story from the second chapter of the Gospel of Luke, passing Rachel's old Bible from one to the next in succession. The wondrous account of the birth of Christ was even more touching when resonated in the sweet voices of the young.

The presents Addie bought for Daniel and Emily were somewhat more extravagant than ones she'd given them in previous years, but she wanted the gifts to be special and hoped the day would cast bright on them, in spite of the overshadowing of recent events.

Emily was thrilled with a bejeweled trinket box that played a tune and a silver-handled hairbrush. Daniel was proud of his new pocketknife and a checkers set, which he promptly challenged all the men to a game of. Laura gave Sarah Beth a gold locket on a chain, Jesse a harmonica and a box of shotgun shells, and Meggie a new baby-doll. The socks that hung on the fireplace yielded candies and fruits. They all were giddy over the gifts they received.

Addie gave all the women perfumed soaps she bought from a shop in Oakdale the day she and Hiram went there together. She also had

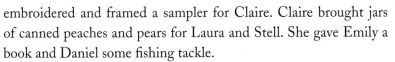

embroidered and framed a sampler for Claire. Claire brought jars of canned peaches and pears for Laura and Stell. She gave Emily a book and Daniel some fishing tackle.

With an impish expression, Claire pushed a huge, wrapped parcel toward Addie and said, "For you, from me."

Addie anxiously tore the paper away. Staring at the gift, she was speechless. Her fingers trembled as she ran her hands over them, and her mind carried her back to that day, the first Saturday in October. She treasured the memory of the hours the three women had spent together over pound cake and coffee, laughter, and tears. In such a short time, they had all grown so close. She raised her glistening eyes to Claire's. Her voice was barely a whisper when she said, "Thank you, Claire. I will forever cherish these." Claire had given her the two beautiful quilts they planned to sell to the mercantile.

Claire said, "When Creenie found out I was giving you the quilts for Christmas, I had to make her take the money she would have earned if we'd sold them to Neelson. She kept on insisting she wouldn't have it, but I wouldn't hear of it. I know she needs the money." She added, "I'm worried about Creenie. She hasn't been well lately."

Addie noted her concerned expression. "I'm sorry to hear that. What's the matter with her?"

"I don't really know. Travis has been going out to see her." Then, with her usual flight of ideas, Claire suddenly remembered something else. "I'll have to tell Emily that I continued on with the lessons she started with Sassie. I've been helping that girl learn to read and write, and let me tell you, she's smart as a whip. But back to what I was saying before, the last time Ap brought the girl to my house, Creenie didn't come along. Sassie said her mama was in the bed, sick. I asked Ap about her, but you can't make heads or tails of what he says. He's like talking to a bannie rooster. Travis told me coming over here, though, that Creenie seemed to be doing better the last time he saw her."

Laura's brother, Asher, his wife, Anna, and daughter, Libby, had joined them for dinner also, and suddenly Anna erupted with a note of jeering in her voice. "I'll swanee! Sassie, Creenie, Ap—I've never heard of such ridiculous-sounding names!"

From across the room, Emily chimed in, "They're all real nice. They're our Negro friends." She added ruefully, "I sure wish Sassie could've come here to spend Christmas with us!"

Anna's mouth dropped open in sly amusement, but before she could come out with what she was fixing to say, Stell cut her eyes in her direction and bridled her tongue with a look that warned her to keep quiet, both of them knowing the reason. Anna was fiercely prejudiced against blacks.

Stell managed to say with both an appearance of calm and elite sarcasm, "Anna, you must stay wore down to a frazzle from wrestlin' with that silly tongue of yours."

Adhering to her mother-in-law's gag, but replying to her caustically, Anna said, "A distinction we no doubt have in common." For a minute or two, she rested a fixed, satisfied smile and narrowed eyes on the woman but controlled the urge to say more.

Stell, sitting bolt upright, had long ago pronounced her daughter-in-law simple and ignorant. Unfazed by her snippety remark, she parted her lips and belched silently.

Until today, Addie had not experienced the displeasure of being around Anna and her chaffing, simpering manner. It took being in the same room with her and Stell all of two minutes to figure out they rubbed each other raw. But no wonder. The woman plainly felt her importance. She seemed inclined to talk of little else than herself, and when she did, it was with calculated slyness and harsh judgment. Even though Asher was Laura's twin in every way—earthy and amicable, and a pleasure to be around—his wife, on the other hand, proved anything but.

Addie looked at Anna blankly for a moment before turning back to Claire to say, "Don't you let me forget to send a big basket of Christmas

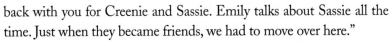

back with you for Creenie and Sassie. Emily talks about Sassie all the time. Just when they became friends, we had to move over here."

At that precise moment, another gift for Addie entered the room. One that proved a worthy rival even to the quilts. When Hiram helped Daniel carry it in, and she realized what her son had done, her heart swelled. She was moved to tears, knowing that he'd crafted it so painstakingly with his own two hands, specifically to give to her for Christmas. That day she admired it in the woodshop, she never suspected the five-drawer chest was hers. Unable to summon appropriate words, she went directly to him and gave him a big hug, making him blush profusely under all the attention.

Soon afterward, the men made an excuse to slip away from the party, and the gathering dispersed. A little while later, Addie observed that Claire had dragged her rocking chair up alongside Stell's, and the two old women sat in amiable conversation. As perversely stubborn and self-absorbed as Stell was most of the time, she and Claire almost immediately struck common ground and spent hours reminiscing about the good ol'days.

Seeing them together made Addie smile, for secretly and affectionately she knew that Claire, like Stell, didn't really have much of a convincing sweet-old-lady smile either. Claire just managed to keep most of her observations philosophic, cleverly dressed up in their Sunday best. Whereas Stell was abrupt and uncouth, Claire carried off a more refined style by putting forth a little effort in making a more graceful presentation of her calling of spades.

Come morning, Addie had every intention of walking up to Stell's house with Claire to present and argue her case about her moving here to live in Golden Meadow.

As the day wore on, and some of the excitement dwindled, Claire and Addie finally got the chance to catch up on all the Collinsville gossip.

While they sat at the kitchen table sharing a sweet, juicy orange, Claire told her, "You won't believe Speck Nobles finally convinced Ruthie Jones to marry him. I would think after all this time she'd

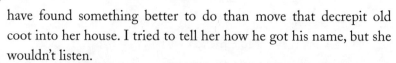

have found something better to do than move that decrepit old coot into her house. I tried to tell her how he got his name, but she wouldn't listen.

"And Tom Dewey, ornery codger, finally lost his fight with the devil. He was determined to live forever; had to have been the oldest man in the county. The last time I saw him alive, his joints creaked like rusty bed springs.

"I'll tell you somebody else who passed on. Lucy James, bless her dear soul. She was the sweetest thing to have had such a disagreeable daughter—disposition sour as a green quince. Lucy was healthy as a horse, but overnight, a growth the size of a gourd came up on her leg, and she was dead within three weeks. I told Travis I was so tired of going to the cemetery; I hoped the next funeral I have to go to is my own. I hope the Lord will wait 'til I'm old, though, before he sets me down."

"And speakin' of Travis, did he mention to you that he's gettin' on pretty thick with a woman named Abigail something-or-other from over in Oakdale? She works in the bank there. To hear him tell it, he's got a few years on her … I sure hope he hasn't pulled one too green."

Upon hearing this, an unexpected twinge of jealously quickly barbed Addie, yet it was equally quick to flee. She was truly happy Travis had met someone.

Her attention went back to what Claire was saying. "Oh, and while I'm thinkin' about it, your flock of guineas has migrated to my place. They roost in my sycamore tree every night!"

Addie's heart was full and content. Not so long ago, she had forgotten about joy, never imagined she would feel it again. But now it had come back to her. She smiled as Claire's flight of ideas led her down the familiar, endearing road of their friendship. She had missed her unbearably.

A little while later, when Daniel came into the kitchen for another slice of fruit cake, his heart skipped a beat when he overheard Claire

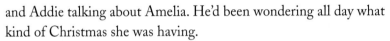

and Addie talking about Amelia. He'd been wondering all day what kind of Christmas she was having.

He curiously inquired, "What's that y'all were sayin' 'bout Amelia, Mama?"

Addie glanced at him with a surprised expression. "Claire just told me the most shocking thing. It seems Amelia is expecting a child most any day now."

At that very moment, the girls came cheerily running through to attack the cookie jar, and with all the racket and activity going on in the kitchen, no one gave particular thought to Daniel as he slipped out of the room. He went straight outdoors on limbs that felt like they might at any moment snap like dry twigs. His eyes smarted, and his throat backed up. He felt smothered and could barely suck in enough air to breathe. He made it just beyond the smokehouse before he bent over double and retched forcefully, vomiting up his Christmas dinner.

The men and boys decided to stay the night at Hiram's house and make the sleeping arrangements more convenient for everyone. Of course, they really just wanted to escape the women so they could be themselves.

As the candles over the fireplace burned low, Addie found a comfortable chair in a corner littered with discarded bows and wrapping paper and sat down to feel the quiet and reflect over the day. As soon as she put her head back and closed her eyes, Amelia immediately came to her mind.

With her pale, creamy skin and just a smattering of freckles across her nose, and those big, brown eyes of hers, Amelia had grown into a beauty. However, when she was little, most times she'd looked thrown away in dirty, threadbare clothes, painfully skinny with long, gangly legs and unkempt hair.

Daniel had never known, but the first time Addie noticed him taking food from his plate and slipping it into his pockets, she'd immediately guessed he was feeding Amelia. That's why she always made certain to cook plenty, so there would be enough for her too. On numerous occasions Addie invited the girl to eat with them; however, she rarely did.

Amelia had been proud but not haughty. She'd had an air of self-sufficiency about her that was both admirable and heart-rending. Addie knew she had it hard at home; might as well say the poor girl raised herself.

She wondered how many times she'd seen Daniel and Amelia come from fishing, his arm slung over her shoulder. *Those two had been inseparable.* She remembered that Daniel gave Amelia a doll one year for her birthday. *That doll made Amelia so happy.* And Addie thought of another thing that seemed to defy explanation; Rachel hadn't taken to most folks, yet she and Amelia reached out to and seemed to understand each other. A rare and beautiful friendship had budded and thrived between the woman and the little girl.

Yes, Amelia had certainly overcome the odds and become a lovely young woman. Addie was heartsick to learn she was pregnant. *I wonder who the baby's father is…*

Thinking back over times past made Addie think of the ones she'd recently lost. Yet in spite of it all, she didn't feel sad. Instead, she felt overrun with blessings. *This is the best Christmas I've ever had.* Sitting alone with this thought, she said a silent prayer of thanksgiving:

Most precious Lord, thank you for family and friends, both old and new, and for your blessings of good health, food, laughter, and this home, this gathering place. Please pour out a blessing on those less fortunate than me. Place your healing hand upon Creenie, and watch over Amelia and her unborn child. Most of all, thank you for love and giving unto us this day when we celebrate the birth of Jesus Christ, our Lord and Savior, the Prince of Peace.

Earlier in the day, after the children read the Christmas story, Wesley had unexpectedly reached for and passed Samuel's fiddle to Hiram. Hiram took up the instrument, put it to his neck, and softly set the bow to the strings. They all listened spellbound as he played "Silent Night, Holy Night."

While the song was so sweetly rendered, something akin to a miracle happened. Addie felt Samuel come back to her and lay his hand gently on her shoulder. She closed her eyes and inwardly wished the tune would never draw to a close. When the music ended, she opened her eyes and turned her face to Hiram's. When their eyes met, he knew and was gratified, pleased of the gift he had given her.

Now as the evening grew late, the wondrous carol and the tenderness in his eyes turned her thoughts from Amelia and lingered in the stillness of Addie's mind.

CHAPTER 25

"For there is nothing hid which shall not be manifested; neither was anything kept secret, but that it should come abroad." (Mark 4:22).

Rain had fallen on and off for the past few days, but it didn't hinder them from attending worship service on New Year's Day. Addie enjoyed the sermon but found herself disinterested and detached as folks stood around on the porch afterward, measuring the glories and disasters that marked the year passed and speculated about the year to come. It all sounded so trivial to her in comparison to her own affairs.

When they returned home, the aroma of black-eyed peas and cabbage filled the house. The meal paled in comparison to the rich feast they had for Christmas, but they gave thanks to God for it and ate heartily of the traditional, humble fare.

The next morning, Stell greeted the day by proclaiming the Christmas tree looked as withered as a jilted bride, so Laura and Addie set about taking down the holiday decorations and putting the house back in order.

After the midday meal, the house fell quiet. Stell retired to her chair and nodded off. Wesley returned to the barn, where he was sharpening implements, readying them for spring. When Laura went to put Meggie down for her nap, Addie wrapped a woolen shawl around her shoulders and slipped outside.

The January day was dreary and overcast, looking about equal of day and dark. The chilly dampness made the temperature seem colder than it really was; the moist air made her nose run.

Addie had a pestering sense of *something*. She couldn't put a name to it, but something was weighing on her mind, making her feel uneasy; a premonition of some kind. Surely there was no reason for this persistent feeling of dread. She thought, *What else could possibly happen?* Determined not to dwell on it, she laid it to the bleak weather and pushed the feeling aside.

She wandered around to the front of the house. A camellia bush, ornate with blooms, drew her close. She lingered there for several minutes, admiring its beauty as one would, appreciative of the work of fine art. Defiant of winter's dullness, each stem held a softly ruffled gift, a bright jewel of ruby red showcased against an evergreen background. The dark, shiny leaves were a rich contrast to the deep garnet blossoms. Shed petals blanketed the ground underneath the shrub, adorning it with a velvety skirt fashioned from the spent blooms.

Bittersweet memories swept over Addie as the camellias made her think of Rachel. Camellias had been her favorite flower. In fact, she knew this particular bush came from a cutting of the one at Rachel's old home place in Collinsville. Planted several years back, now it was nearly eight feet tall. Oh how she missed her mama!

Addie gazed out across the winter view, picturesque in its way. Trees stood before her, naked of their leaves, their limbs exposed. Off in the distance, a wagon rolled slowly along. At first glimpse she didn't pay particular attention to it, but her curiosity stirred when it turned off the main road onto the lane leading to the house. She thought it peculiar anyone would be out visiting on a day so unsuitable. Several minutes later the wagon came to a rattling stop at the front gate.

The driver of the wagon was a Negro man wearing a heavy coat. With his neck wrapped with a scarf against the cold, his hat pulled low, covering most of his face, the man was a stranger to Addie. However, even though his passenger's head was covered with a shawl, as soon as the woman climbed down from the seat and made her way across the yard, Addie recognized her and hurried to greet her. She didn't know what to think.

"Why, Creenie! What on earth brings you over this way?" Addie reached out and grabbed both her hands in hers. She told her happily. "Good gracious, it's so good to see you! Let's go inside where it's warm; your hands are like ice!"

Creenie was weary from the long ride. She felt weak and sick to her stomach. She wasn't really well enough to travel such a long distance, but she didn't have a choice. The angel of death was stalking her. *If I holds on to dis awful secret fo' one mo' day, I knows I gone die.* She was certain that the secret she harbored had been slowly killing her for months.

Creenie squeezed Addie's hands but said nothing. She shuddered and looked over her shoulder, half expecting to see the grim reaper. Not there on a social call, she shook her head firmly and said in a trembling voice, "I ain't got time to go inside, Miz Addie. I'z jus come here 'cauze I'z got somethin' very impo'tant to tell y'all—you an' yo bruther, Missa Wesley." She whispered as if she was afraid of being overheard.

Addie was puzzled. She wondered why Creenie was acting so standoffish and nervous. Maybe it was because she didn't feel well. She couldn't help but notice that Creenie's eyes were jaundiced; her skin was pale and dusky. She remembered Claire told her at Christmastime that Creenie had been sick.

What on earth could Creenie possibly have to say to me and Wesley? In the next instant, Addie knew, and the realization summoned panic. The reason for her premonition, the nameless, persistent feeling of

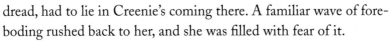

dread, had to lie in Creenie's coming there. A familiar wave of fore-boding rushed back to her, and she was filled with fear of it.

Addie felt her mouth go dry. She could do little but pray for God to be at her side, be her companion in strength for whatever was about to come. She said, "Wesley's out in the barn working." Her mind raced as she led the way toward the barn; Creenie followed a few paces behind.

Seeing Addie and Creenie enter the barn, Wesley stood up, straightened his back, and laid his file in the bed of the buckboard. Curious as to who the Negro woman was and what business brought her there, he waited for an explanation.

Addie glanced at Wesley with an odd expression. The mystery of it all made for an awkward introduction. "Wesley, this is Creenie Boone, an old friend of mine from Collinsville. We sewed together for the mercantile. She said she's got something important to tell the both of us."

Wesley acknowledged Creenie with a nod. She briefly raised her eyes to his face and then quickly looked away. For a seemingly end-less moment, they all stood waiting. Creenie's eyes were downcast, fixed on the ground. Addie's heart was pounding.

When Creenie finally commenced to talking, the words tumbled forth like an avalanche. "I feel awful sorry fo' what I'z 'bout to say, but I caint hold dis in no mo'. Ever since I knowed dis, I'z bin sick. I'z had a fever an' a belly ache so bad I caint eat, an' some days my legs hurt me so bad I caint git out o' bed an' walk. I caint hardly sleep 'cauze I knows da Lawd done laid a curse on me cauze o' dis terrible thang I know."

She dared not look at them but rambled on, "Like I say, I'z sorry, but I thank I'd want to know dis if it wuz my mama."

She had their rapt attention.

Creenie was fidgety, and her fingers picked at the sleeve of her coat. Her voice quavered, she seemed almost unaware of them as she began her narrative: "Missa Alfred, he come up to da house some-time an' drank an' play cards when my cuzin' Peegie wuz dere back durin' da summer. One night, he dere an' drunk an' showin' out; I'z in da back room." She paused and put her trembling hand to her chest. She rocked for a moment and took a deep breath, calling up the courage to continue. "Missa Alfred, he tol' Peegie how he hide his horse in da woods dat day. He say Miz Emily wuz out 'hind da house doin' da washin'. He say he saw you, Miz Addie, head off down to da peapatch totin' a pan."

Addie's heart pounded wildly.

As Creenie talked on, her voice took on a shrill note. She seemed out of her mind, restless, pacing back and forth ... back and forth. She couldn't tell it standing still.

"I heared Missa Alfred say to Peegie how he snuck back up to da house dat mawnin'." Creenie started crying. Addie's chest began to rise and fall with Creenie's every word, her skin took on a prickly sensation.

Tears were streaming down Creenie's cheeks, "Missa Alfred, he jus' laff an' laff. He say he goes in dere where Miz Rachel wuz layin' on da flo'. Oh, dat po' woman! Missa Alfred say he helt a piller on Miz Rachel's face, an' he kilt her til she wuz dead as a doornail. Missa Alfred jus be laffin' an' laffin' like what he done wuz so funny! Den he gone say after Miz Rachel dead, he snuck from out da house an' run to da woods to git on his hoss an' ride off to town like he ain't done nothin'!"

Addie's head was spinning. She felt dizzy and nauseous. She careened and reached out to catch hold of the buckboard to keep from being swept away, but to no avail. She fell in and was swiftly sucked under. She thought she heard Wesley say something, but she couldn't understand what. His voice sounded muffled. She was underwater, caught in an eddy. She couldn't breathe, she was drowning. She thought, *Why won't somebody save me?*

When she finally struggled to the surface and gasped for air, she heard Wesley shouting at Creenie. He was outraged, accusing her of making the whole story up. *It's a lie!* For some crazy, unknown reason, she was lying to them. They'd have to be insane to believe such a far-fetched tale!

Creenie swore every word was true. She screeched back at Wesley, "Now dat don't make no kind o' sense! Why you thank I come all dis way to tell a lie? If it be a lie, Missa Alfred da one dat tol' it, but it sho' didn't sound like no lie! Missa Alfred sound *proud* o' what he done, bragged over it!"

Addie lifted her arms to quiet the argument. Managing to speak, she said, "Stop, Wesley. Creenie's telling the truth. Everything happened that morning just like she described. She couldn't possibly have known lest Alfred told it. Lord how I wish it wasn't so, but in my heart, I know what she's saying is true. From what she's told us, there's no doubt in my mind. Alfred killed Mama."

She could hardly say the words, admit her own husband had murdered her Mama, but deep down inside she knew it was true. Alfred had slain Rachel sure as they were standing there. *Evil lunatic! Madman!* A vision of Alfred's sneering face swam before her eyes. Addie caught a chill and shuddered. *Hell, hold him fast!*

Her every nerve was in shock; her mind swirled in a fog. It was hard to absorb the horror of what Creenie had just confessed to them. It was unthinkable. She thought of Rachel—pitiful, lying on the floor, helpless, and unable to move—and Alfred smothering her to death with a pillow. It was incomprehensible. As she pieced it all together and the reality of it slowly sank in, her heart splintered. A sob broke from her, and she cried, "Poor Mama!" It was like salt poured into a raw wound as her grief for Rachel was renewed. *I can't take any more sorrow.*

Wesley's emotions were wrought, but in a different way. His reaction was spawned more out of anger. He demanded of Creenie, "Why, in God's name, didn't you tell us this before?"

Creenie answered him, sniffling, "Cauze I knows how mean Missa Alfred be. I wuz scart o' him. Peegie say if we say anythang 'bout what Missa Alfred tol', he libel to kill us, too. Split our het wif da ax! So we jus let da Lawd take care o' him. I wuz thankin' Missa Alfred couldn't hurt us no mo' when his leg got chopped off, an' den he burn up in his own house. But den I'z got so sick. I jus' knows I got a hex on me fo' not tellin' da truf 'bout Miz Rachel. Dat why I'z come here … to git shed o' dis so's I can git well."

Wesley could only stare as Creenie pulled an old handkerchief from her pocket and wiped her wet eyes and nose. Her irrational voodoo logic struck him as perplexing and incredible as the story itself. He saw no need to press the woman further, figuring she'd told them all she knew.

From his plain expression, Creenie sensed her dismissal. She turned to Addie and said, "I *iz* real sorry 'bout what happen to yo' Mama, an' I hate I upset y'all."

As Creenie started toward the door, Addie stopped her. "Wait."

Her emotions were churning, but she managed to compose herself enough to form a few trembling words. "God bless you for your courage. I know it wasn't easy for you to come here and tell us this, and I just want you to know, this changes nothing between us. I'll always look to you as a dear friend."

She meant it. Creenie was dear to her, and none of this mess was her fault. She couldn't help what Alfred had done; she was simply the talebearer. Addie wouldn't let something he did come between them.

"I'll be praying for you to get well."

Creenie blinked her eyes rapidly, touched by Addie's benevolent spirit, grateful to be departing on good terms with her. "All right, Miz Addie."

Creenie ran to the wagon and stepped up into it. The man was yet to utter a word. He took up the reins, lightly slapped the horse's back, and they pulled away from the house. Creenie took a deep breath of fresh, cold air. She felt better already, relieved to have her conscience cleared of that worrisome secret.

Actually, she had come there with the intention of baring her soul of two secrets, but she just couldn't bring herself to confess the other thing. She thought, *Miz Addie's a nice lady. She bin through enough already havin' to hear 'bout how Missa Alfred kilt her mama.*

The other thing would just be an added cross for her to bear. *Jus' another thang fo' her to haf to thank back on.* She closed her eyes, hoping the echoing sound of the horse's hooves would intrude upon her thoughts enough to erase the gnawing doubt that left her mind hanging in the balance between right and wrong.

A few minutes later she'd made peace with her decision and was sure she'd done the right thing in not telling Addie the *whole* truth. *What good could possibly come from Miz Addie knowin' 'bout Sassie bein' Missa Alfred's chile?* None.

That settled, she opened her eyes and told the man, "Pull off up yunder in dem bushes. I'z got to pee."

The atmosphere in the barn had the cadence of a pounding heart. Wesley rubbed his hands roughly over his face and through his hair, as if trying to rouse himself from a three-day drunk. For a minute there was a stupendous hush as he tried to quiet his nerves.

He looked squarely at Addie, his blue eyes flashing and stretched wide. For lack of something better, he said, "Well, hellfire! That was a fine how-do-you- do!" Now he really wished he'd beat the stew out of Alfred when he'd had the mind to.

Addie was numb. This couldn't have happened. She didn't know what to say either, except, "Daniel and Emily mustn't know their father killed their granny. They've been through enough already."

Wesley nodded his agreement. "That's all right by me, but you know I don't keep things from Laura. I'll have to tell her. Right now, I'm just decidin' what to say."

Addie felt his dilemma. Far too addle-minded to give an account of such a story herself, she told him, "I gladly leave that to you. I wouldn't know how to start telling it."

His tone was absolute. "And, sister … it'll suit me just fine if we don't have company tomorrow."

CHAPTER 26

"Forsake me not, O Lord; O my God, be not far from me."
(Psalms 38:21).

Addie knew heartbreak again. How she longed to just curl up and quietly fade away. *Oh that I had wings like a dove! For then would I fly away and be at rest.* She thought by now, being so acquainted with pain, she might feel nothing but blessed numbness, but instead the blade seemed blunter this time around. She had been trying so hard, struggling with all the loss in her life, adjusting to all the changes, and just when her spirit was beginning to lift and she felt a sense of restoration, she was blindsided, knocked off balance yet again. Joy was plucked from her bosom, and she was rendered desolate, grief-stricken over Rachel's death again, only this time worse. She was sure she would not be able to bear the agony of knowing Alfred had murdered her mama. The very thought of it overwhelmed her, left her enveloped in utter despair.

Her nerves were taut. The tightness in her throat and in the pit of her stomach made it impossible to eat, but she felt it necessary to be present at the supper table to avoid raising suspicion. Otherwise, the children would surely have asked questions. Questions she didn't have strength or presence of mind to answer.

Laura herself was shocked by what Wesley had told her that afternoon. She couldn't believe that Alfred had killed Rachel. Sitting across the table from Addie, she was sorely concerned. Her heart wrenched as she watched her sister-in-law struggle to hold a fork, staring absently at the uneaten food she pushed around on her plate. Addie took a sip of coffee, her hands trembling so violently the cup rattled sharply against the saucer as she set it down. Seeing the somber, hollow expression in her eyes crushed Laura. She had never seen anyone look so troubled, so distraught. She longed to reach out to her; she wished she could make things better.

By some small miracle, Addie made it through the meal convincingly enough. When they'd finished supper, the children lit around Wesley like flies on honey when he took a knife and started to strip the purple, reed-like rind from a stalk of sugar cane. This provided Addie with an escape, since they all knew she was not fond of the fibrous, wallowing cud left behind after chewing the juice from a wedge of cane. She scarcely had the will to rise from her chair, but she said goodnight to everyone and excused herself.

Oblivious to how much time may have lapsed—it could have been an hour or far more or less than an hour—Addie heard a light knocking on the bedroom door. Without waiting for permission, Laura entered the room quietly. Addie was in a rocking chair, but she sat still; the chair was not moving.

Going over to the five-drawer chest Daniel had made, Laura picked up Addie's hairbrush and went and stood behind her. She gently removed the pins from her hair and shook it loose with her fingers. As she began brushing Addie's long chestnut hair, she felt Addie's shoulders quake and knew she was crying. Laura didn't say a word; she just stayed with Addie and continued to brush her hair.

Finally, in a small quavering voice, Addie softly choked out, "I swear to you, Laura, I honestly feel like I'm losing my mind. It torments me to think how Mama must have suffered at Alfred's cruel hands." Since Rachel's last stroke left her paralyzed and unable to talk, she had been mute and defenseless. "There's no way she could've told me if he was mistreating her." A minute later, she whispered, "Why did God let this happen?" She was profoundly sad. She couldn't take any more.

Laura was afraid, hoping Addie was not growing bitter—*for by sorrow of the heart the spirit is broken.* She placed her hand gently on Addie's shoulder and offered her the best explanation she could think of. "Bad things happen to good people, same as good things happen to bad ones. Mattew 5:45 says, "He maketh the sun to rise on the evil and on the good, and sendeth rain on the just and the unjust." After a moment, she added, "Addie, I won't presume to understand why you've had to suffer through so much heartache, but I stand fast on God's promise that He will not lay more upon us than we can bear. I know God loves you, and I believe in my heart He has good things in store for you." *For no eye has seen the things that God hath prepared for them that love him . . .*

Laura wrapped her arms around Addie and squeezed her reassuringly. "Wesley and I are going to help you through this. We're all bound together by love, and *love never fails.*"

Moved by Laura's compassion for her, Addie said, "I do so love you, Laura. I don't know what I'd do without you."

Laura was right on both accounts. God did love Addie. And yes, He did have good things in store for her. But what she didn't know was that she would have to endure yet another blow with a pickax to her heart in order to receive them.

That same night, over in Collinsville, Travis had made himself comfortable in his favorite chair. A nice, relaxing fire was burning in his fireplace. The room was warm and aromatic with the rich, sweet smell of tobacco from the cigar he finished a while ago. He was not asleep, but it was late enough that he was indeed sorry when he heard someone knock on the side door he used for his practice. He hated the prospect of having to get bundled up to go back out into the cold night.

The man said they needed a doctor and gave Travis directions to a place a few miles out of town. Travis knew the house—he'd been expecting this summons for a week or so now. Figuring there was no need to rush, he moseyed on out there about an hour later.

The girl was glad when he arrived. She was afraid and wanted him there by her side. The pains came and went. They came again and went again; and again and again.

The girl clung to her aunt's hand tightly. The aunt spoke soothingly to the girl and wiped her brow and neck frequently with a cool, wet cloth.

Long into the night, Travis directed the girl when to breathe and when to pant. He instructed her when to relax and when to bear down and when to push. He encouraged her to go with the pain, not fight it, and he praised her progress.

In the wee hours of the morning, the baby finally emerged, and the red, wrinkled face broke into a lusty squall. The girl was crying now, and laughing at the same time. The pain was over; nothing else mattered except her baby. Travis was relieved. He thought the delivery went well, especially considering it was her first and she was so young.

"It's a girl, Amelia. You have a strong and healthy, beautiful baby girl."

CHAPTER 27

"Love beareth all things, believeth all things, hopeth all things, endureth all things ... there abideth faith, hope, love, but the greatest of these is love." (1 Corinthians 13:7, 13).

Ever since Christmas Day, when he'd learned of Amelia's pregnancy, Daniel could think of nothing else. His mind was in turmoil. The night before last he caught himself doing something he'd most likely been doing subconsciously all along, but he just hadn't noticed until then. How could such a small, seemingly insignificant gesture evoke such an intense feeling of sadness? During supper, he'd glanced down at his plate and saw his cornbread torn into halves. He didn't have to wonder why he broke it in two. He'd stared at the cornbread long and hard. The longer he'd stared at it, the more convinced he became of what he must do. He knew he had to find Amelia.

It had become a ritual, early on Saturday morning, before the rest of the household stirred into their routine, Wesley, Hiram, and Daniel made their own breakfast and sat around the kitchen table man-talking, as Laura called it. This morning as Hiram and Wesley exchanged news and discussed their plans for the day, Daniel ate methodically and said almost nothing, his thoughts adrift.

He was anxious for Addie to get up and around. When he finished his breakfast and got up from the table, Daniel headed out the door for the barn. Before he left the house, he asked Wesley to tell Addie he needed to see her as soon as she arose. While he was waiting on Addie, Daniel pulled Hiram aside and proceeded to tell him what he intended to do.

When Wesley relayed Daniel's message to her, Addie leisurely poured herself a cup of coffee and took a biscuit from the pan on the stove and filled it with a piece of fried ham. She then set out casually across the yard, nibbling on the biscuit as she went. Her thoughts had been so preoccupied after Creenie's visit that she had neglected to notice how troubled Daniel had been the last couple of weeks. After what seemed like a long wait to Daniel, she entered the barn.

He was nervously pacing back and forth, back and forth.

Addie smiled and said, "Good morning," but when she saw the strain on his face, she immediately asked, "What's the matter, Daniel?"

Daniel didn't want to waste any more time where Amelia was concerned. Given what he now knew, he'd already dallied overlong.

"Mama, there's somethin' we need to talk about. You best sit down."

Addie stared at him, thinking how serious he sounded and how serious he looked. All of a sudden, she got the feeling she'd hoed this row before. She felt like putting her hands over her ears. Luckily, there was an old church bench against the wall behind her, and she sat down there before her knees gave way. After she sat down, Daniel pulled a chair close to her and perched on its edge. He leaned toward her and reached out and grasped Addie's hands.

"Mama, first I want you to know I love you. I know things have been hard on you lately, just like they bound to've been hard on you puttin' up with Pa all them years." He went on. "The last thing I want to do is upset you an' make things worse than they already are, but I'm afraid what I'm fixin' to tell you might do just that.

217

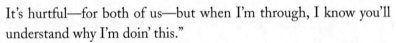

It's hurtful—for both of us—but when I'm through, I know you'll understand why I'm doin' this."

He took a deep breath.

If he felt unsure of himself, it didn't show. Daniel spoke straight from the hip. With bold poise, he recounted the event of seeing Alfred, Cleve, and Pete attack Amelia back in the spring. He also told Addie about confronting Alfred that evening and the fight they had that led up to him leaving.

Hiram walked in quietly but said nothing.

Addie's heart stopped as she found herself listening to yet another astounding account of a heinous transgression committed by Alfred. *I've been here before.* She sat so still she might have been dead. Not once did she so much as blink, lest a movement so slight cause the atmosphere to collapse and suffocate them all. Couldn't Alfred have been content to be just a murderer? No, he had to aspire to being a rapist as well. Was it even remotely possible there was anything left for her to dread hearing about her dearly dead and departed husband? If her heart hadn't been so filled with pain for Amelia and Daniel, she would have burst out laughing from the hilarious absurdity of it all.

But she was too upset to laugh, too upset to think. *I've finally gone crazy!*

Her senses came back to her somewhat when Daniel said, "Mister Hiram's lettin' me have some days off to go an' try to find Amelia ... an' when I do, I'm gonna ask her to marry me, soon as I've saved up enough money to buy the old Lewis place. I'm hopin' we might even be able to rent it in the meantime."

She looked at Daniel, perplexed. So much was being poured over her head at once that it took her a minute to pull her thoughts together. Still somewhat addled, she said, "Why, I know where Amelia is. She's in Collinsville."

Daniel replied, "Not anymore. She moved away from Pete's an' went to live with her mama."

Addie was shaking her head. "You're right about one thing, she did move away from Pete, but not to live with Bonnie. When Claire was here at Christmas, she told me Amelia is living with her aunt, Jennie Grayson, just out from town. By way of the crow, she's not too awfully far from our old place."

Daniel's knees went weak. He realized Amelia must have misled him out of shame about what had happened and to hide the fact she was pregnant. Out loud, but only to himself, he asked, "Doesn't she know how much I love her, an' that none of that other stuff matters?"

Then he started shouting at Addie, not disrespectfully, but out of excitement, "Why didn't you tell me?" His face broke into a smile, and his eyes were shining.

As they looked at each other, she answered, "It never crossed my mind to. I had no reason to think you didn't know where Amelia was. Up until now, I knew nothing of this."

Daniel couldn't be still; he was breathless. "Mama, tell me, where *exactly* does Amelia's Aunt Jennie live?"

"The only thing I know for sure is that she lives on Double Branch Road, just the other side of Collinsville. Once you get over that way, probably most anyone can give you directions to her house."

Daniel felt like he'd been reborn. "Soon as I saddle up Gent, I'm headed that way!" He started toward the tack room with tears of joy in his eyes.

Addie was in better control of herself now. She called after him, "Wait, Daniel."

He stopped and turned around impatiently.

For a moment she thought about giving him a double earful of motherly advice, but on second thought, the look on his face tugged at her heart. She'd never seen him look so happy. He wasn't being forced to marry Amelia out of pity or a sense of obligation; he was making a rational, honorable choice in the name of love. Daniel had spent his entire boyhood making his way to this place and to this time. He and Amelia's hearts had been knit since they were children, and now they would pass through this portal and enter the next phase of their lives together as husband and wife. This was simply meant to be.

Addie's tears came. Remembering the money in the blue fruit jar in the top drawer of the chest he had given her on Christmas Day, she told him, "Let me talk to Laura. We'll work it out somehow so Amelia can stay with us until your place is ready. I'll buy the old Lewis place and give it to you and Amelia as a wedding present."

Daniel couldn't believe what he was hearing. He hurried to her and hugged her with such exuberance, her feet were lifted off the ground.

"I love you, Mama! But I've gotta get goin'!" He kissed her quickly on the cheek and let out an excited, "*Whoopie!*"

As he started to leave again, Addie stopped him again. "Daniel, you can't ride Gent to Collinsville."

He turned around and looked at her in confusion. "Why?"

"Because, son, you and Amelia will be traveling back with a baby. You'll need to borrow a buggy."

Hiram finally spoke up, "You can take mine." He gave Daniel a slap on his shoulder as he ran out to make preparations to leave.

When Daniel went out, Addie stood there quietly. She was emotionally drained. After a moment, she turned to face Hiram, and looking directly at him, she asked, "You knew this?" It was barely a question.

Hiram nodded. He knew without a doubt she was put out with him.

"How long have you known?"

"A good while."

She studied him for a moment, ready to strangle him. Then she asked accusingly, "Didn't it occur to you that was a heavy burden for a boy to carry around all by himself? You should have told me."

Hiram scratched his beard as he contemplated her question and framed up his reply. "I considered it a mite bundlesome. But once he'd told me about it, he weren't totin' it around all by himself anymore. I made a promise to Daniel that I wouldn't tell. I can't rightly apologize to you for keepin' that promise. He needed someone he could trust, and I want him to know he can trust me."

Addie couldn't be mad at Hiram. He did the right thing in keeping his promise to Daniel, and she respected him for that. Having thought about it, she realized that though his situation with his wife had been vastly different, Hiram knew perfectly well how Daniel felt. He not only understood Daniel's pain, but also the depth of his love for Amelia. For yet in the aftermath of a betrayal that wrenched his heart, the love he'd shown for Madeline was likewise infallible.

It was early evening when Daniel walked up on the porch of Jennie Grayson's house. He knocked on the door. Terribly unsure of how he would be received, his palms were sweating and his chest felt tight. He took a deep breath and tried to calm his fears. Minutes passed without a response from inside.

There was smoke coming from the chimney. He was sure someone was home. He knocked again, this time louder. He wasn't leaving until someone opened the door. He waited, his heart hammering.

Finally the door opened slowly, and there stood this incredibly beautiful young woman, looking at him very cautiously, crying. *Amelia!* Daniel's world reeled and his breath caught in his throat. He yearned to take her in his arms right then and brush her tears away.

Amelia turned her face away from him and said tearfully, "Go away, Daniel! I told you not to come lookin' for me."

Daniel took another deep breath and squared his shoulders. "I'd been here months ago if I'd known where to look. I came as soon as I found out where you were … I couldn't stay away." His voice pleaded gently, "Please, let me come in, Amelia. We need to talk."

Amelia shook her head no, a flood of tears streaming down her cheeks. She said miserably, "I can't let you in, Daniel. I'm begging you, please go away and forget about me."

He was insistent. "I'm not leaving here 'til you hear me out."

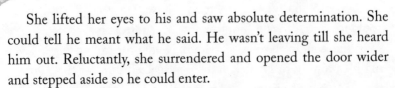

She lifted her eyes to his and saw absolute determination. She could tell he meant what he said. He wasn't leaving till she heard him out. Reluctantly, she surrendered and opened the door wider and stepped aside so he could enter.

Daniel stepped across the threshold into the warm, tidy room. A fire crackled in the fireplace. He was relieved that Amelia seemed to be the only one in the house. He needed to speak with her alone, without interference.

Amelia opened her mouth and started to say something. "Daniel—"

He interrupted her. With intense tenderness, he said, "I'm lonesome without you, Amelia. I'm not whole without you."

This brought on a fresh wave of tears. "I'm not that same little innocent girl you used to sit with on the creek bank."

"Yes, you are. To me, you are," he told her adamantly, gently. He also was brought to tears.

She cried piteously, "Those were wonderful days, but they're over and done with now."

Daniel was crying for her, for him, for everything they'd lost as he said, "They don't have to be."

Wiping the tears from her cheeks, she shook her head and said, "You don't understand, Daniel. If you only knew, you wouldn't even be able to stand there and look at me."

"I do understand." His voice was strained with emotion. "I know what happened, Amelia. I was there. I saw." His heart wrenched as he remembered. "Please forgive me for not stoppin' them." He choked on the words, "Say you forgive me."

Amelia looked at him closely, her eyes round with confusion and surprise as she searched his face, amazed at what she found there, at what he was saying. She took a step toward him, her heart fluttering. Hesitantly, she said, "Daniel, I have a baby."

For the first time since entering the house, he noticed the crib near the fireplace. "W-Well," he stammered, "well … good, 'cause I

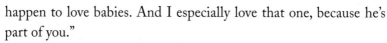

happen to love babies. And I especially love that one, because he's part of you."

He'd made her smile, at least a little.

"Can you stand there and honestly tell me you won't think of that day every time you look at me and that you won't wonder every time you look at my baby whether or not your pa is *her* father?"

Her question was blunt and struck right to the heart of the issue. Daniel took a deep breath, looked into the eyes of his beloved, and instantly knew that her concern didn't matter. Should she accept his offer, this child would be his forever, no questions asked. "I can honestly tell you that nothin' else matters in this whole world except that I love you." It was his turn to challenge her. "Can you honestly tell me that you won't ever blame me for what he did to you or that you'll never hate me just for bein' his son?"

The words caught in her throat. "Oh, Daniel, you're not to blame for what happened. And don't you know I could never hate you? I've loved you with all my heart since I was eight years old!"

Daniel reached out to touch a lock of her hair. He gazed at her deeply and reminded her, "Do you remember that night we lay under the stars, an' you promised to marry me someday when the time was right?"

Amelia nodded.

"Did you mean it?"

Her heart was pounding. In a quivering voice, she said, "Of course I meant it, Daniel."

Daniel exhaled. His smile was triumphant. "Well, Amelia, I say the time is right!"

A little cry escaped her as she slipped her arms around him, and they dissolved into each other. Their second kiss was long and slow, full of tenderness and intimate promise. As they clung together, Daniel asked, "By the way, what's my daughter's name?"

Through her tears, Amelia managed to tell him, "Her name is Rachel … Rachel Danielle."

Jennie Grayson was overjoyed when she arrived home to discover the fortunate turn of events. Amelia had cried on her shoulder many a night over the loss of her beloved Daniel. She'd heard so much about him, she felt as though she'd known him forever.

Jennie knew of Daniel's people. There couldn't have been a finer man than his grandpa Samuel Warren, and if anyone had ever said an unfavorable word about his mother, Addie, she hadn't heard it. Those facts, combined with the adoration in the young man's eyes when he looked at Amelia and Rachel, gave her confidence that her niece and great-niece would be well taken care of.

Daniel graciously declined Jennie's offer for him to stay the night at her house. Though he hated to let Amelia out of his sight again, somehow it didn't seem appropriate. He felt more comfortable going back into Collinsville and spending the night with Travis. But he assured them he'd return at first light for Amelia and Rachel. They'd need to get an early start since it'd take them over half a day to get to Golden Meadow—to get *home*.

Little preparation was necessary for Amelia, since she had so few worldly possessions to pack. Really, there were only her clothes and Rachel's tiny things—most of which had been sown by and given to her unknowingly by Addie through Travis.

Before Amelia closed the lid of her trunk, there was one last thing she buried deep within the folds of her dresses to protect it during their long journey. But before she tucked it away for safekeeping, she couldn't resist hugging close the doll Daniel had given her on her tenth birthday.

The next morning, Amelia smiled at Daniel when he detoured off Monroe Road.

He grinned and defended himself, saying, "Don't make sense to be this close an' not stop in. We just can't stay long."

Claire was pulling up turnips when they pulled up in her yard. She came running. "Well, you young'uns have saved me from myself today!" she exclaimed brightly. "Get down out of that buggy an' come in! I'm fixin' to put these on to cook, and we'll have us some pot liquor and cornbread in jig time!"

"We can't stay that long, Miss Claire," said Daniel. "We just came by long enough for you to gather up your clothes an' come on home with us. We want you to dance at our weddin.'"

They climbed out of the buggy.

Claire was tickled to see them and clearly had no intention on letting them leave before she'd had her say. "Come on in; let me knock the dirt off my hands so I can love on that little sack of sugar. Y'all catch me up on the news." She snorted. "But I got a letter from Stell last Friday. She just had to write and tell me about all her ailments, so we needn't bore each other to death talkin' about her."

After she washed her hands, she sat down in a rocker with Rachel and crooned, "This is a pretty baby."

"We don't want to hinder you from goin' to church, but the offer stands about goin' home with us," Daniel said.

As she cradled Rachel in her arms, she replied, "Oh, I can't go today, but I tell you I've had some blue days since y'all moved off over yonder. When your mama first asked me to move way over there, I thought she'd lost her mind! I didn't think I could. It seemed like the jumpin' off place of the world to me. But now I can hardly wait. I told her to give me a few weeks to get everything settled here and I'd be over there to shake things up."

An hour flew by with them talking, all the while Claire held the darling baby girl, babbling to her lovingly and insensibly. Daniel and Amelia said good-bye about fifty times before they could finally get away from her. Their unexpected visit had made her day.

Again the wheels of the buggy turned over the hard clay of

Monroe Road. The previous day, when he'd come into Collinsville, Daniel's mind was so purpose driven on finding Amelia that he hadn't even realized when he passed by the old burned-out place. As they rolled slowly past it now, he expected, after spending his whole life growing up there, at least some feeling of sentiment to surface from somewhere deep within. However, the only profound thought he had was how hauntingly foreign and forlorn it appeared. He felt no attachment to the place in his heart whatsoever.

As the old home place faded from view, Daniel cast all the things from his past that he'd just as soon forget back over his shoulder and left them behind to settle in the dust. He felt like everything he'd ever need was right there beside him on the seat of the buggy. He and Amelia and Rachel moved steadfastly toward their future.

They had traveled a fair distance when Daniel smiled at Amelia and said, "I bet Miss Claire's still standin' back there in her yard talkin' to us." They laughed, knowing what he said was probably true.

Amelia unwrapped one of the teacakes Claire packed for their journey, broke it in two, and gave Daniel half.

It was Hiram that offered the solution to the overcrowding at Wesley's house. Daniel and Jesse would bunk with him until the new Coulter place was fit to live in.

Wesley begged Hiram to extend the invitation to include him as well, but all his request earned him was a glare from Laura, accompanied with the chastising suggestion that he pile up and sleep in the barn with old Ben. Acknowledging from whence his blessings flowed, Wesley was resigned to lick his wounded ego in a house swarming with females.

Amelia marveled at how her life had turned into a dream. Each new dawn she awoke to find herself playing the role of a fairy tale prin-

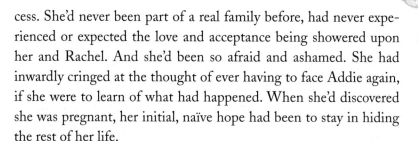

cess. She'd never been part of a real family before, had never experienced or expected the love and acceptance being showered upon her and Rachel. And she'd been so afraid and ashamed. She had inwardly cringed at the thought of ever having to face Addie again, if she were to learn of what had happened. When she'd discovered she was pregnant, her initial, naïve hope had been to stay in hiding the rest of her life.

Any worries proved a waste of time, though, for Addie had somehow recognized all her fears beforehand. As soon as she and Daniel had arrived at Wesley's and she'd stepped down from the buggy, Addie was there waiting. A sense of kinship was already there, waiting. Love, too, awaited. Love had been waiting for her there all along. When Addie saw she was shaking, she folded her arms around her and simply whispered, "Welcome home, Amelia."

Rachel was a beautiful baby. There were no distinguishable features upon her face that gave away the identity of her father. And if there had been, they were all blind to them.

Everyone, especially Daniel, was a fool over her. When he held her, he talked to her like she was already a full-grown person and didn't care in the least if anyone thought he was silly. No one did. Sarah Beth and Emily were always on hand for babysitting duty. Jesse gawked at her awkwardly, fascinated by her smallness. Meggie seemed a little jealous, sensing she was no longer the baby of the family. Regardless of the fact that Daniel had not fathered Rachel in the traditional manner, Addie behaved as the typical, insanely infatuated, first-time grandmother. Stell, of course, who blatantly admitted she wasn't overly fond of babies, went as far as to obligingly stare at her a few minutes, but she otherwise kept a genteel distance and declined the offer to hold her. Laura chided her aversion by saying, "For heaven's sake, Mama. She's not going to eat you!"

Stell mumbled derisively, "I 'spect Jonah had a similar misconception of the whale."

When Wesley and Daniel traveled to Oakdale to finalize the sale of the former Lewis property, the bank secretary, who prepared the documents for them to sign, was named Abigail Langford. During the course of conversation, when she learned the men were originally from Collinsville, it was soon established they all shared a mutual friend in Dr. Travis Hughes.

Men are, by nature, unobservant; so therefore, they are considered blind and generally of little use when called upon to satisfy the curiosities aroused by women concerning other women. That being so, neither Wesley nor Daniel could adequately answer any of the questions Addie raised in regards to Miss Langford. The best description they gave her was that she was very nice, but Addie was nosey to find out what lay hidden behind the conspicuously sly and sheepish grins exchanged between her brother and son. Daniel contributed that he couldn't swear to it, but he thought the dress she was wearing was either brown or pink. *Men!*

There were no idle hands at the old farmstead. Everyone pitched in and did whatever was needed, and within three weeks, the repairs were completed and the house had been cleaned out and scrubbed from top to bottom. Of course, there was still much about the place to be set right, but it presented as a fine enough place and stood ready for a fine family.

On the first Saturday of February, Daniel Warren Coulter and Amelia Rose Riley were wed in a simple ceremony at two o'clock in the afternoon at the Harmony Baptist Church of Golden Meadow.

Wesley escorted the bride down the aisle. Amelia was radiant and looked exquisite in a dove-gray dress made of soft velvet. In honor of the late Rachel, she carried a bouquet of red camellias. Daniel was beaming and strikingly handsome. The happy couple could not take their eyes off each other. Their faces glowed with happiness. The love they had for each other, from the time they were but children, was obvious.

Hiram stood as Daniel's best man, and Amelia thrilled Emily by asking her to be her maid-of-honor. Amelia cried throughout the pledging of vows, as did Addie. She was overwhelmed with emotion as she looked at Daniel and Amelia, then down at the perfect infant sleeping contently in her arms. Baby Rachel looked like an angel wearing a tiny, yellow dress trimmed with lace.

It was remarkable, a miracle how God had worked everything out. In the end, love had conquered all. At that moment, Addie again knew absolute joy. Everything seemed right with the world.

That same evening, as dusk approached in Missouri, a lone traveler on horseback was nearing the place where he planned to make camp for the night. The man had been making his way north for months now. A few weeks back, when he'd crossed over into Arkansas from Mississippi, he had stayed well east of the Ozark Mountains to avoid the rough terrain.

It was cold, and he was weary. But at least he was more familiar with his surroundings now. He told himself, "I'm gettin' close to home—what's left of me, that is." His left arm and hand were badly scarred from being burned, his nub of a leg ached, the ever-present pain hounded him, had become his constant and unwelcome companion. He shuddered to think what would have happened if he hadn't woke up when he did. *I jus' did have time to grab one crutch an' slither out on my belly like a snake.* He'd half-crawled, half-dragged himself through the woods to Pete's house. *I's lucky ol' Pete was willin' to help me.*

The horse he called Judge had proved to be a good mount, but he regretted having to leave Gent behind. *That Gent was one fine horse.*

"Ain't no point in lookin' back," Alfred said out loud to himself and Judge, "'less'n we's wantin' to go that a-way."

CHAPTER 28

During the second week of March, the doors and windows of Stell's little farmhouse were flung open so the fresh air could chase away the musty smell. Every room received a thorough cleaning, swept from ceiling to floor; every inch was scoured and mopped with pine soap. Wesley replaced the rotten steps leading onto the porch, and Daniel built shelves across an entire wall in one room for Claire's books. Addie worked at cleaning the fireplace and hearth, as well as the old wood stove. It took a fair amount of effort to spruce it up, but after a few days, the look of neglect from having stood empty for the last three years disappeared, and the place was once again fit for habitation.

Once the yard was raked, Jesse was elected to oversee the burning of an enormous pile of branches and leaves. There was particular irony in the fact that the fire was still smoking on the afternoon Travis and Claire pulled up in a wagon laden with her possessions,

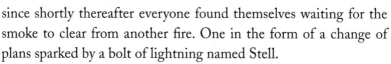

since shortly thereafter everyone found themselves waiting for the smoke to clear from another fire. One in the form of a change of plans sparked by a bolt of lightning named Stell.

As it were, Stell didn't take any useful part in helping unload Claire's things. She dragged a well-worn rocker out onto the porch just out of the line of traffic and became a spectator. Rocking, with her feet swinging up in the air with every backward push, she watched boxes being taken off the wagon and carried into the house. Shooed from being underfoot, Meggie toddled past her grandmother, clutching her baby-doll under one arm. Inwardly, Stell deemed it amusing when she heard Meggie chant part of a silly ditty, "Home again, home again, jiggedy-jog."

She chose that moment to stand up, lean over the porch railing, and announce, "Wesley, when y'all get done here, you take an' go down to the house an' haul the rest of my belongings back up here."

Wesley and Travis were midway from the wagon to the house carrying a trestle table, but the impact of her words caused activity to stop in its tracks. Wesley's eyes were wide as he stared at Stell, unblinking. Not trusting his ears, he slowly shifted his gaze to Laura. Surely he had misunderstood what the woman said. *Lord, if this is a dream, please don't wake me up.*

Laura glanced from Wesley to Stell. Thinking she was joking, she waved her hand in flippant dismissal and told Wesley, "Why, you'll do no such silly thing! Mama's just pulling our leg. She's not being serious."

Stell stoically informed her, "I be-dogged if Mama's not dead serious. If you don't believe me, just ask God. Wesley, you go on an' do as I say. The matter's settled."

Laura looked like a child whose feelings had been hurt. "I don't understand, Mama. I thought you were satisfied living with us."

Stell shook her head in denial. "I wouldn't a-put myself to the trouble an' give up my house from the start 'cept to be a help to you when Meggie came along. Truth is, I wouldn't a-give it up then, 'cept you an' Wesley kept worryin' me, wore me down to a bitter nub."

Wesley choked at the comment and then hastened to disguise it as a cough when Laura shot him a look with her hands on her hips.

Stell continued, "I'm bound to be old one day. Lord knows I'm done set in my ways. But, it's time I move back up here in my house where I'm free to do as I've always done—where I'm free to be myself."

Laura couldn't believe what she was hearing. She tapped her foot testily. "Just what do you mean by that?"

Turning away from Laura, Stell presented her appeal to everyone else as if trying to pull the jury over to her side. "For one thing, she stays all a-quiver over my dippin' snuff." This was true. Laura frowned on tobacco-chewing inside the house. "Futhermore, I don't cherish all the comin's an' goin's—folks a-marchin' through the house day an' night like Sherman's army. All that racket makes my nerves sore as a rizen, not to say how it hinders my commune with the Lord."

Stell was impossible. While they all stared at her in ridiculous wonder, even Laura wanted to laugh, but she wouldn't let herself just yet. For all her practice putting up with Stell, this topped the cake. "Well I never! If only I had known. I had no idea you felt this way. If you were so unhappy all this time, why on earth haven't you said something before now?"

Stell shrugged her shoulders and admitted, "I didn't want to hurt your feelings."

Laura huffed, "Well, you should rest easy now that you got over that."

Laura looked over at Wesley with the slight hope that he might have something useful to say, but he didn't say anything. He was pretending to be distracted. Seemingly, some undetermined object had captured his attention out toward the pasture, for he was gazing in that direction as intently as a young bull would consider a herd of cows.

Seeing that Laura felt put out, Stell set about patching the rift.

Changing her strategy, she said, "Addie's young and able-bodied. She's more of a help to you than I am."

"Indeed she is!" Laura's voice had lost some of its earlier resentment.

Then Claire's character entered the scene, the plot unfolded, and the play really turned into a comedy. As if on cue, she jumped in and began to argue Stell's flimsy defense. The two were soon found out. It became apparent they'd conspired as far back as Christmas to share the house. There was no sense in them denying it.

While the drama played out for the audience, Addie didn't open her mouth. Though inwardly disappointed, she couldn't take offense. What could she say? After all, the house did belong to Stell.

Claire sidled up to Addie and whispered, "You don't mind, do you? If it's true what they say, 'familiarity breeds contempt,' this may be the more suitable arrangement. Should things come to blows, I'd much rather take a swing at Stell than you."

Addie smiled and assured her, "Nothing matters except that you're here." Her family was again intact.

There were no hard feelings, no ruffled feathers. Sarah Beth and Emily were happy as larks to be able to continue sharing a room, and at least this way, Addie would be allowed her own privacy.

The women went about setting up the house in grand style. Wesley and Travis finished unloading the wagon and made themselves available to put the heavier pieces of furniture in place. Then it started. "What if we move this over by the window? Wouldn't that look better over on the other wall? No, on second thought, move it back where it was before." The men soon had a bate of that; they could see they were useless there anyway.

Wesley hollered out over the cackling chaos, "Y'all can get your nest made without us!" They gratefully stomped out of the house. *Women!*

Of course when they left, all the women burst out laughing, glad to be rid of them.

Some time later, Laura whispered to Addie with a giggle, "I overheard Claire and Mama discussing how to make muscadine wine!"

Addie feigned shock, "Good gracious! Now they have their own den of iniquity. Next thing we know, there'll be an old tomcat or two prowling about the place!" It was funny to them now, and a bit scary too, for knowing Stell and Claire, there was no telling what mischief the two might get into now that they'd joined forces.

Sarah Beth's face brightened at an idea. She asked Laura, "Mama, can I call Mrs. Ellis 'Granny Claire'?" She liked the sound of it and said it a couple more times, just to see how it rolled off her tongue.

Stell overheard and didn't like the sound of it one bit. Before Laura could answer, she drew the line. "Don't talk foolishness, girl. You don't have but one granny, and that's *me*."

Claire's initial intent was to kindly reject the title out of respect for Stell, but the woman's overzealous objection struck a sour chord with her. In response, she changed her tune and zealously wrung her neck. "That's right, Sarah Beth, you heed Granny Stell's advice. *Granny* is hardly a suitable endearment for me. I'm nowhere near as old as she." Her lips curled upwards triumphantly.

Stell sniffed. "Hmph! I see I've welcomed nothing but a pure liar into my home! Truth be told, Eve herself couldn't lay claim to bein' more 'n a day or two older than you at most!"

Claire could handle a springy jig. To Stell, she said, "Well, say what you will, young lady, but when my eyes get as dull as your ears, I reckon I can always hold to ol' Ben's tail an' let him lead me from here to yonder!"

Stell lightened up. She cupped her hand to her ear and yelled in jest, "Eh? Speak up, I can't hear you!"

After they all had a big laugh, it was decided right then and there. From that day forward, Claire would be addressed by the children as *Auntie* Claire.

Down at the barn, Travis swung himself from the empty wagon and asked, "You sure this ain't gonna be in the way here?"

Wesley chuckled. "Far as I care, my friend, it can set right there 'til the second comin' of the Lord." He was grinning ear to ear.

Travis studied him for a minute. Dang if Wesley didn't look three sheets to the wind. He gibed, "Man, what's ailin' you? You look downright goofy for a man that don't drank." He knew, but he'd get a bigger kick out of hearing Wesley say it.

Wesley made no pretense. He exclaimed robustly, "Heck, man, are you blind *and* stupid? My ma-in-law just moved out. This could very well be the best day of my life! I could just kiss Miss Claire!"

Gratified, Travis threw his head back and roared.

Winter succumbed. March eased out like a lamb letting spring frolic upon the land in a gentle dance set to nature's song of praise to the Good Shepherd, who so lovingly watches over His flock.

It was a time of renaissance. Daffodils awoke and sprang forth in sweetly scented bouquets that smelled of sunshine and swayed in soft breezes that whispered the promise of warmer days. An azalea bush at the far end of the porch grew impatient of holding its delicately furled buds and finally exploded into a dazzling show of brilliant white. A flamboyant display of pink and lavender lavished the front of the house. Wisteria vine, laden with clusters of lavender blossoms, climbed a wooden trellis and shaded the opposite end of the porch, while perfuming the air with its essence.

Red-breasted robins hopped about on spindly legs, welcoming the rebirth of tender, green sprouts. Fields were tilled. Rich, brown soil lay ready for the planting season.

Addie had never witnessed a more glorious spring. In the afternoon, she set out walking to visit Amelia and the baby but couldn't pass the woodshop without saying hello to Hiram and Daniel. As she approached, she heard Daniel whistling. It pleased her to see him so happy. Married life agreed with him.

When she entered, Hiram glanced up from what he was doing

and drawled mildly, "Well, I heard you drew the short straw up at Stell's place."

She smiled and said teasingly, "I did. But it's probably safer for everyone this way, keeping those two hemmed up in the same house, under quarantine. However, Travis assures me insanity is not contagious."

He and Daniel chuckled.

They talked on for a few minutes before Addie said, "Well, I didn't mean to hinder y'all from your work. I'll be on my way."

She and Hiram saw each other so regularly, she honestly couldn't say if she'd ever noticed the depth of his eyes before, but as she started to leave, Hiram looked at her, and their eyes met briefly. When he turned his attention back to the cabinet he was working on, Addie gave pause as something suddenly caused her to remember. *He's looked at me with those same eyes before. Warm and startlingly blue, with crinkles at the corners when he smiled at her…*

For a fleeting moment, her mind flashed back to the day they'd first met, the day of Rachel's funeral. The thought lasted barely a second, like a slight whiff of something pleasant but indefinite that drifted past unexpectedly on a gentle breeze.

She turned and left the shop and headed in the direction of Daniel and Amelia's place, hardly able to wait to plant some kisses on little Rachel.

Easter was two weeks away. The weather held delightful enough to put even Stell in good humor. Sunday morning, as she clambered awkwardly into the buggy after slapping at Wesley's hand, rejecting his offer of assistance, she bleated out a proclamation. "If you're lucky enough to be alive on a day fine as this, then that's luck enough!" Even though she needed no help climbing into the buggy, Claire gratefully accepted a boost from Wesley, satisfied that it aggravated Stell to no end.

Two Sundays back, when the invitational hymn was sung, both

Daniel and Amelia had walked down the aisle and joined the fellowship of the church, professing their faith in Jesus Christ and accepting Him as their personal Savior—*for except a man be born again, he cannot see the kingdom of God.* Once warmer days settled in, the congregation would gather on the creek bank to witness their baptism in the cold stream of Cedar Creek—*for he that believeth and is baptized shall be saved.*

As was customary, when the worship service ended, folks shook hands with the preacher and filed outside, only to group together again. Meandering about the churchyard, neighbor visited with neighbor, exchanging niceties and chewing on bits of news. There was no hurry to get home for the lazy day, so everyone took advantage of this leisurely opportunity to mingle with their friends.

Laughing children chased one another. Girls wore their best dresses, adorned their hair with pretty ribbons, and muffled their giggles while they whispered coyly behind cupped hands. Boys stood back and watched the girls with hopeful, mischievous grins. Young courting couples walked, fingers entwined, their heads close, sharing secrets and making ideal plans from naïve dreams.

Women talked of quilts, recipes, marriages, and babies. Men mulled over weather, crops, and livestock. Dozens of tales, perhaps even a lie or two, were staged in the shadow of the church house while the amens of the worship meeting echoed still.

It was a perfect day. Addie noticed Hiram standing in the midst of several chortling men. He looked toward her. She smiled. He acknowledged her with a slight nod. They were merely two acquaintances exchanging cordial gestures.

Unexpectedly, their eyes held. Suddenly a feeling swept over Addie that took her completely by surprise. *How did I not notice before how handsome he is?* While the moment lingered overlong, expressions softened and then intensified. Hiram's gaze darkened from blue to almost black as his eyes traveled the length of her body in a bold caress then returned again to her eyes. Feelings which had long lain dormant suddenly stirred within her. Addie felt her skin flush as a tingling warmth sparked in her belly and spread quickly to the very core of her being, igniting a fire that threatened to consume her. Her mind flipped, and she ceased to breathe. Propriety demanded she turn away from his penetrating gaze, but her traitorous body betrayed her; her femininity reveled in the reawakened sensations.

After several seconds, Addie tore free and forced herself to turn away from him. She felt embarrassed and confused and a bit insulted. *How dare he presume to flirt with me so! I've a good mind to go over there and slap his face!*

Moments later, however, somewhat regained of a few shreds of composure, Addie realized there was no sense in denying herself what she was feeling; though she did admit the feeling had crept up and caught her completely unaware. Along with that admission came an instant dismay of her *response* to those feelings. What started out as an innocent glance had ended with her affording Hiram a glimpse of that sensual element within her that God ordained to be private and respected between a man and woman within the sacrament of matrimony. Ashamed, she thought, *What a tart he must he think I am, and at church, no less.* She felt plowed under.

Then it struck her. *Get hold of yourself, you idiot! Hiram doesn't think anything of the sort. How could he possibly see how crazy you are about him from all the way across the churchyard?* She realized it was her inner response to him that was improper, not the other way around. *Thank goodness! He doesn't even realize the effect those deep blue eyes had on me!* She'd only imagined that he had looked upon her so, and she reckoned, subconsciously, she must have wanted him to.

Convinced of this more likely probability, Addie relaxed. At least now she was aware of her vulnerabilities and the powerful undertow that lay in the depths of Hiram's startlingly blue eyes. And for this cause, she decided the most sensible thing for her to do would be to stay as far away from him as possible.

Addie retreated to safety and joined Laura and a group of ladies who were ironing out the details for the Easter Sunday dinner on the grounds and egg hunt. She responded graciously to Anna's curt greeting and was somehow able to alternately tolerate and ignore her waspish comments, all the while yearning to get home to be alone with her thoughts.

She didn't notice when Hiram bid *adieu* to the men and went his way toward home. Nor did she guess he had more on his mind than seed potatoes and corn.

Hiram was glad to be in his quiet, peaceful house. He never worked on the Sabbath, but for a while, he busied his mind with menial tasks to keep from thinking. He sat at his desk and scribbled away in his ledger, tallied columns of figures, and looked over order requests. After that he went and sat on his back porch with a whetstone and sharpened his pocketknife. Finally he resigned himself to explore the thoughts that besot him.

His mind drifted back to his marriage with Madeline. *Madeline and me sure made us a fair share of bad memories.* Built on a shaky foundation of youthful lusts, it hadn't taken long for Madeline to realize she'd made a mistake. Being married to him proved a disappointment compared to the life she'd really wanted. As it turned out, she wasn't the sort of wife he'd had in mind either, but he'd been committed to trying to make it work. Madeline, on the other hand, usually only tried to make it work when she wanted some *thing* from him. He thought, *And in God's eyes, a body's not for barterin.'*

He'd been a man alone for a good many years now. He was settled in, considered himself to have a comfortable life, and had his own business. He enjoyed his solitude, or at least he thought he did until recently. Since Madeline's death, he'd never really considered remarrying, nor had he come across a woman since then that he cared to pursue in that direction. Based on his personal experience, it had seemed sensible to him to accept the opinion of Paul in 1 Corinthians 7:8: "It is good to be unmarried."

His thoughts came to rest on Addie. He remembered feeling drawn to her beauty and sweetness the first day they met. He couldn't just stare at her, but he'd seen something very different in her eyes, an inner light, an alluring something that touched him deep in his soul. He remembered thinking, *I've finally met my soul mate, and she's already married, and pregnant.*

Since she'd moved here, to Golden Meadow, strangely he'd only felt drawn to her as a friend and confidant. He'd told her things about himself he'd never dare tell another living soul. He *liked* her and wanted her to *like* him too. Initially he'd felt sorry for her; she'd been through so much he had felt she needed protection from a friend.

From the beginning he'd known he could trust her. She made him feel comfortable and happy. From his observations and all indications, she was godly, a good mother, and a beautiful woman by anyone's standard.

As he sat there thinking about Addie's fine attributes, Hiram could honestly say he'd not once consciously looked upon her with passionate desire. That is, at least not until today. He couldn't say that now. After what transpired between them earlier at church, there was no denying his physical attraction for her. When he looked at her today, it was like his soul drank in the very essence of her.

Like most men, he craved intimacy with a woman, but he'd made an oath with himself not to let lust cloud his judgment again, as it had with Madeline. He was a man of God and didn't care to compromise his convictions or his morality again for anything less than a love set apart.

But, he *was* a man, and surely not so rusty at romance that he misinterpreted what he saw mirrored in Addie's eyes today. She'd looked at him like a woman filled with longing for a man. Presently, as he sat on his porch and thought of her, he was excruciatingly aware of the long-suppressed need she awoke in him.

Now it was what Paul said in the eighth verse he was contemplating: "For it is better to marry than to burn."

It was an abundant season. Addie stayed plenty busy with gardening and any other form of activity she could use as an excuse to keep a reasonable distance between her and Hiram. Ever since that day in the churchyard, she avoided spending more than a few minutes at a time around Hiram, and never alone.

In her eyes, the feelings he evoked in her had changed everything between them, and for that she was sorry, because she missed their friendship. Still, she was not prepared to accept that she was attracted to him in *that* way. Too much had happened in the past year for her to even think about moving in that direction. In the recesses of her mind, she sometimes wondered if she had anything left to offer a man in the way of love. Right now, it seemed impossible to consider being able to handle such a relationship. Remembering Alfred, sometimes she wondered if she'd ever even want to. One thing she did know for sure was that she liked Hiram way too much to toy with his heart.

Addie's aloofness toward him served only to confirm what Hiram prayed and hoped for to be true. He was sure the strong feelings he had for her were mutual. Even though he understood a lot about what she was going through, it was disheartening for him to watch Addie walk past the woodshop on her way to visit Amelia and Rachel without coming in to speak. He missed spending time with her, and it certainly wasn't his will that made her a stranger. However, to say that her friendship alone would be enough now would be a lie. He wanted more. His interest in her was deeper and burned within him relentlessly. But he would be patient, lest risk losing her completely. He realized that Addie had been tossed about and was vulnerable and afraid. She needed and deserved time to sort it all out. He prayed and had faith that her reluctance would pass.

Addie's coolness toward Hiram didn't go unnoticed by Wesley and Laura. It puzzled them, and they talked in private of it. Though uncommon for men to discuss such issues, Wesley made mention of it in passing to Hiram one day in hopes he could shed some light on the situation. The conversation was, however, brief. Hiram had long since pegged Wesley and Laura for matchmakers. For a minute, he said nothing of the subject. Then he told his friend in a slow drawl, "From what I can tell, Addie's took on her fair share of lead. Sometimes wounds are slow to heal. Let's just wait on the Lord."

May was lush and sweet-smelling. Red clover and black-eyed Susans swayed in balmy currents; magnolia, hydrangeas, and rhododendrons bloomed profusely. The children were out of school for the summer, and the canning season was upon them.

Near the end of the month, Hiram received a letter from his brother, Wilkes. It was to inform him that their father was ill and to ask, if it was at all possible, could he come home?

Hiram left for Virginia before dawn the next morning.

Monday, Travis was returning home by way of Golden Meadow from Oakdale. The morning's mist had hardly lifted when Addie glanced through the kitchen window and glimpsed him nearing the barn on his horse. She dried her hands on her apron and hurried outside to greet him.

He was hitching up his wagon when she strolled up behind him. He looked at her and said, "Mornin', Addie."

She teased him brightly. "You're up early. What's wrong— couldn't sleep?"

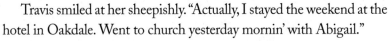

Travis smiled at her sheepishly. "Actually, I stayed the weekend at the hotel in Oakdale. Went to church yesterday mornin' with Abigail."

Travis seemed happy; his face beamed like a kid's in a candy store. She said, "I'm sure Abigail mentioned that she met Wesley and Daniel when they went to the bank in March to sign the deed to the old Lewis place. I'm anxious to meet this Abigail who, I am assuming, is responsible for that spring in your step."

"Maybe soon," was his short reply.

Travis was tempted to tell Addie that Abigail's birthday was at the end of July, and he was studying hard on surprising her with a marriage proposal, but that was a secret he decided to keep close to the vest for now. Anyway, he was too distracted. He was worried about a patient and in a hurry to get home. He'd simply come by for the wagon he'd stored in their barn the day he helped Claire move.

"How's Claire gettin' on … and the newlyweds?"

She laughed. "Claire and Stell get up every morning at sunup, sharpen their claws, and take turns despising each other till sundown. Daniel and Amelia are impossibly young and in love. Now ask me about Rachel," she suggested primly.

Travis mocked her playfully, "Why, I do believe this new role becomes you, Addie. I guess I never painted you in this light before— the doting grandmother."

She invited him in, saying, "There's coffee made. Come in, and you can tell Laura and me all about Abigail … and I'll tell you all about my grandbaby."

He shook his head. "Much obliged for the offer. Any other time I'd take you up on it, but not today. I really need to hit the grit back to Collinsville … to look in on Creenie."

Addie didn't miss the concern in his voice. "Surely, you don't mean Creenie is sick again. Claire thought her condition had improved."

Travis nodded. "It had for a while, but then her symptoms recurred last week, only worse. She's runnin' a high fever, weak as rain water, in terrible pain. When I saw her Thursday, she was debilitated to the point of just about not bein' able to walk. Hopefully, I left enough morphine to keep her easy till I get back over there this evenin'."

Travis scratched his head. "I've seen the same group of symptoms only a few times before. The disease seems rare … seems to only affect Negroes." He shook his head sadly, avoiding Addie's eyes.

Addie could tell he was guarding something. "What are you saying, Travis?"

He stopped what he was doing and rested his arm against his horse and told her remorsefully, "What I'm sayin' is there's nothing more I know to do for Creenie except treat her pain, keep her as comfortable as possible. I'm afraid she's dyin', and there's not a thing I can do about it, Addie." He couldn't hide his frustration at being powerless to help her. Despite his rough hide, he had a tender spot for his patients. He added sadly, "In fact, she was mighty low last week. She may very well be gone already."

Addie flinched. She was stunned. How could this be? "But, she's so young. Surely there's something …" But she knew if there was, Travis wouldn't be standing there telling her this. She asked him quickly, "Who's looking after Creenie?"

"Sassie's doin' the best she can, poor thing. Creenie doesn't have anybody else."

Addie thought of all the time and energy she'd spent tending to Rachel. Caring for the sick is hard, demanding work. Her heart went out to Sassie. "Sassie's but a child." Her mind was racing. She remembered how Claire told her Sassie bawled her eyes out when she learned she was moving away. It had pierced Claire's heart to see her cry and carry on so.

"Travis, don't leave till I get back." Addie rushed from the barn.

By the time she reached Stell's house, she was out of breath. She found Claire down on her knees, puttering in a flowerbed.

Addie didn't waste words. "Claire, how soon can you be ready to travel?"

Claire straightened up and searched Addie's face. She recognized

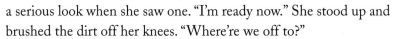

a serious look when she saw one. "I'm ready now." She stood up and brushed the dirt off her knees. "Where're we off to?"

Addie's tone held a sense of urgency. "Collinsville. Travis says Creenie's bad off, and Sassie needs our help. He's waiting for us in the barn."

Claire had heard aplenty. She went hastily into the house for a change of clothes.

The evening was fading when Travis, Addie, and Claire reached Creenie's primitive little cabin. When they entered, they were met with the overpowering stench of sickness. Sassie ran to Claire and threw her small arms around her waist. She buried her face in her chest and released a wave of gulping sobs she'd been holding back for days. The girl was exhausted and overwrought with pent-up emotion. Claire put a comforting hand on Sassie's curly head and patted her back as they held each other close until the tears subsided.

Creenie was alive, but barely. Her breathing was raspy and ragged. It took effort, but Addie was careful not to let her facial expression reveal how aghast she was at Creenie's appearance. There was no doubting they had come into a dire, desperate situation.

Relief flooded Creenie's face when she saw Travis. She reached a trembling hand out to him and managed a weak smile for Claire and Addie. Creenie's skin had an unnatural pallor; deep lines of distress were etched into her face. Her eyes were jaundiced, and she was shaking with a fever. There was vomit in a slopjar beside the bed. A large bald patch on one side of her head gave explanation to the clumps of hair lying on the floor and on her pillow. It was obvious that Creenie had pulled out handfuls of her own hair during episodes of intense and excruciating pain.

Addie turned to Claire. "Let's heat some water. Creenie will feel better after a bath."

Claire nodded. She spoke gently, "Sassie, show me where we can get some water and some firewood." Sassie took her by the hand and led her outside.

Travis mixed a little packet of a white powder in a small amount of water and spooned it into Creenie's mouth. "For the pain, Creenie." He held a cup of water to her lips so she could drink.

Creenie accepted it gratefully and then lay back and closed her eyes to let the medicine take effect.

Waiting on the water to heat, Addie went to find fresh bed linens and a clean nightgown for her.

Travis had a couple of other things to tend to. Confident that he was leaving his patient in capable hands, he told Addie he would return a bit later and gave her instructions about the pain medicine, should Creenie need another dose before he made it back. Addie assured him, "We'll be fine."

Addie bathed every inch of Creenie's body with warm, soapy water. She removed the soiled bedclothes and remade the bed. While she did that, Claire and Sassie cooked them a light supper of grits and eggs. They had built a crackling fire, and the house now felt and smelled clean and cozy. The morphine had eased Creenie's pain. She was drowsy but coherent.

In a soft voice, she told Addie, "You don't know how I 'preciate y'all comin' here. I wuz so 'fraid fo' Sassie to be here all by herself when I die."

Addie's throat tightened, and she was unable to answer. She nodded and squeezed Creenie's hand. There was sad irony in what she was thinking. She, Creenie, and Claire had spent all those hours together quilting, and now they didn't have a thimble full of hope that their friend would live to see another day.

Creenie said, "I feel so much better now, Miz Addie. Thank-you fo' da bath."

After they cleaned up the supper dishes, Claire heated another pan of water so Sassie could take a bath. It was a heart-wrenching scene when a freshly-scrubbed Sassie crawled into bed with her dying mama and nestled her head on her chest. Creenie folded her arms around Sassie, and mama and daughter lay crooning affectionately to each other until Creenie drifted off to sleep.

Claire and Addie teetered on a tightrope of dread and sorrow. Their beloved friend was dying. On the verge of tears, they avoided eye contact, knowing if they looked at each other they would give into the emotions of the other. They couldn't let that happen. Sassie's state of mind was dependent upon their composure.

Before Sassie got into her own bed, she insisted on reading a few pages from a book Claire gave her before leaving for Golden Meadow. Her progress was remarkable. She had truly become a good reader. When Claire and Addie praised her, her smile lit up the room.

It wasn't long before the tired girl fell fast asleep.

Claire looked down at Sassie's sweet, peaceful face and whispered to Addie, "That's probably the first sleep this baby's had in days." Not long afterward, Claire nodded off in a chair near Sassie's bed, leaving Addie to keep vigil over Creenie. It was pitch dark, except for the smoking, leaping flame of a single oil lamp.

Sometime later, Addie watched Creenie's legs draw up and spasm uncontrollably. She groaned in a fitful sleep. She was burning up with a fever. Addie dipped a rag in cool water and squeezed it out and placed it lightly on Creenie's forehead.

Creenie's eyes fluttered open. At first she didn't know where she was, but she felt like she'd traveled from somewhere very far away to get there. Everything looked hazy. Once her sight adjusted to her surroundings, she saw Addie sitting in a chair close to her bed and smiled as she remembered.

Addie whispered, "Do you need some medicine?"

Creenie indicated no. There was something she needed to tell Addie while they were alone, while she was coherent—*before she died.*

"I'z at Miz Claire's house one day, an' she started talkin' 'bout da Lawd an' what all He done fo' her. I tol' her I bin hearin' 'bout da Lawd all my life in church an' I jus' figure He dere an' if I ever need

Him I'z to let Him know. But dat day when Miz Claire tol' me 'bout God's love an' how Jezus died on da cross to save me—my heart broke in two. Miz Claire axe me wuz I saved? I say no, but right den, I heard God callin' me, tellin' me He would save me. All I haf to do is axe Him to come into my heart.

"Miz Claire an' me got down on our knees, right dere in Miz Claire's house, an' I axe Jezus to come into my heart. It feel *so* good, Miz Addie, fo' Him to live dere all da time now. You know, I bin scart of dyin' all my life, but I'z not scart no mo'. Dis ol' Creenie done died one time—right dere dat day in Miz Claire's house. I know I'z gone be wif da Lawd when I die dis time."

Tears slid from the corners of Addie's eyes. Creenie wasn't finished yet. "Miz Addie…"

Addie sensed alarm and started trembling inside. Somehow she knew in her heart what was coming. Had she but allowed herself, she would have seen the truth long ago. She wanted to stop Creenie from saying it, tell her it didn't matter. But she let Creenie have her say, because she realized it was her way of purging her soul, making her peace with this world before she left it.

"I'z walkin' from town one mawnin'. I wuzn't nothin' but 'bout sixteen." Her voice broke. "I run in da woods to hide, but he seen me an' run after me… *he so strong*…" She let out a sob. "I'z so sorry, Miz Addie."

Addie reached over and patted her arm. "I know, Creenie. I know. I'm sorry, too." She felt her pain and her shame. She knew how brutally forceful and degrading Alfred could be. Creenie couldn't help what happened. She and Sassie, they were just two more innocent victims of Alfred's horrible meanness.

Creenie said, "Miz Addie, Sassie don't know who her daddy iz. She don't haf to know, but I want you to know, I ain't never regretted havin' her. She always bin my shinin' star. Da thang I hates most 'bout dyin' iz not bein' able to stay here wif her an' see her grow up, 'cauze da most special thang in dis life iz bein' wif da ones you love."

Both women were crying openly.

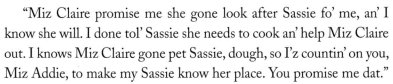

"Miz Claire promise me she gone look after Sassie fo' me, an' I know she will. I done tol' Sassie she needs to cook an' help Miz Claire out. I knows Miz Claire gone pet Sassie, dough, so I'z countin' on you, Miz Addie, to make my Sassie know her place. You promise me dat."

Addie nodded and wiped her eyes on her skirt. "You don't have to worry about that, Creenie. After you're gone, I'll see to it that Sassie always knows her place. I promise, after you're gone, she'll always know her place is with us. Her place will be with her family."

Creenie smiled weakly at Addie, "Don't fo' the life o' me know why we bof' cryin' like lil' babies. Ain't like we never gone see each other agin. We gone be up in Heaven together one day."

Too soon, the morphine wore off. A mournful, tormented whimpering sound escaped Creenie as the pain worsened and attacked her with a vengeance. Addie hurriedly medicated her, just as Travis instructed. She massaged Creenie's back until the agony numbed and she floated out again, back to that place very far away. *Please, God, be merciful, end her suffering.*

Creenie passed away the following day around noon. Claire, Addie, and Travis were in attendance at her funeral and burial at Soul's Chapel, the little clapboard church up on Nigger Ridge. Sassie clung to Claire's hand like a lost child, her heart rent.

As they loaded Sassie's belongings onto the wagon, among them were an assortment of heavy, thick-rimmed crockery bowls, cast iron pots and baking pans, and an array of utensils—all of which had been passed down to her from her late great-auntie Dorrie.

The next morning, on their way out of Collinsville, Addie asked Travis to pull over at Eminence Cemetery. She went immediately toward the weathered headstone of Samuel. Beside it was a newer one marking Rachel's grave. The small plot next to Rachel was where her baby was buried.

She had lost so much. Standing at her mama's grave, Addie wept bitter tears, her anguish multiplied now that she'd learned the circumstance of her death—*her murder.* Her grief brought so many things back to her. *I loved Mama so... why didn't I try harder to understand her when I was younger, while she was alive?* Now she was gone; it was too late.

Anger and resentment welled up within her, threatened to smother her, as she thought about Alfred and the unspeakable acts he had done. How many had suffered at his cruel hands? Words could not measure what she felt. She thought, *He murdered my mama, killed my unborn son, and raped Creenie and Amelia.*

She thought of Daniel, Emily, Baby Rachel, and Sassie and how interwoven their lives had become. In fact, Alfred had intertwined them. *Alfred fathered them all.* Her son was raising his half sister as his own daughter. It was almost more than she could fathom, too complicated to grasp. She looked heavenward and cried, "You can't possibly expect me to forgive Alfred for all he's done!" Her mind screamed, *Why did you let all this happen?*

Travis watched as Addie wandered about the cemetery, regarding her with both sympathy and admiration. He knew she was hurting, but he also knew her strength was a match to—if not greater than—that of any mortal man. Life had made her strong. He only hoped it wouldn't make her hard as well.

When Creenie realized she was dying, she'd confided to him the details of Rachel's murder and told him about Alfred molesting her years ago. He knew Alfred was Sassie's father. One of ethical discretion, bound to the confidentialities of those he doctored, he had no intention of ever broaching these private matters with Addie.

After a time, she came back through the rusty iron gate wearing a brave smile on her face. A few minutes later, Travis's wagon pulled slowly onto Monroe Road, setting out with yet another orphan and with all she had in this world, on a pilgrimage toward Golden Meadow.

God was with them.

Three weeks after Hiram left for Virginia, Wesley received a letter from him. It was short and to the point:

This is to let you know I am in Virginia with my brother, Wilkes. I was fortunate to have arrived timely and was able to spend some time with my father before he passed on. Those were precious hours, and I thank God I have them to memory. I have a few things to settle here yet. I look forward to being home in three or so weeks.

Hiram

He enclosed an additional note to Daniel, detailing certain things he needed him to take care of concerning the business and around his place.

Addie saw a huge smile spread across Daniel's face as he read the note from Hiram. There was a particular sentiment for the man cast in his features; his respect for his boss was obvious. Addie was warmed by Hiram's consideration of her son. He was a good man, and Daniel would do well to model himself after him. It was a sad reality that Daniel had never gotten a foothold in his own father's heart. Alfred had been so harsh and unyielding, so hateful.

In the middle of the night, Addie slipped out of bed and went out on the porch. The night smelled of honeysuckle and manure. She sat down on the steps and gazed up into the sky. The stars didn't seem as bright tonight for some reason. An owl hooted from a tree-top out beyond the woodshed. The stillness of the night bore down on her. Ben ambled up noiselessly. She reached out and stroked his head. His sleek coat was warm and slightly damp; dew was falling. For a while, she and Ben sat and kept each other company and listened to the hoot owl.

The next morning, not long after breakfast, Addie was sitting down to churn. Laura was at the well drawing a bucket of water. Just minutes before, Emily, Sarah Beth, Jesse, and Sassie lit out to the barn to play in the loft. All of a sudden, the children began hollering at the

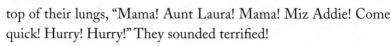
top of their lungs, "Mama! Aunt Laura! Mama! Miz Addie! Come quick! Hurry! Hurry!" They sounded terrified!

What on earth? Thinking the worst, Laura and Addie took off running toward the barn to investigate, afraid of what they might find when they got there, praying, *Lord, let them be all right!*

Hearts pounding, they hurried into the barn to see what all the ruckus was about. Ah, but they were flooded with relief. No one was hurt, no one had fallen from the loft, and there were no broken bones or necks. Laura half-heartedly scolded them. "For heaven's sakes! Y'all scared the living daylights out of us!"

There was no big emergency, except in the eyes of a child. They had all entered the barn and made a startling discovery. Jesse's hunting dog, Lady, was charged as the culprit of all the commotion. Proved undeserving of her name, she was lying in a bed of hay with a brand-new litter of pups. Even though he was nowhere to be seen, there was no disputing the sire. Each and every one of the snoozing, fat puppies were identical to Ben.

The children were overjoyed. When Addie and Laura left the barn, they were already fussing over which pup belonged to whom.

As they walked back toward the house, Laura smiled at Addie smugly and said, "I have a secret. I know something they don't know." In answer to the question on Addie's face, she replied, "Callie has five brand-new kittens hid in the woodshed."

CHAPTER 29

Thursday evening after supper, when Wesley headed out to the barn to take a last look at a new calf and smoke, Addie followed close on his heels.

"Wesley, is there something going on that I should know about?" she asked.

Earlier in the day she went into the central hall, the door having been left open to catch any breeze that might stir. Looking out, she'd seen Laura and Asher standing near the well. She'd paused and, for a moment, watched them curiously. As she stood watching, she noticed that Laura looked upset. Though she couldn't hear what was being said, by their attitudes she got the distinct impression they were engrossed in a heated argument. She wondered what they could be arguing about.

At first, Addie thought maybe she had simply misjudged the situation, but after Asher left, for the rest of the afternoon Laura acted preoccupied and somewhat distant, without her usual manners and humor. The more she thought about it, Addie was certain that something was wrong. Thinking back, it dawned on her that Libby had not come to play with the other children lately. And too, she remembered just days before she'd overheard Wesley tell Jesse sternly, "I can't help how they feel, son...how many times have I told you not to meddle..."

Never one to beat around the bush, she got right to the point. "Why are Laura and Asher quarreling, and why isn't Libby coming here to play anymore?"

Wesley's eyes avoided her face. Given his druthers, he would have welcomed a throbbing toothache over this suffering discussion with her. He could already imagine how she was going to react. He sighed heavily, exhaling a big billow of smoke.

"Addie, pullin' calves makes for a mighty long day. I really wish we didn't have to have this out right now."

With her suspicions confirmed, she said, "I say we do, especially since I have a strong feeling the reason has something to do with me." And she intended to find out what it was.

Wesley had hoped she wouldn't press him on the matter, but he knew his sister. *I might as well just get this over with.* "It's not so much to do with *you*," he said. He frowned, shaking his head. "Addie, you gonna stand there an' tell me you didn't foresee this happenin'?"

She did not understand. Her expression said *for heaven's sake, will you just tell me what's going on!* So in a measured tone, he did. "One day you an' Claire just up an' light a shuck, take off to Collinsville with Travis. Next thing we know, a few days later y'all come traipsin' back with Sassie. Without so much as a nod, y'all move her in like she was close kin. Now *surely* you must've figured that was bound to cause some folks 'round here to get all bent out of shape."

Addie stood with her arms folded. Her nerves were jumping, but her face showed nothing as she let the impact of his words penetrate. When she was certain she had it right in her mind, she said, "I see."

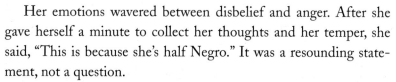

Her emotions wavered between disbelief and anger. After she gave herself a minute to collect her thoughts and her temper, she said, "This is because she's half Negro." It was a resounding statement, not a question.

After another thoughtful pause, she asked, "So this is how you and Laura feel?"

Wesley became defensive. "How can you ask me that? You know me, and you know Laura. I sure ain't gonna lie an' say we thought it was all hunky-dory to start with … it took a considerable minute for us to come to terms with it, but no, that's *not* how me or Laura feel."

Addie's mind raced ahead. "What about Stell?"

"You've been around Stell long enough to know that if she had any quarrel with Sassie, you wouldn't have to ask. Me, you, and the whole state of Mississippi would have heard about it by now. Stell thinks the world of that little girl."

"So we're just talking about Asher and Anna, then?"

"It ain't so much Asher, either." Not trying to make excuses, more in the way of explanation, he said, "They say hate is learned, but I'd swear to Moses it might be inherited. Anna, well, she sees folks the same way her pa did … he had two brothers who died in the war—"

It was futile for him to ponder the particulars. Addie interrupted him right there. "As I recall, the war ended a great many years ago, long before Anna was even born. Maybe I should go see her myself, inform her that Lincoln freed the slaves back in 1865," she fired sarcastically.

Wesley fired back more gently, "Lincoln might have freed the slaves, Addie, but he didn't change the color of anybody's skin. Neither did the war put an end to the conflict between the races or do away with any prejudice. I know the Bible says in Christ all men are equal. … *there is neither Jew nor Greek, there is neither bond nor free, for ye are all one in Christ Jesus* … but all men and women don't believe that."

Addie said, "I don't like any of this … I never considered … I swear, if Anna were here right now I'd—"

Wesley stopped her. "I'm not takin' sides, but before we get all judgmental and overly self-righteous here, let me ask you a hypo-thetical question ... an' I don't expect you to give me an answer ... it's just a thing for you to think on."

Addie looked at him and waited to hear what he had to say.

"Think about whether or not you might feel any different about this situation if Sassie was a twelve-year old *boy* instead of a girl. Do you reckon then you'd be as agreeable to *him* bein' raised up in the same house with your daughter?"

As Addie considered the question, it made her realize she didn't have the answers to all the complex social issues between the races. In truth, she was at a loss. *I cannot say for certain how I would feel under those circumstances.* She experienced a sudden twinge of hypoc-risy and frustration. What she was seeking was a definite solution for what now appeared to be an unsolvable situation, and for all their talking, nothing had really changed or been accomplished.

Albeit, out of fierce loyalty, she came to Claire's defense. "I can't answer your question, but I can tell you this: Claire's only faults are trying to live up to a promise made to a dying friend and loving a beautiful, innocent child. Claire's a peacemaker, and if she had any idea that bringing Sassie here had caused dissension of any sort between Laura and her brother, she'd probably take Sassie away from here tomorrow and move back to Collinsville with her ... and I don't think I could bear that." *Let anyone who dares tangle with me on this.*

Wesley put out his cigar. "Face it, Addie, this old world is full of prejudice; always has been, probably always will be. *'Cause some folks cling to it like hope.* I'd be willin' to wager they'll be havin' this same conversation a hundred years from now." There was another impor-tant question on his mind that he did not ask, one that had crossed his thoughts frequently. He couldn't help but wonder if Addie and Claire didn't know who Sassie's father was. He had a nagging suspi-cion, but figured if he was right, there was a can of worms best kept the lid on. He threw his arm over Addie's shoulder. "Bet I know something that will make us both feel better … another piece of that chocolate pie we had at supper."

She smiled. She hated it when her brother was right. Arm in arm, they headed for the house without another word.

They hadn't understood everything they'd heard but enough. The four friends—Sarah Beth, Emily, Sassie, and Libby—were up in the hayloft, huddled close, wiping away their sad, little tears.

The following morning, in the peaceful reverie of dawn, Asher and Anna came looking for Libby. It took only minutes to establish that not only she, but Sarah Beth and Emily as well, were in neither the house nor the barn. The girls were nowhere to be found.

Amid Anna's hysteria, Laura and Addie pulled wrappers over their nightgowns, Laura, Addie, Anna, and Asher set out on foot toward Stell's house to see if the girls were up there or if Sassie might know anything of their whereabouts. Of course, common sense assured Addie that Sassie was gone as well, but they had to start somewhere.

Wesley gratefully stayed behind with Jesse and Meggie, not wishing to have any part of the family squabble that was most certainly about to take place up the lane.

As they walked along, Anna ranted every step of the way, carrying on as if the very worst that could befall the girls had already been proved. "Horrible! Just horrible!"

Addie was practical and kept her wits about her. She had been through enough crises in her life that this one did not appear particularly catastrophic so far. She was confident that Emily knew how to take care of herself. So did Sassie. *We'll find them.*

Claire saw them coming and had, in fact, been expecting them ever since she'd discovered Sassie wasn't in her room. She met them at the door with, "They're not here, but come on in." Anna brushed past Claire brusquely. Stell was sitting in her rocker, immensely displeased by the unruly intrusion at such an unseemly hour.

The room erupted with a storm of questions and speculation. It was obvious the girls had run away for some reason, but why? Where would they go? How long had they been gone?

Trying to ignore Anna's harrowing tone, Addie asked Claire, "When's the last time you saw Sassie?"

"When she came home last night about dusk-dark. She had hay in her hair, told Stell and me she'd been playin' in the barn with the rest of the girls. Bless her heart, she looked worn-out... went directly to bed."

"There's no telling where they could be by now if they've been gone all night!" Anna hollered.

Addie raised an eyebrow, astonished at the woman's nerve. *Did she just holler at Claire?* Addie stared at her, frowning. *Why does she have to be so mean-spirited and rude? And prejudiced!* She couldn't imagine. "There's no point in us yelling at each other," she said. "That won't accomplish a thing in helping us find the girls."

Laura was wide-eyed with concern but not panicked. Asher proved to be somewhat of a solid presence, but like everyone else, he failed to get a word in edgewise over his wife.

After hearing what Claire said about the girls being in the barn, Addie understood immediately. *They must have heard Wesley and me talking.* Managing to call together some semblance of order, she briefly explained and ended with, "They obviously got their feelings hurt and ran away to teach us a lesson."

Anna responded curtly, "Such lessons we've been spared until you two dullards came along and degraded the proper order of things. No doubt this is our penance for allowing our children to skip about with that horrid little Negro!"

The words stung Addie's ears like briars. Before she could stop herself, she stepped forward and slapped Anna soundly across the face.

"Cease, I say!" It was a command.

There was a sudden hush in the room as Stell rose from her chair abruptly. "This is *my* house, and I *will not* stand for such!"

In a rare display of affection, she reached over and clumsily grasped Claire's hand. "This dear soul here is my friend, and I'll not hear another foul word uttered against her! And the same goes for Sassie!"

She hesitated, daring anyone to say more. She let another long moment pass for effect, allowing her silence to chastise them all.

"Y'all ever one ought to be ashamed of yourselves. Come stompin' up in here at this unholy hour with all your pretty talk… While them girls is out yonder wanderin' around lost as geese in tall grass. You have verily come to blows over some fearsome nonsense that wouldn't amount to a hill of beans if you was to die tonight. Again I say, shame on you!"

The search began.

Wesley saddled a horse and rode toward Oakdale. Addie went with Asher and Anna in the opposite direction, they turning west on Longview Road toward Collinsville.

As rightfulness would have it, it was Anna who spotted the girls. They were hardly two miles away from home, three of them sitting on the creek bank in the shadow of Cedar Creek Bridge, while Sarah Beth soaked her sore feet in the icy water.

Relieved to have found them so quickly, Asher and the women climbed down the steep embankment leading to the sandbar. As soon as she came near to her, Anna asked Libby harshly. "Just what do you think you're doing?"

Libby edged away.

Emily wasn't as easily intimidated. "We're sittin' here waitin' for Sarah Beth's silly feet to cool off. She didn't wear any stockings an' got a blister on her heel," came her spunky reply.

Addie went over and cupped Emily's face in her hands. "Are you all right? We were sick with worry not knowing where y'all were. You shouldn't have run off like that."

"I know, Mama. I'm sorry, but—"

Sassie blurted out, "Don't be mad at dem. It's my fault. When I tol' dem I wuz leavin', dey all tagged along behin' me like a pack of stray dawgs."

Anna barked at Libby, "You're gonna get it when we get home, young lady!"

Libby hung her head and replied meekly, "Yes, Ma'am." She gave her pa a quick, apprehensive glance.

Rubbing his neck tensely, Asher glanced unbelievably at his wife then back to Libby. "No, young lady, you're gonna get it right now." He kneeled down and held his arms open wide. "Come here, pun'kin." Libby ran to him, and they hugged tightly.

"I'm starving," he said. "How 'bout let's all go home an' have some breakfast?"

"I'm so hungry I could eat a horse!" Emily exclaimed in agreement.

"Lucky for you, that's exactly what your Aunt Laura is making," Addie teased.

Everyone started making their way toward the wagon except Sassie. Addie stopped and turned around and extended a hand to her. "You coming?"

Sassie raised her chin stubbornly and shook her head. "I ain't goin' back dere . . . 'cauze of *her.*"

Addie knew she meant Anna. She gave Sassie a small, wistful smile and said, "If you don't come home with us, Claire's heart will be broken, as mine will be. And Stell's . . . It just won't be the same without you there . . ." She let her voice trail off and stared out at the creek.

Sassie didn't say a word. She fought, trying her best not to cry, but a single plump tear rolled down her cheek and left a wet line on the side of her face. It made Addie remember the tear that rolled down Creenie's cheek on the day she told her and Claire about how her daddy and little brother had drowned. *The day we quilted.* The memory tugged at Addie's heart.

"Where will you go?" she asked softly.

"Back to Mama's house," Sassie answered. Her big, green eyes were filled with sadness, her chin trembled.

"Sassie, your mama's not there anymore," Addie said gently.

"At least she *wuz* dere! Her hands never touched the first thang here!"

"That's not true." Addie put her hand to her heart. "I have her handprint right here, where she touched my heart, and so do you … and I see her every time I look at you. You're mama lives in you, Sassie. Creenie lives inside your heart and mine."

Sassie couldn't hold back her tears any longer. She ran and flung herself into Addie's arms, sobbing. "Oh, Miz Addie, I miss my mama so bad!"

Addie felt the girl's grief, and it tore at her heart as she held her. "I know you do, honey. So do I … so do I."

A few minutes later, Sassie turned her face up to Addie's and asked, sniffing, "If I go back with y'all, iz we gone quit all dis fussin'?"

Addie answered her honestly. "Probably not. That's just how it is sometimes with people. We don't always get along; God didn't make us perfect. Sometimes we let foolish and ignorant disputes come between us and cause strife. But, even so, that doesn't necessarily mean we don't care about each other; it just means we're human."

As she stroked Sassie's hair, Addie thought about what she'd said and had an idea. "You know what? I don't for the life of me know why I didn't think of this before, but when we get home I have something to give you, something your mama's hands were all over."

Sassie looked up into her face hopefully. "What iz it?"

"Remember that beautiful star quilt she pieced together? The one we all worked on last October?"

Sassie nodded.

"Well, I want you to have it. *She* would want you to have it, 'cause she told me you'd always been her shining star."

Sassie's face brightened. "Miz Addie, I love you!"

"I love you too. Now let's go home."

Later that day, with everything back to normal, Stell settled comfortably into her rocking chair. She leaned her head back and closed her eyes. With hearty satisfaction she called back the memory of Addie slapping Anna across the face.

The vision so delighted her, she remembered it a second time.

Then thrice.

Soon, with the corners of her mouth curved slightly upward, she snored.

CHAPTER 30

"They shall obtain joy and gladness, and sorrow and sighing shall flee away." (Isaiah 35:10).

The days passed, and it was summer. They were in the middle of the main harvest and canning season. On this particular hot and muggy morning during the last week of June, a denseness in the air foretold of rain.

Just before the break of dawn, Addie began stirring from an untroubled sleep. Her mind yet lingering in a pleasant dream, she heard a voice say, "Sometimes you have to fall in love more than once ... I've never stopped prayin' for the chance ..."

The voice, which she recognized, evoked within her a sense of melancholy, and even before she fully awoke, a pang of emptiness and loneliness jabbed at her heart.

To the distant rumblings of the approaching thunderstorm, she opened her eyes and got her bearings. As she lay in bed and stared at the ceiling, the deep male voice from the dream lingered in her mind. She thought of how the voice sounded like the man it belonged to— strong and very masculine.

Addie missed Hiram. While she went through the motions of her days convincingly enough, her mind constantly courted thoughts of him. In him, she had found a friend, and until he had gone away, she hadn't realized just how much his friendship meant to her. Lately, he seemed to be everywhere she looked. She saw him standing in her yard in Collinsville the day of Rachel's funeral. She saw him working tirelessly beside Daniel the day her house burned down, and she saw him standing up as Daniel's best man on his wedding day. She saw him slumped back in a chair in the woodshop with his long legs stretched out before him, telling her of his late wife, Madeline, *and playing Pa's fiddle on Christmas Day.*

Even if he seemed to always be there in the back of her mind, sadly though, *Hiram* was far away, somewhere in Virginia. Inwardly, Addie hung her head. How she regretted the way she'd treated him before he left. He'd been nothing but kind to her, a true gentleman. He hadn't deserved the way she'd treated him. She'd practically shunned him for the last three months. Now she was sorry she'd shut him out. Now she missed him terribly, and she missed their talks, hungered for the sustenance of their friendship.

Determined to set things right between them as soon as he returned, she ciphered the weeks in her head according to the letter he'd sent Wesley and Daniel. Realizing the time grew near, maybe even in the next few days, she rejoiced silently before she rolled out of bed to start the day. *He'll be home soon! It'll no doubt seem like a lifetime, but hallelujah, Hiram will be home soon!*

The following Tuesday, Jesse darted quick as a rabbit up the lane to the house, bounded up the steps and onto the porch, and interrupted the quietness of the afternoon. He was nearly out of breath when he exclaimed to Laura, "Mister Hiram's back! Mister Hiram's back!" Without taking time to say more, he ran across the backyard toward the field, shouting, "I'm goin' to tell Pa Mr. Hiram's back!"

From inside the house, Addie heard Jesse's announcement and flew to her room. Nervously she twisted her hair up in a loose knot and secured it with pins. She hurriedly looked in the mirror. She didn't have to pinch her cheeks; they were already flushed with the anticipation of seeing him.

Laura was at the stove stirring a pan of squash as she strode down the hall past the kitchen. "Addie, let's invite Hiram to supper tomorrow night…Where are you going in such a hurry?" But she knew. The sparkle in Addie's eyes gave her away.

Addie breathlessly tossed a reply over her shoulder, "I'll be back directly. I've got a fence to mend!" She practically ran out of the house, letting the door slam behind her.

A few minutes later, finding the door to the woodshop ajar, Addie went right on in, welcomed by the pleasant scents of pine and cedar. All the way there, she'd rehearsed over and over in her mind what she planned to say to Hiram when she saw him. And now there he was, right before her. Her heart leapt at the sight of him! He looked even more handsome than she remembered. Suddenly, her mind went blank. She went toward him with the prowess of a cat approaching a sparrow.

Hearing someone enter, Hiram turned toward her. Not expecting Addie, but very pleased to see her, as she stepped near, he smiled and fixed his thoughts to speak. However, before he had time to utter a single syllable, she reached up and took his face in her hands, pulled his head down, and pressed her lips to his. Hiram, eyebrows raised in surprise, didn't know what to make of this unforeseen quirk of fate, but neither was he fixing to deny himself such a fortuitous opportunity. Seizing the moment, he slid his arm around her and drew her firmly against his chest. His mouth moved over hers in a kiss that quickened his very soul.

Addie leaned into him for support. She thought she might faint from the thrill of the soft pressure of his lips moving slowly, warmly upon hers. The masculine smell of him permeated her senses; she felt the warmth of his skin through the cloth of his shirt.

For a moment, time stood still.

Suddenly, the spell was broken when a resounding *hrrrumph* echoed within the walls of the shop as someone cleared his throat. Addie jerked away from Hiram with a gasp and spun around to see Daniel standing with his arms crossed, grinning in amusement. So intent she'd been upon seeing Hiram, when she came into the woodshop, she hadn't noticed Daniel over in the corner, busy setting handles on a cabinet door.

She was stunned. It took a brief moment for the realization of what had happened to float back to her. When the full impact of her actions sank in, she was appalled, shocked at what she'd just done. *What came over me?* Never in her wildest imaginings had she behaved so. *I've had a total leave of sanity!*

Hiram was staring at her wearing a broad, boyish grin. Even though she had shaken him deeply, he managed to speak in his usual calm drawl. "Well, Addie, I was just tellin' Daniel how good it is to be home, but now that I've received a proper welcome, I believe I might have sorely understated that fact." He didn't even try to wipe the grin off his face.

Her ears roared with embarrassment, and she blushed under his intense gaze. Her mind raced. She figured she had two choices here, and since Hiram looked so enormously pleased—almost like he was gloating—her pride wasn't about to let him know for sure how rattled she was. *I can pull this off.*

Collecting herself, she swallowed hard and put on a confident smile as if what she'd done was an ordinary, everyday occurrence. She couldn't quite meet his eyes, and it took her a minute to find the words, but in an unfaltering voice, she said to him, "I just came up here because Laura wanted me to invite you to supper tomorrow night." She glanced over at Daniel. "Of course we expect you,

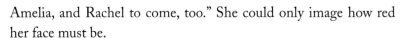

Amelia, and Rachel to come, too." She could only image how red her face must be.

Still smiling, Daniel nodded his head and said, "We'll look forward to it, Mama."

She turned and started for the door.

Hiram, immensely entertained by her novel attempt at landing on her feet in the face of adversity, couldn't let her go without calling after her teasingly, "Addie, tell Laura I said much obliged for the supper invitation. And, there's one other thing you can pass on to her for me. Tell her from here on out if she has anything else she wants me to know, I'll thank her to send you to tell me. I must say, you have a particular knack for deliverin' messages."

She heard Daniel chuckle softly in the background.

With unruffled poise, Addie slipped out the door into the warm, bright sunshine. Once outside, she exhaled deeply, a huge smile spread across her face. *Now I know what it feels like to make a complete fool of myself,* she thought. *And I can hardly wait until tomorrow so I can do it again!*

As foolish as she felt, she had never been so happy. The woman within her that she had been denying was beginning to resurface. She walked home beaming, her heart reawakened and filled with gladness that Hiram had come home.

The following morning, Hiram and Daniel were in Oakdale making the delivery of a corner cabinet Daniel had made to special order. As they were crossing the street, headed toward the general store, Travis spotted them and rode up alongside on his horse.

He pulled back on the reins and vaulted down from the saddle. "Just the hombres I need to see."

While they all shook hands, Travis hurriedly inquired after everyone—Addie, Claire, Sassie. He asked about Rachel and Amelia. Daniel assured him all the family was well.

Dispensed of niceties, he got down to the business at hand. "I kept thinkin' one day I'd mosey on out your way and extend the invitation in person, but now that I've run up on y'all, that won't be necessary." Hiram and Daniel listened as Travis told them about his engagement and upcoming marriage to Abigail Langford. Arrangements were in place for Judge Harvey Strauss to perform the nuptials in his chambers at the courthouse just before noon the last Friday of the month.

Hiram joked, "Congratulations to you; or my condolences, whichever the case may be!"

Travis's jolly mood bore proof he was without reservation or qualms when it came to the idea of his upcoming marriage. He said, "Abigail's spreadin' a rumor that she's havin' to hog tie an' drag me to the altar, but there's not a drop of truth to it. Truth is, I'm one lucky fool for findin' her, an' I figure if I don't marry her pretty quick, she might come to her senses an' leave me holdin' my hat in one hand an' my…" Thankfully, the clatter of wheels and hooves from the street drowned out the rest of that statement.

Laughing at his own wit, he continued, "Y'all be sure to tell everybody me an' Abigail want y'all to come an' stand as witnesses. After the lynchin'… I mean the hitchin'… we'll go mark the happy occasion with a fine meal before we have to leave town." Travis said they planned to be gone several weeks on their honeymoon, with one of their destinations being Memphis, as he was taking Abigail to meet his son. "This old pawpaw has a new grandson he needs to lay eyes on!" he boasted.

As they talked on for a few minutes, Travis told Hiram and Daniel he was on his way to look at a building on the next street that he was contemplating to purchase. Abigail already owned a house just on the outskirts of town, but he needed a place for his practice.

A few minutes later he swung himself onto his horse. As he cantered away, he hailed to them in departure, "See you all at the funeral… I mean, weddin'!"

Hiram and Daniel lumbered on into the general store. While

Daniel wandered about for a few minutes, looking with casual interest at this and that, Hiram walked directly to the back of the store, where he knew he'd find the grindstone he intended to buy for sharpening his shop tools. When he approached the front counter to pay out, Daniel was covetously inspecting a handsome rifle, not the first time he'd shown an interest in the gun.

"It's a dandy. You lookin' to buy it?" Hiram asked.

Daniel shook his head, not that the gun didn't meet with his approval. "Nope, today I'm just lookin.'"

Hiram urged him, "Go on, man, buy it. Reward yourself for the sale you made this mornin.'"

Daniel paused only a second before passing the rifle back to the storekeeper. He told Hiram, "I already spent more than I can afford." He counted out what he owed and picked up a box that was sitting on the counter. He started smiling because he already felt the ribbing that was coming as Hiram peered curiously into the box.

"Dishes! You mean to tell me that when confronted with the dilemma of choosin' between buyin' a box of dishes or that fine rifle back there, you picked the box of *dishes*? Boy, you got it bad!" He ragged Daniel mercilessly.

Daniel didn't care; he was stoked over his purchase but was willing to play along for the heck of it. In his own defense, he reasoned, "Well, we gotta eat to live, an' we gotta have dishes to eat off of." Then he caved in. "I can't lie. I'd rather have the rifle, but Amelia's birthday is just around the corner and I don't have money for both."

Hiram was having too much fun to let him off the hook just yet. He chuckled, "Let me just go ahead and tell you what's comin' your way next, my young friend. Soon as Amelia lays eyes on her pretty new dishes, she's gonna start beggin' you to make her a china hutch to display them in. You wait and see if I don't know what I'm talkin' about."

It was Daniel's turn. Now that he'd fed him enough slack, he jerked the line and reeled him in. "Go on. You best pick on me all you want to while you can, old man. Judgin' by what I saw yesterday, I reckon you'll be buyin' dishes an' makin' your own hutch here sooner than you think!"

Hiram grabbed his chest and carried on in mock injury, but Daniel noticed the turn about in prediction didn't really seem to bother him much, if any at all. And the prospect of Hiram and his mother getting together didn't bother Daniel in the least. In fact, nothing would please him more.

He slid the box onto the wagon while Hiram bought a newspaper from a boy on the corner. After they climbed up to the seat, Daniel shortened one rein and loosened the other, turning the horse and wagon into the street. Grinning, he could hardly wait to see the look on Amelia's face when she saw the dishes.

The next evening, their guest arrived promptly. His being received as practically a credible member of the family since moving to Golden Meadow, everyone was so glad Hiram was back that even without the food, the night still would have been like a party. However, Laura's kitchen had been host to a flurry of activity all day as she and Addie prepared a welcome home meal worthy of a celebration.

There was a steaming pan of peppery, buttermilk-baked chicken that made its own creamy gravy, which they spooned over fluffy buttered rice. Field peas were seasoned with just the right amount of both salt and sugar. A bowl was mounded high with yellow squash fried with onions, and there was moist cornbread that melted in their mouths. Addie baked a delicious dish of sweet potatoes drizzled with sugar and butter, topped with toasted pecans. Sarah Beth and Emily picked a pail of blackberries that Sassie turned into a sweet, juicy cobbler. The sumptuous meal justly awarded compliments to all the cooks.

The children snickered every time Stell declared, "A spoonful

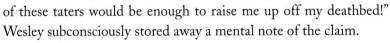

of these taters would be enough to raise me up off my deathbed!" Wesley subconsciously stored away a mental note of the claim.

Hiram wasn't much of a talker and had never been particularly fond of big gatherings, but he politely endured and satisfied all the questions asked of him about his trip to Virginia and about his family there. He told them his brother, Wilkes, had mentioned coming for a visit next spring. Of course, the main topic of conversation while they ate was the news of Travis and Abigail's upcoming marriage, and Travis's plan to move his medical practice to Oakdale.

Hiram was seated next to Addie, and though it may have been purely unintentional, in passing a platter of food, his fingers ever so briefly brushed against her hand. The roughness of his skin rubbed against the softness of hers in the merest whisper of a touch, making her heart skip a beat. Every now and then, their eyes met and a look of quiet understanding ebbed between them.

When they left the table, everyone dragged their chairs out to the porch to enjoy the light, nighttime breeze. Daniel and Amelia said goodnight and headed home to put Rachel to bed. Jesse beat Hiram at a game of checkers, while Wesley proved a more worthy opponent.

While everyone else talked and laughed, Stell shifted irritably in her chair. That was her way of letting them know she didn't approve of their loud talking. It disturbed her. She preferred to sit without conversation after a meal. Used to her contrariness, Claire and the others ignored her and talked anyway as she rocked in her chair and alternately snored and broke wind silently, holding an empty buttermilk glass on her lap.

Idly moving to and fro in the porch swing, Addie watched as the girls ran about the yard chasing fireflies. They were having themselves a time running through the cool grass barefooted. It had already been settled with Laura and Claire that Sassie could stay over and they could have a pallet party. Hearing them squealing with pleasure and girly silliness, she sighed dreamily and made the comment, "Wouldn't it be wonderful to find such joy again in the simplest of things?"

All agreed.

With the air sweetened with petunias and bee balm, everyone was happy and content on this warm summer evening.

It was nearly pitch dark before Stell and Claire decided it was time for them to go home. When they arose from their chairs and said their goodnights, Wesley stood up, stretched, and said, "Allow me an' Hiram the pleasure of walking you ladies home." He was hoping to score some points with Laura to redeem later on that night.

Stell rolled her eyes and snorted, "Horse hockey! You can just set your hinny back down. Me an' Claire are plenty able to look after ourselves, she just looks feeble. There ain't a cussed thang between here an' my house that has the guts to tangle with either of us!"

Wesley bit his tongue, thinking, *If the Gospel ever passed over your lips, there it was.* "Oh, I know you're more than able, Miss Stell, but we can't take a chance on any harm comin' to y'all, now can we? Who'd ride herd over the rest of us if somethin' were to happen to you?"

"You make a good point, but I still don't see the use in it," she acknowledged stiffly.

Fueled by determination and stubbornness, the lithe old women went sprinting across the yard toward the gap, Stell just muttering to herself, "I guess I'm bound to die one day—an' I'll be glad of it—but I can tell you when the day comes I'm done in, it won't be said Stell fell over dead from bein' scared of walkin' home in the dark!" Seeing the men in pursuit, she called over her shoulder, "But I can see you've got to be stubborn about it! You can waste your time if you've a mind to, but try to keep up, for mercy's sake! It's past our bedtime!"

Wesley and Hiram *followed* Stell and Claire home.

A little while later, as the men were strolling leisurely back down the lane enjoying a cigar, Hiram exhaled a curl of smoke and said,

"You know, Wesley, your sister's startin' to remind me a lot of my second wife."

For a moment, Wesley was taken back. "Dang, how many wives have you had?"

Hiram grinned at his friend and replied, "Just one … so far."

CHAPTER 31

"And the Lord God said, It is not good that the man should be alone." (Genesis 2:18).

It was about dark-thirty on the third Friday in July.

Earlier in the week, when Addie was walking home from Amelia's house, Hiram was waiting outside the door of the woodshop, watching for her to come back by. He lifted his hand and waved, motioning her toward him. As she headed in his direction to say hello, he came out and met her halfway. He didn't waste any time in asking her to come to his house for supper on Friday night. A smile played at the corners of her lips as she eagerly accepted without a moment's hesitation. He gentlemanly offered to fetch her in his buggy, and though she appreciated the gesture, she declined and told him, "That's kind of you, but it's such a short distance. I believe I'll just enjoy the walk."

Having so looked forward to this night all week, her excitement had made the days seemingly drag by at a snail's pace. Now she was finally walking to his house.

Dusk, her favorite time of day, wrapped softly and sweetly around her. A meadowlark warbled faintly, but the birdsong was fading, and insects had begun heralding the coming night. Honeysuckle and wild roses trailed along the roadside and infused the air with their rich, heady scents. As their fragrance penetrated her senses, she felt almost intoxicated by the pungent smells and peaceful sounds of summer, and the anticipation of spending the evening alone with Hiram.

Addie paused on the road and gazed up into the velvet sky and inhaled deeply. Her mind became flooded with the memory of another summer night not so long ago when she stood searching the heavens for answers. *That night seems like a lifetime ago.* While the memory brought her suddenly to tears, she prayed, *Lord, you've led me far in the year past. Please continue to lead me.* Her heart had made an incredible journey down a troubled road to get to this place.

When she arrived at his house, Hiram was waiting for her just inside the picketed gate. Holding the gate open, he greeted her with a relaxed smile as his eyes touched her face warmly, tenderly. "I'm happy you've come." Everything about him looked handsome. He was wearing a crisp blue shirt that matched his eyes. His beard was neatly trimmed. He smelled fresh and male.

Addie was a bundle of nerves but was glad to be there. Her heart was pounding as they went up the steps and onto his front porch. Hiram held the front door open and stepped aside for her to enter. It was her first time being inside his home, and it looked exactly as she suspected it would—neat and orderly with finely crafted furniture, but with the stark decor one expected from a man living by himself. *In need of a woman's touch,* she thought.

Supper smelled good. A pot was simmering on the stove, and the oven door was ajar. "It's too nice a night to let go to waste," Hiram told her. "I was thinkin' it might be fun if we eat outside."

Addie followed him from the kitchen through the screen door onto the back porch, where the table sat ready. Surprised, her breath caught in quiet awe at the sight of it. Hiram pulled her chair out, and she sat down.

Wildflower petals were strewn about the table, and at the center of it, a wreath of roses encircled a large glass jar. The jar was aglow and blinking—a lamp, primal in origin—alight and burning with the lively flickering of at least two dozen fireflies.

Drawn to her womanly air, Hiram bent near to her ear, his breath warmly fanned the side of her neck. He murmured a soft promise, "It is my aim, Addie Virginia, to bring you joy again in even the simplest of things."

Overcome with emotion, Addie flushed, and her heart raced out of control. Silently she repeated her prayer, *Lord, please continue on with me.*

The meal was delicious. They dined on roasted chicken seasoned with garlic and pepper and potatoes in a buttery cream sauce. Complimenting his effort, Addie said, "When you asked me to supper, I wondered if you could really cook."

He chuckled and told her, "I learned out of necessity. But I'll admit, I've choked down many a burnt suppers and failed experiments along the way—some worse than others. It's a small miracle I didn't kill myself!"

They talked and laughed for hours. Their conversation was easy and unhurried. They listened to each other with keen interest, and little by little, many truths were stirred and discovered—not only about each other but about themselves as well. By evening's end, they'd pretty much shared their life's stories, most everything lay bare between them. Their friendship warmed and comforted each other, not unlike a fire on a cold winter day.

It was late when Hiram walked Addie home under a hazy, magical moon. As they approached the house, he reached out and drew her hand possessively into his. Their fingers interlaced and fit together intimately. As they came to the end of the short walkway and stopped at the bottom of the steps, his face was very close to hers. Addie felt breathless in anticipation of the kiss she sensed was coming. In this close proximity, she could feel the heat radiating from his body, and the sensation of it seemed to press upon her skin.

She closed her eyes and reveled in the pleasing, manly scent of him as they bathed in the sultry mugginess of the July night and the nearness of each other.

Just as he was preparing to take Addie into his arms, Hiram heard a bump from somewhere inside the house. Did he imagine it? He looked toward the house and frowned. There was certainly no ignoring all the windows facing him. The thought crossed his mind that he and Addie might possibly be being innocently spied upon by several pairs of inquisitive young eyes. Children did that sort of thing, he knew.

While he stood there looking at the house and all those windows, his better instincts strained against his ardor. After a minute, he swallowed hard and came to a painful, exasperating decision. Rather than chance doing anything to jeopardize Addie's character, just in case the girls were watching them, he gallantly surrendered to sacrifice. Before turning loose of her hand, he gave it a tender, remorseful squeeze and muttered something under his breath she didn't understand.

With his jaw clenched, he said, "I really enjoyed tonight. I want you … I want you to come to supper again real soon." He turned to go and said a regretful, "Goodnight."

She had really expected him … had really *wanted* him … to kiss her. Baffled by his reluctance, Addie replied, "I enjoyed it too. Goodnight, Hiram." For heaven's sakes, was it really too much for her to think that they might share a simple goodnight kiss? Flustered and disappointed, she climbed the steps and went into the house.

On the long walk home, with his head filled with thoughts of Addie, Hiram mentally kicked himself over and over and groaned, "What is wrong with me? Why didn't I kiss her while we were in the privacy of my own house?"

It was a mistake he wouldn't bear repeating.

CHAPTER 32

On Sunday afternoon, Travis brought Abigail Langford to call.

When the buggy pulled up and came to a stop, Travis hopped down and reached up with outstretched arms to help Abigail down. The woman didn't simply step down; instead she jumped into his arms, letting him catch her about her waist and swing her around, twirling them like they were on a dance floor at a ball. When the dance came to an end, she collapsed on him, full of mirth. To those observing from the porch, it was apparent from the way they were carrying on, Travis had found the perfect mate for his devil-may-care attitude. The couple sashayed toward everyone, laughing in a light, carefree mood, his arm thrown around his fiancee's shoulder in a playful display of affection. Laura's eyes met Addie's briefly with one eyebrow raised slightly—cocked and loaded.

Out of the corner of her mouth, Addie whispered to Claire, "I reckon you can lay your fears aside. It doesn't much look like he

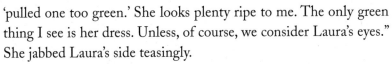

'pulled one too green.' She looks plenty ripe to me. The only green thing I see is her dress. Unless, of course, we consider Laura's eyes." She jabbed Laura's side teasingly.

On first sight, Addie was skeptical. She had not had any expectations of how Abigail might look, but she certainly hadn't expected her to look like *that*. The auburn-haired, green-eyed beauty was downright ornamental. Her features were exceptionally appealing, almost too perfect. Her tall, striking figure was clothed in a light green muslin dress, undoubtedly very costly.

However, once Abigail removed her hat and gloves and came toward them with her hands outstretched, it soon became obvious to them all that not only was she very lovely and self-assured in her physical sensuality, she also possessed the ability to draw folks to her with the personable warmth and openness she exuded. The effect she had on them, especially the men, was near mesmerizing. *Like flies to honey.*

In a cheery lilt, she exclaimed, "I'm so very pleased to meet you all at last. Travis has told me so much about you. I feel like I'm already part of the family." She looked around and gushed, "And what a beautiful place you have out here. I just love to ride out in the country!"

After introductions were made, she was invited to sit with them on the porch. Laura excused herself and went inside to get everyone pie and coffee. Of course, the men folk drifted off to smoke. Travis could always be counted on to be packing a pocketful of good cigars. Once the children hurriedly said a dutiful hello to the fancy, perfumed lady, they ran off to play.

Abigail commented, "I told Travis after I made acquaintance with Wesley and Daniel at the bank that day what a small world it is indeed. Until I met Travis, I had never known a single soul from Collinsville, and now here I sit with all you precious people. Life is odd, isn't it?"

None could agree more with that statement than Addie. *Yes, life is indeed odd.*

Claire asked sweetly, "How long have you worked at the bank, dear?"

Abigail replied, "Practically all my life. My father built the bank in Oakdale and ran it until he passed away. Now my brother and I own it."

Addie thought, *Not only is the woman beautiful, she's filthy rich as well.* It almost irked her that she was so down-to-earth and likeable. Yet at the same time, she couldn't help but feel an instant kinship to her. Clearly she and Travis shared a joyful romance; even a blind man could see the sparks fly between the two of them. And taking her privileged background into consideration, Abigail was born and bred to be a doctor's wife. Without doubt, the striking pair were custom-made for each other.

Abigail pretty much carried the conversation. She was charming and hospitable and generous with information about herself and her family. It was evident she was making every effort to make a good impression and was seeking approval and acceptance from Travis's friends.

She must have sensed some reservation in them, for she admitted, "It's been my incredible luck to have found Travis. He's a wonderful, fun, and caring man—and I adore him. At first I resisted his wooing because I was sickened at the possibility that I might ever again be so terribly wrong about a man—as I had been previously." She went on to confess, "You see, I was married before for a few years, to a tyrant. My first husband was a cold, poisonous, mean-spirited man that made my life a living hell, until I finally got up enough courage to divorce him. I thank God every day for Travis. He's taught me to trust again, and to love again."

Addie had heard enough, she was sold. As far as she was concerned, the stunningly gorgeous Abigail was the newest member in the circle of the sisterhood. And she wouldn't dare ask for fear of the answer, but she couldn't help but wonder if her first husband's name was Alfred.

Travis purchased the building in Oakdale he'd mentioned to Daniel and Hiram the week prior, but before he could set up shop, the place was in need of some renovation. He hired them to do the job for him and was hoping for completion of the work by the time he and Abigail returned from their honeymoon.

A while later, as the buggy departed, Abigail turned around in the seat and called back, "It was so wonderful to be here!"

Claire said, "What a delightful and energetic person!"

Addie replied, "She certainly is, and not a shy bone in her body."

Stell piped in, "And speakin' of body, the way that girl's pieced together would make Queen Esther feel clabber-faced."

As the buggy pulled off the carriageway onto Longview Road, Laura stood with her arms crossed, drumming her fingers on her forearm and watching as they slowly rolled from sight. Inwardly tapping her foot, she thought, *That woman is as loose as a goose's bowels.* Aloud, she asked cattily, "Do you think that girl can even boil a kettle of water?"

It was Wesley's turn to speak. "No doubt—just by lookin' at it!"

Even Laura laughed at her husband's tongue-tied, infantile fawning over the beautiful creature named Abigail Langford. The good doctor was going to have his hands full with that one.

And knowing Travis, delightfully so!

The following Friday morning, Wesley, Laura, Claire, Addie, and Hiram rode into Oakdale and witnessed the marriage of Dr. Brandon Travis Hughes and Abigail Catherine Langford. Following the ceremony, the celebration continued over steak dinners in a private dining room at the hotel directly across the street from the courthouse.

Shortly after the meal, the newlyweds left town on the stage en route to Memphis. After spending a couple of weeks in Tennessee, they planned to travel to Natchez and extend their honeymoon for a time at the stately antebellum mansion, known as Monmouth Plantation. Abigail had ties with the family who owned it, a friendship which had been established years before, when her father's business dealings took them to Natchez and Vicksburg

As they were waved off amid shouts of congratulations and wishes for happiness, Travis called out to them exuberantly, "See y'all 'round the first of September!"

Shortly after two o'clock on that very same afternoon, Cleve Walls led his limping mare into the livery in a rat hole of a town in western Missouri. The horse had thrown a shoe several miles back. The farrior told Cleve he'd have the nag ready in about an hour, so he had time to kill.

A recent, heavy downpour had passed, and the sun broke out, causing a muggy, suffocating vapor to rise off the hot mud. Cleve's clothes were still damp from being caught in the rain, and his unwashed skin gave off a strong, rancid stink kin to that of a buck polecat.

Standing in front of the blacksmith shed, Cleve rolled a smoke and looked up at the weathered signs painted on the buildings on either side of the road running through town. He didn't have the foggiest idea what any of them meant. He couldn't read a lick, so none of the lettering made a bit of sense to him.

As he stood there taking in the sights, he paid attention when a huge black steed pranced by with a man sitting straight and tall in the saddle. Something seemed awfully familiar about the rider. *If I didn't know better, I'd swear I jus' seen Alfred Coulter.* He blinked rapidly and thought, *Either mine eyes is playin' tricks on me, or I sho' done an' seen me a ghost.* But dead men didn't ride horses. Superstition caused his shoulders to flinch, and he shuddered as a chill ran over him. *A'possum jus' scurried 'cross my grave,* he thought.

Cleve watched as the man awkwardly dismounted the horse. He squinted and peered, trying to get a clearer image. *Well, kiss my black...*—that's when he knew for certain—*an' call it Christmas!* He slapped his hat against his dirty pants leg as realization seized him. "If dat don't beat all!" he exclaimed. He couldn't get over it. "I's stumbl't 'cross me a gold brick in dis here sorry place." It was a stroke of luck. His perfect white teeth flashed in a wide grin. Jubilation! *Alfred Coulter, alive!*

From across the way, he watched Alfred tie the reins to the hitching post and then hobble stiff-legged with an uneven gait, using a walking stick for balance. *Dat dirty dawg done got hisself a wood leg,* he mused.

Alfred pushed through the swinging door of a tavern across the road. Cleve waited a calculated time and then tracked through the mud and followed behind his old partner, his simple mind making a game of sneaking up on him.

Inside the saloon was dark and dank-smelling, permeated with a heavy, underlying stench of stale smoke. Except for Alfred and the woman behind the bar, the place was empty. Not many fools drank this early in the day. The barmaid was a fat, sagging woman with big red hands and a butt as wide as a door. She wore signs that proved she'd spent her whole life just shy of the bottom rung of society's ladder. Alfred was standing, propped up, his elbows resting on the bar.

Cleve ventured inside on his tiptoes, side-stepped a table and chairs, and eased up beside him. He dove in headlong, trying his best to sound clever, "Scuze me, suh, but is yo' name Jezus? 'Cauze you sho' do look like somebody done bin raized up out da grave." Cleve was tingling. He knew he was fixing to be entertained with an amusing tale of survival over a few shots of whiskey.

Alfred turned to stone. When he recognized the voice at his side, he felt like he'd been doused in the face by a cold gust of wet wind. Inwardly he flinched, but outwardly he stared straight ahead. He hadn't seen this coming. It'd been months now since he'd mulled over the possibility of being discovered. Silently he cursed. His mind was racing, but he willed himself to appear bland and indifferent.

Cleve was feeling important and sang gleefully, "Yassuh! You sho' made a name fo' yo se'f down in Mis'sippi!"

Alfred hardly blinked. His every nerve was standing at attention, but he stayed still enough to actually be dead. He inquired dryly, "Do tell."

"Good Lawd a'mighty! The whole town wuz talkin' 'bout how you wuz fried crisp as a cracklin'! *Tee-hee-hee!*" Cleve still couldn't believe his eyes. "Yassuh, ol' Ap wuz sangin' like a canary at yo' funeral," he cackled.

After a long pause, Alfred asked suspiciously, "Cleve, what you doin' way up here?"

"Ain't got no mo' friends lef' in Mis'sippi. I'z headin' up north where I'z got peoples to stay wif."

Alfred threw back his whiskey and waited. An awkward silence passed.

Cleve remembered something he felt compelled to tell. "Pete's girl done had a baby. White as cotton." He grinned. "Sho caint be none o' mine."

He was really starting to irritate Alfred. "Don't mean the bastard's mine neither."

"Ain't no bastard, boss. Naw, suh. Yo' boy an' her done moved off an' jumped da broom."

Suddenly he thought of something else. He poked Alfred's arm, which chapped him to no end. "Adder you an' yo' house burnt, Miz Addie an' yo girl moved off to stay wif her bruther. But din, not long ago, I seen Miz Addie at Creenie's funeral. Her an' da doc wuz dere together."

Alfred felt unwell. These noxious bits of news hit his stomach like a bitter cup of gall, and his mind reeled with the sour aftertaste. A dull, thudding ache set up in the leg and foot that was no longer there. He needed to get off to himself, far away from the jibber-jabbering of this ignorant, pestering nigger, so he could think. He wondered why Addie would go to Creenie's funeral? Had that crazy coon blabbered it around that he'd raped her? *Shoot, that was a hundred years ago!* And why was she dead? But he didn't really care about any of that. It just incensed him to think about the doc with his wife. He despised Travis vehemently. *He's bin a burr under my saddle since I first laid eyes on him.*

Testily, he told Cleve, "Ain't nothin' back in Mis'sippi I'm wantin' to be worried with, you hear? We finished with each other. Me an' you got no business, so you best be gittin' on up north, if you get my meanin.'"

Seeing the scowl on Alfred's face was enough to wipe the grin on Cleve's clean off. He'd seen that look too many times before. Still, his lack of gumption forced him to ask, "What iz you sayin', man?" But the weight of Alfred's words had already sunk in, and he was beginning to feel the noose tightening around his neck. Too late, he realized he'd made a devil of a mistake.

Alfred spewed scornfully, "Don't play big, dumb nigger with me, you big, dumb nigger. I'm studyin' hard on how I'm gone git rid o' you—bein's you run up on me like this. Right now, I'm thankin' hard on slittin' yer throat with a butcher knife. Be a sorry waste of a bullet if I's to blow yer brains out."

Cleve's guts got all balled up and twisted. In one hot minute, his day had turned to crap. Before he left, he blurted out a scared promise, "I ain't gone say nothin' to nobody 'bout seein' you."

With the cloud of Alfred's threat hanging over him, Cleve hurried to the stable for his horse. Distant thunder made him glance up nervously at the sky. Another storm was brewing. Shaking, he told himself, *Cleve, you iz one big, dumb nigger, jus' like da man say.*

What he'd considered earlier a stroke of luck had quickly turned into a curse. For the rest of his days, he'd be looking over his shoulder with the fear of seeing the madman back there in the bar stalking him like prey. *Dat be's one crazy white man!*

Inside the bar, now that he was alone, Alfred turned it over and over and over in his mind. Like the approaching lightning, the vision of Addie and Travis together flashed time and time and time again. The searing pain in his phantom limb shot up toward his head. His raging thoughts ricocheted, striking first one side of his mind and then another, until he was overtaken by a blinding headache. The wrath he had pent up inside rose like a festering boil, making his hands tremble so violently he couldn't lift his whiskey, lest it spill over the edge of the glass.

Right then and there, Alfred settled the notion in his head. He'd had several long and bitter months to think on it, and now it was decided.

He was going back to even the score with the man who'd months ago took off his leg. *The man who's now took up with my wife,* he thought. *An' while I'm there, I might as well pay a visit to my new young'un.*

Alfred said aloud to himself, "I reckon me an' Judge are headin' south." It was time for atonement.

CHAPTER 33

"This is the day which the Lord hath made; we will rejoice and be glad in it!" (Psalms 118:24).

With the main harvest and heaviest canning all but done, Wesley and Hiram planned a special outing for the whole family. For weeks they had been promising Daniel and Jesse a trip to Leaf River to go catfishing, so they set aside the first Saturday in August to go.

By mid-morning, picnic baskets laden with food, a couple of watermelons, jugs of tea and water, and a few more necessary supplies were hoisted onto a wagon. Even Ben jumped aboard and plopped down, slobbering. His tail thumped on the wagon floorboard in eager prospect of the unknown. Laura tried to persuade Stell and Claire to go along with them, but Stell crowed, "If I wanted to finish dyin' today, I'd go to the river." But then, looking ahead to supper, she added heartily, "Claire an' me will have the grease hot when y'all drag in."

Days before, when Addie first learned they were taking the children to the river, she instantly remembered the tragic account of Creenie's brother and father drowning and voiced her concern to

Laura. "Pa always warned us to be cautious of the river. He said it had dangerous sinkholes, and though the water may look calm on the surface, its underlying currents could suck you under." She knew some things weren't always as they appeared on the surface.

Laura smiled and assured her, "I promise—it's safe where we're going. You're gonna love it, you'll see."

Hiram took the cut-through road behind his place and drove about seven miles before he turned the wagon onto a narrow, rutted trail and followed it about a half mile into the woods. The trail came to a dead end in a grove of hardwoods. After he tied feedsacks over the horses' heads, they were left stomping their hooves and swishing their tails. They'd spend the better part of their day swatting at horseflies. Everyone was given something to carry as they walked down a path the last quarter mile to the river. Ben trotted ahead of them, marking his territory on low-growing bushes. When the river finally came into view, the children shrieked with excitement.

As Addie stepped out from the cover of the woods and climbed down the low embankment at the path's end, she could only stare at the idyllic setting before her.

On either side of the wide, lazy current stretched a long, pristine sandbar. The sand was brilliant white, almost blinding in the bright, glaring sunlight. Here, the water was shallow and lapped gently upon the shore. Anchored in the middle of the stream, the trunk of an old fallen tree divided the current, making a slight rushing sound as the water channeled around it. Just downriver, a steep red bluff towered above an interesting limestone formation, and near the edge of a quiet pool grew a clump of cypresses and willows with gracefully sweeping limbs. The intruders disturbed a pair of red-tailed hawks and a long-legged crane, all which took flight and soared to light on trees that were perched high upon the bluff.

The girls raced across the warm sand to test the temperature of the water and frolicked where the riverbed was rippled by the current. Addie helped Laura spread a coverlet on the sand to sit on

while the men made a make-shift tent from a bedsheet, to provide shade for when the sun climbed high in the afternoon.

A short while later, the grown-ups ate informally, directly from the picnic baskets, but the children gave little consideration to the food that was brought. They were too captivated by the river to eat. Sassie, Emily, Sarah Beth, and Meggie went into the bushes and changed into their swimdresses and waded across the river to the opposite sandbar to explore. Laura followed to keep an eye on Meggie.

Rachel fussed with the tie strings when Amelia covered her fuzzy little head with a bonnet to protect her from the sun, but as soon as the baby was allowed to wiggle her toes in the sand and splash in the tepid shallows, she became so engrossed in this new activity she forgot all about the confining headdress. For a while, everyone was content to laze on the sand and relax in the serenity of this beautiful place.

Two weeks had passed since Hiram and Addie supped alone at his house. Since that night, they had not spent any time together except for the few hours last Friday when they attended Travis and Abigail's wedding with the others. Hiram and Daniel had put in a long week at Travis's new office in Oakdale, and while work may have been keeping Hiram's hands busy, thoughts of Addie occupied his mind.

He no longer bothered denying to himself that he was in love with Addie. He cared for her more than he'd ever cared about anyone before. He knew she'd come a ways to get to where she was and deserved to have a man who would treat her the way God intended for a woman to be treated. He wanted to be that man. He'd been praying about it for months now, and before this day was through, he aimed to tell Addie how he felt.

Reclining on his elbow on the sand beside her, he regarded her quietly. He wished he could read her mind and know what she was thinking. She sat with her knees drawn up under her chin, her feet pressed into the sand, absently gazing across the river to the opposite shore. The summer sun left a healthy glow upon her skin, and a soft wind played with a few tendrils of her hair that had worked loose

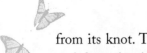

from its knot. The freed silken strands cascaded over her shoulder and down her back. Struck by her womanly beauty, he fought the urge to reach up to touch her face.

Addie felt Hiram watching her. She turned her head and glanced at him and noticed the seriousness in his eyes. She smiled and sighed, "It's so pretty here. Have you ever been here before?" The sunlight danced off the water, sparkling like jewels. An occasional fluffy white cloud floated by.

He told her, "I came here once before with Wesley to fish," and meant every word when he added, "but to tell you the truth, today it seems lit up in a different sort of way."

His words tumbled over in her mind. However plain he said it, the implication was unmistakable. Addie's heart beat a little harder as a thrill of satisfaction surged through her. There were things she wanted to tell to him, just now didn't seem like the right time to say what she wanted to say. It seemed awkward and too personal with everyone else so close. She always felt happy when she was with him, felt ever closer to him as time went by. She longed to be with him again in private. *Maybe next time he'll kiss me.*

After that Sunday back in the spring when their eyes met in the churchyard, she'd done everything in her power to deceive herself into thinking her response to him was merely a misfire of emotions. However, ever since he'd returned from Virginia, she realized she'd only been fooling herself. Hiram was in her heart. She loved him, and she loved the man he was. She now realized he was the man she'd been searching for all along, the man she'd prayed for all along, a man anchored on the Rock. Without warning, tears stung her eyes as she was overcome with her feelings for him. Not wanting him to see, she looked the other way. Once she had composed herself, she changed the course of her thoughts and steered the conversation toward a different topic.

"How's the work for Travis going?"

"Movin' along. There's enough work to keep us busy there for at least three more weeks." Inwardly he smiled. He knew she'd deliberately changed the subject. He would be patient and respect her boundaries for now. If he'd learned anything from his dealings with women, he remembered they were likened to working a crosscut saw. Don't waste strength pushing; they'll buck every time. Just pull toward you when it comes your turn. Unless he was completely illiterate and misreading the signals she'd been sending him since he got back from Virginia, he figured his turn was coming up directly.

He asked, "Why don't you ride over to Oakdale with me next Friday and see what we've been doin'? I was thinkin' we could have dinner together while we're in town."

Just the thought of it made her smile. She wanted to jump up and down for joy, but she tried to act casual as she accepted his invitation. "I'd surely enjoy that. Friday it is."

The girls called to Addie and pleaded with her to wade over to the opposite sandbar and see what they had discovered. Hiram stood up and said, "Come on, let's both go." He held out his hands, and she laughed softly as he grabbed her and pulled her to her feet. He waited as she gathered her skirt hem up and tied it in the front with her belt strings; then he again reached for her hand and grasped it lightly as they crossed the calf-deep river to where the girls were collecting smooth, colorful pebbles and mussel shells. Emily turned a shell in her hand to catch the light so Addie could see its pearly iridescence.

"Buttons are made from those."

Wesley yelled across the river to Hiram, "Come on! It's time we caught some fish!" Though reluctant to leave Addie, he heeded the call.

Daniel was baffled as they followed a path upstream to go fishing without poles, tackle, or bait. They walked along the bank until they came to a still pool above a beaver dam. Here, the water's edge was outlined with reeds, tall grass, and several huge oaks. The tangled roots of the mighty oaks trailed into the murky water which was dotted with craggy stumps and snags. It looked snaky.

About an hour and a half later, Amelia, Rachel and Meggie

were napping underneath the tent. A small swarm of yellow jackets frantically assaulted the sweet melon rinds. Laura and Addie lazily basked in the beauty and warmth of the day and the pleasantness of the place. Dragonflies skimmed the surface of the shallows as the girls continued to amuse themselves and each other, playing in the water and the sand.

The sound of distant hollering grabbed their attention and then brought forth chuckles as they recognized the source of the commotion. They listened as it gave over to absurdity. The jovial shouts and ridiculous, tribal-like chanting became louder and more distinct as the fishermen made their way downriver toward them. Finally they came into view, behaving more like rowdy juveniles than grown men. The foursome was balancing a sturdy sapling over their shoulders, proudly displaying their catch. And their catch was quite impressive! Tied to the pole were two croaking, monstrous-looking fish.

They held up the whiskered, white bellied fish and bragged, "These will easily weigh thirty-five to forty pounds apiece." The fish were bigger than Meggie!

Everyone gathered around to gawk at the grunting catfish. The girls wanted to touch their slick skin, but Wesley warned them to be careful of their spined fins. His and Daniel's chests, arms, and hands were marked with bleeding cuts and red welts—battle scars from wrestling with the angry fish as they noodled them from their hiding places. Addie was less than enthralled with the disgusting-looking creatures and said with a wrinkled nose, "They sure are ugly!"

Daniel was exuberantly telling the tale about how they waded and dove into the muddy water and grabbed the fish from underneath sunken logs with their bare hands. The way he described roundering with the mad, thrashing fish made the sport sound exhausting. All the while, Jesse described with outstretched arms and wide eyes the size of all the cotton-mouthed moccasins they'd scared off. The story of their adventure held everyone's rapt attention. Everyone's, that is, except Addie's. She had become distracted. Her attention had drifted elsewhere …

Hiram's pants were saturated from swimming in the river and clung to him like a second skin. His hastily donned shirt still lay open and exposed a tanned, naked torso. When he noticed where Addie's gaze was drawn, he purposely hesitated in buttoning his shirt. He figured right here and now he could lay one mystery to rest.

It seemed lately sleepless nights were a recurring event for him. Some nights he lay in bed while mentally pacing the room. Of course he knew the reason sleep deemed impossible was because his mind was obsessed with Addie; lately she was foremost in his thoughts. The certain lingering looks that passed between them, the sweet taste of her lips on his the day he returned home from Virginia, a brush of skin here, an inviting smile there … Of late, his celibate life proved to be but a tortuous, fleshy prison. Indeed, he wanted Addie to look.

And look she did.

Her eyes continued their slow ascent from his muscular thighs and narrow hips and roamed appreciatively over his hard, flat belly before moving upward to take in the expanse of his broad, hairy chest. *No doubt this was exactly what God had in mind when He created Adam.*

Her thorough appraisal of him finally led her to look upon his ruggedly handsome face. Here, her warm, liquid eyes were met with an intense and fiery stare. Hiram almost became lost in the deep pools of blue that so boldly beheld him. His heart thundered fiercely as his eyes bore into hers and held them magnetically. His eyes asked her hungrily, "Curious?" He was satisfied she was.

Under his heated gaze, Addie's heart was pounding, and her face felt hot.

At that moment, Laura put her hand on her arm and warbled cheerfully, "Yes, they are ugly, but just wait till you taste it. You won't be disappointed." Addie pretended to turn her attention again to the hideous-looking fish, but her mind was consumed with far more arresting things.

The jaunt to the river left everyone as lethargic as a dose of laudanum. On the way to the river, the girls had belted out silly rhymes, played annoying hand-clapping games, and repeated the dreaded 'how much longer till we get there?' at least a hundred times. On the way home from the river, however, the wagon ride was markedly quieter.

When the wagon rolled to a stop in the yard, Claire and Stell came out to see the fish and help them unload everything. Then, while Jesse watered Hiram's horses, the men started skinning and filleting the fish. As for the girls, especially since they had church the next morning, the women proceeded to draw water and sequestered the children inside the house to bathe them and wash their hair.

All day long there hadn't been a cross word spoken among them. Now, tired and irritable, the girls commenced to bickering. Sarah Beth started the fight when she told Laura accusingly, "Mama, Emily took my prettiest shell an' she won't give it back."

"Liar!" Emily retorted.

Sassie chimed in, "Yes, you did. I saw you."

"No, I didn't!"

Addie told her gently, "Emily, if you've got something that belongs to Sarah Beth, give it back to her."

Emily adamantly denied it. "I don't, Mama—she's lyin'!"

Sarah Beth whined, "Am not! Sassie saw you take it, too!"

Laura scolded, "We've had a good day. Let's not ruin it now by fussin' over a pile of silly old shells. Y'all just share them and get along."

"Well, you can't spend the night, so don't ask!" Sarah Beth told Emily prissily, sticking out her tongue.

Emily shot back, "You can't tell me what to do! Anyway, I *live* here! So there! *Ha!*" Addie gave Emily a look of warning.

Sarah Beth lunged at Emily and yanked her hair. Emily squealed and started crying like she'd been slapped across the face, but her wails sounded fake and exaggerated.

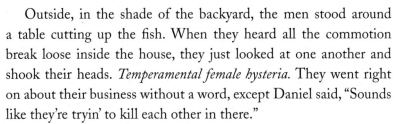

Outside, in the shade of the backyard, the men stood around a table cutting up the fish. When they heard all the commotion break loose inside the house, they just looked at one another and shook their heads. *Temperamental female hysteria.* They went right on about their business without a word, except Daniel said, "Sounds like they're tryin' to kill each other in there."

Back inside, all of a sudden, Sassie decided to side with Emily. "I wouldn't spend the night with you for all your dumb ol' shells, meanie!"

Sarah Beth ordered Emily, "Hush up, you big cry baby!"

Sarah Beth whimpered when Laura swatted her behind and demanded, "Young lady, you tell Emily you're sorry for pullin' her hair!" In all the noise and confusion, Meggie started to whimper. Rachel fretted.

"I'm not a crybaby!" Emily sniveled.

Sassie defended Emily. "You better quit, Sarah Beth!"

The arch of Laura's eyebrows should have been a dead give away. She'd heard enough. She snapped and yelled, "Everybody shut up! Right now! And I mean it!"

It became silent as a tomb.

Wesley cast a doubtful look toward the house and said, "Sounds like the massacre's over. Hope you boys are hungry. They's a mess of fish here."

Addie rubbed a thick, soothing salve on the girls' reddened faces and arms. Freshly scrubbed and soap scented, they slipped into their nightgowns, relaxed and ready for bed as soon as they ate supper. By the simple redemption of soap and water, they were all friends again.

The fish was rolled in cornmeal and fried crisp and brown. Claire had prepared a large bowl of potato salad and tossed together a cabbage slaw. Stell added bits of chopped onion and bell pepper to the cornbread batter and fried it on top of the stove. Jugs of chilled sweet tea were pulled up from the well and poured into glasses.

The meal was served outside. Wesley said grace for the food, and everyone dug in, starving after the long day at the river. Laura was right, the fish was delicious. Even Stell awarded Wesley a rare compliment by proclaiming, "This fish is so good I'd gladly eat it with somebody's teeth, should the Lord see fit to command such a happenin'!"

Quickly deciding how unlikely it was that God would concern Himself with her teeth, she offset the compliment by registering a complaint with Claire. "You was sure heavy-handed with the sugar when you made the tea! It's so sweet it makes my teeth ache. If they ever' one fall out here directly, I'll know who to credit!"

By now, Claire was used to Stell. She may have drawn first blood, but Claire was no victim. She smiled and replied nicely, "Well, if all your teeth were to fall out, I'd have to forfeit the glory knowing I had indeed missed my mark…" She paused a moment while passing the slaw to Stell. "…'cause I was aimin' at your tongue, not your teeth!"

Wesley smiled as he enjoyed a joke with himself.

Stell turned her nose up at the slaw and grunted, "Raw cabbage gives me the bellyache!"

Claire mused primly, "Pity."

During the meal, Jesse and Daniel told the fishing tale again for the benefit of Stell and Claire. Only this time around, the river had risen a few feet, the fish had grown more than a tad bigger, and the snakes were at least a foot longer!

Notwithstanding, the fish did the men proud. Everyone enjoyed themselves and had their fill, including the cats!

In accepting a cup of coffee from Addie, in a discreet gesture for her alone, Hiram let his fingers glide across the back of her hand in a fleeting caress that made her heart skip a beat. A short time later, she was disappointed to hear him offering Daniel, Amelia, and the baby a ride home in his wagon.

Laura told them politely, "Y'all don't have to leave so soon." Of course she knew everyone was tired; it had been a long day.

Hiram replied, "I best be gettin' on. These tired old horses need to be put to bed." He yawned broadly. "And so do these tired old dogs."

As farewells were exchanged, for a moment his eyes touched

Addie's. In leaving, he told her, "I really enjoyed today. I'll see you in the mornin' at church."

As soon as the dishes were done, though it was still early, Addie said goodnight and walked down the hallway to her bedroom, feeling lonely. At the washstand in her room, she poured water from the pitcher into the large bowl and bathed. After she put on a nightgown, she dampened and perfumed her hair and brushed it. Clean and relaxed, she stretched out across her bed, which tonight seemed larger than usual. She dozed off thinking back over the fun day and about Hiram, and his deep voice, his handsome face, his strong hands…

Shadows lengthened then disappeared. While twilight dwindled, Wesley and Laura sat together quietly on the porch swing, holding hands and flirting with each other. The moon rose, and the stars came out, and the soft and gentle rhythm of night descended upon the place like a sonata to their souls on this languid summer's eve.

It had been a good day.

Addie was dreaming.

> A storm was coming. She felt the distant rumbling of a thunderstorm. The approaching storm was ominous, big, and black. It was coming, coming, coming, closer and closer. The storm was thundering toward her. No, it was galloping toward her. The rumbling storm was a big, black horse galloping toward her, its hooves thundering. The horse called her name. No…someone on the horse called her name. Addie tossed fitfully in her sleep and turned onto her side. The horse rumbled past her and galloped off into the distance. The thunder faded as the storm moved on; then it was gone.

Addie was asleep.

"Addie." It was little more than a faint whisper.

Again, this time only louder, "Addie."

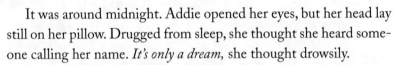

It was around midnight. Addie opened her eyes, but her head lay still on her pillow. Drugged from sleep, she thought she heard someone calling her name. *It's only a dream,* she thought drowsily.

"Addie." Now the voice sounded closer.

Her senses awakened abruptly. The voice was real. Someone was there. Startled, she sat up in bed, and a sense of apprehension filled her. Her pulse quickened. Her eyes, adjusting to the darkness, darted about the room. Moonlight filtered through the transparency of the curtains, causing the furniture to cast eerie shadows across the floor and ceiling. When her eyes moved toward the window, she gasped silently. Cold fear gripped her—her breath froze in her chest. Clutching the sheet close to her body, her hands began to tremble. In the pale light, she made out the silhouette of a man peeping through her window. She inhaled deeply to fill her lungs with enough air to cry out to Wesley for help.

"Addie, are you awake?" Suddenly, she realized. The low, hoarse whisper belonged to Hiram. Hiram was standing outside in the dark, talking to her through her bedroom window.

Upon recognizing his voice, relief swept through her, and fear was replaced with confusion. She slid from the bed and padded over to the window and whispered, "Hiram, besides scaring me half to death, what on earth are you doing here? Is something wrong?" She was bewildered by his unexpected presence in the middle of the night.

"Come outside, Addie. I need to talk to you."

There was a feeling inside her she'd never known. But that didn't matter right now. Without further question, barefooted and in her nightgown, she tiptoed from her room and made her way noiselessly down the hall, careful not to wake the sleeping household. Hiram was waiting for her on the porch when she slipped quietly through the front door.

They were standing very close. Her back pressed against the house as he leaned in toward her. She didn't know what to think as he moved in closer and braced both his hands on the wall behind

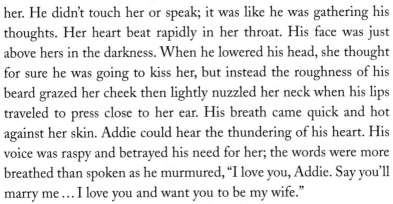

her. He didn't touch her or speak; it was like he was gathering his thoughts. Her heart beat rapidly in her throat. His face was just above hers in the darkness. When he lowered his head, she thought for sure he was going to kiss her, but instead the roughness of his beard grazed her cheek then lightly nuzzled her neck when his lips traveled to press close to her ear. His breath came quick and hot against her skin. Addie could hear the thundering of his heart. His voice was raspy and betrayed his need for her; the words were more breathed than spoken as he murmured, "I love you, Addie. Say you'll marry me … I love you and want you to be my wife."

For several moments, silence wrapped around them while time stood still and waited. They both knew there was no turning away from each other. From the first day they met, they were drawn together like magnets. Entranced and trembling, Addie whispered her answer against his neck. "Yes, Hiram, yes … I love you, too. Yes, I'll marry you." Her eyes swam with happy tears.

It was with a feeling of triumph that Hiram gathered her up into his strong arms and melded her to him. His mouth came down hard upon hers and moved over her lips hungrily, passionately, and without restraint. He kissed her savagely and greedily; he was starved for her.

Addie welcomed and returned his kiss eagerly, savoring the taste of him; his breath was warm in her mouth. She slid her arms around him and pulled him closer. Her hands stroked the back of his neck, and her fingers wove through his hair. Feeling her response, Hiram tightened his grasp about her waist and drew her womanly softness yet more snugly, crushing her against the steely length of his body. Her knees felt weak, she swayed and clung to him, hoping the moment would go on forever.

Hiram breathed in the fresh lavender fragrance of her hair and huskily muttered something unintelligible against her ear as his mouth moved to lavish kisses on the silken flesh of her neck and nestle in the hollow above her shoulder. His beard rubbed pleasantly against her skin, causing her to shiver at his burning intensity.

Hearing Addie moan softly beneath his lips, he realized her passion matched his. His mouth took hers again, and they were swept up in an overpowering, soaring whirlwind of desire for each other.

The stirring within her was maddening. Addie was a mature woman with instinctive needs and desires. The intense power of lust threatened her reasoning. Her body yearned for her to surrender her principles and yield to the sweet sensational craving, enticed her to give in to her carnal desires.

All the while, her mind struggled to think beyond this moment and toward a lifetime of pleasure. It was almost beyond her will to resist the flame kindled by Hiram's touch. Suddenly she was brought back to reality when, in the heat of his passion, he moved boldly and seductively against her with raw and intimate suggestion, proving the strength of his desire for her.

No! We aren't married yet! I can't let this happen! It was no simple task, but her good judgment overcame. She fought for and regained her self-control. Made aware of her immodest dress, she broke their deep kiss, turned from his arms, and pulled away from his passionate hold—not because she was angry with him or ashamed. She understood what he was feeling, for she was filled with the same physical longing as he. They responded to each other the way God intended them to—*as a husband and a wife!* She told herself, *We'll be married soon.* But for now, she knew they must guard their hearts and not let their attraction for each other hinder their personal relationship with the Lord.

Addie went and sat down on the steps.

After she pulled away from him abruptly, Hiram knew utter frustration. However, they worshipped the same God, and he understood why she made them stop. *But* even though he wouldn't intentionally do anything to dishonor this woman that would soon be his wife, he certainly hadn't wanted to stop when they did. He was a man, flesh and blood, and a man had certain needs! Of course, God knew this, for He created man and ordained marriage for just such a reason.

Hiram stood there with his chest heaving like a horse rode hard and ground his teeth while his mind and manhood sparred, waiting for his better nature to win out and take control of the reins. He saw it wasn't going to be easy for him not to act a fool when he was alone with Addie. He wanted her. At the same time, considering the manner in which she had responded to him, he figured he'd made a glad discovery, not a sorry one. It seemed both he and Addie had a few fires to put out. Mentally he rubbed his hands together in greedy anticipation of their wedding night and all the nights to follow.

A few minutes later, Hiram went and sat down on the steps beside Addie. He leaned over and nudged her playfully with his shoulder. Grinning broadly with a glint in his eye, he teased her in his low drawl, "Must be the beard, huh?"

Addie could still feel the flush of desire on her cheeks but refused to be bested by him. She chuckled and asked, "What else could it be?"

He reached out and pulled her to him. "Come here." He put an arm around her shoulder, and she snuggled close, pressing her cheek to his chest to listen to his heart beat. Never before having been so blissfully happy, Addie looked up at Hiram in the moonlight and murmured, "I love you."

He kissed her chastely on her forehead and whispered, "I love you too, Addie."

The next morning, Claire and Sassie were just clearing the table after finishing breakfast when Addie knocked once and strode into Stell's house.

Stell rolled out a welcome to her, saying, "Well, pull yourself up a chair an' set a spell before we have to head off to church an' suffer through another long, drawn-out sermon. I woke up filled with the dread that Lizzie Ainsworth will beller out a solo today. She sounds like a dyin' calf in a hailstorm. You can rest assured—we'll be spared neither boredom nor headache this day!"

Addie ignored Stell and marched over to where Claire and Sassie were. She was bubbling over, unable to contain her happiness a moment longer. "I've come to ask my best friend to stand up as my matron of honor, *and* I'm also looking for someone to make me a wedding cake!"

The announcement was music to Claire's ears. She replied gaily, "You've come to the right place on both accounts. We'll be there with bells on!"

As realization dawned upon Sassie, her mouth flew open and her face exploded into a bright smile. She rushed and threw her arms around Addie's waist, and the three embraced excitedly.

Stell expressed her disinterest by belching loudly.

Hiram wanted to get married that very afternoon, but Addie wouldn't hear of it. She wanted a church wedding and needed time to prepare. The date they settled on was the first Saturday of October.

Trying to reason with his impatience, she asked, "We've waited for each other all our lives, what's eight more weeks?"

He answered her agonizingly, "Fifty-six days." Inwardly he groaned, *Damn near an eternity!*

CHAPTER 34

"I am my beloved's, and my beloved is mine." (Solomon's Song 6:3).

Proprietors John-Ott and Leah Owens had come up with the name of the restaurant they opened in the former dwelling place on Sparrow Street long before they'd actually acquired the rambling old house from Parson Tilly's family after the beloved reverend passed away.

They knew whether prodded by manners, custom, unwritten law, or general rule, it's a given that most God-fearing folk feel inclined, at some time or another, to wring a chicken's neck, fry it up in a skillet, and feed it to the preacher. However, only a suspected liar wagering to prove himself would foster the bold-faced claim as to having been a *guest* for a meal at the preacher's house. Such an occasion was near unheard of.

With this notion in mind, the Owens figured it would be an amusing turnabout from the expected if it were to become common around Oakdale to hear folks say, "I ate dinner at The Preacher's House yesterday," or, "Let's go get some vittles over at The Preacher's

House." Thus, it seemed only fitting that the place on Sparrow Street continue to be referred to as it had been in the years past when Parson Tilly resided there. The restaurant was fondly referred to as The Preacher's House.

First, Hiram took Addie to see Travis's office, and they then went to The Preacher's House for dinner. The restaurant was a popular place, and the dining hall was near overflowing on this Friday noon. The atmosphere was stimulating and alive, bursting with the robust chatter among patrons and the noisy clattering of dishes and silverware as tables were being alternately served and cleared. Since arriving at the restaurant some forty minutes ago, their meal had been interrupted a few times, as first one then another stopped by their table to wish them well and congratulate them on their upcoming marriage.

For a seemingly endless while, Maude Thorne, the church organist, and Lizzie Ainsworth and her plump daughter, Priscilla, stood over them taking the liberty of peddling their opinions of and advice on wedding etiquette. Lizzie was a disagreeable, overbearing woman with a thin moustache, tiered chins, and a voice that Stell claimed would curdle milk.

Hiram's face stuck in a polite smile as he stared across the white linen-covered table at Addie, doing his best to hide his annoyance and endure the intrusion. When the two elder women's prattle gravitated toward their personal trials and illnesses, Priscilla noticed a small tic on his jaw, proof of his aggravation that they'd tarried overlong. She tugged at her mother's sleeve, urging her to move on to pester her next victim.

As the women bustled off, Hiram picked up his fork to resume eating. Addie leaned toward him with an apologetic smile and whispered, "News sure travels fast."

His hardy response was, "Tel-a-graph or tell-a-woman!"

Addie didn't try fast enough to suppress an uncontrollable giggle. She voiced a prediction. "Given a few more years, Maude and Lizzie will be a mirror image of Stell and Claire!"

Hiram easily envisioned such and nodded his agreement. Eying her plate, he asked, "How's your food?"

Addie had just about finished every morsel of her tender roast beef, mashed potatoes, and stewed okra and carrots. She tore off a piece of a delicate yeast roll, buttered it liberally, and answered, "Delicious." When his blue eyes caught hers devilishly, she realized he was teasing her about her hearty appetite. She wasn't one of those women who picked at her food to impress a man into thinking she was a light eater. She was by no means slight, however, not fat either. Her figure was trim but full and womanly in ways that Hiram found extremely disconcerting. She smiled at him playfully. "Whenever you're ready, sir, we can order dessert."

The creamy rice pudding was laced with just enough vanilla, rum, and citrus to make an otherwise dull dish interesting. They finished their coffee and made their way out of The Preacher's House feeling full and satisfied. As they left, Hiram charmingly offered Addie his arm, and she slipped her hand into the crook of it as they strolled along the boardwalk in amiable conversation. They were having the best day together, celebrating their love for each other.

All of a sudden she caught a glimpse of something at the edge of the street that made her stop dead in her tracks. An eerie sensation of impending doom washed over her. Her breath caught in her throat, and her surroundings became blurry and disorienting with an almost surreal aura. She felt lightheaded, felt the color drain from her face. She thought if she could but blink she might be able to chase away the vision of the apparition, but her eyes were fixed and wide open. Dumbstruck, she could only stare at the haunting image standing a mere few feet in front of her. *It is the black horse from my dream!* The memory of the rolling, thunderous beating of hooves was deafening to her ears. Alfred was here! She sensed it. He had somehow come back from the dead and was here!

She pulled back sharply on Hiram's arm and intuitively moved to stand behind him so that his body might shield her, protect her from the onslaught she felt was coming. Her mind was stretched taunt with dread, and an intense spasm of fear moved through her as she braced for the worst. She waited, expecting for them to come face to face with *Alfred* at any minute.

Hiram felt her stiffen beside him and looked at her tense, pale face with a concerned frown, thinking she had become ill.

"Addie, what's wrong? Are you all right, sweet? Do you need me to take you home?"

Startled by his voice, she jerked her head up to look at him. Before she could answer a lanky, blond-haired man that looked to be in his mid-twenties sauntered toward the smut-black horse and untied the reins from the hitching post. He swung himself up into the saddle with ease and rode the horse down the street. Moments later, they had vanished from sight.

It was then that Addie realized her foolishness. She let out a heavy breath and reprimanded herself silently. *It is only a nightmare. A horrible, bad dream! I've let my imagination run wild and conjured up a monster.* She inhaled deeply in an attempt to tame the furious racing of her heart. *Heaven help me! Alfred has been dead for almost a year.* She chided inwardly, *I'll not let a silly ghost from the past spoil this perfect day.*

Hiram was still awaiting a reply. With a worried frown, he asked again in a hushed, urgent tone, "Addie, are you ill? Do we need to go?" He stroked her arm, trying to soothe whatever it was that besieged her.

She shook her head. Forcing the disturbing image of Alfred and the black horse from her mind, she fought to overcome her nerves and recapture her composure. Touched by Hiram's concern and attentiveness, she felt herself relax a bit and, after a moment, became inwardly amused at the absurdity of it all. Feeling somewhat embarrassed, she gave him a trembling smile. "No, I'm sorry, Hiram. Forgive me. I'm fine. Really, I am." She managed a soft laugh, "I never figured myself as one to have the pre-wedding jitters!"

Hiram looked at her uncertainly for a few seconds and was

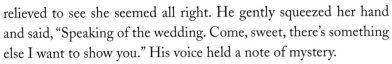

relieved to see she seemed all right. He gently squeezed her hand and said, "Speaking of the wedding. Come, sweet, there's something else I want to show you." His voice held a note of mystery.

Addie searched his face with an inquisitive sidelong glance as he guided her down the walkway.

A bell tinkled as they entered the door of a dress shop. The tall, smiling woman who greeted them recognized Hiram immediately. She remembered him from a few days ago and guessed why they were there, all the while thinking, *Be it my fervent prayer that I won't anytime soon forget that handsome face!* Just because she was some years older than him, she was still young enough to appreciate a handsome man when she saw one. She gave Addie a quick, appraising glance.

Addie could tell even by their brief exchange that the willowy clerk and Hiram were acquainted with each other, but he made no effort to introduce them, which she found a little odd. In fact, she detected perhaps a meek secrecy between them. *Maybe she's an old girlfriend.* That could explain the censor.

He addressed the woman, "Madame, if you would be so kind…?"

She nodded rapidly and hurried toward the back of the shop, disappearing through a curtain into the storeroom.

Addie looked at Hiram questioningly. She still didn't understand why he brought her here, and he wasn't talking. His expression showed nothing. While they waited for the clerk to return, she wandered about a table stacked high with several bolts of assorted fabrics, feeling somewhat dejected.

"Here we are," the woman crooned in a sing-song voice as she burst through the curtain and eagerly flounced toward them holding up a fancy gown. She cleared a place and, in a sweeping motion, spread the gown across one of the tables, proudly displaying the full length of it before them.

"Oh!" Addie was immediately drawn to the gown and inspected it with awe. It was the most beautiful garment she'd ever laid eyes on. The dress was made of smooth satin. The bodice had an ivory lace overlay embellished with tiny seed pearls and a scooped neckline adorned with a frothy ruffle of ivory lace. The long lace sleeves were sown to reach almost to the wrists where the bottoms flared slightly and were trimmed with more frilly ruffles. The dress gathered at the waist with a wide satin sash that tied in the back. A train of soft ivory lace fell from the back waistline and trailed at least an arm's length longer than the satin hemline of the full skirt. The gown fastened in the back with a long row of dainty pearl buttons.

A few minutes later she became aware there was a definite quietness about the shop. She looked up uncertainly. Hiram was standing near with his arms folded across his chest. The clerk stood quietly, her lips curved in a slight, knowing smile. They were both regarding her intently... expectantly... in anticipation of...

As Addie glanced at their faces, suddenly their secret revealed itself. Her heart began to race as it became clear. Now she understood perfectly well why Hiram had brought her here! He and the clerk were holding their breath awaiting a response from her, hoping the gown met with her approval!

The woman chirped, "The color is perfect for you. Would you like to try it on?"

Hiram gazed at Addie lovingly, his eyes twinkling, while hers swam with tears. "Do you like it?" She was at a loss, giddy and dumbfounded, so overcome she couldn't form words. Tears spilled silently down her cheeks.

The woman turned away ever so slightly and tried to appear distracted to allow Hiram and Addie a private moment, but she couldn't resist watching them out of the corner of her eye. The two made a good couple. Blinking rapidly to squelch her own tears, she felt caught up and swept away, honored to be privy to such a romantic scheme. She was almost begrudgingly envious of Addie, wistful that it was she being so chivalrously wooed and courted by this fine specimen of a man. She sighed dreamily.

Hiram's eyes bore into Addie's and held them magnetically. He closed his fingers around hers and spoke softly, almost shyly, feeling a bit clumsy with words in the presence of the clerk. "When I passed by and saw the dress in the window last week, it was so pretty it made me smile. So naturally I thought of you. I want to buy it for you, my love . . . for you to wear when we marry. That is, of course, if it suits you."

Overcome with emotion, Addie turned to again look at the dress. She touched it with trembling fingers and ran her palm over the smooth fabric. Hiram continually surprised her. Once again he'd tenderly traced a path to her heart and come upon a place never yet tried, stirring her to the very depths of her soul. Tears of profound joy spilled over and rolled down her cheeks. She tingled with delight as she fingered the glossy satin of the beautiful gown, thankful that she'd never mentioned it to him, glad that he didn't know. For if he had known, it may have made a difference in his choosing, which made her even more thankful and glad because his choice—his taste and wonderful sense of style—astounded her. She couldn't possibly have found a dress more suitable for herself or more suitable for the occasion.

Addie lifted adoring eyes to him and murmured in a strangled voice, "Oh, Hiram. I've never owned anything so lovely, and I don't believe I've worn anything yellow since I was a little girl." Her eyes were shining as she gave him her best smile and whispered, "It's absolutely perfect."

As they traveled home that afternoon and came upon a long, straight stretch of road with cleared fields on either side, Addie nudged Hiram and posed a provoking, hypothetical question. "Do you think since we're out here in the wide open, in broad daylight, where all the world and God can see us, if you were to stop the buggy and kiss me right now, do you suppose we could behave in a more appropriate manner than we did the last time?" She smiled at him impishly. Her recollection of *the last time* was forevermore and most fondly branded upon her mind.

Hiram pulled back on the reins so hard the horse turned his head to give him a damning glare. But he didn't pay any mind to the horse. He had far more pressing business on his mind.

Grinning at Addie fiendishly, he swept her into his arms and swore, "Sweet Lord, I hope not!"

CHAPTER 35

"Behold, thou art fair, my love; behold thou art fair."
(Solomon's Song 4:1).

The fair city of Natchez, built on bluffs overlooking the Mississippi River, was home to many wealthy planters and grand antebellum mansions. Of course, when the city was surrendered to the Union army during the Civil War, countless lives were wasted, and many of the grand properties were either seized by the enemy and ravaged or lost.

Days before, after bidding *adieu* to his son Brandon, Travis and Abigail boarded a steamboat in Memphis and traveled downriver to Natchez. The bells of St. Mary's cathedral were tolling when they disembarked at the most notorious landing on the entire Mississippi River, the port known as Natchez-Under-the-Hill. There a carriage awaited and had driven them to Monmouth Plantation.

Built in 1818, by Postmaster John Hankinson, the stately Monmouth was situated on a high hill about a mile from downtown Natchez. A few years later, John Anthony Quitman purchased the property for his bride, Eliza. Quitman, who served as a major general in the Mexican-

American War, was awarded a gold sword by President James Polk for his bravery in combat, and went on to become the governor of Mississippi in 1850. He and Eliza had seven children. Under a veil of suspicious circumstance, Mr. Quitman died in 1858.

Two of John Quitman's granddaughters, Eva and Alice Lovell, had recently moved back to Natchez and were once again living at Monmouth. Weeks before, when they politely issued an invitation encouraging their childhood friend and her new husband to come for a visit, Abigail and Travis had happily accepted. Now, their honeymoon was drawing near an end; they would be leaving on the stage bound for home the following morning.

Just before noon, Travis left the central hall of the mansion through the front entranceway, which led him onto a wide, columned portico. A giant, spreading live oak heavily draped with Spanish moss shaded the carriageway where a driver was waiting to take him to Dunleith. Travis was on his way there to call on his old friend Joseph Carpenter, a prominent banker who had hosted a reception in honor of the newlyweds the night before.

After dining outdoors on the courtyard, Eva, Alice, and Abigail took a walk about the grounds before retiring to their rooms for their afternoon naps. A winding garden path led them past the croquet lawn to an arbor canopied with wisteria vines that provided somewhat of a cooling shade from the oppressive heat.

Across the way, a wind chime tinkled on a charming gazebo that stood in wait to offer a private sanctuary for still moments. A gently sloping terrace crept to the water's edge of a small duck pond. Louisiana irises and elephant ears stayed within a fair margin of its banks, while cypress trees with fluted trunks waded out and sat in the shallows with their bald, knobby knees emerged. Crepe myrtles were in bloom, as was the rose garden, which lent a sweet perfume to the atmosphere. Beyond the pond, the beautiful gardens were bordered by the wild, green beauty of the surrounding woods, thick with hardwoods with an underlay of palmettos.

As they strolled along the floral paths, Abigail sighed. "No wonder Mother loved it here. It's so enchanting."

Eva looked around and replied wistfully, "Yes, but nowhere near as opulent as it was in the old days before the war."

Alice agreed. "God preserve us! What *would* poor Granddaddy say if he knew his beloved home had been occupied by those lecherous Yankees! Or that his descendents had to pay wages to his own house servants! He would surely have gone out to the woods and hanged himself... and been spared the fate of being poisoned..."

Abigail knew full well how their grandfather died, but spirited as she was, she didn't care to talk of dismal bygones. As they neared the green-shuttered veranda of the mansion, she exclaimed cheerfully, "Well, war or no war, Monmouth is still a grand place!" With genuine affection, she added, "You are dears for allowing Travis and me to stay here. You've been the perfect hostesses, and it's been wonderful to see you both again." She suggested amiably, "I *insist*—you all must come and visit us in Oakdale some day soon."

"How I wish y'all didn't have to leave tomorrow. It seems you only just arrived," Eva protested remorsefully.

Abigail slipped her arm through Eva's and said, "Travis and I simply mustn't delay any longer. Jonathan's been running the bank all by himself for almost a month now."

Having been reminded of Jonathan, Alice smiled and replied coyly, "And speaking of that handsome brother of yours, I suppose he's still the most eligible bachelor in town..."

The evening thunder cracked and rumbled as the winds changed slightly and blew in a cooling rainstorm from the southeast that tamed some of the air's sultriness. In a lofty, beautifully-furnished room, Travis and Abigail lay tangled in the sheets of a huge four-poster bed with an intricately carved headboard and swathed in yards of mosquito netting. Moonlight streamed in, and the breeze

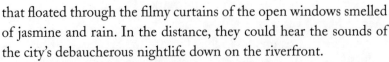

that floated through the filmy curtains of the open windows smelled of jasmine and rain. In the distance, they could hear the sounds of the city's debaucherous nightlife down on the riverfront.

While Travis puffed on a cigar, Abigail's flushed face lay on his shoulder while she idly stroked the mat of hair that covered his chest, savoring his clean, masculine scent.

"You happy, darlin'?" he asked huskily.

"Mmm...yes...blissfully," she purred contently. "I've had so much fun. I'm glad I got to meet your son and his family. Can you believe of all the places I've visited, I'd never been to Memphis before?"

Her chattering was hindering him from dozing off. He mumbled sleepily, "Yep, I've had me a time, but I'm ready to get home. I'm hopin' them boys have got my office ready so when we get back, I can start playin' doctor in Oakdale."

Abigail pushed up on her elbow and murmured brazenly in his ear, "Well...if you're just wanting to play doctor, I've got all the practice you need right here, Dr. Hughes."

Travis regarded her with a gleam in his eyes and chuckled. "Honey, I'm your man an' there ain't nothin' I'd like better, but as bad as I hate to admit it, I'm afraid you're gonna have to give me a while to catch my second wind. You know, you didn't exactly marry a spring chicken!"

Abigail sat up on the bed in all her dazzling splendor, her flaming hair a wild mass of soft curls tumbling over her shoulders, her ivory skin glowing in the moonlight. She reached and took the cigar from Travis and put it to her mouth and inhaled deeply. A moment later, when she blew out lightly through her pouting lips, a billowy ring of smoke encircled her head, very much *unlike* a halo.

With smoldering eyes and a seductive smile, she looked at him and said, "What girl would want a spring chicken when she's married to the cock-of-the-walk?"

Turned out, Travis wasn't near as old as he thought.

CHAPTER 36

"For it is the Day of Atonement, to make atonement for you before the Lord your God." (Leviticus 23:28).

Jesse slipped out of the house into the foggy dawn, carrying with him three things—a passion for hunting, a fanciful imagination, and the shotgun his Pa gave him some days back on his ninth birthday. Naturally, Ben jogged alongside the boy for company.

They hadn't gone far when the hound jumped a covey of quail hiding in a briar thicket. As the flock of birds scattered through the tall, dewed grass, Jesse fired and managed to kill a couple. He grinned with a heightened sense of prowess as he knelt and put them in his burlap game sack. He petted Ben's head in a gesture of comradeship and in celebration of their good luck. On a map of extraordinary adventures that existed only in Jesse's mind, he marked the place as hallowed, since he'd killed an acorn-fat tom turkey in almost the very same spot last Christmas morn. Before they proceeded on their way, both boy and dog faced the red eastern sky and peed on the sacred hunting ground.

They then picked their way through the woods and came out near a large chinquapin tree at the edge of the dead cornfield behind Daniel's. With summer getting on to an end, it was dove season. Every morning, just after daybreak and again in late afternoon, an abundance of birds flew in to feed on any stray kernels left among the dried stalks in the field. On this particular September morning, the intermittent thunder from Jesse's shotgun went on for about an hour as he blasted away at the doves that flew overhead. Finally his young arm gave out. His shoulder was bruised and stung from the force of the gun's recoil. He wandered around the field and gathered up almost a dozen doves. Before heading home, the hunters crossed the field to Daniel's house.

Amelia was out behind the house hanging the wash on the line to dry. She greeted Jesse and patted Ben's head. "I heard you shootin'. How many'd you get?"

Jesse was proud to let her look inside the bag. "Got a good mess an' two partridges." He looked around and asked, "Daniel's done an' gone?" He wanted to show him his kill.

Amelia smiled. She knew Jesse worshipped his older cousin. "Yep, he's already at the woodshop. Stop by there an' see him on your way home."

Jesse accepted her offering of a cold biscuit and berry jam. When he rose from the table, he spent a little time playing with Rachel. Readying to leave, he told Amelia, trying his best to sound older than his nine years, "I was plannin' on givin' y'all these." He emptied out the coarsely woven sack and gave her the birds.

"Well, much obliged, Jesse. Why don't you come back this evenin' an' have supper with us?"

He shrugged as he took up his gun and set to leave. "If Pa will let me, I'm comin' back over this a way huntin' this evenin'. I might stop by."

The boy and the dog headed down the stretch of road toward home. Amelia watched them go and smiled to herself when Jesse picked up a long stick and began to randomly whack at weeds as he

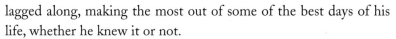

lagged along, making the most out of some of the best days of his life, whether he knew it or not.

After that, the morning hours fled into late afternoon.

Amelia felt lighthearted and free as a girl as she started their supper. Humming to herself, she wrapped a piece of bacon around each of the doves to season the meat and keep it moist while it roasted. She slid the pan into the hot oven and wiped her hands on her apron. She stirred the rice and covered it with a lid to steam.

As she set the table with the dishes Daniel had surprised her with a few weeks ago, she thought about how in his spare time he was making a hutch for her to display them in. *Daniel's so good to me and Rachel. I love him so.* Now and then, when her mind drifted back to her childhood days and she remembered how hard her life had been back then, she would bow her head and thank God for the cocoon of blessings He had woven so tightly around her.

When she looked in on Rachel napping peacefully, she was suddenly reminded of the clothes she'd washed and hung out on the line that morning. She slipped out the back door into the golden light of the afternoon, scattering the chickens as she went across the yard. Feathers littered the grass like confetti around the table where she'd plucked the doves a while ago. Amelia looked happily toward the clothesline, noting that most of the sun-freshened clothes belonged to her sweet baby girl.

Then, without a whisper of forewarning, the ease of the day ended abruptly.

A slight sound that seemed to come from the corner of the house made her turn her head casually to look. In the next instant, she whirled around and shrieked as a huge black horse rumbled toward her at great speed. Instinctively, her arms flew up as the horse lunged toward her violently. The armload of clothes fell about her feet.

Then she saw *him.* She gasped in disbelief upon recognizing the leering face of the man who sat astride the horse. Terrorized, her mind screamed, *This is not really happening! It's not possible! He's dead! He burned to death!*

Alfred urged the horse toward her in a lurching movement. Prancing, it circled her.

"You bin missin' me?" he sneered.

Fear possessed her. She let out a half-choked sob as she tried frantically to dart past the horse and run to the house. Alfred snatched at the braided leather reins and wheeled the steed around, blocking her path.

"I heared you growed up some. Ain't near scrawny as you wuz." He smirked as he eyed her lewdly. "Yessir, I'm fixin' to have me anuther fine time with my boy's purty lil' wife!"

Amelia tried to get away as he steered the horse and plowed over a high row of bright yellow sunflowers. Heavy hooves stomped roughly upon Rachel's sweet, little dresses and ground them into the dirt.

Her memory flashed back to the rape. What this monster had done to her was too horrible to think about, and now here he was threatening to do the same again.

"No! I can't; *I won't!*" Amelia had no intention of going through that again.

Time and again, Amelia dodged the horse. She'd go first that way, then another, trying to get past; but every time, Alfred jerked the reins, spun them around, and cut off her escape. She didn't realize he was purposely tiring her out.

The powerful horse pawed at the ground in angry frustration. It snorted and blew fiercely through its nostrils, rebelling against the rough handling. The harsh pulling and yanking of the bit was cruel and painful and tore at the sensitive corners of his mouth. His flesh was raw and bleeding.

Alfred laughed wickedly as he steered the menacing horse toward Amelia. He taunted her, toyed with her like a puppet on a string. Finally he played upon her biggest fear.

"I might as well take a peep at my baby while I'm here!"

Even though posed with the grave threat of being trampled to death

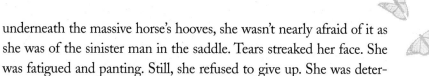

underneath the massive horse's hooves, she wasn't nearly afraid of it as she was of the sinister man in the saddle. Tears streaked her face. She was fatigued and panting. Still, she refused to give up. She was determined to keep this madman away from her baby. *Think! Think! Think!*

At last, it occurred to her. In order to keep him away from her baby, she must lead him away from the house. She made a daring decision to run in the opposite direction, away from the house, into the open field.

Driven by fear and determination, Amelia pushed onward into a battle she had feeble hope of winning. Of course, her desperate attempt to outrun the huge beast proved futile. Her fear excited Alfred. He laughed wildly and dug his heels into the horse's sides, making it charge after her, its hooves throwing up dirt clods all around, showering her with dirt. He took pleasure in terrorizing her. He was the hunter, she his prey. What chance did she possibly stand against him?

Finally, overwhelmed with exhaustion and despair, Amelia stopped. In dire desperation, she threw her head back and cried out, "God! Oh, God! Please help me!" Somehow she managed to fill her lungs with air and let out a long, loud scream. And another and another!

In the distance, Daniel was heading home from the woodshop. He was whistling as he walked along; he couldn't wait to see Amelia and Rachel. He didn't have to wonder what they were having for supper that night, Jesse'd come by and told him about the doves. He could almost taste them now.

Suddenly, the sound of Amelia's screams echoed across the way, and the fineness of his day shattered like glass.

Daniel broke into a hard run. When he rounded the bend in the road the length of the field stretched out before him, and from afar, he viewed the dangerous scene being played out. Recognizing Alfred, he thought his eyes were deceiving him. *How can this be?* In a panic, he went flying across the divide, calling out her name, and calling on the name of the Lord.

And Alfred heard.

He whirled the horse around. His eyes narrowed as he looked across the field and saw Daniel coming toward them. With an evil grin on his face, he told Amelia, "A'fore I kill him, I caint thank o' nothin' no sweeter 'n seein' the look on his face when he hears the thangs I'm gone do to you an' his mama—a'fore I kill y'all, too."

Amelia's mind careened as she saw Daniel running toward them, toward his death. "Go back! Go back!" she yelled until she was hoarse, but to no avail. As a last resort, she turned to Alfred and pleaded with him to spare Daniel. Alfred reached down and pulled a rifle from a sling hanging on the saddle. He lifted the gun, and with a murderous expression, he pointed the barrel. Amelia's breath came in quick gasps. With a sob and all her strength, she turned and started running.

Over the way, Daniel saw Alfred raise the gun. From the depths of his heart, he cried out beseechingly toward Heaven as he continued to arduously run toward them. A hush fell upon the earth as even the angels turned imploring eyes upon the Maker. All held their breath, in hope and faith, waiting for His answer.

An instant later, the crack of a single shot pierced the air.

And time ceased.

Daniel stopped in his tracks, petrified. He inhaled sharply, painfully. From across the distance that separated them, he watched helplessly as Amelia, his love, fell slowly, face-forward, to the ground. His features became twisted and contorted, revealing the anguish he felt deep within as his heart was wrenched. He let out a cry, but there was no sound. A deafening silence prevailed. The world stood agonizingly still.

Amelia lay on the ground, quivering, shaking uncontrollably. Her heart was like a drum in her ears. After resting for a few seconds, she rolled onto her back. The great horse loomed over her and reared. Alfred's balance was thrown. Dropping the rawhide reins, one of his hands went to the front of his shirt, the other grabbed blindly at the horse's mane in

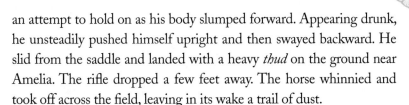

an attempt to hold on as his body slumped forward. Appearing drunk, he unsteadily pushed himself upright and then swayed backward. He slid from the saddle and landed with a heavy *thud* on the ground near Amelia. The rifle dropped a few feet away. The horse whinnied and took off across the field, leaving in its wake a trail of dust.

Alfred lay still, bleeding from a gunshot wound to his chest.

He looked at Amelia with a dazed, startled expression. Watching him warily, she reached down and snatched at her torn skirt, freeing her shoe. When he had raised the gun and she turned to run, her foot got caught up in the hem of her dress, causing her to clumsily trip over it and fall. Amazingly, she was unharmed, except for scraped skin on both elbows and a tender gash on one knee. She pushed herself to her feet, gathered up her skirt, and with renewed strength, ran as fast as she could toward the house. She had to get to her baby.

Daniel's heart soared with joy when he saw Amelia get up and run to the house. *Thank you, Lord, for sparing her!* He still didn't understand what had happened. He took up a heavy, knotted fence-post and approached Alfred slowly, cautiously, keeping his eyes on him and on the rifle that lay just beyond his reach. But as he drew closer, he could tell he was hurt bad. He wasn't going anywhere.

Alfred deliberately closed his eyes and refused to acknowledge his son's presence. Thinking it was Daniel who had shot him, he thought, *I never would-a pegged him for a killer.*

Daniel went over and moved the gun, just as a precaution. As he looked at Alfred, no useful words came to mind, and nothing came to mind of anything that could be undone. The kind of acts Alfred committed had the tendency of cutting a lot of ties, and other than suffering the temptation to shoot him a few more times, Daniel had no further interest in his pa. But it wasn't what the Bible said about vengeance belonging to God that kept him from it, nor was it the commandment not to kill. So long as Alfred was suffering, Daniel wanted him to live. So long as he was slowly and painfully dying, no way would he deprive him of one second of misery after what he'd done to Amelia. He turned away from Alfred and started looking around in a bewildered search for the one who had shot him.

After a moment, his eyes glimpsed movement at the field's edge. His spirit sank as the source of the valor that saved their lives was revealed. The price of their ransom proved great. *He's but a lamb!* Innocence lost is oft times costly, but always irretrievable.

Ben was trotting toward Daniel, wagging his tail; and not many paces behind was nine-year-old Jesse, on wobbly limbs, sobbing uncontrollably, toting his gun. He had come to the field to shoot doves and ended up a witness to all hell breaking loose. By the time he reached Daniel, the boy was as pale as a sheet and near hysterical.

"I didn't know what to do, Daniel! I saw that bad man chasin' Amelia an' tryin' to hurt her! I saw he had a gun! I jus' didn't know what to do!" It dawned on Daniel that Jesse had not a wink as to Alfred's identity. *This was good.*

Daniel felt sick as he put his arm around the boy's quaking shoulders and drew him close. He spoke to him soothingly, "It's all right, Jesse. You did right. Ever'thing's gonna be fine now. You're a hero. You saved us—Amelia and me."

Jesse wailed, "No! I didn't, Daniel! I was too scared!" He sniffled as he wiped his eyes and nose on his sleeve and pointed toward the house. "Soon as I saw him ride up, I knew he'd know what to do, 'cause he's a doctor!"

Perplexed, Daniel looked to where Jesse pointed. Walking toward them was Travis, carrying a rifle! It was Travis who had shot Alfred, not little Jesse. Travis was the avenger!

He sauntered up and greeted them in a calm and casual way, as if nothing had happened. He drawled, "I come to let y'all know we made it home. Had us a time, and Daniel, I need to pay you an' Hiram for the work you did for me. Y'all did a fine job." He cast an insolent look over toward Alfred. "Looks like I happen'd by at a right fine time. Luck of the draw, I'd say." He told Jesse, "Son, run home an' tell your

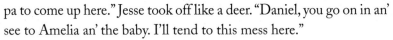

pa to come up here." Jesse took off like a deer. "Daniel, you go on in an' see to Amelia an' the baby. I'll tend to this mess here."

He didn't have to say it twice. Daniel didn't waste any time in hurrying toward the house to where his family was.

With them gone, Travis swaggered over and stood over Alfred. He was dying but was not dead yet. For a dying man, he cast a mighty cold, hard stare up at Travis, his face a mask of hatred. Travis saw his bet and raised him. He pointed to the oozing hole in his chest and, seemingly without an ounce of pity, said, "That's bound to hurt." Making no effort to conceal his disdain for the man, he added, "It's regrettable it cain't hurt bad enough to make up for all the trespassin' you've done against folks over the years."

Unwilling to let go of his pride, Alfred snorted at the remark.

Travis said, "I be-dogged if I didn't think we cremated your sorry hide." He was fishing for information about how he'd escaped the fire, but Alfred was too smart to take the bait. When he didn't comment, Travis mentally shrugged and changed the subject nonchalantly. "Alfred, I done took me a wife."

Alfred spat, "Ain't legal. She ain't free to marry long as I'm alive."

For a few seconds, Travis stared out across the field thinking about what he'd said. He smiled inwardly as he realized, *He thinks I married Addie.* And he intended on letting him die thinking it, too. He boasted, "That bein' the case, we sure had us a time breakin' the law. Yes, sir, that wife of mine is quite a woman."

Alfred grimaced as he heaved and coughed. Blood sprayed from his mouth. He challenged gruffly, "Finish it."

Travis saw the amount of blood that soaked the ground underneath Alfred and knew he was a goner. He observed sarcastically, "You are one foolhardy son- of-a-gun to be in such a hurry to depart from this world, consider'n where you're off to."

Alfred's voice was bitter as gall as he taunted Travis, "You ain't man enough to do me in!"

Travis pushed his hat back and laughed. His tone was patronizing as he said, "I beg to differ. While I truly cannot claim to be a cold-blooded murderer—like some we know—I have, in fact, studied on killin' you for a good, long while."

Alfred started shaking like wet dog; his teeth chattered, his chest wheezed. Travis looked on blandly. He tapped his wooden leg with the toe of his boot.

"Studied on how it'd feel to kill you that night. Always figured it'd favor somethin' sweet an' savory…like a fine woman…or a fine cigar…" He reached into his vest pocket. "One of which, coincident'ly, I happen to have right here." He rolled the cigar between his fingers and then sniffed it. "But, I'm done wastin' my time studyin' on killin' you, Alfred…" He bit off the pointed end and spit it to the ground. "'Cause I done know how it feels."

He struck a match, lit up, and inhaled deeply. A minute later he exhaled, and a lazy curl of smoke formed a cloud around his head. Addressing the smoke with a satisfied smile, he conceded, "It feels mighty fine."

Alfred had gone to hell.

However, as Travis looked down again at the dead man he'd so mortally despised over the years, in that moment he learned something about himself. Though he would never have given Alfred the satisfaction of knowing it, in his heart he deeply regretted that it had come to this.

His eyes smarting from the smoke, he dropped his cigar to the ground and crushed it underneath his boot, for presently it had lost its sweetness.

A few minutes later, Wesley, Hiram, and Addie arrived on the scene. There were many questions in everyone's mind, but answers were few, or rather none. They were all left stranded in the midst of a perplexing mystery.

Seeing Alfred shook Addie to the very core of her soul. To think, he'd been alive all this time! Trembling with the effort, it took every ounce of her courage to walk over to where his body lay. She couldn't stop herself from asking, "Is he *really* dead this time?"

Staring at his face opened a floodgate of memories, all bad. As she thought about all the atrocious things he had done, her contempt for him spread through her veins like ice water. Anger and resentment stung her eyes, but she denied herself a single tear. He had been the cause of far too many tears already.

She shuddered to think what might have happened had Travis not come along when he did. She tried to convince herself that all that mattered now was that Daniel, Amelia, and the baby were safe and well. There should have at least been some comfort in knowing that no one would ever have to fear him again, but somehow that didn't seem enough. She just couldn't seem to let it all go. Even though Alfred was dead, peace eluded her.

There was a collective agreement that it would accomplish nothing for the children to know the identity of the bad man, as Jesse had referred to him. At least for now, this would be kept secret from them, though Jesse would not soon forget what he'd seen.

Travis, Wesley, Hiram, and Daniel, with Alfred's body tied across the big black horse, headed out for the sheriff's office in Oakdale to tell of the occurrence. Since Oakdale was the county seat, the sheriff had but to summon Judge Strauss from the courthouse down the street. All the men sat around a big table and talked in length, purposing to put the case to rest.

Upon completion of the inquiry, all the facts having been presented and considered, Strauss proclaimed, "So far as I can see, the matter is settled. From what I've learned here today of the man Alfred Coulter, the scales of justice would not be balanced had he been killed a hundred times multiplied by five score. The killing was most certainly justified."

Travis was vindicated. There would be no trial, nor any judgment against him. It was declared justice had been served, atonement granted.

Alfred would be quietly laid to rest the following morning, buried in a lonely plot in Oakdale Cemetery. No one else would ever know, but it would be Travis who, over the years, would see to it that his grave was carefully tended.

In the stillness of midnight, unable to sleep, Addie went outside on the porch. It was drizzling rain. She was still having a hard time believing that Alfred had not been killed in the fire that destroyed their house and that he'd evidently come back there with the sole intent of harming them. *Alfred was demonic.* The thought made her shiver. But as she pulled her shawl closer against the chilling thought, although she tried to deny it, deep down inside she knew she'd been wrestling with a formidable demon of her own for months now, long before all the drama that took place that day.

She had every reason to be happy, and she was, except for that one persistent thorn that constantly pricked at her conscious and made her miserable. For a minute she tried to think of Hiram and how much she loved him and how she could hardly wait until they were married. But still, there was something amiss. There was a place in her heart where she ached, and that place gave passage to a sorrowful, hollow feeling that seemed to creep into her very bones.

And she knew why.

God, please stop asking this of me. You expect too much. I can't do it . . .

Addie sat down and pulled her knees up under her chin. Unable to hold back her tears any longer, she let them flow freely and drop to her hands like rain dropping from the eaves of the house.

CHAPTER 37

"Train up a child in the way he should go; and when he is old, he will not depart from it." (Proverbs 22:6).

Short of divine revelation, Hiram would never have thought six months ago that he'd be getting married a couple of weeks from now. Of course, in the back of his mind he'd known full well by marrying Addie he would also be taking on the shared responsibility of raising Emily. But now with the wedding date just around the bend, he was starting to get nervous. Doubt washed over him as he realized his life was fixing to be changed forever. He'd never had children of his own, and all of a sudden he felt like he was marching into battle armed with nothing but a slingshot.

A few days ago, he'd mentioned his concerns to Addie, but she assured him, "Hiram, we're going to be just fine. Emily thinks the world of you." Even so, he rightly realized that there was a big difference in Emily's approval of him as a friend of the family as opposed to her acceptance of him as her stepfather. Once he and Addie were

married, his and Emily's relationship would take on a whole new meaning. They needed to get to know each other.

After careful thought, he came up with an idea. He asked Emily out on a date. She'd never eaten in a restaurant before, so on Saturday he took the two of them to Oakdale to have dinner at The Preacher's House.

Over the clatter of dishes and the low rumble of the other diners' conversations, they enjoyed fried chicken, rice and gravy, cucumber salad, and snapped beans. Emily, feeling *so* grown-up, did most of the talking, while Hiram listened attentively. The way she told the story about the snake in Rachel's room set them both to laughing. But then she became serious and said, "Granny died the next day after that."

Hiram said gently, "You probably don't remember, but I was at your granny's funeral." Before she had a chance to answer, he added on a lighter note, "That afternoon, you came home with your Uncle Wesley. I still think about those delicious cookies you and Sarah Beth brought to me that mornin' while I was workin' on my house. You told me your mama claimed she could see clean through to a man's heart by way of a hammered thumb." The proverb made him chuckle again.

She nodded and smiled as she remembered. After a moment, she said, "I didn't see you at Granny's funeral, but I remember you were there the day our house burned down." She started to add, 'The day my pa died," but she didn't like to think about what had happened to him; it was too horrible. Sometimes it seemed to her that he and her granny died only yesterday; other times it seemed long ago.

As Hiram looked across the table, he couldn't ignore what he saw in Emily's eyes. For a moment she looked sad, and his heart went out to her. He thought of how in a short period of time she'd lost two people she loved very much, or at least she thought her pa had died in the fire. She had no idea that Travis shot him just recently. Anyway, things had changed abruptly for her, and he realized she'd learned at a tender age that life could break your heart.

By the time their cake was served, she was once again full of cheerful animation and went into a long story about why she wasn't going to make Callie move again, since she'd not too long made friends with all the cats in Wesley's barn. Instead, she had chosen a gray kitten named Shadow to take with her. Emily's bright-eyed imagination captivated and amused him. Hiram thanked God that this sweet, precocious child, who was going to change his life forever, had crossed his path. She was like an unexpected gift.

As they left the restaurant, Emily instinctively reached out and grabbed his hand. There was a new, unspoken certainty between them. She skipped along beside him, chattering nonstop.

It was Saturday, and the town was bustling. Emily took it all in—all the sights, sounds, and smells, having the time of her life. Walking along the busy boardwalk, they came to a shop, and Hiram told her, "Let's go in here. I need to buy a ring for my best girl."

While Hiram spoke with the clerk at the counter, Emily looked around curiously.

A few minutes later, satisfied he had found the perfect ring to surprise her with, Hiram paid the man and walked over to where Emily was browsing. When she glanced up at his face, she wondered why he looked so serious all of a sudden.

Hiram took a deep breath. "Emily, I just want you to know I thank God every day that I met you, and Daniel, and your mama. I'm a firm believer that if we trust God and abide in Him, He puts us where we belong. I believe He brought us all together because He knew we were meant to be a family."

Emily blinked hard, feeling her eyes wanting to well up unexpectedly.

He continued, "Here, in a few days, I'll be puttin' a ring on your mama's finger, promisin' my love to her, promisin' to be good to her, and promisin' to look after her the best I know how for the rest of my life." He reached into his pocket and pulled out a small box. "There's only one other thing that would make me happier." He knelt down in front of her on one knee.

Opening the box, he proposed to her tenderly, "Emily Victoria Coulter, it would please me greatly if you would accept this ring from me as a promise of my love for you and your mama. I promise I'll be good to you and her an' look after the both of you the best I know how for the rest of my life."

For several stunned seconds, Emily stared at the ring. She thought they had come here to buy a ring for her mother. Her wide eyes met Hiram's for verification. He had kept a straight face as long as he could and was now grinning at her like a fox in a henhouse. Her face broke into a happy smile, and she blurted out a loud *yes!*

In a grand gesture, Hiram took her hand, slipped the birthstone ring on her finger, and made much to-do about kissing the back of her dainty hand with a loud smack that sent her into a fit of giggling.

CHAPTER 38

"Forbearing one another, and forgiving one another, if any man have a quarrel against any; even as Christ forgave you, so also do ye." (Colossians 3:13).

Laura was putting the finishing touches on the dress Meggie would wear to the wedding. She glanced up just in time to see Addie make a beeline for the door. Addie was not herself at all today. She was usually in command of her emotions, but she'd been an irritable bundle of nerves all morning.

Laura went back to her stitching, dismissing her mood. After all, it was understandable with all the preparations and the wedding just two weeks away, she was bound to feel a little pent up and unraveled around the edges. Fresh air could do wonders to clear one's head.

Addie cut across the yard and headed down the carriageway toward the road, carrying with her the key. Once away from the house, she didn't try to hold back the tears. They came, but they were not comforting. Joy should be hers, yet it seemed far away. She'd kept her heart locked for too long, for too long she'd held fast to the key. Only she could release herself and conquer *the little foxes that spoil the vines.*

A burning need deep within her compelled her forward. With a purpose-driven sense of urgency, she made her way toward Hiram's house. She had held herself away from him for too long, resisted what he commanded for too long. In denying him, by her own doing she had forfeited peace in her heart, had denied herself a sweet blessing from on high. *Ye have not because ye ask not…*

Despair filled her soul; the weight of it bore down on her heavy as a gravestone. She was weary from carrying the burdensome load of it. She sought a resting place. *For I will give you rest…*

She went through the gate and bounded up the steps to Hiram's house. No longer would she deny herself or *Him.* She had come here to surrender it all to Him, to surrender it all into His open arms. She had come here knowing Hiram was not at home. He had taken Emily to Oakdale for dinner at The Preacher's House. She entered the quiet house and shut the door behind her, shutting out everything and everybody else in the world. *In quietness and confidence shall be your strength.* She swallowed hard against the stubborn lump in her throat. *Stubborn pride is hard to swallow.*

Addie went over to a small bench near the hearth and dropped to her knees. He was already there, waiting for her at the foot of the Cross. In submission to His will, she bowed her head in His presence, her face rested on the bench—*upon His promise*—and she wept as she prayed.

Her heart was rent as she laid her petition at the Savior's feet, saying first a humble prayer of acclamation: *O Lord God and Heavenly Father, thank you for loving me and being so faithful to provide my needs. Your goodness to me is great…*

She gave thanks for answered prayers. *You have yet again given answer to my fervent prayers. How many times I asked you to give unto me a godly husband to share my life with. How wrong I was to believe you denied me. Thank you for sending Hiram my way, dear God…*

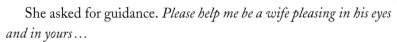

She asked for guidance. *Please help me be a wife pleasing in his eyes and in yours…*

And she confessed. *Forgive me, O God, where I have failed you, for I know the forgiveness you ask me to give is slight in comparison to the forgiveness you have bestowed upon me…*

She asked the Holy Spirit: *Fill me with a spirit of forgiveness, for my heart cannot offer retreat for both—the abundance of love I feel for Hiram and the hatred I bear for Alfred. Remove from me this stain of resentment and the bitterness that has taken root in my heart, for I know an unforgiving spirit destroys the soul…*

In repentance, Addie sobbed. *By your strength and in accordance to your will, dear Father, I lay all grudge aside…I forgive Alfred!…I forgive Alfred!*

His mercy failed her not; under the canopy of God's grace, joy belonged to her.

It was both an end and a beginning for her, but for her and Hiram, it was only the beginning.

CHAPTER 39

"What? know ye not that your body is the temple of the Holy Spirit…?" (1 Corinthians 6:19).

Five days before the wedding, Addie entered the woodshop briskly and found Hiram running a plane across a board, shaving its surface, making it smooth in preparation for use. He barely glanced up as she approached.

Slightly out of breath from the walk from Wesley's, she stood for a moment watching him. Looking around, she asked, "Where's Daniel?"

"I sent him to town on an errand. He took Amelia and the baby with him into Oakdale."

That was just what she wanted to hear. "Good. I was hoping to speak to you alone."

Hiram looked up and regarded her for only a moment. Noticing the gentle rise and fall of her chest, he asked teasingly, "Did you run all the way here?" He turned his attention back to the board, running his hand over it, testing its roughness.

Not understanding what he meant, she looked puzzled. "What?"

He had been acting strange for the last few days, and she was here to get to the bottom of things. "Is there something wrong, Hiram?"

Not really listening, and not noticing that she was upset, he replied casually, "I don't reckon."

Exasperated, she asked, "Then why have you been avoiding me the past few days?"

He shrugged and answered, "I didn't realize I was."

A little irritated at his disinterest, she said, "Well, you have, and if I've said or done anything to make you mad, I wish you'd tell me so we could clear the air."

"Addie, it's nothing."

"How can you say it's nothing? Even now you won't put that stupid board down long enough to look at me."

In the next instant, Hiram threw the plane aside and closed the distance between him and Addie in a few long strides. In one rapid movement, he swept her into his arms and covered her mouth with his in a blistering kiss. Lifting her feet off the ground, he backed her toward a large, oak table in one corner of the shop, and before she knew what was happening, she found herself atop the table, Hiram climbing on top of her.

His mouth took hers again as he lowered himself to fit intimately against her so that every inch of their bodies touched. Under the fevered, insistent kiss, he pressed his hips hard against her. There was no disputing his ardor.

For several pleasurable moments, Addie forgot herself in his embrace.

Struggling for restraint, and finding it with great effort, Hiram raised his head. With eyes burning with passion, he looked at her. His face was near to hers, her lips full and moist, their breath warm in each other's mouths. "This is why, Addie. This is why." His breathing was labored, his voice ragged and hoarse. "I am but a man, flesh and blood. Your nearness only fuels my desire for you. You offer no dissuasion." It was no longer easy for him to play the gentlemanly monk.

Addie's body ached for fulfillment. "Because I yearn the same for you," she murmured softly. *Burn* was a more apt description for the fire that threatened to consume her.

He gave her half a smile. "And I praise the Lord for that, but I, we, must honor God, and ourselves, and each other, and wait." Reluctantly, he pulled away from her, saying, "And if that means avoidin' you 'til we meet at the church to marry, so be it."

Addie watched as he headed toward the door. "Where are you going?"

He called over his shoulder, "To the cussed creek for a swim!"

"It's October—the water's like ice. You're going to freeze!"

He answered gruffly, "Yes, I know. You might consider joinin' me!"

CHAPTER 40

"Husbands, love your wives, even as Christ also loved the church, and gave Himself for it... and the wife see that she reverence her husband." (Ephesians 5:25, 33).

The first Saturday in October dawned fair and glowing. The day itself was cause for celebration. During the night, the winds had shifted ever so slightly from the north, and a crisp, autumnal breeze drifted gently across the unclouded, azure sky, bringing an enticing foretaste of fall to Golden Meadow. Such a fine and glorious day it was, one would be hard put to mourn the passing of the season faded and spent as summer bade farewell.

Everyone had worked like ants all week in preparation for what the community hailed as the social event of the year. The Warren place looked fitting for the festivities that would follow today's ceremony. The yard was swept, and two lines of tables were set up underneath the oaks just beyond the side porch. On the porch were tables for the wedding feast and, of course, another for the beautiful wedding cake.

Sassie received exclamations of joy and even respect for her spectacular cake. It was truly awe-inspiring. By using a variety of sizes of baking pans and her imagination, she created a multi-tiered cake, which she frosted with a sweet, fluffy confection made of egg whites and sugar, beaten in a pan over boiling water, just like she'd watched her Aunt Dorrie do. She piped a border around the edge of the cake with additional frosting and added decorative swirls and curlicues. It was evident the she had taken great pains in making the delightful cake. The cake was a gift to Addie, straight from Sassie's heart.

The day before, a few of the men had gathered and dug a bar-beque pit out behind the smokehouse. They pulled several layers of chicken wire across the pit, staked the wire taunt, and made a grill. Three large logs had been burned down to smoldering coals. Asher and a couple of his friends had been mopping and tending a pig and half dozen wild turkeys over the pit since before daybreak. As the day wore on, the tantalizing aroma of the roasting meat spread through the air, as did word of it, and first one, then another, felt obliged to happen by to pay their respects to the cooks.

The house buzzed with excitement. Just before noon, Sarah Beth, Meggie, Emily, and Sassie all took their turn on the stool in front of Laura's dressing table and watched as their hair was tortured with hot curling irons. After their hair was arranged, they sat around impatiently, preened and prim in their petticoats, waiting until the last minute to put on their wedding frocks so they wouldn't get wrinkled.

Combing his hair, Laura gave Jesse a strict speech about staying clean, and she put Wesley in charge of seeing to it that the boy stayed presentable while she finished dressing. "Yes, ma'am," was still echoing in her ears when she looked through a window ten minutes later to see Wesley doubled over laughing in jovial conversation with Asher and the other men, oblivious to Jesse dancing a jig in the smoke and ash around the grill pit. *Men!*

Shortly after one o'clock, Addie was in her chemise putting the finishing touches on her hair. There came a light rapping on her bedroom door. It was Claire. She came in and closed the door

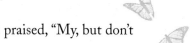

behind her. Addie smiled at her warmly and praised, "My, but don't you look nice all dressed up in your finery!"

Claire frowned and took the compliment with a grain of salt and scoffed self-critically, "I feel silly. Who on earth looks at an old woman at a weddin'? But there again, who's ever seen a bridesmaid old as Methuselah?"

Addie thought she was beautiful and said so. Then, "I'm glad you're here. You can help me with my dress." The beautiful yellow gown was spread carefully across her bed.

"First thing's first," Claire said. She reached out and placed an object in Addie's hands. "Something old, something blue, something borrowed... your dress is new." In a soft, quavering voice, she said, "This belonged to my mother. I thought you might want to carry it." Claire's eyes misted.

Addie looked at the faded blue, satin-covered prayer book. Tears welled up, but before she could say anything, Claire said, "Here, let's get you in this pretty dress. They're out yonder waitin' for me, an' you know what a cantankerous old bird Stell is—bustin' a stitch to get there early so she can perch on the front pew. I told her sittin' closer to the preacher won't get her one hair's breadth closer to the Lord. Claims she cain't hear, my foot! Stell can hear a mouse dooky through a brick wall. Now, be careful not to mess up your hair." She held the dress while Addie slipped it over her head and slid her arms through the sleeves.

The rustle of satin fell around Addie like a softly spoken whisper. Her skin tingled from the mere touch of it; her face felt flushed. Giddy, she did her best to stand still while Claire fastened the back of the gown. With trembling hands, she smoothed the skirt down and adjusted the flounce of lace where the neckline scooped and the lace ruffled at her wrists. She inhaled deeply and turned around to face Claire.

Claire breathed a sigh as she looked on with approval. Her voice held a touch of melancholy as she said, "My gracious! You are a fetching sight! You look like a queen!"

It was true. Addie was radiant. The gown hardly deserved her.

Claire added, "You and Hiram make a fine couple. I know you're going to be happy!"

"I already am," Addie whispered. *For in me is a new heart and a new spirit.* "God is so good." Tears sprang up again, this time spilling over. She reached out and took both Claire's hands in hers. "You're a wonderful friend—*my best friend*—and I hope you know I love you dearly."

"I reckon we have seen the sun rise and set on a right smart." They both laughed at the sober understatement. In leaving, Claire leaned over and kissed Addie fiercely on her brow. "I do so love you, Addie." In a choked voice, she added softly, "See you at the altar, child!" Her face was wet with tears.

All the women and children climbed into Wesley's four-seated rockaway carriage and headed to the church. As planned, when Hiram left his house, he went by for Daniel, Amelia, and Rachel, and they rode with him. Daniel would return a short time later to drive Addie to the church.

When everyone had gone, Addie walked out onto the porch. For a moment, she looked around thinking how everything in the world looked so absolutely perfect today. Leaves ruffled lightly in the breeze, and ladybugs whirled over a multi-colored bed of zinnias. Everything seemed sweet and tender, infused with joy.

She glanced down the carriageway expectantly, waiting for Daniel. While her thoughts were on him, she had to admit that she was worried about her son. She knew he had hard feelings for Alfred bottled up inside. A few days ago, she tried to talk to him about it, but he'd told her firmly he didn't care to hear what she had to say. She wished she could make him see how much richer his life would be if he could only forgive, as she had. Yet she didn't blame Daniel for the way he felt. Alfred had trampled on his heart where it hurt the most. Daniel loved Amelia fiercely, and he hated Alfred just as fiercely for hurting her, for *raping* her.

She understood. Oh how she understood!

Maybe in time, she thought. *Maybe in time.*

And of time, she also knew sooner or later she would have to deal with the matter of Sassie's parentage. She wondered how it would affect the family to learn that Alfred was her father. How would Daniel and Emily react? Theirs was already a divided family due to prejudice. Anna rarely came around, and when she did, things were strained and tense.

Addie lifted her eyes to the sky and said, "Lord, I'm turning these things over to you. Please, just see us all through the fallout."

She was getting impatient. What on earth was taking Daniel so long? She felt so happy, so at peace, and so looking forward to marrying Hiram. And she was certainly looking forward to their honeymoon. Once again, he had surprised her by planning a romantic trip for them to New Orleans. She sighed. All she longed for was a simple life with this wonderful man of her dreams.

She hadn't really thought about it until he brought it up a few nights ago, but Hiram was hoping they would have a child. Actually, he said *children!*

Finally!

Daniel had arrived.

He pulled up and reined the buggy to a stop in the shade of the yard. He hopped down from his seat and waved to the men who were barbequing out behind the smokehouse. When he saw Addie, he stopped in mid-step, and for a minute he just stared and shook his head in amazement. He had never before, he swore, seen his mother look as happy or as beautiful as she did at that moment. Her eyes were dancing, fuller of joy than he'd ever seen.

He went toward her, and mounting the steps, he exclaimed with sincere admiration, "I 'spect there couldn't be a prettier bride anywhere! Just wait 'til Hiram lays eyes on you."

Smiling brightly, she went to Daniel and kissed his cheek. She stepped back to inspect his appearance. He was wearing a new black suit. With motherly pride in her voice, she bragged, "What a handsome man you are!" Then, with a laugh, she pointed toward the buggy, "And, that's a mighty fine-looking horse, too!"

Daniel explained sheepishly, "That's Amelia's doin.'" Hiram's horse had a thick garland of autumn leaves and flowers looped about its neck.

Addie focused her gaze on Daniel. She knew her son, and there was *something* in his manner—she couldn't put her finger on it. Her eyes searched his face, trying to guess what was on his mind. She could tell he was hiding something. Daniel had a secret.

She demanded lightly, "Daniel Coulter, you tell me right now why it is your feet have not touched the ground since you got here—and don't try to tell me it's on account of the wedding. I know better!"

Daniel felt elated, like he was walking on a cloud. Just remembering the sweet, shy way Amelia had told him made his heart swell. "I hadn't thought of sayin' anythin' just yet…I didn't want to steal any thunder from yours an' Hiram's big day…*but*…" he gave Addie a broad, boyish grin that lit up his whole face, "I'm about to bust! I can't keep it to myself a minute longer." He beamed. "Amelia told me this mornin'…she's pretty sure…we're goin' to have a baby come spring!"

The announcement pleased Addie. "Oh, this is wonderful news! You and Amelia have christened this day and made it even sweeter…as impossible as that may have seemed!" She hugged him tightly.

He reminded her of the time, saying, "We'd better get goin' if I'm to get you to the church by two!"

She didn't tarry. Barely able to contain her excitement, she said merrily, "Give me just one minute." She almost skipped into the house to get her bouquet and Claire's prayer book.

They proceeded to the church.

Harmony Baptist Church sat in a little valley surrounded by white-barked sycamores and several sweetgum trees. Foliage was just beginning to salute the season with a subtle display of the beauty forthcoming. An impromptu breeze led a scattering of fallen leaves in a delicate waltz about the churchyard.

Daniel slowed the horse a bit as he approached the church with

Addie, allotting time for the last ones who were slowly filing inside to find a seat. The church was full, near to overflowing.

When they came to a halt in front of the church, he helped her down from the buggy. Organ music wafted through the open windows. Addie's heart was in her throat. Daniel gave her a gentle smile and asked, "You nervous?"

Her eyes were swimming with tears. "A little."

"Happy?"

She nodded. "A lot. I keep pinching myself to make sure I'm not dreaming." *Happy are the people whose God is the Lord!*

For a fleeting moment, Daniel thought of Alfred. He swallowed hard against the memory and said, "Mama, if there was ever one who deserved to be happy, it's you. Hiram's..." His voice trailed off. Daniel knew Hiram to be among the best of men, decent and respectful. He was everything that Alfred was not. Daniel was certain he would also be the best of husbands for his mother. However, be it left unspoken, Daniel loved Hiram in a son-to-father sort of way. He simply said, "Hiram's a good man."

For the first time, Addie noticed Daniel had dropped the 'Mister' when referring to Hiram. She knew the bond between them surpassed friendship. She felt a surge of gratitude to Hiram for reaching out and catching her son and holding him up when he'd needed it most.

She whispered, "I love you, my son."

Daniel cleared his throat and said, "I love you, Mama, an' you best know, just because I'm walkin' you down the aisle don't mean I'm givin' you away." *Her children rise up, and call her blessed...*

Hand in hand, mother and son walked up the steps.

The music changed as Maude struck the first chords of the wedding march.

Addie shivered with anticipation. Daniel offered her his arm, and together they took a deep breath, smiled at each other, and entered the church. In unison, the congregation rose to their feet, and every head turned to see the bride come down the aisle.

When Hiram saw Addie, his breath caught in his throat. He couldn't take his eyes off her. His gaze moved over her warmly, appreciatively, lovingly. *She's so beautiful,* he thought. *Inside and out.* He felt the blood rushing through his veins, his pulse throbbed. Their eyes met and held in a mirrored promise of love and adoration.

As Addie walked down the aisle toward him, she could scarcely breathe for the pounding of her heart. She was mesmerized, lost in the eyes that beheld her, forgetting all but the two of them. She didn't see the lit candles or the lovely flower arrangements, nor was she aware of the faces of those in attendance. She missed the wink Travis gave her as she passed by him and Abigail. All she saw was Hiram waiting for her at the altar. He looked so handsome, regally attired in a black suit and a crisp white shirt. A slow smile played across his features, and she melted under his warm gaze.

At the altar, Daniel kissed her cheek and offered her hand to Hiram. His strong fingers curled around hers. He gave her a reassuring squeeze as he drew her with him to the altar steps where Wesley, his best man, and Claire joined them.

In a firm, steady voice, Rev. Orin McElreath began the marriage ceremony by reading the thirteenth chapter of 1 Corinthians, where the Apostle Paul spoke of love. He then turned to the fifth chapter of Ephesians. "Husbands love your wives even as Christ also loved the church and gave himself for it . . .

"Do you, Hiram, take this woman, Addie, to be your lawfully wedded wife, to live with her according to God's ordinance, in holy matrimony, to love her, comfort her, honor and keep her, in sickness and in health, forsaking all others, keeping yourself solely unto her, so long as you both shall live?"

Looking tenderly into his bride's shining eyes, Hiram answered in a deep, clear voice, "I do."

"Addie, do you, take this man, Hiram, to be your lawfully wedded husband, to live with him according to God's ordinance, in holy matrimony, to love him, comfort him, keep him, in sickness and in

health, forsaking all others, keeping yourself only unto him, so long as you both shall live?"

Her heart fluttered. She promised softly, "I do."

The preacher turned to Wesley, took the ring, and handed it to Hiram. He repeated the words as Rev. McElreath instructed, pledging himself to Addie, saying, "With this ring, I thee wed … *my beloved.*" His fingers caressed her hand as he slid the gold wedding band upon her finger. *You are the keeper of my heart; I, the keeper of yours.*

After Hiram received his ring, the preacher turned again to the Scriptures and read from the book of Ruth. "For whither thou goest, I will go; and where thou lodgest, I will lodge; thy people shall be my people, and thy God my God."

Then he concluded. "Hiram and Addie, as you both have so solemnly promised in the presence of God and these witnesses, in accordance with the laws of the state of Mississippi, I do hereby pronounce you, Hiram and Addie, husband and wife." The preacher looked at Hiram over wire-rimmed glasses and stated with an unexpected glint, "It is customary for the groom to kiss the bride."

Addie lifted her eyes to his as Hiram gently cupped her face in his hands and lowered his head. His mouth moved upon hers in a tender kiss. He longed to take her into his arms, but aware of all the eyes upon them, his lips didn't linger. *Tonight,* he solaced.

When the kiss ended, she gave him a quick, breathless smile and tried to stop her head from spinning. Grasping hands, the newlyweds hastily made their way down the aisle past a sea of shining faces, taking their leave through the front door of the church. In the background, the choir jubilantly serenaded them with an age-old song of eternal promise:

> "There's a land that is fairer than day,
> And by faith we can see it afar;
> For the Father waits over the way,
> To prepare us a dwelling place there.
> In the sweet by and by."